W. James Besemer
1-22-'99

FLIGHT PATH

A NOVEL

Jan David Blais

highpoint press

FLIGHT PATH

Publisher's Cataloging in Publication (Prepared by Quality Books Inc.)
Blais, Jan David.
    Flight Path : a novel / Jan David Blais.
    p. cm.

1. Airlines -- Fiction.   2. Aviation -- Fiction.   I. Title.
PS3552.L35F55 1996   813'.54
                    QBI96-40338

ISBN 0-9654607-0-3

Book and page design and production by Nieshoff Design, Lexington, Massachusetts. Published by Highpoint Press, Cambridge, Massachusetts. Printed and bound in the United States of America by Thomson-Shore, Dexter, Michigan. This book is printed on recycled paper, using soy ink.

For Barbara – *sine qua non*

Contents

Author's Note

This is a work of fiction. It is entirely a product of the author's imagination. Except for obvious references to existing companies and institutions, known individuals, and publicly-reported events, any resemblance to actual companies, institutions, individuals, or events is entirely coincidental. I've taken liberties with certain locales and the sequence of certain historical events, as well as simplifying some airline market situations, but straying not too far, it is hoped, from reality.

This book has had many friends. It is not possible to acknowledge all of them, but I wish to single out some who helped with generous encouragement and comment. Any errors and all editorial judgments are the author's.

My special thanks go to Dennis Hanlon for showing me that airline insiders would like the story, and to Liz Reilly and Paula Blais Gorgas for showing me that others would, as well; to Alice Volpe, who was there at the beginning; to Gino Francesconi, Carnegie Hall Archivist; to Marion Mistrik, librarian for the Air Transport Association; to staff of the Boston, Cambridge, Monterey, and Seattle Public Libraries; to staff of the Manteca Historical Society and the Manteca Public Library.

To my editor, Joyce Engelson, for her clear-eyed appraisal of the manuscript and advice, and David Tompkins for editorial assistance; to David Barber for copyediting; to Lynn Simon for proofing and editing; to Deborah Rust for jacket design; to Pat Nieshoff for book and page design; and to Judith Appelbaum and Florence Janovic of Sensible Solutions, Inc., for their astute marketing assistance.

Also, for their advice and support, my thanks to Samuel C. Butler, Deborah Coffey, John Corcoran, Tom Elin, Murray Gartner, William P. Kennedy, Bill Lawder, Martin Lobel, Skip Lutz, Andrew K. McCusker, Alexander J. Moody, Jr., the late Len Morgan, J. E. Murdock III, Rosemary O'Connell, Allan Paulson, Gretchen Ritter, J. Stephen Sheppard, Robert P. Silverberg, Manny Solomon, Mervin K. Strickler, Jr., and Bud Travers. And to a book whose portrayal of flying and the natural world has been an inspiration for years, Guy Murchie's *Song of the Sky*.

Finally, with love and appreciation, to Barbara, Annie, and Andrew, for their advice, candor, and good humor throughout.

Cambridge, Massachusetts. November 1996

Sometimes I feel a strange exhilaration up here which seems to come from something beyond the mere stimulus of flying. It is a feeling of belonging to the sky I fly, of owning and being owned – if only for a moment – by the air I breathe. It is akin to the well known claim of the swallow: each bird staking out his personal bug-strewn slice of heaven, his inviolate property of the blue.

GUY MURCHIE • *Song of the Sky*

...Vaulting ambition, which o'erleaps itself
And falls on th' other side.

SHAKESPEARE • *Macbeth – Act I, Scene VII*

"It has always seemed strange to me," said Doc. "The things we admire in men, kindness and generosity, openness, honesty, understanding and feeling are the concomitants of failure in our system. And those traits we detest, sharpness, greed, acquisitiveness, meanness, egotism and self-interest are the traits of success. And while men admire the quality of the first they love the produce of the second."

JOHN STEINBECK • *Cannery Row*

Aviation in itself is not inherently dangerous. But to an even greater degree than the sea, it is terribly unforgiving of any carelessness, incapacity or neglect.

TRADITIONAL

PROLOGUE

"**M**R. BELL." The flight attendant placed her hand on the armrest. The seat-belt sign had been lit for most of the flight.

"It's five o'clock, Mr. Bell."

He looked so peaceful sleeping, not at all how she pictured him doing battle in the airline wars. He was breathing quietly, his mouth partly open. His reddish-gray hair was tousled, and the top button of his white shirt was undone, a striped tie at half mast, in the airline's red, white, and blue. She had hung his jacket, of course, when the flight boarded in San Francisco.

Eight years with the airline but still relatively junior, this was Dana Sharpton's first month serving in the first class cabin of the 747. Most of the airline's top executives avoided red-eyes like the plague, but here in 2A was the founder, chairman, CEO, and president of her company, and she was supposed to wake him up. She'd never met the big boss before, though his wife, Dee, a retired stewardess, as they were called in her time, was a frequent visitor to flight attendant gatherings.

She decided she'd better chance it. Reaching across the sleeping gentleman in 2B, she gently shook Bell's shoulder.

"It's five o'clock, Mr. Bell. You wanted me to let you know."

This time he stirred and opened his eyes. After a moment he looked around.

"I must have nodded off," he said, his voice thick with sleep.

He glanced at his watch. "Guess I did more than nod off." He raised the window shade and peered out...still dark. Then he reached into the seat pocket where he'd stowed the complimentary toilet kit the airline provided its first class passengers. By now his seatmate was also stirring. Bell motioned that he needed to get by. Looking confused, the man lifted himself in his seat, and Bell scraped past. The flight attendant stood aside to let him by.

"Thanks," he said, stifling a yawn. "Give the crew a call, will you. Tell them I'll be up in a couple of minutes."

The flight attendant smiled. "Consider it done."

She glanced at the Fasten Seat Belt sign but decided not to mention it. He knows what he's doing, she thought. Even if he doesn't, I'm not about to tell him.

Bell opened the lavatory door and stepped inside. One of life's most underrated pleasures, he thought, as he stood over the toilet. Twenty-nine seconds later, for he sometimes kept track of the time as a sort of challenge, he zipped his fly. Not bad for an old guy.

He glanced quickly at the mirror over the small sink. God, do I look awful... I really hate these trips. This one was important, they said, a fundraiser for Reagan, stockpiling cash for a presidential run in 1980. Somebody at dinner made a joke about the former "acting governor," but fact is, he surprised everybody in that job. Turned out to be the real McCoy. Sure put those long-hairs in their place. But president? Dunno about that. That's not the same thing, not the same at all.

Bell steadied himself as the plane hit a patch of turbulence. Better see about a contribution... do what we can, but we need to be careful. Some of the fellas got tangled up with that Nixon crowd, got their knuckles rapped. Never liked Nixon. Too liberal for my taste, as it turned out. Just shows, no guarantee you'll get what you pay for.

He ran the hot water for a few seconds on his right hand until it started to hurt, then the cold water on his left. He dried his hands on a paper towel, then wet the towel and wiped his face. For the first time, he gave the mirror a good look. Damn. It's a good thing I don't feel as old as I look.

It's a tough business we're in... helluva lot harder than it used to be. Harder than it ought to be. He shook his head. I really should have stayed at home, with Dee going in next week. A chill went through him... they know it's cancer. They don't know how bad or, God forbid, if it spread. He shook his head. What a trouper... don't know how she does it. I sure couldn't. Deep down, though, I know she's terrified. You don't live with a person all these years and not know what they're feeling. He closed his eyes. Please, God. Let her be all right.

Bell took a deep breath. He reached in his shirt pocket for a comb and slicked back his hair. A lot more gray the last few years. Barber's after me to try some of that coloring crap but not a chance. I am what

I am, and that includes my hair. He snapped open the toilet kit and removed a small toothbrush and tube of paste. He brushed his teeth vigorously, rinsed out his mouth, and spat into the wash stand. Finally he wiped the basin with a dry towel.

Please Be Thoughtful of the Next Passenger. He stared at the sign over the basin. Damn right, he thought, and the one after that, too.

Bell opened the lavatory door and stepped across to the circular staircase leading to the 747's upper deck. One hand on the metal rail, he mounted the stairs. Stiff...stiff...been sitting too long. At the top, he surveyed the upper-deck lounge. In the dim light he could make out a couple of people asleep in their seats, one stretched out on the circular leather sofa to the side of the stand-up bar. Like to get rid of this, put in some seats we can sell. Another sixteen, twenty passengers we could get in here, first class fares. That'd help a lot. Trouble is, most flights we don't sell out in first, as it is. Mostly pass riders and deadheads.

He gave a knock on the cockpit door. A moment later it opened. The second officer was holding the door for him.

"Morning," the pilot said, retreating into the cockpit and taking his seat at the side-facing instrument console.

"I believe you're right," Bell replied.

As Bell stepped in, the captain turned around. "Hey, Charlie. Where've you been?"

"Asleep, no thanks to you guys. When are you going to learn how to give us customers a smooth ride?"

"Didn't know you wanted one," the pilot laughed. "Damn! You should've told me."

Bell leaned forward against the pilots' seat backs, an arm on each. Don Goodwin and Al Boudreau. Good men. Been with me a long time, both of them. The second officer, I met him at the start of the flight, but the name escapes me.

"What's going on?" Goodwin asked.

"Not a whole lot. Just thought I'd check up on you guys."

"We're about crossing Lake Huron. Looks close to on-time."

Bell straightened and sat down in the jump seat behind and slightly above the captain, one of the two auxiliary seats for deadheading crew and FAA inspectors. He looped his arms through the shoulder harness and locked it tight. On the flight deck, he could feel the side-to-side motion of the giant aircraft's front end, typical in turbulence.

The first officer turned around. "Want to listen in?" He pointed to a headset hanging on the side panel next to Bell.

Bell shook his head. "Thanks anyway."

He looked ahead. Sandwiched between the main instrument panel and an array of switches above the pilots' heads along the roof, was the 747's wrap-around windscreen, the flight crew's window on the world at thirty-three thousand feet. The sky was beginning to take on a pink glow, though he could see a line of dark columns silhouetted against the brightening sky.

"Some pretty good buildups ahead," Goodwin observed. "They've been vectoring everybody to the north for a better ride. I know how much that means to you."

In a few moments, the plane banked left, then rolled out on a new heading to skirt the line of thunderstorms. Bell folded his arms as they droned along, watching the cloud tops slide by on the right. This was not a talky crew. A remark here and there, dialogue with air traffic control. That's all right with me, he thought. Nice to have some quiet up here. Peaceful.

The dim flight deck, air whooshing past the cockpit, the up-and-down, side-to-side motion...it was hypnotic to Bell. He closed his eyes and his mind drifted back in time.

Travel Air...our first plane, in '36, it was. Found it in Missouri, two more outside Chicago. Took some fancy footwork to pay for them. Mail was it, at the start. The passengers didn't come until I started collecting Tri-Motors. That Ford was a real step up, bought eight of them, all told. He chuckled. Never did pay them off. By the time we got close, the DC-3 had come along. First plane I ever bought new...finally started making some money. About time, my investors said. Honey of an airplane...liked it so well we pretty much went with Douglas from then on. The Four, the Six, the Seven. Though we came close on the Electra.

Then our first jet. He smiled, recalling the takeoff from Boeing Field on that demo flight. Unbelievable airplane, the 707, then that long-range one for international. Stayed with Boeing after that except for the 'Ten, of course. 727, 737, this big bird, more coming down the line. They get better all the time...

"Will you look at that!"

Bell snapped out of his reverie. He looked ahead... how beautiful can it get. Forty years of sunrises. I will never tire of this.

At all levels, the sky was filled with clouds backlit by the dawn. Oranges and yellows and reds... fantastic shapes and sizes. Six miles down, behind this unbelievable display, the sun, commencing its march across the vault of the sky.

Bell unlocked his shoulder harness. He leaned forward against the captain's seat back, resting his chin on his arms. I am not a religious man. I do not like Sundays. This is my church. It has always been my church. If there is a God, he'll know I tried, I did the best I could. His eyes became moist.

Please let Dee be all right. Please, God. Let her be all right.

PART ONE

A High Wire of
Their Own Making

1

OCTOBER 1979. *Rogers Park, Chicago's North Side.* It was a small wood-frame building behind a three-story walk-up, just south of the Evanston line. Whenever it rained, water seeped through the foundation, creating a pattern of rivulets that led under the car, a black '72 Eldorado that dominated the space from its cinder-block platform. Normally, the owner parked his new Corvette in the second bay, but this evening that was empty, a dark rectangle in the inner wall seen through a door frame with no door.

Against the back wall a workbench was mounted, an oak plank chipped and stained from decades of home improvement and car repair. A cobwebbed bulb hanging from the ceiling threw a weak, shadowless light. Squeezed in the confine between the bench and the car, a man worked intently, an athletic bag draped over a vise at his elbow. His tools were spread across the bench – needle-nose pliers, screwdrivers of several types and sizes, insulated wire, a pocket knife, a soldering iron – defining his workspace and, from the absorption he brought to the task, from the feverish cast of his eyes, his entire being.

Periodically the man bent forward and stared at a creased piece of paper, photocopied from a technical manual of some sort. His eyes narrowed, darting from the drawing to the bench and back again. Each time, after a moment he nodded, his face relaxed, and he forged ahead. Gradually his construction was taking shape.

The man leaned back against the Cadillac's grille and let out a deep sigh. He glanced at his watch. Nine-thirty. Nearly an hour I've been at it, he thought, nonstop. Need to wrap it up. They'll be back soon. Movies. For a moment his mind wandered, and he stared blankly at the pieces of alarm clock and the other parts of his assembly. When's the last movie I ever went to? Can't remember. Must be years.

Hard to figure, old Jackie making out like this. Him and me, we go back a long way, growing up without two dimes to rub together,

both our families. Now look at him. Married, a kid, got three buildings, renters, big bucks every month and that's on top of his regular
job, but there's *no way* takin' care of them's as much work as he says.
He always was a complainer, Jackie, but at least he lent me his place
tonight, have to give him that. In his mind the man pictured his
friend's house, one in a row of look-alikes, staple of Chicago's blue-
collar Near North. Absolute fucking palace compared to that dump of
mine. Not even counting the woman and that kid of hers, a midget
couldn't turn around in mine. Can't tell me that's right. *No way* that's
right, somebody works as hard as me and considering what they put
me through. Not fair, not fair at all. He shook his head. . . before long
we'll even up *that* score.

He set to work again, his eyes straining in the poor light. Medium
height, in his early forties, thin bony face, receding dark, coarse hair,
a light sweater showing above his jacket collar. The man shuddered,
overcome for a moment by the dank chill, by the enormity of his plan.
He shook his head hard and blinked. C'mon, get with it. Get *with* it!

He snipped a length of wire and stripped the yellow insulation
from the end. In a smooth motion he reached for the spool of solder
and the iron, careful to avoid its hot tip sticking out over the edge of
the bench. Drop of metal, press the wire in to set the connection.
Good old clock, he thought sadly, had it for years. Got me up for a lot
of early shifts. Sorry to see you go. Would've used one of those fancy
electronic timers, but better you stick to what you know. Be different
if I was an avionics type, but all I am's a dumb dogface mechanic. All
I ever been.

Waiting for the solder to harden, the man's gaze strayed to the
light bulb. As he stared at it, the bulb seemed to pulsate, slowly
expanding and contracting, then rays of colors began shooting out of
it in all directions. He blinked, squeezing his eyes shut. That pain
again! That goddamn pain behind my eye. Jesus! Don't let it happen
now! He lowered his head. Be quiet, be quiet, don't move. Put everything down. Careful! Rub 'em hard, both hands. Spots everywhere
now, everywhere. Open 'em. . . that's better, some. Still hurts like a
sonofabitch. Bastards, all of them. It's all their fault.

Through his haze he looked at the assembly on the bench. Got to
finish, close it up, but I better see if it fits, first. Gently he lifted the
clock and wire and placed them in the box next to the dry cell. Jam

the piece of towel in, cushion it, make sure it can't move. It'll get bumped around plenty, you can count on that. His mouth tightened. Ramp rats – no pride, nothing but mouth, any of 'em. Damn box. Couldn't find an empty one anywhere, two fucking dozen cigars I have to buy, just to get a box! Make me sick to my stomach, always did, the smell's enough, just *looking* at them's enough. Fifteen bucks down the toilet, but there'll be more where that came from, a *lot* more!

He stared at the packet of plastic explosive nesting in its bed of towels. Unbelievable, something that small, what it can do. How much it *cost*. What I had to go through to get hold of it.

He smiled grimly. This fucker goes right to the edge. Bastards never gave me a chance. I'll show them what I can do but I can't let nothing go wrong. Christ, I don't want nobody to get hurt! He swallowed hard. Whatever I am, I'm not. . . that.

Suddenly he heard a rattling, grinding noise. The overhead door! They're back! Frantically he wrapped the loose lead with electrical tape and stuffed the scraps of cloth around the edge. Shut the lid, heavy rubber band around it one way, then the other. He cocked his head, staring at the box. It's a cross. A crucifix! He swallowed hard. I didn't need that.

Big towel around the box, into the bag with it. Tools in the kit, press shut the Velcro flap, tie the cord. *Shit!* That damn soldering iron! He stuck his finger and thumb in his mouth, angrily yanking the cord from the socket. Hands shaking, he pushed the iron into the metal case, jamming the cord inside and forcing the lid shut. Look around. Check around!

Suddenly a figure appeared at the doorway.

"Hey man, how's it goin'!"

He zipped the bag shut. Made it. Just in time.

2

A SLENDER, DARK-HAIRED WOMAN sat at her dressing table, putting the final touches on her makeup. After a long look she nodded approvingly. The person in the mirror was ten years younger than her own thirty-eight, *at least* ten. A delicate bone structure, near-perfect skin – admittedly, a few worry lines about the mouth and at the corners of the eyes – a trim figure accentuated by a blue silk dress with a hint of the East, fourth-generation sapphire pendant with paired earrings, the entire presentation tasteful, understated, and certain to be admired, precisely as planned. She permitted herself a smile.

Then, thinking of all the crowded evenings and weekends that culminated in this evening, Elaine Hartley sighed. But at least an event like tonight's was some payback for her many volunteer hours, a benefit sponsored by her principal charity, New York's Young Professionals for the Arts, for the Midtown Chamber Orchestra. After an early-evening concert, a good cross-section of the city's business and cultural elite would be treated to a lavish buffet, a thank-you for their four- and five-figure generosity. These events made her life a constant pressure cooker, on top of her responsibilities as a key interior designer for a leading New York firm. But she knew very well that moving in these circles, showcasing her husband's rising star and, by her choice, her own lesser light, was what it was all about.

"You ready yet?"

Her husband came up behind her, placing his hands on her shoulders. As she rose, she touched his hand lightly. "Everyone says what an elegant couple we make, Philip. And you know, I do believe they're right."

With mid-length dark hair neatly trimmed, a noticeable flattening at the bridge of his nose suggesting a past injury, and gray eyes set rather broadly apart, Philip Hartley's features could be counted as regular, possibly even handsome, though not matinee-idol quality.

"And who will I have the pleasure of seeing tonight?" It had been a demanding day, and Hartley was not looking forward to another evening of mingling. Elaine stepped to a table and picked up a program.

"Same idea as our Little Theater thing last spring, but more music people, of course. Not to mention the bankers, business types, and so on. Your crowd."

Hartley followed her across the room. He moved with the balance and coiled energy of an athlete. The cut of his tuxedo jacket revealed a muscular torso.

"My crowd which happens to foot the bills for these artists you like to collect." He ran his eye down the acceptance list. "Say, Arthur Winston's on here! I've been wanting a chance to get him aside."

"He was easy. Catherine's on the orchestra's board."

Hartley nodded appreciatively. He glanced at his Rolex chronograph. "The cab should be downstairs. We'd better get going."

Feeling better about the evening, he held Elaine's full-length mink for her and tossed his dark gray topcoat over his arm. They stepped into the foyer, garnished with nineteenth-century New York scenes and period furniture. A vase of dried autumn flowers stood on a table next to a long brass-framed mirror that invited final adjustments as they awaited the elevator.

The Hartleys' brownstone was in a choice Manhattan neighborhood, a quiet street in the East Fifties overlooking FDR Drive and the East River. At its First Avenue end, the short block opened onto a colorful scene – greengrocers, dry cleaners, neighborhood restaurants. For the most part, these leafy cross streets intersecting the fast-paced avenues were home to citizens of established wealth, but with a growing population of younger executives, lawyers, and bankers enjoying early success in the big time. Convenient, pleasant, and reasonably secure, not to mention a very, very good address. Even in bad weather, Hartley walked the nine blocks to the BellAir Tower, except on travel days when a company limo called.

At forty-three, Philip Hartley's ascent in BellAir, one of the nation's largest and oldest airlines, had been unusually rapid. In his previous position as an assistant vice-president with Salomon Brothers, Hartley had had passing contact with the BellAir account.

But it wasn't until 1977, while serving as the airline's advisor during its acquisition of a failing smaller carrier, that BellAir's senior management became aware of him. Hartley's acumen and boardroom demeanor so impressed Charlie Bell that he started calling on him for advice, bypassing senior members of the Salomon team and causing some unpleasantness for Hartley in the firm. After an off-again, on-again courtship, Bell prevailed on Hartley to sign on as his special assistant, and within six months the chairman made good on his promise and named Hartley the airline's chief financial officer with the rank of senior vice-president. Clearly, Philip Hartley was one of the favorites on Charlie Bell's fast track.

In the lobby, the Hartleys were greeted by Mullins, the white-haired security guard who was a fixture in the Dunston Building, as it was informally known, after the real-estate magnate who built it before World War I. No one ever used Mullins' first name. After so many years of neglect, Elaine sometimes wondered whether he still had one. They settled into the taxi for the short ride to Carnegie Hall.

"Philip, remind me, what is Arthur Winston's position on your board?"

"Vice-chairman," Hartley nodded. "Head of the executive committee, too. That's the only important job Charlie hasn't kept for himself."

As they rode along he reminisced. "We met in '73, that International Metals deal. He picked up a nice fee and the bank got some very good press." He looked out the side window. They were crossing Central Park, the bare trees glistening in the oncoming headlights. The fall had been colder than usual, with morning frosts, and it was only mid-October. "I have a very good feeling about Arthur, the kind of interest he's taking in my career."

Elaine smiled, pleased at her matchmaking. She knew Winston was important. "By the way, their daughter was at Wellesley the same time I was, two years behind, actually. Catherine and I should get along fine."

THE MUSIC AND APPLAUSE died away, and soon the glittering crowd began flowing down the circular staircase from the Carnegie Recital Hall to the Blue Room just below. As leaders of the city had for the better part of a century, Elaine Hartley's guests gathered under a magnificent crystal chandelier in the elegant, smallish room. Inside the door, a tall, robust woman waited, her jet-black hair a striking contrast to her brilliant red-satin pantsuit.

"Philip! So *good* to see you. And Elaine, don't you look *wonderful!* I hardly *recognize* you from this afternoon! Mmmm-uhh!" She embraced Elaine, then, with a smooth, well-practiced maneuver, offered her cheek to Hartley. "Mmmm-*uhh!*" She drew back. "Philip! Wasn't that a *fabulous* concert, tell me the truth. Personally, I can't stand Bartok, but at least the rest of it sounded familiar. Music is not my strong suit. Well, don't just stand there, you two. Come in! Have a drop of the bubbly!"

Hartley eased into the room and looked around. "No Harry tonight?"

"Missing in action." A shadow passed over her face. "London. This time it's something to do with computers. At least that's what he says." Suddenly all smiles again. "Maybe his next trip I'll show up and surprise him." She winked at Hartley. "What do you think of that idea, Philip? You're a man of the world. You're going places."

"I'll pass on that one, Gretchen. You figure it out yourself."

"Say, I wonder. . . " She peered over Hartley's shoulder. "Who *is* that cute guy, the one Ruthie's with? I'd better check him out. Excuse me, you two." She gestured toward the far side of the room. "The bar's over there. . . oh, Elaine, can you believe I'm telling *you* that! As if we weren't here all afternoon setting up the damn place! Well, 'bye now!"

She swept away in a flourish of red. Hartley shook his head. "Easy to see why Harry spends so much time on the road."

Elaine suppressed a laugh. "You're most unkind, darling. Even if she is a motormouth, Gretchen's a very sweet person and she certainly puts a lot of herself into these benefits."

"Does that make her easier to take?"

He picked a glass off a passing tray. The waiter paused. "Champagne, madam?"

"Chivas with a splash of soda, if you please."

"Very good, I'll be right back."

"Phil Hartley!"

A short, stocky man, not a hair on his head, was clapping Hartley on the back. "Phil Hartley! It's you! As I live and breathe, it's *you!*"

Hartley dried his hand on a paper napkin. "It's been a while, Barry. El, this is Barry Kaplan, an old teammate of mine from Cal. He's with Merrill here in town."

"Come on, not all that old." Kaplan put his arm around Hartley's shoulder. "Your friend has a great memory, Mrs. H, but have you noticed how selective it is? So, how is it we never see you at alumni meetings anymore? You lose the address or what?"

Hartley nodded at his wife. "Barry always had a way with words. And his Yul Brynner act, that's as good as it ever was."

Kaplan shrugged. "I'm halfway there anyway, why not go all the way? But seriously, Phil, where've you been hiding yourself?"

The waiter reappeared. "Chivas with a splash?" Elaine took her glass.

"I'll catch up with you boys later. Need to see some people."

Kaplan turned to Hartley. "Hey, I wasn't trying to give you a hard time, it's just, well, your name came up the other day and the fellas and I, we were wondering how you were doing. Anyway, who do you like in the Big Game? Stanford hasn't been all that great this year. Maybe our guys have a chance."

"I haven't followed the team that much. This new job really keeps me hopping. Though there's an outside chance I might get out there this year. There's some kind of alumni program they want me in."

"Yeah, I heard about that. I'd go, if I were you." Kaplan stood back. "Say, you're looking great, Phil. What do you do to stay in shape these days?"

"I get over to the Racquet Club a couple of times a week, work with the weights, play a little squash. Not as much as I'd like, but it's better than nothing. The knee's holding up, only time I notice it is if I run on it too hard."

Kaplan frowned. "I tell you, what a tough break that was for you, hell, for all of us. We were never the same after that first year when you were healthy, not that we were all that great anyway. Hey! Howyadoin'!" Kaplan grasped the hand of an older man walking by. "Powelson," he remarked under his breath. "Canadian. Big-time developer. *Megabucks,* if you get my drift." He took a sip of champagne. "By the way, I was meaning to ask, how do you like being with the airlines, you know, compared to Salomon?"

Hartley shrugged, "I'd topped out there, the way things were heading." All those years at the firm, he thought. Like a caged animal, no chance to break out, no chance to make a mark.

"I was kind of surprised to hear you'd moved over. Figured you'd be there forever. Well, you'll do great, Phil, you always do." Kaplan leaned forward. "So. You got any hot airline tips?"

Hartley shook his head. "That's your job. You tell me!"

"C'mon, how do you think I find out about things?" Kaplan waved his hand around the room. "You think I'm here for the music?"

"Maybe the food." Hartley lowered his voice. "All right. I'll give you one. Here's a million-dollar idea. Keep your eyes on BellAir. We're going to surprise a lot of people, these next couple of years." He paused. "Your airline analyst at Merrill. Greenberg. How well do you know him?"

"Only slightly. That's a whole different department. But he has a good reputation, very big on research."

Hartley reached inside his jacket and extracted a card from a small leather case. "Have him give me a call. . . "

"Ladies and gentlemen! Attention! May I have your attention!"

Hartley looked up. It was Elaine's friend in the red suit. The room began to quiet.

"Your attention please! Thank you! Thank you! Welcome, all, and thank you for joining us tonight. Wasn't that a *fabulous* concert!" A few people started clapping, but she held up a hand. "I'm Gretchen Bond, President of Young Professionals for the Arts, your hosts this evening.

"First, let me recognize my two co-chair*persons* who worked so hard to make this evening a success. Please give them a big round of applause for putting together this wonderful event. Elaine Hartley and Rudy. . . " She looked around the room. "Oh, Rudy, where *are* you? Ah, over there, on the side. Rudy Vitale!

"It's really wonderful to see so many friends here tonight. Please enjoy yourselves and be sure to say hello to the members of the orchestra who are circulating around the room. You'll recognize them from these." She held up an oversized blue button with white lettering.

Hartley looked up. A tall, distinguished-looking man was approaching, his long, slender face framed by precisely waved, silver-white hair.

"Philip! Isn't that your wife they just recognized?"

Hartley greeted the older man warmly. "Yes, that's Elaine, all right."

"We just met. Had a pleasant chat, very pleasant indeed. I didn't realize this was her evening. It turns out she and our daughter were at Wellesley together."

Hartley thought quickly. "Is that so!" he exclaimed, feigning a look of surprise.

"Small world, isn't it." Winston glanced around the room. "I don't know about you, but I'm just window dressing at these events. Catherine is our family patron of the arts, though somehow my check-writing skills never seem to go out of style. I must say, however, as benefits go, this is very well done. My compliments to Elaine."

"No question, she has a flair for this." Hartley noticed Kaplan shifting his weight from one foot to the other. "By the way, this is a friend of mine, Barry Kaplan of Merrill Lynch. Barry, Arthur Winston."

Kaplan looked at Winston quizzically, as if he knew him from somewhere. "A pleasure," he remarked, shaking Winston's hand.

"Are you in the investment banking side at Merrill, Mr. Kaplan? I have some old friends over there."

Kaplan shook his head. "More retail than anything else."

Gretchen Bond was moving the program along. She tapped the microphone for quiet. "Now I'd like to ask Maestro Stefan Kroll to come up here. Please join me in giving him a warm welcome."

Someone shouted "Bravo!" and the crowd began applauding. Suddenly, one corner of the room was flooded in brilliant light as the Channel 2 camera crew swung into action. The conductor's shaggy white mane bobbed in the glare, his eyes flitting from side to side, tracing the path of the paper Gretchen Bond was waving at the crowd.

"Maestro, rather than just tell you of our appreciation, I have a check here for *one hundred thousand dollars,* from the arts and business leaders of our city which I am *delighted* to present to you!"

"I am overwhelmed..." The conductor's words were drowned out by cheers. "You cannot begin to know what this means to me, to the orchestra."

Winston nudged Hartley. "What I hope it means is they get current on their loan one of these days. Philip, let's slide over to the bar. This is apt to be a long one."

Hartley turned to Kaplan. "See you, Barry. Let's stay in touch."

"Yeah, Phil. Let's do that." Kaplan watched his friend move away with Winston. His eyes narrowed... we've lost him for good.

3

AN EARLY WINTER STORM down from the Arctic by way of Manitoba was tightening its grip on the Chicago area. A few inches at most, according to the afternoon news, but for Henry Kowalski any snow was too much snow.

"Son of a bitch!" The heavy wrench slipped out of his hand and clanged off into the shadows. "God-*damnit*-all!"

Kowalski backed down the ladder, blowing on his fingers as he peered around the massive landing gear of the DC-10. Hunched over, he stepped around the oversized tires. No wrench. Nowhere in sight.

"Yo! Freddie!" Kowalski shouted to his partner. "Gimme a light! Fast!"

Being able to see helped a lot. Right away he found the wrench, but it was already tacky from its exposure to the cold air. Kowalski rubbed his hands together. Much longer on the ground, it would have ripped off a chunk of skin, for sure. It's nights like this... Next time I really got to remember those gloves.

It was a messy repair, with purple Skydrol spraying all over and stinging the mechanic's eyes as he searched the line for a pinhole leak. The hydraulic system powered the DC-10's landing gear and control surfaces, a definite no-go item if it wasn't right. As Kowalski labored, shafts of light from lamps on the terminal wall pierced the swirling snow, but even with a tug next to his ladder, engine running and head-lamps trained on his work area, there was barely enough light to do the job. Kowalski wiped his forehead with the back of his hand and peered into the wheel well, his head and lungs filling with fumes.

"Fifty below and sweating like a pig," he said under his breath. "Un-fucking-be-*liev*-able!"

"Hey, what's goin' on down there?" The voice of his lead mechanic boomed through the headset. "Twelve minutes! That's all we got left!"

Kowalski fumbled for the mike hanging loosely from his belt. "I'm hooking her up now. This one's a real sonofabitch!"

"Better move it, I'm tellin' you! We're runnin' outta time!"

We're running out of time, Kowalski snorted. Here I am freezing my ass off and he says *we're* running out of time! I lay you odds that bugger's in the cockpit drinking coffee, warm and dry, playing up to the stews.

Now giant wet flakes were falling, whitening the wing and tail surfaces of Kowalski's DC-10 and the other aircraft parked nearby, but the crystalline beauty of the scene was marred by jet engines screaming, the growl of tugs, the clatter of baggage carts racing past. The air reeked of spent jet fuel. The DC-10's auxiliary power unit added its muffled roar, powering the plane's electrical systems and warming the passengers held captive by Henry Kowalski as he ministered to the plane's hydraulics.

Inside the cabin Joe Maravich was feeling the pressure of the clock, but true, he wasn't freezing. Quarterback of the repair, Maravich cursed repeatedly under his breath. It was so stupid! Right away, Henry'd found the hole. No problem, should've been a piece of cake, but damned if Maintenance Supply wasn't missing the size line he needed to splice in. So it was get hold of United across the field and borrow one. Good thing, Maravich thought, a *damn* good thing that at least on the ramp there's still some cooperation. Like the old days. Sort of.

Under the plane Kowalski struggled with the new line. If he didn't close it up by 1915 – 7:15 Chicago time – the flight would be canceled and the passengers who thought they were heading to San Francisco on Flight 159 would be handed over to the competition by a very unhappy BellAir management. United would grab most of them and a later American flight the rest. Any strays would be put on BellAir's last departure, the ten o'clock onestop through Denver. Worst of all, Kowalski thought, it's us that'll be tagged with the cancellation. But if I can only finish in time...

By now Henry was working one wrench against the other, carefully tightening the nuts so he didn't split that precious replacement line. Christ, he thought grimly, don't let *that* happen.

In the cockpit, the captain leaned over his seat back toward Maravich. "We gonna make it? We've got a helluva load tonight, twenty in first, couple hundred in back. Be a damn shame to lose them."

"We'll make it, all right," Maravich replied, nervously glancing at his watch. "That's one of my best men down there. Hell, you'da been out of here by now if they had the part like they're supposed to."

"Being an optimist," the captain drawled, "I'll tell them to get ready to de-ice."

Maravich lifted his mike. "We're down to four minutes, Henry. Where the hell are you?"

Half-blinded by sweat, Kowalski was by now working mainly by feel. He ignored the radio. Better I finish the job than stop and talk about it.

"Henry! You reading me? What's happenin', man?"

Still no response. "Aw, shit. I better go see what he's doin'." Maravich turned to leave, but his path was blocked by a beefy young passenger in a business suit, a linebacker gone to seed.

"Don't you people know what time it is? We're an hour late! *An hour late!*"

Maravich felt himself getting hot. Easy. . . easy. . . he took a deep breath. "Like the captain said, we're working it as fast as we can." You think it's some kind of picnic down there, he muttered under his breath. Goddamn lardass.

But the linebacker wasn't through. "Excuses! Excuses!" Now he was waving his arms. "Last time you'll see me on one of your planes!"

Big fucking deal. Maravich lowered a shoulder. "Nobody's going nowhere if I don't get through." As he pushed by, his radio gave a loud squawk.

"Joey! I *got* the motherfucker! Turn on number three pump!"

"All *right!*" A smile began to creep across Maravich's face. He quickly stifled it and glared at the linebacker. "We got it. You happy now?"

"I'll believe that when I see it," grumbled the big man. Maravich rushed to the cockpit. He motioned the second officer out of the way, squirmed into the side-facing seat at the instrument console, and hit the switch activating the plane's hydraulic system. Immediately the pressure shot up. Maravich squinted at the fluid quantity indicator. . . holding steady. . . holding steady. Beautiful! He reached for the red Out of Service tag he'd placed on the control wheel an hour earlier.

"I'll collect that!" This time he couldn't contain his grin.

The flight attendant who'd been lounging in the jump seat behind the captain stood up. She yawned and stretched. "Time to put the animals back in their cages. What do you think, Bill, ten minutes?"

"More like twenty, with the de-icing," he replied. "With any luck, we'll make up some of the delay. Headwinds aren't too bad tonight."

Just then a grimy figure appeared at the cockpit door. Henry Kowalski's quilted BellAir cap with its long peak and earflaps was crusted with snow. The airline's winged B logo was all but invisible. His eyes and nose were red, but success was written all over his face.

"Nice going, fellas," the flight attendant said. She nodded at Maravich. "Don't mind that bigmouth. We've had him a coupl'a weeks running, nothing's ever good enough for him." She touched her finger to her temple. "I believe the man has a problem."

"All in a day's work," Maravich grunted. "Lemme call Maintenance Control. Henry, I'll stand you a coffee if there ain't nothing going on."

Kowalski took off his cap and slicked back his dirty-blond hair with a comb, adjusting it toward the thinning center.

"Coffee. I'd sooner pour it on my hands about now."

THE READY ROOM for BellAir Line Maintenance was on the lower level of the O'Hare terminal, a short step from the windswept ramp. Beneath the passenger concourse, its overpriced shops and snack bars, grade-school art displays, round-the-clock watering holes, and disembodied PA voices, there existed a very different world – home base for the nuts and bolts of operations, the rough and tumble, sometimes dangerous action that drove the airline forward, forcing square pegs into round holes, routinely performing miracles. A wide variety of trades and characters made up this workaday world. Bag schleppers and aircraft movers known as "ramp rats"...cleaners and provisioners... "honeybucket" lavatory crews...green-eyeshade dispatchers calculating weight and balance, passing the weather word down the line... pilots checking charts and papers, bad-mouthing the hangar queen about to be foisted on the next unfortunate crew... flight attendants between engagements...the company's station manager tearing out what hair he has left... supporting-role clerical types... and, not to forget, the Henry Kowalskis and Joe Maraviches of Line Maintenance.

At small airports, the day is generally shorter, since few flights transit the city each day. Many functions are carried out by phone and telex or deferred to a full-service station downline. But even a twenty-four operation like O'Hare, as night falls the workplace slows and a smaller shift is left to handle the late flights positioning aircraft for the next day's early departures. About the time Kowalski and Maravich finished their ordeal on the ramp, there was a break in the action. BellAir's peak-time flights had been dispatched, and another bank of arrivals wasn't due in until eight.

An indispensable feature of this underground airport is the employee cafeteria, good any hour for coffee, a fast meal, or a sandwich. Hot food, plenty of it, edible, for the most part, and priced right, all for flashing an airport ID.

"How come you're on this shift, Henry?" asked Maravich, spooning sugar into a heavy ceramic mug, webbed with scratches from years of industrial-grade dishwasher abuse. "Don't see much of you since you went on days."

"Yeah, this is unusual." Kowalski lit a cigarette. "Vince Costello, he asked me to trade a couple of weeks, so I figured what the hell, I can use the extra money, with Christmas and all."

"Vinnie. What's he up to these days?"

"Dunno." Henry shook his head. "That shit he picked up in 'Nam keeps coming back. Anyway, that's the word." Henry wrapped his hands around the steaming mug. "So, Joey. You're doin' all right these days. How long you been a lead, anyway?"

"Since June. Yeah, it's okay but, you know, there's so much bullshit. It's like you're the meat in the sandwich all the time, you know what I mean? Sometimes I wonder if it's worth it."

"So what's next for you? Management? Sure, that's it. I can see you in management."

Maravich gave him a punch on his shoulder. "C'mon, Henry, gimme a break."

"Hey, don't try to shit me, Joey. I know you're in tight with those new friends of yours. So tell me, whadda they say's going on?"

Maravich made a sour face. "Nothin', absolutely nothin'. No, I'm serious. Only way you find anything out's from the union, same as before."

"Sure, sure. So, tell me, we goin' out like United?"

"Nah, not a chance..."

"Hey, man! What's goin' on?" A slim, dapper black man in a BellAir ticket agent uniform was standing beside their table. He set his tray down. "I trust you gentlemen can use some intelligent conversation for a change?"

"Sure, Leonard, you just tell us where to get some." Maravich moved over and made room. "So. Once again we are honored with a visit from one of our fancy people from upstairs. You know Henry, here?"

"Sure." The ticket agent slid his chair out and sat down. "Howyadoin', Henry."

Kowalski nodded, automatically straightening in his chair. Even after so many years working with black people, in the air force, at O'Hare, he still felt uneasy around them. Why was that, he sometimes wondered... maybe if I knew some of them better, in the neighborhood, something like that.

"Man, you couldn't pay me enough to go out there tonight." The agent dug into a mound of pie and ice cream. "It's a real bitch."

"Henry, I believe we just received a compliment." Maravich leaned back in his chair with a deadpan expression. "Candyass ticket agents wouldn't last five minutes on the ramp, for Chrissakes. But as for us, it is our pleasure, our *distinct pleasure,* to freeze our ass off so we can make you people upstairs look good. Hey, Leonard, nothing personal."

"Freeze whose ass!" Henry shouted. "Fuckin' A! Who's the one outside hanging onto the damn ladder? One guess. Me, that's who!" He held up his hands. "Look. Frostbite! Third degree at least. And what is old Joey doin', old Joey's nice and warm inside, makin' out with the stews. Leonard, I tell you, from now on I am sticking to day shift."

"Shit, man," the ticket agent replied between bites, "you think the counter's some kind of a picnic? Two-hour delays! The whole system! I got pissed off people everywhere, kicking my ass like it's goin' out of style and I'm supposed to be *nice* to them? You wouldn't last five minutes up there."

The men were quiet for a moment. "Say," Maravich turned to Henry, "I ran into Artie Mathews today. There's a meeting about the negotiations. Thursday night. They got a copy of the United contract.

Maybe we'll get some idea what management's thinking about for us."

Henry snickered. "Fucking union. I tell you, I never count on the union. Far as I'm concerned, those guys spend their whole time sucking up to management when they're supposed to be working for us."

"You fellas heard about the layoffs," the ticket agent interjected.

"Layoffs! You're shittin' me. *What* layoffs?"

"I wish I was. Old man Thompson's figuring the cuts, even as we speak. Ten percent across the board is what they're saying. Systemwide."

Maravich slumped in his chair. "Hell, that's no surprise. Anybody could see it comin', the way traffic's been so lousy. It's a rotten year all around."

"Maybe I'll go to that meeting, after all," Henry grunted.

Maravich wadded a paper napkin and stuffed it in his mug. "We better get back." He stood up. "Take it easy, Leonard."

"You too, my man. Keep 'em flying!"

4

OFF O'HARE ninety minutes late, Flight 159 climbed through the storm, finally bound for San Francisco. Beneath the clouds, spinouts, fenderbenders, gapers' blocks, the usual rush-hour bedlam clogged Chicagoland's streets and expressways, delaying cocktail hour for thousands of commuters.

Perched on the tip of an aluminum tube some hundred eighty feet in front of the DC-10's tail-mounted rear engine, the flight deck was buffeted by the storm, but the crew paid little attention to the bumpy ride. Bill Van Dusen was a thirty-year BellAir veteran, had flown every aircraft in the fleet and then some. With his lightly salted dark hair, Van Dusen was the model airline captain, rock-steady, reliable as they came. In fact, he had been pressed into a BellAir TV commercial the year before, to the delight of his colleagues, who ragged on him mercilessly until the ad finally ran its course and disappeared.

Earlier in the year Ken Jarvis had upgraded from 727 first officer to right seat in the DC-10, gaining a better pay scale and more flexible hours, as well as progressing in the profession. A member of the pilot union's safety committee at BellAir, Jarvis brought a thoughtful and critical perspective to the ground school and simulator training he'd just completed on the 'Ten.

The third member of the Chicago-based flight crew, the second officer, or flight engineer, occupied a side-facing seat before a complex array of switches, dials, and lights. The appearance of this particular pilot was guaranteed to confound airline old-timers, for though the gray BellAir uniform was standard issue, this one was cut somewhat differently, and Lori Mitchell wore it with undeniable flair. For nearly a year, she'd been flying the line, one of BellAir's pathfinding first class of women pilots. Actually, "flying" was a poor choice of words to use around Mitchell, for despite responsibility for the aircraft's critical operating systems – engine performance, fuel consumption, and the like – the aircraft's standard cockpit layout denied Mitchell and her fellow second officers any chance of touching the flight controls, much less ever making a takeoff or landing. In fact, the hard-earned flying skills that qualified them as pilot-hires in the first place could actually deteriorate unless maintained on personal time. Mitchell's credentials were impressive. Forty-two hundred hours, first instructing, then captaining a commuter aircraft in the Northeast – high-density airspace, dozens of takeoffs and landings every day, often squashed down in the freezing rain and thunderstorm action – some of the most demanding flying anywhere.

Passing through twenty-three thousand feet, the DC-10 began scooting along the ragged cloud tops. Suddenly it popped into the clear, starry night. The only vestige of day was a faint reddish line lying across the horizon, fading through orange to deep blue then, overhead, pitch black. After the rocky start, above the clouds the ride was perfectly smooth, a rush of wind the only reminder of the huge machine's passage through the air.

"BellAir 159, contact Minneapolis Center on 134.5."

"134.5, BellAir 159. Have a good one, Chicago."

Jarvis flicked a switch that rang a chime at the first flight attendant's station. "Now that we're out of the crud, I believe the crew can commence working."

Van Dusen nodded. "How'd you like the ride, Lori?" he asked.

"No problem," she replied. "I've seen a lot worse."

Van Dusen glanced at Mitchell. He considered himself a modern man, in sync with the times, yet it startled him to see a woman so at ease on traditionally masculine turf. Still, at least he took some pride in recognizing the discomfort his instincts caused him. This was progress, of a sort.

"You getting along okay these days?" Van Dusen ventured, "or are we neanderthals still giving you ladies a hard time?"

Mitchell thought a moment. "Everybody's been really helpful. For the most part, that is. Some exceptions, but I guess that's par for the course."

Gratified, Van Dusen turned to Jarvis. "Say, Ken, how low was that ceiling when we finally got off?"

Jarvis consulted a handwritten sheet. "Three hundred. Visibility eighth of a mile."

Van Dusen paused, as if unsure whether he should express his thought. "You know," he finally said, "after that American flight went in last May, it got so I hated visual departures off that runway... the burnt ground and all. I always tried not to look, but I couldn't help it." Van Dusen shook his head as if trying to empty it of the memory. Too close to home. More than once, he'd hung on the edge of disaster himself. Though not recently, knock on wood.

"Take it from this old-timer," he said with feeling, "you people ought to tip your cap to Charlie Bell. Sometimes that bugger didn't know where our next paycheck was coming from, but he sure was there for us when it counted." He looked around the cockpit. "Good equipment, extra training, anything to give us an edge up here."

Jarvis looked at Van Dusen, "What scares me, Bill, with this deregulation business the company seems to be getting so wrapped up chasing the almighty buck. I mean, you've got to be real careful not to lose your edge. I'll tell you, the safety committee's watching that one *real* close."

"I hear you." Van Dusen paused again. "You know, the boss's hat size was always twice as big as anybody else's, but give the man credit, he put strong people in Operations and he backed them up. If you ask me, that took real balls!" Van Dusen caught his breath. He reddened, then turned to survey the damage.

"Sorry, Lori," he said sheepishly.

Mitchell shot him a look. "I am familiar with the term."

"Well, ah... right. I guess we've all got some learning to do around here."

Mitchell frowned. "Mind if I ask you guys something? Why is it, you talk about Charlie Bell like he's not around anymore? I mean, the last time I saw him he looked fine to me."

"Oh, well, I guess it's just a habit I sort of fell into." Van Dusen nodded, "I guess I just remember the good old days a lot clearer than I should. When we were a small outfit, everybody seemed to pull together better. I don't know... mainly I'm worried about the company, and the industry for that matter, so many changes happening and business so bad. I don't even know half the people Charlie has flying for him these days. Who knows where it's all heading."

"Did you know United's furloughing pilots?" Jarvis asked.

"I heard something to that effect. What's the deal?"

"I rode over on the crew bus with a couple of United guys today. They're saying the number's ninety-five and it could go higher."

"Sign of the times," said Van Dusen gloomily. "Wouldn't surprise me if we're looking at that ourselves pretty soon. There's even talk about management layoffs, if you can believe it. All I know, something's got to give. Our loads are terrible, TW and Continental are cutting way back, now United, too, it looks like. No sir, things definitely do not look good."

Van Dusen was quiet for a moment. He stared at the array of dials and gauges on his panel. How different everything was, compared to just a few years ago. It was only a few years, wasn't it? Those times seemed simpler than they really were, he mused. Somehow the difficulties, the austerity, tended to fade with the years.

"Damn!" Van Dusen suddenly said, slapping his knee, "I was really rooting for those maintenance guys tonight. We don't see many loads like this anymore."

Jarvis nodded. "Trouble is, if we take a furlough and they put some Tens on the ground, I'll have to bump back to the 727." He shook his head. "What a pain in the ass that'll be! All that training down the drain. Then I'll have to go through the whole drill again."

"Pain!" Mitchell broke in. "I'll be out of a *job*! Try *that* for pain!"

Van Dusen nodded solemnly. "Yeah, well, it's a bad situation, no question."

A horn sounded, warning that the aircraft was nearing its initial cruising altitude. In an older plane, Van Dusen and Jarvis now would be preparing to push the control wheel forward, to retard the throttles to the selected power setting and trim for cruise configuration. In this cockpit, however, the pilot and copilot needed simply to fold their arms and watch the electronic wizard of an autopilot fly the DC-10, which it did with a smooth precision no human crew could match, even on a good day. It took some getting used to, the first few times an aggressive, take-charge individual had to sit back and watch the control wheel moving forward, the cluster of thrust levers retreating and the heavy trim wheel rotating eerily, all on their own.

"Lori, why don't you call for coffee and find out about our meals," Van Dusen asked. "And it's probably time to talk to the people. How about taking it, Ken? Lately you've been doing a lot better."

"Better!" Jarvis scoffed. "Didn't you hear about my tryout with WGN? You know, a second-career kind of thing."

Van Dusen laughed. "I wouldn't be quitting my day job just yet."

Clearing his throat, Jarvis adjusted a dial and pressed the transmit button on his control wheel. "Ladies and gentlemen, this is your first officer speaking. On behalf of Captain Van Dusen, Second Officer Mitchell, and myself, we want to thank you for flying with us tonight. We're sorry about the delay and the bumpy ride, but we hope you'll sit back now and enjoy BellAir's fine inflight service. We've leveled at our initial cruise altitude of thirty-five thousand feet, and after we burn off some fuel we'll be climbing on up to thirty-nine thousand for the remainder of our flight to San Francisco. We're expecting a smooth flight the rest of the way, so I've turned the seat belt sign off and you're free to get up and move about the cabin..."

A chime sounded. Van Dusen casually picked up the handset connecting the flight with ARINC, the airlines' private communications network.

"159 here. Yeah, Steve, this is Bill. What? So, what's different about this one? I see. Who's there? Okay, call us back. We'll be here, we ain't going anywhere."

Van Dusen took a deep breath, then turned to his crew. "Well, people, seems like they found another way to screw up our evening."

Jarvis stared at him. "What are you telling us, Bill?" he said slowly.

"There's a bomb threat against the flight. That was Ops." Van Dusen frowned. "For some reason, they think this one's for real."

5

ARTHUR WINSTON elbowed his way through the crowd, with Philip Hartley close behind. *"Artistes!"* Winston snorted, "I've had my fill of them! People like this Kroll may perform a useful function," he glanced ahead, his way blocked, "but what really troubles me... excuse me, if we can get through there... what troubles me most is their total lack of business sense. I have never met one who knows which end of a balance sheet is up. Ah, here we are!"

Winston plucked a glass of champagne from the bar. "Always looking for a handout, which is bad enough, but the lack of respect, no, let me be candid, the *arrogance* toward their benefactors, is what really galls me. Just because we take seriously the mundane little detail of how things are paid for."

"No business sense," Hartley nodded. "Sounds a lot like airline people."

"Well, now, that's right," Winston responded between sips, "but the root of *our* problem, why this illustrious industry of ours is a disaster, is its years of government subsidies and controls. And now that we're finally deregulated, my banking colleagues, for one, are worried about what they call 'destructive competition' among the airlines." Winston shook his head. "Can you believe, they actually *liked* the old protectionism!"

"They're not the only ones," Hartley replied. "You see a lot of long faces around our shop these days."

"So I understand." Winston took another sip. "However, I take a different tack. Professor Kahn was quite right, all those years the government protecting the weak, holding the strong ones back. Now that's what I'd call destructive!" He looked at his young colleague. "It's high time we rolled the dice and found out what we're really made of. If this company of ours can pull itself together, my goodness, there is *no limit* to our earnings potential!"

Winston studied the hors d'oeuvres table a moment, then reached for a stuffed mushroom. "People are just kidding themselves. Deregulation isn't about competition, not at all. Competition is a myth, though a very useful one. In the end, it comes down to making money. *Making money,* pure and simple, however you do it. That's what counts."

Hartley smiled grimly. "When the industry gets through this shake-out period, it's going to pay off big for the survivors."

"That's a useful way to put it. The strong and the clever, those with resources and vision. Like ourselves, let us hope." Winston surveyed the table again. "Nothing for you?"

"I try to go easy on this kind of thing. Don't get much chance to burn it off these days."

A miniature pizza disappeared into Winston's mouth. "Well, whatever you do seems to be working, Philip. I understand athletes have a special problem staying fit. Football was your sport, wasn't it?"

"Second team All-America my sophomore year. Then next season, opening game, I caught my cleats and twisted a leg going down. Somebody landed on top of it, tore the knee up. Couple of operations, they put everything back together. I gave it a try senior year, but it didn't work. They said I'd be a cripple for life if it happened again."

"This was on the West Coast, I take it."

"The University of California. Cal to its friends, Berkeley to everybody else."

"Before the troubles out there?"

"Things didn't start coming unglued until the early sixties. I got out in '58." Hartley paused for effect. He'd been over this ground many times. "I was about as low as you can get when they told me I couldn't play ball, but all of a sudden, I had time on my hands and started cracking the books for real. Everything just seemed to fall into place. I thought I knew something about competition, but it turned out I didn't have a clue until I got to the B-School."

"Well, we're pleased you're with us. It's no secret how highly Charlie thinks of you. In fact, I might say some of us on the board are more than a little interested in how you handle your new finance assignment." Winston looked at Hartley intently. "My greatest concern is that some of our people care more about flying planes than running a business. As I say, they've never been called on to make a real honest-to-god profit in their lives. Till now, that is. Leather jackets and scarves? Come, now. Hardly the tools of the trade these days!"

Hartley noticed a change had come over the older man. His eyes were cold and hard.

"Good people in their own way, but many of them will be asked to step aside. We need new blood, people who know how to win. People who know *what* to win!" Winston gestured with his empty glass. "Profitability. Shareholder value. *That's* what it's all about! You mark my words. If this company of ours doesn't wake up soon, it will be remembered as a victim of deregulation. And I can assure you, I, for one, do not intend to let that happen."

Winston smiled. "These days, there is a wealth of opportunity for a man with your drive, your eye for the bottom line. You have all the tools, Philip, and if I may be candid, friends in high places who want you to succeed. There is no limit to what you can achieve, how far you can go." The older man raised his glass solemnly. "Let me offer a toast and a word of advice: here's to communication!"

Hartley looked at him, puzzled.

"That's right, communication. If you learn nothing else, know that the higher you go, the more important it is to communicate! Of course, I mean with the people who matter. Many a CEO has neglected this simple little rule and paid the price for his arrogance. Or his stupidity. As for your career at BellAir, you will be your own best friend, or your worst enemy. It's entirely up to you. And whatever you do, don't let yourself be dragged down by guilt, feeling sorry for the people around you. When changes have to be made, well, by God, make them! And I offer you this: anytime you want to chat, just pick up the phone, anytime at all. Some of our directors prefer the arm's-length approach, but that's not my style. As I see it, whatever goes wrong eventually winds up on my doorstep, so I want to stay abreast of things."

Winston edged closer. "One more thing, Philip, and this is strictly between us, if you will. I have serious doubts about our esteemed marketing vice-president and his crowd. I've made my concerns known to

Charlie, but the old-boy network is, shall we say, rather rampant there, if you know what I mean. I'll be interested in your opinion. Take a look around that shop and tell me what you see."

"I hear what you're saying, Arthur."

Winston put his glass down and looked around. Hartley had the distinct impression the conversation had just come to an end.

"Time to round up Catherine." Winston rubbed his hands together. "Sorry we can't stay longer. Nice chatting with you, and take care of that Elaine. You have a good one there."

The crowd was beginning to thin. As Philip Hartley returned his glass to the bar, he realized he was perspiring from his few minutes with Arthur Winston.

"Philip!"

Gretchen Bond came rushing up.

"Philip! You have a call."

Hartley frowned. Only BellAir's operations team knew where he was, and he wasn't to be disturbed except in an emergency. She pointed toward the entrance. "The phone's outside, around the corner."

He made his way through the crowd to an alcove next to the men's room.

"Hartley here."

"Mr. Hartley, this is Tim Ryan at Ops. Sorry to bother you, but we received a bomb threat against a flight out of O'Hare about fifteen minutes ago. I'm calling all the officers to let them know. We just activated the war room and Mr. Mueller's on his way in. It looks pretty serious."

"Okay, Tim. Thanks."

Hartley replaced the phone, resting his hand on the receiver for a moment. The airline's normal procedures didn't require the presence of BellAir's chief financial officer at this kind of emergency, but Hartley was keenly interested in how operations chief Fritz Mueller handled the pressure-cooker situation. It would provide an excellent chance to observe this key rival and his people in action. In Philip Hartley's expansive view of his career, everything that affected BellAir was his turf. If not now, later. Hartley was a fast learner, and a slow forgetter.

Just inside the entrance, Elaine and Gretchen Bond were chatting. At once Elaine noticed his serious expression.

"Is there a problem?"

He drew her aside. "There's a bomb threat against one of our flights. I'm going back to the office."

"Of course," she replied. "I hope everything will be all right."

Hartley smiled and gave her a peck on the cheek. "They'll be fine. Don't wait up," he said over his shoulder, making for the coatroom. "I'll be late."

6

POLISHED SHIP-GRAY linoleum floors, a low, sectioned ceiling for access to the maze of computer cabling overhead: this was Operations, BellAir's nerve center, Floor Forty-five of its midtown Manhattan headquarters. On the far wall of the long room, an array of oversized clocks kept time for the airline's worldwide system. Geneva... London and its familiar Greenwich Mean Time identifier... New York at ten-thirty eastern standard time... Los Angeles, then westward across the Pacific... Honolulu... Tokyo... Taipei. Beneath the clocks, a bank of teletype printers spat out weather reports and wind forecasts to fifty-three thousand feet, all monitored by the airline's staff of trained meteorologists.

Despite the late hour, most of the desks in Ops were busy. Although BellAir's European activities were largely buttoned up for the night, many flights were still airborne, coping with delays from the upper Midwest storm pounding Chicago. In the Pacific and Far East, the new day was about to dawn. At the largest cluster of desks, the company's flight controllers sat in their "pen," keeping radio contact with every BellAir aircraft, save for certain gaps overseas, an electronic umbilical for the airline's flights as they traversed the globe.

In the far corner, a glass partition separated a small room from the main work area. Normally dark, on this night, BellAir's "war room" was swarming with activity. It was only forty-five minutes since the bomb threat was called in, shortly after Flight 159's departure from O'Hare, but in that brief time BellAir's emergency team had been assembled, and the FAA and FBI alerted. A senior controller, Steve Avery, was working a radio console. Jack Murchie of BellAir's twenty-four-hour technical-support staff was making final adjustments to his radiotelephone network. Brow furrowed, Murchie looked as if his life depended on what he had just cobbled together. He pulled a microphone across the table.

"Let's make sure everybody's patched in. FAA Washington?"

"Sturgis and Jones."

"FBI Chicago."

"Andreozzi here."

"BellAir, Chicago."

"Yo. Joe Thompson."

"159?"

"We're with you."

Satisfied, Avery looked around the room. "We've got Axelrod from Maintenance and Vern here for Flight Ops. Security, O'Brien. Who's handling PR tonight? Right. Milt Collins. Okay, Fritz just showed. I'll turn it over to him."

A burly man settled into the chair at the head of the table. His forearms were bare under a short-sleeved white shirt, and he wore a nondescript tie, thin and dark, loosened at the collar. Fritz Mueller was one of the old hands, a BellAir original. A line pilot for an airline acquired by Bell in the thirties, Mueller had risen through the ranks to his present position, executive vice-president and chief operating officer. For over ten years, he had headed the nuts-and-bolts side of the airline's operations – flying, maintenance, security, airport activities worldwide. Despite an acquired management perspective, he remained a pilot favorite, and the affection was mutual. After a very long day Mueller had been halfway to his home in suburban Larchmont when his pager went off. Directing his driver to stop at the first pay phone they came to, he received a fast briefing and immediately turned the company limo around, back to Manhattan.

Slipping into the room behind Mueller was Philip Hartley. His formal attire raised a few eyebrows, but otherwise he was ignored by Mueller's people, intent on their crisis. Since this was Fritz Mueller's show, Hartley took an observer's seat at the rear, a respectable distance away from the table.

Mueller's face was impassive as he took command. He had made a career of playing "Mr. Inside" to Charlie Bell's "Mr. Outside," his laserlike approach complementing the diffuse focus that the airline's many "publics" forced upon Bell. Mueller used a sardonic sense of humor to sculpt his people into shape, and his temper was legendary, although in recent years, it seemed more practiced in the threat than the exercise.

"All right," Mueller began hoarsely. "Let's go over what we know. First off, Bill, you hearing me okay?"

"Sure thing, chief," replied Flight 159. "Loud and clear."

"Don't worry, we'll get you guys out of this. We'll go by the book and it'll turn out fine. Everything normal? How's your fuel holding up?"

"We're long on fuel. So, what can you tell us about our little, ah... difficulty?"

"We can't be certain." Mueller looked at O'Brien, his security chief, as he began recapping the briefing he'd received on the fly while rushing from the underground garage to the war room. "If it's anything, it's probably a barometer-type mechanism, the kind of thing that could be set to blow when you descend through a certain altitude. We have to be concerned maybe there's a time delay on it, too. It didn't sound like a regular timing device or we'd have brought you in right away. George, what about the phone call?"

An FBI alumnus, George O'Brien was a white-haired Irishman with a florid face and a pockmarked, bulbous afterthought of a nose. He reached for a table mike.

"The call came in to Reservations at 7:55 Chicago time," O'Brien began in a flat, nasal tone, reading from a small notebook. "The girl that took it, a Sandra Duffy, she did a nice job following the checklist, got as much as she could outta the guy. Normal-sounding voice, no particular accent, not colored, not foreign, nothin' like that." He flipped through several pages of his notebook. "He spoke very slow. She said it sounded muffled, like he was talking through a handkerchief or something. Best she could remember, his words were, 'I put a bomb on 159 at O'Hare today. It's big enough to bring it down.' Then he says, here's the important part, he says, *'It's set to go off when the plane's descending.'*"

"What altitude?" Mueller shot back. "What about altitude!"

"I'm getting to that. 'What altitude?' she says, but he says, 'Nothing doing, that's for you to find out.'"

"What makes you think this isn't just a crank?" Mueller asked, frowning. "Hell, we get a couple of calls like this every week."

Andreozzi, from the Chicago FBI office, spoke up. "Thing that worries us is the details he knew about your operation."

"Such as?"

O'Brien consulted his notes again. "Such as, the res agent asked him, 'Where's the bomb?' He says, best she could take it down, 'I'll tell you, but it won't do you any good. It's in a brown suitcase I put aboard. The flight's a DC-10...'"

"A DC-10!" snapped Mueller. "Hell, anybody with an OAG can figure *that* out! Put aboard? What the hell's *that* supposed to mean?"

"Wait one, Fritz," O'Brien held up his hand. "It's what he said next. He says, 'Right now it's sitting in a container in the center cargo compartment. It's in an LD 3. Ask Joe Thompson. He'll tell you. This friend of mine, he told me to say that.'"

Thompson, BellAir's O'Hare station manager, broke in. "How the hell's he know my name? What is this, an inside job?"

"Any mention of a ransom?" asked the FAA official. "An organization or anything?"

"None at all. She asks him what he's after, but the bastard says, 'I already told you too much.' Then he says, 'God have mercy on their souls,' and he hangs up. Just like that!"

"What about the trace?"

"The call originated from a pay phone in Bensenville, that's just west of O'Hare, but the guy was gone when the police got there. Naturally."

The FBI spokesman jumped in. "Bensenville police and the Cook County Sheriffs are on it, checking for prints, witnesses, all the usual stuff, anything out of the ordinary."

"Son of a bitch," said Mueller in a low voice. "That's it? No ransom, no reason, no nothing." He thought for a moment, then shook his head. "This is just so weird...we'd better take it serious, but shit! We don't know if the fucking thing's set for ten feet or ten thousand!" Mueller rubbed his forehead. "Bill, whereabouts are you now?"

"J-84, abeam Omaha. We've been at thirty-five thousand since your wake-up call. Figured we'd just stay here in case we needed to get down quick."

"That's good," Mueller said, looking around the room. "We'll take him into Stapleton. That's the highest place around with good facilities. Steve, what's the Denver weather?"

"Clear and unrestricted under a high cloud deck, wind from the south at ten, a few gusts. Nice night."

"Why not Cheyenne?" asked Swensen. "That's seven, eight hundred feet higher."

Mueller shook his head. "I'll trade that for the options Stapleton gives you. He has a lot better shot at landing into the wind there, too."

"Cheyenne's three thousand overcast and five miles, gusts to thirty," said Avery. "No change forecast either place."

"Well, that does it," Mueller snapped. "Bill, you catch all that? You comfortable with Stapleton?"

"Sure. Know it like the back of my hand."

"Okay. Like I said, you go by the book unless there's a damn good reason."

Avery threw a copy of Stapleton's Jeppesen chart on an overhead projector and the airport's runway layout flashed onto the screen. Mueller studied it a moment.

"Bill, here's the deal. The winds the way they are, they'll give you the ILS approach for 17 Left, then they'll take you over to the far corner of the field, southeast side as far away from the terminal as you can get. This one, I think you better pop the slides and get everybody out. We won't know we're okay till we search the plane. And one other thing."

"Yeah, Fritz?"

"No heroes tonight. You understand me?"

"Don't worry, boss. We'll handle it."

"You get yourselves the hell away from there. I mean it!"

"Okay," Van Dusen replied. "Sounds like a plan."

Mueller looked around the room. He noticed Hartley for the first time. A flicker of irritation crossed his face as he turned back to the microphone. "We'll talk more as we go along, and do I need to say this better be the smoothest landing you ever made? None of your usual shit, bouncing it in."

Van Dusen chuckled. "No sweat, I'm in a groove. Been greasing them on all week."

VAN DUSEN AND JARVIS looked at each other. "Get Donna up here right away."

A moment later the first flight attendant knocked on the cockpit door. "What's up? You people aren't still hungry?"

"Not anymore." Van Dusen flashed a crooked smile. "We got a little problem. Some nut made a bomb threat against the flight."

Her face dropped. "Jeez, you gotta be kidding."

"I wish I was, but Ops is acting like this one's for real. For all they know it is. The thing's supposedly in the cargo hold, they don't know, it could be some kind of pressure device that'll blow when we're descending but they don't know what altitude! Terrific. Just terrific."

"How should we handle the passengers?"

"Nothing about any bomb, not even a hint. What we'll do, I'll get on the PA when we're starting our descent and tell them we've got a mechanical problem but nothing to worry about, the usual bit, we're setting down in Denver as a precaution."

"What about the crew?"

"Can they keep their mouths shut?"

"God, how would I know? When's the last time anybody kept a secret around this place?"

"Well, let me put it this way. The more the crew knows, the better, but not a word to the passengers about the bomb part. Understand?"

She nodded.

"One other thing. We'll be using the slides, soon as we park. I'll mention that in the announcement, then you take 'em through the procedure. Keep them busy, but try to keep it light. Look at it like this, it's inflight entertainment, right? What the hell, it's probably some idiot with a warped sense of humor. That's how these things always turn out."

She laughed nervously. "Entertainment, huh. I suppose you're handing out the Oscars afterward."

"You're on. We'll talk when we get closer in."

The flight attendant took a deep breath, then opened the cockpit door. "Wish me luck," she said, biting her lip.

Lori Mitchell forced a smile. "Luck."

As the door closed, Van Dusen turned around. "This'll be a normal approach except we'll need to dump fuel, let's figure about twenty-five minutes out. Lori, you ever done that on this airplane?"

"Never had the pleasure, Bill."

"Let's go through the checklist in a couple of minutes. In fact, why not pull it out now and start taking a look. Ken, you handle the approach to the outer marker, then uncouple the autopilot and take over the radios. I'll take it in from there."

"What'sa matter, you don't trust me?"

"C'mon, if I'm in charge, I'm in charge. Right?"

" 'Course. I'd do the same in your place."

"Hope you never have to."

"I wouldn't bet against it, the crazies we get these days."

FLIGHT 159 DRONED ON, two hundred miles east of Denver and less than an hour away, approaching Colorado's eastern plains, wrinkled threshold to the great mountains just beyond. As it approached the town of North Platte, air traffic control instructed the aircraft to slow and enter a gradual descent, a twinkle in the firmament on its earthward course.

Van Dusen ran his thumb over the intercom transmit button, his thoughts wandering. First time he was ever in this part of the country, a flatlands kid driving west with his father in their old Ford. Just sixteen, the ink still damp on the driver's license in his back pocket. To this day he could picture his dad, straight face, nodding, leading him on, admiring the line of puffy clouds the boy pointed out so enthusiastically, a white band stretching from one end of the horizon to the other.

"Nice clouds, Billy. Real nice clouds."

Many times Van Dusen had replayed that scene. How, as the Ford neared his clouds, they were transformed, amazingly, into the snow-capped front range of the Rockies, rising sheer and majestic from the plain. He never told his dad, of course, but Van Dusen was always thankful for the chance to figure that one out, learning something about himself in the process, about his father too. This night it was too dark to see the mountains. Van Dusen couldn't help wonder if he'd ever see them again. He swallowed hard. Time to do it. He pressed the button.

"Folks, this is your captain. You may have noticed the aircraft has slowed down and started to descend, and that's what we're doing. Wish I could tell you we're almost to San Francisco, but fact is, we're east of Denver, and we'll be landing there because of a mechanical situation that's come up that needs to be checked out on the ground.

So I'm going to put the seat belt sign on now, and we want you to give the flight attendants your full attention. They'll be showing you the procedures for using the escape slides you saw on the video before we took off. This is just a precaution, to expedite leaving the aircraft."

Van Dusen's thumb relaxed. He stared grimly ahead, then jabbed it again, hard. "Be sure you follow their instructions to the letter. We'll be on the ground in forty minutes and as soon as the problem's fixed we'll be on our way to San Francisco. Oh, and by the way, drinks are on the house when we're airborne again out of Denver."

In the crowded cabin, the passengers looked around, fear and alarm on their faces.

"What's going on, miss?"

"Why the slides?"

"What's the big hurry?"

"We're going to crash, aren't we?"

Others reacted differently. "I knew it! I knew it! This scumbag airline!" The hefty young linebacker, now several drinks more obnoxious, was planted in the aisle, waving his arms and shouting at the top of his voice. "Can't you people do *anything* right?"

A slender flight attendant with a pixie haircut put her hand on his arm. "Sir, please take your seat."

"Don't touch me, lady! I know my rights!"

"*Sir!*"

Still he wouldn't budge.

Smiling demurely, the flight attendant began walking toward him, backing him toward his seat. "Sir, I'm sorry, but if you don't sit down, right now, I'll ask the captain to come back here, and, sir" – reaching up, she cupped her hand to his ear – "when we land, I'll have the cops throw your ass in the slammer. *So – take – your – goddamn – seat – like – everybody – else!*"

The man looked at the diminutive woman, still smiling at him. "Oh, all right. It's just, I really need to get to San Francisco." He slumped into his seat, covering his face with his hand. "This is terrible. I'm so late already."

"Nice going, Maggie." Donna Ward was passing through. "Score one for the good guys. Last check, everything's picked up. It's almost show time!"

By twos and threes, she briefed her cabin crew. There was no hint of the real problem as they went about their routine, only an occasional telling look. And the young stewardess who turned chalk-white and began crying when she heard. Take five, Donna said, then report back. The woman was still hiding in the rear galley, furtively lighting her third cigarette with a trembling hand.

Assuming their positions about the cabin, the attendants went through the safety demo, rehearsing procedures. Head down and forward, hands around the ankles. Shoes off to prevent snagging on the slides. After the drill, an air of calm seemed to come over everyone. Donna was surprised, pleased, actually, to see determination on most faces. There's a time and place to tell all, she thought, but this sure ain't it.

"THIS IS ANDREA BARNETT, reporting live from Denver's Stapleton Airport with a developing story…" A gust of wind blew the reporter's hair and she smoothed it back with her free hand. Behind her stretched a dark expanse. Colored lights flashed in the distance.

"Channel 7 has learned that a flight from Chicago, BellAir 159, is about to make an emergency landing here in Denver because of the threat of a bomb on board. Reportedly, the DC-10 is carrying over two hundred passengers and crew, but unfortunately, airport authorities have denied your Eyewitness News Team permission to go on the airfield. So we're forced to make do from this observation deck atop the terminal building, though this does afford us a bird's-eye view of the field. We should be seeing the plane in about fifteen minutes."

She extended her arm and turned toward the airfield. "It is indeed a dramatic sight, the yellow and blue runway lights and the fire trucks and ambulances standing by for any eventuality."

The reporter put her hand to her earpiece, listening to her producer's voice. "Details are sketchy, but we can report airline officials are concerned that enough high-powered explosives may be on board to destroy the aircraft. On the other hand, it's possible this is just a hoax – most of these situations turn out to be nothing more than that. As I say, our latest information is that the flight is expected in fifteen minutes. Needless to say," she added soberly, "we all pray it will land safely."

IN THE COCKPIT, Bill Van Dusen and his crew were readying Flight 159 for its approach and landing. Our "final approach," he thought grimly. A horn sounded, alerting the crew that they were within five hundred feet of their eleven-thousand-foot clearance altitude. The autopilot began leveling the aircraft.

"BellAir 159, Denver Approach. Descend to nine thousand and turn left two-three-zero degrees. You're twenty miles east of the localizer course for One-Seven Left. We'll be turning you in for the intercept shortly."

"Left two-three-zero and down to nine thousand," Van Dusen responded. "Sure you couldn't let us enjoy eleven a while longer?"

"Sorry about that, fellas. Wind's variable 160 through 170 at ten, occasional gusts to fifteen. Stapleton altimeter 29.85."

"Rog. We have the airport. We'll take the full ILS tonight. Want to keep this one nice and smooth. By the way, we could get used to this personal treatment real easy."

"Always happy to oblige."

The chime rang on the company line. Van Dusen picked it up. "Van Dusen."

"Bill, this is Fritz. Everything on track?"

"So far, so good. Pretty much routine, considering this bad joke you threw at us. We're down to, let's see... eight-point-five, not a hitch. Lot of worried folks in back, though, and they don't know the half of it."

"So they get mad later, that's life. Talk to you when you get down."

"Right."

"And remember, give 'em hell!"

"BellAir 159, turn left two-zero-zero degrees, cleared for the approach. Descend to *seven* thousand, intercept the 17 Left localizer, contact tower at the outer marker, wind now variable 165 through 175 degrees at twelve. Good luck, you guys."

"We'll do all that, BellAir 159."

"What the hell," Jarvis said, looking at Van Dusen. "Let's throw a couple thousand chips in the pot." He dialed 7000 on the autopilot control. The altimeter clicked off the numbers... 8400... 8300... 8200... a gentle 800-foot-per-minute descent.

"Localizer needle's coming in . . . here we go." The aircraft rolled into a left bank, angling toward the electronic course extending out from the runway. "Here comes the glideslope . . . we're just about there." As the aircraft rolled back, wings level, the stylized imaginary airplane in the flight director instrument nested precisely in its target. Now they were lined up on a heading of 175 degrees, pointed slightly to the right of the runway to compensate for the wind.

"Okay, Ken, disengage the autopilot. My airplane."

"Disengaged."

"Gear down, flaps thirty degrees."

"Gear down and flaps thirty," replied Jarvis, reaching for the landing gear lever, then the flap control. "We have three in the green."

"I hope those maintenance guys nailed that repair. Be a hell of a time to belly one in." As the aircraft slowed to 170 knots, Van Dusen advanced the engines against the drag of extended flaps and slats, and the landing gear dangling in the airstream.

"Outer marker." A blue light on the panel began flashing. Dash-dash-dash – the marker beacon.

Jarvis spoke into his headset. "Stapleton Tower, 159's at the outer."

"BellAir 159, cleared to land One-Seven Left. Emergency vehicles standing by. Just in case."

"Full of laughs, aren't you. Yeah, we see 'em. Looks like Christmas down there."

"Can you make the last high-speed turnoff?" asked the tower controller. "Zulu Five. That gives you ten thousand feet of runway."

Jarvis looked at Van Dusen, who nodded.

"Yeah, that's okay."

"Watch for the airport truck with the follow-me sign when you exit the turnoff. Stay with me this frequency, keep it rolling and follow that truck. He'll take you back across the runway and over to the remote apron. Park there and shut it down. We have buses waiting for your passengers."

"Can't hardly wait."

"I know what you mean. Good luck. We're rooting for you."

6100 . . . 6000 . . . 5900 . . .

"Radar altimeter bug set."

Approach lights coming up fast. A bit of jouncing in the mild southeast breeze.

"Wind check."

"170 at twelve," intoned the controller.

"Hot damn, right down the runway," said Van Dusen.

"I'll call it out," said Jarvis, peering at the radar altimeter. "Three hundred above... two-fifty... two hundred... "

"C'mon, baby," Lori Mitchell pleaded, "c'mon..."

"...one-fifty... one hundred... "

"Beep!" The radar altimeter sounded. Van Dusen pulled back on the control wheel. "Easy... easy... throttles coming back... "

"Go for it... go for it... "

The nose of the aircraft rose. Its wings planed their cushion of air. The landing gear reached... down... down for the runway.

There was a thud. The airplane shuddered. They were down.

"Reversers. Spoilers."

Van Dusen eased the DC-10's nose down and touched his brakes gently. Rolling along the runway, the big plane began to slow. Applause and cheering erupted through the cockpit door.

"Damn, that was good!" said Jarvis. *"Bodacious!"*

"Smooth as a baby's bare ass!" Mitchell beamed at Van Dusen.

"That keeps my winning streak alive." Van Dusen expelled a huge breath. "But that was the general idea, wasn't it? My steering, Ken."

Slowing through eighty knots. "Stow reversers and spoilers."

"Rog."

"Stand by to open the doors and deploy the chutes, soon as we park. I'll say when." Van Dusen lightly tapped the brakes to further slow the plane. As he neared the taxiway turnoff, he pivoted the huge machine with a turn of the tiller wheel at his left hand, nosing up behind the emergency truck that was accelerating to the speed of the aircraft, now rolling about twenty knots.

"I have the throttles, Ken. Got to keep up with our escort."

"You said it, *mon capitaine.*"

FROM THE OBSERVATION DECK, the broadcast crew had its camera trained on the flashing lights across the field.

"What a *beautiful* landing!" exclaimed the reporter. "Thank *God* they're down safely! The aircraft is rolling down the runway, and in just a few minutes passengers will be getting on those buses you can just make out over there. We have a Channel 7 camera crew inside the terminal, so stay tuned for live passenger interviews. You'll want to hear what was going through their minds at such a traumatic time. We'll also talk with the crew who brought the huge DC-10 to a safe landing after a bomb threat that, thankfully, seems to have been a hoax."

Surrounded by emergency vehicles, the aircraft lumbered to the parking area where several buses stood by, engines running. As the plane came to a halt the doors on the near side could be seen opening. Yellow chutes spilled from the doors, inflating and flopping on the ground like children's toys.

"The emergency slides!" chirped the broadcaster. "Again, we apologize for any lack of detail in your picture at home, but as we reported earlier, the airport manager here, a Mr. Tom Schneider, refused our Channel 7 crew permission to cover this event down on the field. We're using a powerful telephoto lens, but even so, it's difficult to make out everything from this distance. Now... yes! I believe I see the passengers sliding down the chutes!"

The broadcaster held a hand to her earpiece. "Right. Right. Okay."

The camera swung back to her. "We have a BellAir company official on his way up here, he's agreed to talk with us about this incident. Meantime, looking out there, now we can see passengers boarding the buses and still more are sliding down the chutes." She looked around. "Ah, here he is! This is Sam Chaffee, BellAir's..."

"*Stan* Chaffee," the man in a tan topcoat interrupted. "I'm public affairs manager for the airline here in Denver."

"We appreciate your joining us here, Mr. Chaffee. Now, what can you tell our Channel 7 audience about the dramatic events we've just witnessed?"

"Dramatic, I don't know, but the flight, 159, originated in Philadelphia this afternoon, then it stopped in Chicago and was headed for San Francisco."

"What can you tell us about the bomb threat?"

"Well, the phone call came in to the company shortly after the flight left O'Hare. We decided as a routine precaution to continue to Denver, take the passengers and crew off, which you can see we're doing, then check out the situation. That's really all there is to it."

"Why didn't you just check it during the flight?"

He shook his head. "It's not that easy to get access, not the way it's designed."

"I see. Well then, what exactly did the caller say?"

"Sorry, I'm not at liberty to give you anything on that. The police and FBI are involved. You'll have to talk to them."

"Why didn't you simply have the plane return to O'Hare?"

"Sorry."

"Can't you at least confirm our information about the passengers? I understand there were two hundred sixty on board and a crew of fifteen."

"Two sixty-two. Two hundred forty-seven passengers, crew of fifteen."

The newscaster turned and looked out over the airfield, the camera following. "Perhaps you can tell us what's going on. It's hard to see, but the buses have pulled away, and some other vehicles seem to be moving toward the plane. What's happening now?"

"I can make out two ground-service vehicles, and there's the bomb disposal unit, probably Adams County or it might be the Denver Police. It's a reinforced armor truck, like a Brinks truck, only heavier."

"But why? Isn't it clear the whole thing was a hoax?"

"Well, it looks like that, but we have to go through all the procedures. Next they'll be taking off some of the cargo, you know, suitcases and so on, whatever's in the cargo compartments underneath. Then they'll sort through it, get some dogs in to sniff around, X-ray it and so on."

"I thought you did that before the flight."

He shook his head. "We have security procedures, but passengers won't buy slowing everything down for a one-in-a-million situation."

"I should think security would be your number-one consideration."

"It is," Chaffee shot back, "but we have to move the operation along. Like I said, people just won't wait. Heck, even your station's been on our back for delays. You people did a piece just last week, if you recall, and not very complimentary, either."

"Well, whatever," the broadcaster replied, again looking toward the field. "What's happening out there now?"

Chaffee peered through a pair of binoculars. "Looks like one of our ground-support vehicles, a container loader. It's like a forklift. A platform raises up, then the ground crew rolls the container out of the airplane onto it. Normally it goes to the terminal for sorting out the suitcases and so on. In this situation the police will check it out, I expect."

"The container?"

"Right. Sorry, that's our name for it. It's sort of like a . . . you know, a *container*. I can see one on the lift now. It's flat on top and more rounded on the bottom so it fits the shape of the plane's underneath. They're working the cargo compartment just back of the wing on the starboard side, the right side. Now they're driving over to the bomb truck and lowering the platform, I can see them sliding the container into the back of the truck."

"How many containers are there on a normal flight?"

"Depends on the kind of aircraft. Also how full the flight is with bags and cargo. For a DC-10 fully loaded, I'd say there could be as many as fifteen or sixteen."

"Won't it take a while to unload all of them?"

"No, not that long, actually. Now they're moving another container out of the plane. I'd guess they'll just check the ones loaded in Chicago, that seemed to be where . . . "

Suddenly a burst of yellow-white light erupted on the airfield, followed immediately by the sound of a muffled explosion. The newscaster spun around. The container loader had disappeared from view, engulfed in flames.

"The container blew up!" Chaffee was clawing at the railing. "Jesus! Get the foamer on it!"

A cloud of chemical spray was already pouring toward the blazing vehicle.

"Holy Christ!" Chaffee pressed his binoculars to his eyes. "I . . . there's fuel coming out of the wing! A tank must've ruptured! I got to get down there!"

Suddenly, Chaffee froze. The newscaster ducked and threw her arm up as the airplane's wing blew apart. Men and equipment scattered in all directions, driven by the inferno. A fireball shot hundreds of feet into the dark sky.

The reporter was shouting into her microphone, her face lit by the brilliant flash. Helplessly, Chaffee leaned over the railing.

"The plane's going up!" cried the reporter. The fireball roared overhead.

"The whole plane's going up!"

7

MOST OF BELLAIR'S people learned about Flight 159 on the late news. Then, at sunup, it was to work as usual. Thirty thousand passengers were counting on the airline to be there for them, as it was the day before, as it would be the next. The wheel keeps on turning.

But this day was different. They lingered in the ready rooms, talking quietly, gathering around the bulletin boards to mourn those killed in the explosion, thankful a major loss of life was averted but uncomprehending. Who could have planted the bomb? What kind of person? Irrationally, many felt a sense of personal guilt. Scattered across the globe, they cared deeply about the company and each other, though it took something extraordinary to make them realize how much.

So even in the face of tragedy, the operation was king. Aircraft took off, and aircraft landed. Normalcy served to dull the pain.

AT NINE-THIRTY, after a short sleep and a cold shower, Philip Hartley walked into BellAir's executive conference room. Fritz Mueller was leaning over the long table, pouring coffee into a large BellAir mug. He motioned with the chrome decanter.

"None for me," Hartley said, taking a seat next to Wally Robertson, the airline's marketing VP. Hartley noted Robertson's tweed sport coat slung across a chair, but as was his practice, he kept his own on. Unshaven and obviously in the same shirt as the day before, Mueller took his chair across from the others.

"Two of our people killed," Mueller began, "both of them rampers. Guy named Pete Jensen, he was driving the loader. A Michael Rodriguez was inside the pit with the cop who was killed. Poor Jensen. . .there wasn't much left of him. Rodriguez died on the way to the hospital. Couple of passengers screwed up the evacuation. One broke her ankle, dumb broad still had her heels on. Another guy fell off the slide and got bruised up, some loudmouth they were having trouble with the whole flight. Some cuts and burns. That's about it."

Mueller rubbed his bloodshot eyes. "Obviously, the plane's gone. Once the tank blew, that was it. You saw the pictures. Nobody could get close enough to do anything. It's been an all-time lousy night. Soon as we're done, I'm outta here."

"I spoke to the adjuster a few minutes ago," said Hartley. "It's a total loss. They won't give us any argument on that."

"Our first one in six years." Mueller stuck a cigarette in his mouth. He snapped the gunmetal lighter shut and inhaled deeply.

"Any word from the police?" Hartley asked.

"Not a damn thing. I got O'Brien on them like a glove. Personnel, too. This has the smell of an inside job. We're checking everything, people we fired the last few years, malcontents and the like. And I told George to get me a plan for screening checked bags better." He glanced briefly at Hartley. "I don't give a shit what it costs, or about delays, either, and when I find the bastard who tipped off the TV!" His right hand beat a cadence on the table. "*God-damn!* The whole fucking country watching."

Mueller was silent for a moment. Robertson was fidgeting with a pencil. "Wally, the TV ads, where are we on that?"

Robertson nodded quickly. "The agency pulled them on news shows until Monday so they wouldn't get crosswise with footage of the wreck. Standard policy."

Hand on his chin, Hartley studied Robertson. Before taking over marketing, Wally Robertson had amassed a less than brilliant record heading the airline's regulatory department, whose task it was to petition Washington for fare increases and new routes. The advent of airline deregulation and the competitive marketplace undermined the need for this function and, coincidentally, BellAir's long-time former marketing VP was reaching retirement age, so Charlie Bell eased Robertson into that slot. The move stunned everyone, because Robertson was utterly lacking in sales and marketing experience. But then, the two men went back a long way together. In Hartley's view, it was a terrible appointment. If he'd been around at the time, he certainly would have let Charlie know it was a mistake.

Mueller grimaced and ground out his cigarette. "Well, enough rehashing. We still got an airline to run." He handed across two sheets of paper. "This is the last goddamn thing I need about now, but the boss wants some answers." Mueller's eyes glazed over as he looked at his handout. "Phil. The profitability forecast. What's the story?"

"Preliminary numbers are ready, but we're on hold until Wally gives us his fleet plan." Hartley turned to Robertson.

"Another week, maybe two," Robertson replied. "We had some delays."

"You gotta do better than that," Mueller barked. "Get it to Phil tomorrow, I don't care what shape it's in." He turned to Hartley. "Can you turn it around in a day?"

Hartley nodded. "No problem. Soon as I get Wally's input."

Mueller pressed on. "Speaking of that," he growled, "what the hell is happening in our transcon markets? Your forecasts are way off. They make no sense." Hartley watched Robertson shrink in his chair.

"Look." Robertson put his hand on a stack of computer printouts. "We all knew traffic would be soft to start with, given the recession and all. Then FAA puts our DC-10s on the ground after the American accident, just as we were moving into summer..."

Hartley leapt in. "But you must have taken that into account. That's what a forecast is all about."

Robertson tugged at his collar. "Okay, okay, maybe our crystal ball isn't as good as it should be. Sure, we should have canceled more trips when fuel started going out of sight, but we just didn't know which trips to cut. Aside from the obvious losers, we still don't. We just don't have good enough data. We're nowhere, compared to what American's able to do."

A fish out of water, Hartley thought, a skewered fish at that. Better he should have been a professor or a low-level accountant, not a senior officer in one of America's leading corporations.

Mueller interrupted impatiently. "All right, sorry I brought it up." He looked at his notes. "You heard Charlie the other day, he wants to bring in a consultant to look at the organization. He thinks we could use some outside help."

"We can handle that ourselves." Robertson poked his index finger at the bridge of his glasses. "That's nothing but a red herring. If we were making money, nobody'd give a damn about the organization. We all knew it'd take time to get our act together with deregulation, but we're coming along as well as could be expected. I mean, face it, nobody's doing very well. It's not as if everybody's making a ton of money and we're not."

Hartley leaned back. "I favor outside reviews. When I was at Salomon, our clients used consultants all the time for just this kind of thing. I'll check around. I still have the contacts."

"Okay," said Mueller, scratching his head. "I'm not convinced either, but the boss wants us to get back to him on it."

"It's a damn waste of money," said Robertson glumly. "What do we have a personnel department for?"

"Well, that does it." As Mueller rose, Hartley caught his eye. "Hold it till next week," Mueller said.

Hartley shook his head. "This is something we've been putting off too long. I'll make it short. It's become clear to me, we have to change how we handle the commuter airlines. Sure, we've always limited ourselves to marketing relationships, no ownership interests, no financial support, but that whole area's a disaster waiting to happen. We need a new approach, and we need it fast."

"What are you saying?" Suddenly Robertson was all ears. This was his turf.

"I'm saying, our arm's-length approach isn't good enough." Hartley and Robertson locked stares. "We need to tie up the best commuter in every one of our big-city markets. JFK, La Guardia, the Boston operation, San Francisco, not to mention that mess in L.A. Charlie's talking about cutting back our short-haul flying, but if we sit back and do nothing, we'll lose that traffic to American and United. Simple as that. The last thing we need is them to make a move on those outfits and we end up holding the bag. We need to cut some deals. Whatever they cost, it'll be better than running our jets into all those little towns like we do now."

Mueller broke in. "Not a chance. Charlie's off base on this one. Over my dead body will we ever drop the short-haul flying."

Robertson was becoming redder by the second. "You've got to be kidding! You're saying we should put good money into those two-bit outfits, paint their planes our colors, all that crap?"

"You got the picture," Hartley replied brusquely.

"We've looked at that harebrained idea a hundred times and it never made any sense." Robertson shook his head. "Okay, Phil, you're the one started this, what *about* that mess in L.A.? That guy, what was his name? Steiner? What a disaster! He never heard of on-time performance, and that bunch of longhairs he had running around! I had a stack of complaints a foot high! Our system may not be perfect, but it's served us damn well, and I'll tell you something else. You ask the attorneys what they think about getting in bed with those little outfits." He stood up and grabbed his jacket. "Our real problem is, you think you've got all the answers!"

Mueller slammed his hand on the table. "Look, Wally, I'm fighting Charlie on this one. But if for any reason we decide to use the commuters more, mind you, I'm saying *if* that happens, we damn well need more control than we have now. Forget Peterson's legal mumbo jumbo. May I remind you, those are *our passengers* in those little planes!"

Mueller spread his hands wide. "What do we know about their maintenance? Next to nothing! Or their training? For Chrissakes, Wally, get real. It's got nothing to do with what color their uniform is or when was their last goddamn haircut! This company's willing to take what those guys give us, but we want no part of making sure they do it right." He scowled at Hartley. "Mister money man, you better look your great idea straight in the face. It'll cost one ton of cash if we ever go that route!"

"We will keep that traffic feed," Hartley retorted, "and we'll do it for less, not more!"

"Horseshit!" The room fell silent as Mueller and Hartley glared at each other. Mueller got to his feet. "Wally, let's take Mr. Hartley at his word. Start nosing around. Find out what American and United are up to along these lines. And while you're at it, since Phil's so hot on California, stick my hometown in there, too. Give us a report on Chicago."

"But you're from Milwaukee," Robertson grumbled.

"Don't give me any shit!" Mueller snapped.

Robertson turned scarlet. "Aw, I was just trying to give you a hard time."

"Yeah, I know. That you were. I'm sure you were." Mueller shook his head wearily. "Keep an eye on things. I'm going to bed."

As he and Mueller walked out, Robertson stabbed his glasses into his jacket pocket.

"Hartley, no doubt," Mueller observed.

Robertson nodded. "That bugger is really getting on my nerves. Let him figure out how to do his own job before he tries to take over everybody else's."

Mueller put his arm around Robertson's shoulder. "Hey, don't take it so personally. It's a lot easier doing somebody else's job instead of your own. Hell, we're all guilty of that." He shrugged. "Fact is, the boss says Phil's a player around here. That makes him one."

Robertson looked at the floor gloomily. "I don't know. It's just, well, the guy just rubs me the wrong way."

"Ah, don't let him get to you. It's a tough time. Everybody's on edge." Mueller paused. "Say, I hear your shop's got a new secretary with a terrific set of knockers. Why don't I stop over for a cup of coffee one of these days? They say it's good management practice to inspect the troops once in a while. Whaddya think?"

"Sure, why not... what else is new?" Robertson stared straight ahead, his mouth a small hard line turned down at the corners.

In the conference room Hartley gathered his papers, arranging them in a slim leather folder. The meeting had gone well. The airline was in trouble. Confusion was rampant; everyone could sense it. Frayed tempers, things beginning to unravel. There's opportunity everywhere. A little chaos is just the ticket.

THAT EVENING, the Hartleys were relaxing in their elegant front room, watching the lights on the East River and in Queens beyond. This was unusual, both of them at home with no obligations, no plans. Hartley had changed into a crew neck sweater and slacks, Elaine was sunk in a large soft chair, her shoes off, feet curled beneath her. He switched off the ten o'clock news. Flight 159 was the lead story, as it had been in all the papers.

"Any leads yet?" she asked.

"Not a thing. How about a refill?"

She held out her glass.

He stepped to the wet bar, pouring her an Irish Creme over fresh ice and replenishing his drink from a nearly empty bottle of scotch.

"Thanks," she said, swirling the ice in her glass. "By the way, I noticed you and Arthur Winston were getting on famously last night."

Hartley leaned back in the sofa. "Remember a while ago I told you about Wally Robertson and his cronies? Well, Arthur and I are on the same wavelength. He wants my advice on how to handle the situation." Hartley paused, sipping his drink. "Until last night, I didn't realize how much Arthur is in my corner."

"But what about Charlie?"

"Charlie belongs to the past. If you want to know, he's the airline's biggest problem, himself."

"Just how do you intend to deal with *that* little difficulty?"

"Don't know yet. There are signs he'd like to ease up a little."

"But if he doesn't..."

"We'll deal with that when the time comes. The fact is, even with Arthur's support, this Wally thing is going to be tough, with him and Charlie so thick. But we have to get on with it. American and United'll have us for lunch if we don't make the right moves, and damn quick, too."

She nodded, pleased at his enthusiasm.

"At least I won't have to be out front on this one. The plan is to bring somebody in from outside to look around." He arched one eyebrow. "Somehow, I'll be *very surprised* if they don't recommend canning Wally."

"That's smart. Let somebody else do the dirty work."

"Exactly. Oh, by the way, you remember Roger Bankhead? We ran into him a couple of weeks ago in the Plaza."

"The fellow from McKinsey?"

Hartley nodded. "I had lunch with him today. Roger's one of the smartest marketing men I've ever run across. I couldn't do better than to have him on my team."

"After Wally's taken care of, that is."

"Of course." He smiled. "Timing is everything."

She sipped her drink. "You know, Philip, we do make a good team. You've always been the star, the crowd pleaser. I wish I'd known you back then. I'd love to have seen you play. Imagine, fifty thousand people screaming your name. You really must have been in your element."

"On a good day, eighty thousand." Hartley fell silent, suddenly pensive. *And, my loving wife, there is no way in hell you will ever understand how it hurt to lose that, for everything to fall apart on me.*

To start over, to remake my life. You may think BellAir is for us. That doesn't begin to tell the story.

"You and I are so different," she mused. "I like being back of the camera, moving people around, playing with them, making them do what I want."

"Ah, don't be so dramatic. Everybody manipulates everybody else. You're just better at it than most."

"Thanks, I think. But tell me this, Philip. Do you know my deepest, darkest secret? Have you any idea?"

He made a show of thinking. "As a matter of fact, no. Will you enlighten me?"

"You see, I don't mind if people underestimate me. In fact, I *want* them to. Nobody believes I have a mind of my own, much less an agenda." She folded her arms, hugging herself. "There! Now you know. *That's* my secret."

"The innocent flower," Hartley smiled. "But you don't fool everybody, El. Arthur Winston was very impressed last night. He made a special point of saying so."

She paused, savoring the comment. "What you said before, that's good news, but don't kid yourself, he's not about to do you any favors. He's not the type. There's a certain...streak in him. Playing with fire is how I'd describe being around that man."

Hartley looked at her severely. "That may be, but that man is going to help me get to the top in this company. Don't worry about Arthur. I can handle him. I keep a close watch out for Number One."

He set his drink down and came up behind her chair, reaching down and caressing her neck and hair. She looked up and their eyes met. She smiled faintly, then shook her head. He withdrew his hand and slowly walked across the room, standing framed in the glow of the city lights. As he gazed over the East River, he could sense his wife sitting in the chair behind him, still sipping her drink. Finally, he put his glass down. He turned and, without a word, left the room.

8

APPEARANCES TO THE CONTRARY, BellAir was not a long-time member of New York's business establishment. Founded in Springfield, Illinois, by a youthful Charles Duncan Bell with a stake from his father, a prominent merchant, the company's dusty-boot, midwestern roots were never far beneath the surface. Once up and running, Bell's Flying Service grew rapidly, and by 1936, its second year, it was flying the U.S. Mail in three well-worn Travel Air aircraft. Two years later, Bell burst on the national scene with major passenger routes out of Chicago, now the company's headquarters and hub. Renamed Bell Air Lines, soon service was launched to the east coast, to St. Louis, Kansas City, and other midwestern points, then came the long reach west to Denver and San Francisco.

During the war years, Bell Air Lines took another giant leap, ferrying supplies into all theaters of war and carrying servicemen by the thousands to the peril of combat and then, the fortunate ones, on their return home. Many of these men fell briefly but memorably in love with the Bell stewardesses who ministered to them during their vulnerable hours aloft. To Charlie Bell these weren't just soldiers, they were the executives, accountants, and salesmen of tomorrow, his future customers who would use air travel in far greater numbers than before.

"After we win this war," Bell preached incessantly, "I want these guys *back*! Never forget, what you do today builds our future for tomorrow!" And his people did not forget.

For the airlines, the fifties were an exciting but jittery decade. The nation's first commercial jet aircraft were springing from the drawing boards, Boeing's fabulous 707 debuting in 1958. Leapfrogging Britain's ill-fated Comet, the 707 and its Douglas and Convair counterparts would revolutionize air travel and forever alter the face of the globe. But paying for such advanced equipment brought tremendous financial pressure on those airlines with enough temerity to make the attempt.

By the mid-fifties, Bell's instincts were telling him that to position the airline for the critical times ahead, he needed to move his base to New York City. Though reluctant to relocate, he believed an eastern presence was necessary for day-to-day contact with key players in the nation's financial capital as well as for easier access to the Washington political scene. Thus "New York's Own" Bell Air Lines stepped smartly into the jet age while shedding its reputation for midwest insularity that had become a handicap to Bell's worldwide ambitions. A name change to "BellAir" along with a streamlined version of the company's familiar winged B logo and livery – red, white, and blue on polished aircraft aluminum – symbolized its emergence into the era of international jet travel. For their part, New Yorkers were pleased to claim three of the nation's largest airlines as their own, American, TWA, and BellAir, as well as Pan American, the world's premier international flag carrier.

Assuaging his midwestern pride, Bell kept his pilot training complex at Chicago's South Side Midway Airport, and began investing what would turn out to be millions in a major maintenance center at O'Hare, the emerging giant in the western suburbs. So Chicago remained the key traffic exchange hub on BellAir's domestic system, to some extent mollifying Chicago's disappointed civic leaders while allowing Bell, as he put it, to "keep a foot in the old backyard."

Dedicated in 1957, for a time BellAir's fifty-five-story steel and glass building on Park Avenue dominated its part of the Manhattan skyline. Eventually, other construction rose around it, but today the BellAir Tower remains a notable example of fifties architecture. In 1961, when BellAir modernized its corporate structure and created a holding company for the airline, its headquarters was renamed the BellAir Industries Building. But Charlie Bell failed to anticipate the stubbornness of New Yorkers, who simply ignored the new name. So, except in legal documents and the memories of company publicists, to this day the building remains the BellAir Tower. Even city guidebooks draw the line. None has ever carried a listing for a "BellAir Industries Building."

It wasn't long before the Tower's top floor became known as

"mahogany row." Opulently furnished, Fifty-five was home to Charlie Bell's suite and the first-class offices of his senior executives. BellAir was known in the industry as a high-cost, service-oriented outfit that didn't skimp on the little things or, for that matter, the big ones, either. According to Bell, class begat class, so he treated himself and his top officers well. Six times a year BellAir's board of directors met in a spacious conference room adjacent to Bell's offices, which commanded a panorama of the midtown area until that side of the building was hedged in by upstart neighbors. Floors Fifty-four down to Forty-six housed lesser executives, mid-level managers and staff. Operations was located on Forty-five.

In every headquarters office a certain area serves as a magnet for ambition, and the Tower was no exception. The airline's folklore held tales of bright young men and, though to a much lesser extent, women, rising through the floors to the Fifties and, for an elite few, all the way to Fifty-five. This ascent mirrored their career progress so accurately that company wits, for the most part cynical old-timers with little ambition left and not much to lose, likened the process to salmon migrating upstream. From this jaded perspective, the career life cycle was completed through the periodic layoffs, demotions, and terminations that generate the waste products of the corporate organism.

Airline planning is a contradiction in terms, so the saying goes, its horizon something between a month and a minute, reacting to unforeseeable events or, less charitably, those that just didn't happen to be foreseen. From the beginning, BellAir's course had been set by Charlie Bell's personal vision, and for years the airline traced a consistent and productive path. Even as it grew into a major international force, the company continued to be run Bell's way. When it suited him, he used its complex structure, but otherwise he ignored it. In recent years, Bell came to distrust the organization, blaming it for the company's difficulties.

Bell's frustration was capped by Congress' deregulation of the airline industry in 1978. His opposition to the new legislation was one part disdain for the "woolly-headed professors" who laid the theoretical foundations, one part distaste for the "shortsighted and opportunistic politicians" who so eagerly built upon them. Bell's deepest concern, however, was that the leadership mantle he had worn so many years no longer fit. To its forty-six thousand employees Charlie

Bell still personified the company, but he realized he was drifting, as the old familiar landmarks grew dimmer.

The company's involvement in the politics of deregulation reflected Bell's personal stamp. The airline's financial results over the years owed much to his and his industry colleagues' creative, nurturing use of government for their private gain. The protective framework of regulation gave BellAir a fighting chance to make a profit, not that it succeeded every year, but even in the worst of times it was never very far off.

To Bell it was sheer insanity, this threat to open his route monopolies and protected markets to all comers, and permit the competition to cut fares at will. But as the debate quickened in Washington, Bell noticed where the parade was headed and was agile enough to jump in before it passed him by. Bitter gall indeed, but Bell's hearing testimony and other public statements earned the company valuable credits with the congressmen and staffers whose views ultimately prevailed. The airline industry would never be the same, but Charlie Bell clung to an axiom that had always served him well – it pays to have friends in high places.

Compounding Bell's discomfort, stranded as he was on this unfinished playing field, the grumbling in BellAir's ranks was beginning to resonate even in the rarefied air of Fifty-five. For the first time in years, sharp questions were being asked, and nagging skepticism was widespread. How did the company mean to deal with aggressive moves by United and American? And what about those computer reservation systems with their biased displays, directing travel agencies away from BellAir, whose own CRS lagged far behind?

As a matter of fact, BellAir wasn't standing still. In 1979 it initiated service on several important routes and sloughed off some unprofitable old dogs. Serious efforts were underway to modernize key management functions. Nevertheless, the undercurrent of doubt all too well reflected Bell's own fears. He knew he wasn't setting the tone and direction for the company. For the moment, nobody was.

Since its inception, the airline had suffered its share of accidents, though its safety record was among the industry's best. Charlie Bell's lost planes and crews and passengers still haunted him, and some nights he awoke, trembling and bathed in sweat, reliving an event forty years distant. Flight 159, its mystery still unsolved, had taken its place in this gallery of horrors.

Thus, much was riding on Bell's elite task force, his old comrades Mueller and Robertson, and the newcomer Philip Hartley. These trusted advisors would provide direction and strength. With more trepidation than real hope, Charlie Bell awaited their help in his struggle against the new, deadly forms of business warfare spawned by deregulation and driven by modern technology.

9

ROSS MACLEOD PACED THE SIDEWALK, barely noticing his breath hovering in the frigid November air. Although chilled to the bone, MacLeod kept moving, fists deep in his overcoat pockets, ignoring the company limo running and warm nearby. For twenty-five years quarterback of BellAir's dealings with the federal establishment, MacLeod was the acknowledged dean of the airlines' capitol contingent. Everyone knew Scotty MacLeod, Mister BellAir in Washington, and for his part, he knew anyone in town who mattered, plus more than a few who didn't.

Despite Charlie Bell's distaste for the political scene, which he considered populated by duplicitous, self-serving egos, he faithfully attended the regular gatherings of airline chieftains at the New York Avenue headquarters of their trade group, the Air Transport Association. Whenever the boss was in town, Scotty MacLeod was at his side, though he was excused from these meetings when the ATA Board went into executive session. Today's meeting broke about three, but Charlie ducked into a vacant office for a private chat with United's Dick Ferris.

"Damned weather, fit for neither man nor beast." MacLeod clapped his gloved hands. "What can be keeping that man?"

Just as he decided to make for the building, Bell emerged through the revolving door escorted by an ATA official. Bell quickly approached the car.

"You might make the four-thirty," MacLeod said, glancing at his watch.

"Right," Bell muttered.

The driver, a student working part-time in MacLeod's office, pointed the limo toward National Airport. Rush hour traffic was beginning to build, and with a storm forecast, the commuters were fleeing, anticipating the gridlock even the thought of snow brings to the District.

"Jesus, am I bushed." Bell rubbed his forehead. "These meetings are such a pain in the ass."

MacLeod looked at his old friend . . . how worn he seemed these days. Years ago, Bell's hair, once carrot-red, had darkened. Now it was streaked with gray, and lately the ruddy face seemed paler, the worry lines deeper. Although the eyes, MacLeod took slight comfort in observing, at least Bell's trademark pale-blue eyes were clear and alert as ever.

"You know," Bell said wearily, "none of my old crowd shows up anymore. These new people, they're from some other planet."

"But they know you, they respect what you've done."

Bell snorted. "Don't kid yourself. Same time those guys are kissing my ass, they're figuring out how to carve it up. They are no friends of mine or the airline."

"Hey, Charlie, that's what deregulation's all about. Remember?"

"*Fuck* deregulation!" Instantly, Bell's face turned a bright red. "I never should've let you talk me into it! Goddamnit, this isn't some kind of game. These are peoples' lives we're responsible for! And I'm supposed to worry, does American have a leg up today or what new way did United find to screw us? Nearly fifteen hundred flights a day, we depart. *Fifteen hundred!* And it's not good enough that everything's working right, look what happened in Denver! We nearly lost a planeload of people, two of our guys dead as it is, and we still don't have a line on the bastard that did it. Deregulation. Goddamn fucking waste of time, that's all it is."

"I take it you're finished."

Bell glared at MacLeod. Suddenly he broke into a hearty laugh and slapped him on the knee. "You old sod, you're the only one could get away with that and live!"

The limo was approaching the Lincoln Memorial. Bell leaned forward and put his arm over the front seat. "What's your name, son?" he asked.

"Jerry. Jerry Curtis, Mr. Bell."

"Well, Jerry Curtis, here's what I want you to do. Go around that circle there, then come left onto Independence Ave. You'll be dropping me off at the Smithsonian." Bell sat back. "I don't know what came over me, Scotty, but after sitting through all that bullshit, I need some time in there. What about it? Want to walk around with me?"

"Sure. I'll switch you onto the next flight."

"Nah, I'll just take the shuttle. See what the competition's up to."

They drove by a line of drab government buildings, past the red brick structure that for years housed the nation's collection of aviation memorabilia, and made a U-turn in front of the marble and glass Air and Space Museum.

"This is good," MacLeod said to the driver as they pulled alongside the curb. "I'll give you a call when we're ready."

Exiting the car, the two men strode by the hot dog and pretzel stands, the souvenir vendors packing up for the day, and crossed the low stone steps into the museum building. In the glass-ceilinged entrance gallery they stopped to admire the Wright Brothers' Flyer and the *Spirit of St. Louis* overhead, hanging side by side. But Bell's thoughts were miles away.

"I was fifteen when Lindbergh came through on that tour of his," he said wistfully. "Biggest damn thing ever hit our town. That's when the bug bit me."

Bell started toward the next gallery. "Over here, Scotty..." He gazed up at the ancient airliners. "I have to admit some of your ideas were all right. Damn! If I'd only listened to you, that'd be *our* DC-3 up there instead of American's."

"Our Tri-motor doesn't look too shabby."

"Yeah, but it's not as modern as the Three." Bell smiled. "I should know, I got a ton of hours in both of 'em." He swept his hand about. "If they go ahead with that expansion, I want one of our jets in it. In fact, get hold of them tomorrow and tell them we're on board for a 747!" Bell laughed wryly. "We'd do better parking it here than flying the damn thing, the way things're going these days." Suddenly Bell frowned, looking around the gallery. "Where the hell's our World War II exhibit?"

"Next floor up, in back. Where it's always been."

"Oh, yeah... sure. Well, let's go take a look." Bell led the way to the escalator and mounted it briskly. At the top, when MacLeod caught up, Bell was breathing heavily.

"You set a mean pace," MacLeod observed.

"The legs are fine, but still too many smokes. I'm down to half a pack a day, though."

"For you that's the same as quitting." MacLeod pointed at the far wall. "We're over there."

They stepped across to a small display of photographs bearing the title *The Airlines' Role in World War II*. Between a photo of a Pan American Clipper refueling on a stopover in the Azores and one of FDR in a cockpit, was a shot of a young man waving from the cockpit window of a DC-4 Skymaster.

"Scotty! Recognize that good-looking guy?"

"You haven't changed a bit, chief."

Bell shook his head. "Damn. That is when we really hit the big time! Two hundred miles an hour! Twenty-five hundred miles! And *forty passengers!*"

"May I remind you," MacLeod said dryly, "I was well acquainted with that aircraft long before I had the misfortune of meeting up with you. Many an hour I spent commuting from London on your equipment."

"MI-6," Bell chuckled. "Damn spook. No wonder you always knew what I was going to say before I did."

"Nothing magic about it. All part of the training."

"Hey, Charlie Bell! You old bandit!" A tall man was striding toward the two men. He was wearing a blue windbreaker over a pilot uniform.

"Paul! Jesus! How are you!" Bell threw his arms around the pilot. "I haven't seen you since... I can't even remember. Scotty, you know Paul Harrington, don't you?"

Bell stood back, performing the mandatory inspection. "Captain, you're in uniform, more or less. So why aren't you working?"

The pilot winked at MacLeod. "I sneak in here whenever I get a chance. Have to say your scheduling people are getting smarter, though. There's not as much dead time on the road anymore."

"That is music to my ears," Bell responded. "Somebody's got to make you old buzzards earn those handsome salaries you pull down. What're you flying these days?"

"Best line in the company. Over the pole to Tokyo, a Honolulu trip once in a while, enough to keep up the tan." Harrington paused. "Anything on 159 yet?"

"Not yet, not a damn thing," Bell said grimly.

Harrington nodded. "Well, keep on it. It's only a matter of time. By the way, tell me, Charlie, how's Dee doing?"

"Ah, thanks for asking, Paul, she's doing fine now." Bell shook his head. "You know, that woman's unbelievable, what she went through. The operation, then all that business with the chemicals. It was sheer hell, but she's back on her feet, you wouldn't know anything was ever wrong." Bell grimaced. "I tell you, it was awful, seeing her hurting so bad and not a damn thing I could do about it. But thank God she's all right, now."

"Everybody was pulling for her. She's a very special lady. You know, it's funny running into you like this, I was just thinking about her the other day. Remember that ladies' group she started, those baby blankets of theirs?"

Bell chortled, "I thought it was the dumbest thing I ever heard, but it turned out to be one hell of an idea."

"Well, let me tell you something about that," Harrington said animatedly. " 'Course we got a blanket when our daughter was born, a little pink one with her name on it and the winged B in the corner. Shoot, I hadn't thought about that for years, it's put away somewhere with our things, but you know, one thing leads to another, Kath graduates college, and she gets on with the company as a stew." Harrington shook his head and smiled. "We're a two-generation BellAir family now. Can you believe it? Anyway, the other day she takes me into her little boy's room, he's already four months old, and here is this blue BellAir blanket on his crib with his name. Kevin!"

Harrington paused. "I tell you, Charlie, it's going to be very tough to give all this up. I'll be sixty next year."

"Yeah, but sooner or later us old coots have to step aside. Hate to admit it, but the young people deserve a shot at it, just like we had."

"That doesn't make it any easier." Harrington rubbed his palms together. "Well, it's about that time. It sure was good running into you guys. Remember me to Dee."

"See you around, you old bastard." Bell wrapped his arms around the pilot. "I wish I was flying out with you tonight. I really mean that." He held Harrington at arm's length. "Listen. Come by the office next time you're in New York, I'll show you around. You won't believe some of this fancy computer stuff I got on the drawing boards."

Harrington smiled. "You're on. And that's a promise. So long, Scotty," the pilot said over his shoulder as he walked away.

The late afternoon sun slanted through the dust, silhouetting the Mustang and Corsair that once ruled the skies, now casting shadows on the floor, their engines stilled, the stuff of memories.

Bell exhaled deeply. "Let's sit down a minute."

"Are you all right? You look kind of pale."

"It's just, well, those meetings are getting to me." They sat down on a bench. "All those young tigers. Ferris, what a sharp guy he is. He hasn't been around that long, but boy, is he learning fast. It's people like them...what confidence they've got, and they take shit from *nobody*! Worst thing is, they remind me of myself forty years ago." Bell shook his head. "I ask you, how the hell can we make it when we're up against guys like that? When the best we've got is an old fart like me."

MacLeod scowled. "Come on! What have those guys ever done? You built a *company,* for God's sake! How many cities do we serve? How many paychecks go out with your name on them? You heard Paul, you know what people think about you! What'd those guys ever do?"

"Scotty, the truth is, I don't know how long I can keep it up. I'm just not doing the job anymore. Maybe other people don't know it, but I do. That's what counts. I know."

MacLeod put his hand on Bell's shoulder. "Get hold of yourself, man. You've got plenty of good years left. Don't let anybody hear you talking such rot!"

Bell shook his head. "Things are changing too fast. You hear me talking about computers? Shit, what do I know about computers? I'm an airline guy, not a damn engineer!" Bell wagged a finger in MacLeod's face. "Take today. We had this presentation. You know that fat staff guy, the one with the thick glasses? I followed what he was saying, sort of, but *Ferris*! Five steps ahead of him the whole way! He was asking questions that little creep couldn't even *answer*!" Bell paused, silent for a moment. "What I'm trying to say, Scotty, it's about time somebody else was running the show."

MacLeod's face darkened.

"No, no, I'll never quit! I would never do *that*! I'll stay on as CEO, but I need somebody new to be president, somebody who can run with this crowd, keep up with them."

MacLeod gazed at the ceiling. He sighed deeply. "Well, I suppose that wouldn't be the end of the world." He faced Bell. "I've never pulled any punches with you, Charlie, and I won't start now. The fact is, I've been thinking, too. You mentioned that computer business. United and American are peddling those res systems of theirs like they're going out of style, and here we are still trying to figure out which end is up. Hell, if we don't get out with a product, we'll be so bloody far behind we'll never catch up. There're plenty of other things, too. We both know it. So, I guess what I'm saying, I agree with you, we could use some new blood. And I don't mean to exclude myself, either."

Bell looked at his old friend. "Just between us, I'm going to start preparing the board for a change next year."

"Who do you have in mind?"

"Well, that's the problem. I guess I never gave much thought to when I wouldn't be running the show." Bell frowned. "I'd like to give Fritz a crack at it, but I can't."

"Why not? He's certainly earned it."

Bell shook his head. "Tell the truth, I've never been sure how much I could trust his judgment, outside of running the operation, that is."

"You mean the deal with that stew in Cleveland?"

"Yeah, and there was another one you never even heard of. Sixty years old and the man still can't keep his pecker in his pants! Shit, if he wasn't so damned good at what he does, I'd have had his ass years ago. As it is, I've spent a small fortune covering up his little mistakes. I mean, none of us is a saint, but at least we never put the company at risk the way he did."

MacLeod frowned. "Not Wally, certainly."

"No. Poor old Wally." Bell looked at the floor. "His days are numbered as it is. My being so lousy with all these gimmicks, I need somebody who knows what he's doing, and Wally's even worse than me. I should never have put him in that marketing job, though I didn't see it at the time."

"But who does that leave? Peterson? One of the younger officers?"

"That's about the size of it. I don't want to go outside if I can help it." Bell glanced sideways at MacLeod, "Scotty. . . what would you think about Hartley?"

"You can't be serious. He hasn't been with the company a year!"

"That's a year more than somebody we'd bring in from the

outside."

"Don't con me," MacLeod replied sourly. "Phil's a beginner, for God's sake. It's not like bringing in a guy who's done the job somewhere else."

"Look at it this way," Bell countered. "What I'm saying, it's not good enough anymore just to run the operation. Phil, now he's a modern guy, he understands these new ideas, he gets along with the bankers and so on, all my favorite people." Bell pointed his finger at MacLeod. "And he knows how to get what he wants! He's a *winner*! Fact is, if he had a couple more years in, there'd be no question in my mind, none at all."

"But he knows nothing about operations. He's a numbers guy!"

Bell nodded. "That bothers me some, but if we keep Fritz happy a couple more years, he'd cover the operations side and balance Phil off real well. I mean, these days you don't need to be an operations guy. Look at Ferris, for God's sake, or that fella Crandall they're bringing along at American. See, Scotty, I've been testing Phil. Even if he won't admit it, he's in there over his head, and I did that on purpose. There's a lot more to that finance job than he thinks – politics, arm twisting, dealing with outsiders, but he's doing fine so far, real well. As a matter of fact I'm thinking about giving him some more assignments. Anyway," Bell said conclusively, "it won't happen tomorrow. There's plenty of time to get a good fix before I move on it."

MacLeod shook his head. "Phil Hartley could be Superman himself and people would still think you were off your rocker."

Bell looked at his watch. "Yeah, well, I haven't made up my mind yet. I can always go outside if I have to."

"Your attention, please." Bell looked up. "It is now five forty-five, and the museum will be closing in fifteen minutes. Thank you for visiting the National Air and Space Museum. I repeat, the museum will close in fifteen minutes."

"We'd better move it unless you want to spend the night in your Tri-Motor," MacLeod said glumly. They began walking toward the escalator. By now the crowd had thinned, and the two men were among the last to leave. An iron latticework gate was being drawn across the entrance of the museum store. The bands of schoolchildren were gone, home to dinner, TV, and homework, but perhaps this day a seed was planted. A future Lindbergh? An Armstrong? Possibly even a Charlie Bell.

"I'll give Jerry a call, let him know we're ready."

Bell shook his head. "Don't bother, I'll get a cab."

They moved slowly toward the entrance, "Scotty... about Phil. There's something inside him. I know he could make the hard decisions. Personnel actions, that sort of thing." Bell hunched his shoulders and shoved his hands in his pockets. "I'm just too soft nowadays. Maybe it was Dee being sick and all, but something like that changes you. Now all I can see is our people, what they've done for us, their families, all that pride. Worst thing, I see them one by one. I know too many names. I see their faces." He sighed. "To do this job you need blinders, and mine don't fit any more. Not even close."

The men stepped onto the sidewalk. "You know what I mean, Scotty? Do I make sense?"

"Yes, I think so."

"It bothers me, knowing what we'll have to go through, getting lean and mean like everybody says we have to." He glanced at MacLeod. "Remember the last time we took a strike?"

Bell answered his own question. "Sixty-six it was. Thirteen years ago. That's a long time."

A cold wind whipped about them. A few flakes were beginning to fall. "Outside of Dee, you're the only one I'd say this to." Bell paused. "Don't bet we won't have another one in the next couple of years. A big one. One we force, ourselves."

Bell stared at his old friend. "What I'm saying, it's really getting to me, knowing we'll have to tell our people we're cutting their pay and their jobs, tell 'em we've been lying all these years, they're not worth what we said they were. I'm just not enough of a bastard to take that on."

Bell shook his head slowly. "I'm tired, Scotty, bone tired. I don't have it in me. But I have a hunch our young Mr. Hartley does."

10

VINCENT COSTELLO sat on the edge of his bed in a small flat on Chicago's South Side. It was several weeks after the destruction of Flight 159. Costello's eyes were bloodshot, his back was bowed. Why, he asked himself again and again, why does everything I touch always turn to shit? It wasn't like this before. My job's not that bad, even with those assholes I have to deal with, and there's never enough money, but still, it wasn't until last summer, last summer when the headaches came back. So bad, worse even than when I got hurt and the buzzing in my head so loud, it just wouldn't go away. Costello looked at the window. Even the sun coming through that damned shade she wanted me to fix, it stabs me in my brain.

The television was on. Phony Santa hawking used cars, some broad dressed up like a reindeer. Not even Thanksgiving and already they're at it. Merry Christmas, suckers!

He dragged himself into the bathroom. Christ! Three days I haven't shaved... when was my last haircut? He ran his fingers through the dark, matted hair, lifted an arm for a fast sniff. Got to get cleaned up. Ah... on the floor... cigarettes. Got to pull myself together.

He halted, looking at the burning match. The bomb. His hand began to tremble... the bomb. A thousand times he'd been over it. That ramper, that stupid, *stupid* ramper! He must've banged the belt loader. That *had* to be it, it wasn't supposed to go off, he cried silently. *It was never supposed to go off!* I never meant to hurt anybody and now, now I got murder one staring me in the face. My plan, my great, foolproof plan. Like everything else I ever did, just a piece of shit. He inhaled deeply, holding the smoke as if it were his last breath... then he released it slowly.

One more time. I had to get a bomb on a plane. I had to show them I could do it. Costello shivered. The damn wiring wasn't hooked up, I mean, how could it be? But it must have been, somehow, or something touched. . . I was in such a hurry at the end, maybe that was it. But I had to make it look real so next time they'd do what I told them, no questions asked.

Costello smiled slyly. That was the beauty of the plan. Next time I wouldn't even've had to put one on a plane. Just say, here it is, and go collect the money. I wish I knew what happened. But what the hell, what good would it do? It was a bad day, I remember that, the buzzing so bad and there was a lot of other noise, too. Couldn't sleep the night before, so jittery, rushed and everything. I could've put it off but what if somebody found my gear, found out what I was up to? There'd have been hell to pay, I'da lost my job. He shuddered violently. Nothing like what I'm in for now, though.

He took a long drag on the cigarette. Only good part, next time they'll damn well know who they're dealing with, you better believe it! He slumped on the bed. . . if there *is* a next time. The cops, everybody snooping around. I know they been interviewing people. And all those stories in the papers. I got to lie low for a while. Can't risk it again, not so soon. But at least they didn't find out it was me. . . not yet. He shuddered. Got to give it more time, let it blow over. Christ, what lousy luck I got. But damnit, next time they'll know they'd better listen. For damn sure they better.

The door opened. A woman walked in, followed by a small boy carrying a wrinkled piece of paper, its colors smudged and runny, like the boy.

"Well, well. So you decided to get up." She avoided Costello's eyes as she passed through to the kitchen.

"Hey, Uncle Vince," the boy said. "Wanna see my painting?"

Costello squinted through the smoke rising from the cigarette in his lips. "Yeah, Eddie, that's good. That's real good."

The woman returned with a glass of milk for the boy. "I gotta get ready for work," she said sourly. "You can watch Eddie."

"Hey wha? Whaddya mean, watch Eddie? I got things to do, you know!"

"Things to do, huh? Well, you'll have plenty of time to do them if you keep calling in sick. What's this, third time this week?" She shook her head, and her long, dark hair flew about her shoulders. "Just look at you, layin' around, feeling sorry for yourself. And what's *this* I found!" She held up a small vial.

"Those're my painkillers! They're for my headaches! I got them at the Osco. Give 'em back!" He got to his feet and advanced menacingly.

She backed away. "Keep mixing this stuff with the booze, we'll be finding you face down in here one of these days."

"C'mon! Give it back! I mean it!" He'd backed her against the wall. The woman held out her hand, palm up. Costello took the vial and dropped heavily onto the bed. "And goddamnit, you quit talking to me like that in front of the kid. It's not right."

"He's *my* kid! I'll say whatever I want!"

She looked at Costello for a long silent moment. Then her face softened, becoming sad, almost sweet. "Aw, Vinnie." She went over and cradled his head in her arms, caressing his hair. "Vinnie, Vinnie, Vinnie. What am I going to do with you? You're not the only guy the war ever messed up but here you are, every day you're still fighting it, every day. Please do what I said, call the doctor, go see him, just this once. Please. For me?"

Costello stared straight ahead. "If I told you once, I told you a hundred times, I had my fill of them quacks in the army. What if the company found out I went to a shrink? They don't want guys with problems. Anyway, how'm I supposed to pay for it? Look, there's nothing wrong with me a little luck won't fix. I tell you, this deal I been working on, when it finally comes through we'll be outta this hole so fast . . . "

"Oh, no," she backed away, shaking her head. "Oh, no! No more betting! You said you'd quit! You promised me!"

"It's nothing like that," he protested. "This's more like a . . . a business proposition."

Her eyes narrowed. "You're lying. I know you still talk to that guy Lennie."

"That's got nothin' to do with it. It ain't what you think. Listen. When this deal goes through, he's off my back for good. All's I need is a little more time to work it out."

"This's no way to live, and you with such a talent." Suddenly she brightened.

"Maybe that idea you had, you know, start a repair shop, work on cars and stuff, maybe you could do that when this deal comes through." She straightened and brushed her hair away from her face. "I been thinking, I could even help out with the books. I'd like that. I'd like that a lot!"

"Sure, sure. You can't keep the money straight now. How the hell you gonna help out with the books!"

The woman began to weep. "That's not fair. I'd learn. I would. You shouldn't put me down. Just 'cause I didn't finish school and all, it's not like it was my fault."

Costello looked at her. "Aw, I didn't mean it like that." He touched her lightly on the shoulder. "Sure you can help. You can help and I'll bet you'd do real good, too."

They sat quietly, side by side on the bed. The woman wiped her eyes. "I better get down to the restaurant. Maybe you'd take Eddie to the park later on. When you have time?"

"The park! The park!" the boy shouted, leaping in the air and spinning around.

Costello pondered her proposition. He looked at the boy, and a smile flashed across his face. "Him and me, we go to the park a lot, don't we?"

"Uncle Vince! Will you swing me this time?"

The man fumbled on the floor for his pack of cigarettes, stuck one in his mouth and lit up.

"Yeah, Eddie. Goddamn right I will. I'll swing you."

PART TWO

What Is This Thing Called Love?

1

T HE NIGHT FOLLOWING the loss of Flight 159, a conserva-
tively dressed, middle-aged man traveled from San Francisco
to the central coast city of Monterey. During the short, bumpy
flight, while other passengers read or chatted, this man, seated in the
first row of the small commuter airliner, would lean forward and peer
at the plane's instrument panel. As the plane slowed and began
maneuvering for its final approach, he sat back and massaged his eyes
with his fingertips.

Here I am, he thought, fifty-one years old, senior partner in one of
San Francisco's best law firms, respected confidant of the city's
corporate elite – what am I doing bouncing around the sky like
this? By all rights I should have my hands wrapped around my first
martini of the evening.

And that is exactly where Will Cartright would have been, secure
in the warmth and camaraderie of the Pacific Union Club but for the
death of a law partner several years before. That untimely event had
brought him a new client, Monterey Bay Air Services, or, as everyone
in the area knew it, Bay Airlines.

Early in his career, every capable attorney learns how to fashion
arguments proving that the law is on his side, at the same time obscur-
ing his client's real purposes. Indeed, this mindset can become so
ingrained that it is difficult for a lawyer to switch it off. For example,
in a recent partners' meeting, Cartright was queried about Bay, whose
billings were modest at best and seemed understated in view of the
hours he spent on that account. He cited Bay Airlines' indispensable
service to the central coast and valley and its stimulation of local business, which meant more legal services, some of which fell to the firm,
and so on and so forth. Correct as far as it went. But Cartright's wife
had a different view of the matter.

"Walter Mitty, Will. Pure Walter Mitty."

Of course, she was right. Aviation held a lifelong fascination for Cartright. He'd been up many times with friends and clients, eagerly taking the controls whenever offered the chance. In fact, in the recesses of his mind lurked the thought that someday, if he could ever ease up a little, he might take flying lessons himself, perhaps even buy a plane of his own. Meantime, Will Cartright contented himself with his periodic trips to Monterey, a welcome change of pace from the more prosaic, though far more profitable legal work that was his stock in trade.

Actually, Cartright's comment about Bay Airlines and its owner, Frank Delgado, was no exaggeration. Area residents relied on Bay for their business ventures and visits. Bay linked the peninsula's wealthy with San Francisco, jumping-off point for their world travels. It carried tourists who flocked to the region, which translated into jobs and income. The locals also appreciated Delgado's willingness to provide a plane and pilot, usually at great inconvenience, to ferry an emergency case bound for one of San Francisco's great hospitals.

Frank Delgado's roots were in Salinas, over the hills from Monterey, up the broad coastal valley. Home from Korea with his sergeant's stripes and a dream, Delgado set about nursing his fledgling operation from a flight-instructing, charter-flying, crop-dusting, do-anything-for-a-buck outfit into a thriving company with three hundred employees and a fleet of eight-passenger, twin-engine Cessnas. Most of his people were based in Monterey, with the rest scattered across a modest network stretching from Santa Rosa to the state capital and down to Bakersfield at the foot of the San Joaquin Valley.

Bay provided Delgado and his family a reasonable, if at times erratic, living. He was already counting on '79 to be his best year ever, despite the sluggish economy. The cost of aviation fuel had nearly doubled in a year, but increases at the service station meant business travelers could fly for less than driving and in a fraction of the time, not to mention saving the price of a hotel room. However, the onset of deregulation represented a serious threat to Bay's prospects, like those of the other commuter airlines. Freed of many governmental restraints, the large carriers were eagerly grasping new markets, though to their dismay, a crop of low-fare, no-frills airlines had sprung up, and were busily undercutting fares, upsetting the established order, brashly challenging traditional niceties.

No corner of the country was too remote to be untouched by the landmark deregulation law and no airline too small to escape its reach, certainly not Bay with its profitable little niche. Frank Delgado's years developing and serving his markets would offer him no immunity from the revolution sweeping the industry. Attempting to keep up, Delgado had reluctantly concluded that his old Cessnas simply weren't big or fast enough anymore. They cost too much to operate for what they brought in. If he didn't exploit the emerging opportunities, he knew somebody else would. Grow or die. It was as simple as that. As the company lawyer, Will Cartright was a key player in Delgado's plan to replace his fleet with more modern aircraft.

Cartright stared out his window at the droplets streaking sideways as the plane descended through the clouds. Soon, smudges of light began to appear in the undercast. Looking ahead, he spotted the approach lights over the nose of the aircraft. In a few seconds they were over the runway threshold, and it was power back, right wheel...left wheel...nosewheel. A firm touchdown on the wet surface. Cartright recognized the pilot's correction for a stiff right crosswind, an insider's insight that pleased him. After a short taxi, the aircraft came to a halt, and the pilot shut down its engines. As the copilot stood and squeezed past Cartright, opening the door and lowering its built-in staircase, Cartright saw a sodden figure in a blue and green parka with *Bay Airlines* across the chest, waiting at the foot of the steps.

"Watch your step! Inside the terminal for your bags! Stay between the yellow lines! Mr. Cartright!" the agent shouted over the shriek of a nearby jet. "How're you doin' this miserable evening?"

"Good, Ernie. And you?"

He shrugged. "Can't complain, wouldn't do no good anyway. Go on in. We'll get you a ride soon as we turn this bird around."

Walking across the rainswept ramp, Cartright paused and looked around. What a contrast between the Cessna and a towering BellAir 737 lumbering by. It saddened him to think that these stylish little workhorses would soon be retired, overcome by financial necessity, their productive lives cut short before their time. Cartright shook his head ruefully. And we call that progress.

THIRTY MINUTES LATER, the blue and green van slowed in front of a long, low building on Cannery Row, only a few steps from where Mack and the boys hung out, where Doc, Dora, and Lee Chong once thrived. Then the heart of Monterey's vigorous sardine-processing industry, for years the canneries had lain dark and silent, forcing other establishments that serviced the needs and desires of the local people to close their doors in turn. However, as even a vacant lot may bring forth wildflowers amid the weeds and junk, Monterey's waterfront was awakening. Many of the derelict corrugated iron buildings were taking on new life, this time as smart shops and restaurants in search of a different prey, the tourist.

Cartright stepped onto the sidewalk and looked around. Puzzled, he turned back to the driver. "This can't be the place. There's some mistake."

"No mistake at all, Mr. Cartright. This here's one of Frank's new hangouts."

Unpersuaded, Cartright surveyed the scene as the rain beat down. Hedged in by a leather-goods shop and an arts and crafts boutique, here was his destination, the Blue Heron Bar and Grill, a gritty, dilapidated throwback to the old days – the *really* old days. A blue neon sign patterned roughly after a long-legged bird hung over the front door. All things considered, the Blue Heron was not the sort of establishment an out-of-towner would dream of patronizing. Surely, no tour bus had ever darkened its door.

The entrance was weathered wood and glass, dark one moment, bathed the next in a flickering blue glow from the sign. Taking a deep breath, Cartright elbowed open the front door and stood, dripping, in front of a counter where a young woman was filling sugar shakers from a large sack. Except for a family at a table near the door the restaurant appeared to be empty.

He dropped his bags and peeled off his raincoat. "Is Frank Delgado here?" he asked. There was no response.

"I'm looking for Frank Delgado," he repeated. The girl's powers of concentration were getting on his nerves. It had been a long day.

"I heard you," she said without looking up, carefully wiping the mouth of a shaker with a paper towel and tightening the chrome top. "Follow me."

She picked up a worn menu and stepped to a swinging door that connected the main eating area with a barroom. As Cartright pushed through, the visage of Walter Cronkite greeted him, beaming down from a television on a shelf over the bar where several rough-clad men sat hunched over their drinks. Intent on toweling glasses, the bartender did not greet him.

"Kind of a slow night," Cartright remarked.

"Still early," the girl answered with a yawn. "Not that it matters. They're lousy tippers around here. Bunch of jerks, mostly."

She slipped the menu under Cartright's arm and pointed at the rear of the long, narrow room. "He's in the last booth. Stick your bags over there, if you want." She gestured toward a coat rack outside a door marked *Señoritas*. Cartright stared at the sign for a moment, suddenly feeling the need to know where *Señors* might be, but the girl had already disappeared.

As Cartright put down his suitcase, a man rose in the far corner and started toward him. He was short and blocky, with black hair whitened at the temples and a square, dark face wrinkled about the eyes and mouth from many hours in the sun. He looked fit, though a slight paunch could be seen under his white shirt, worn open at the neck. His left wrist was obscured by an oversized aviator's watch with a complex array of dials and several buttons sprouting from the case.

"Will! Whaddya say, counselor! How was your ride?" He pumped Cartright's hand, throwing his other arm around him.

"Terrific! How's the family? Mariel, the kids?"

"Great, really great," Delgado replied, beaming. "Couldn't be better. Hey, did I tell you about Manny? That little turkey's starting at quarterback, for the varsity, no less! His picture was even in the *Herald*. I'll show you tomorrow."

As the men settled into the booth, something that had been nagging at Cartright during his flight forced its way to the surface. "Too bad about that BellAir plane," he ventured.

Delgado nodded solemnly. "That was a tough one, wasn't it," he replied. "Too early to tell what it really means."

Cartright saw that his question had altered his client's mood and not for the better. After a moment, he sensed Delgado wasn't about to elaborate, so he picked up his menu.

"What do you recommend, here?" Cartright opened the menu. It wasn't seafood as, for some reason, he had expected. He nodded, then a faint smile came across his face. For him, Mexican food was an acquired taste. He was trying but he wasn't there yet.

"I've got this thing memorized, but take your time, take your time. Everything here is excellent."

Cartright closed the menu and looked at the electric-blue bird on the cover.

"Why do they call this place the Blue Heron?"

"Well, since you ask, this was a seafood place until Miguel took it over. Miguel's my cousin." Delgado shrugged. "He does what he knows best, which is Mexican. Can't say I blame him."

"But the name." Cartright tapped the menu.

"A lot of people consider the bird to be a landmark, a work of art even. It's been on the building as long as anybody can remember. Also, you're talking big bucks to put up a new one, so Miguel decided to stay with the sign and concentrate on cooking instead. Anyway, what does that matter, *mi amigo?* Tell you what, let's have a couple of cold ones to start us off. We have serious business to conduct tonight."

In a few minutes the waitress brought several colorful, steaming platters to the table. Delgado lifted a light cloth covering a basket of flour tortillas. "Not bad, not bad at all. Miguel does a helluva job, doesn't he? Well, dig in!"

After eating in silence for a while, Delgado looked up from his plate. "Well, counselor, it's time to talk." He took a swallow of beer, then sat back. "You know how I hate dealing with banks. Only thing worse than banks is giving up a piece of the airline, even a little piece. But it looks like it's coming down to that, too."

"True, but you'll still be able to run everything essentially the same way you do now. The thing is, when you're using somebody else's money, you have a lot more explaining to do..."

Delgado broke in. "If it was just the new airplanes, I'd have it made, but look at all the terminal work we need, then there's our maintenance hangar busting at the seams." He spread his hands helplessly. "It just goes on and on. That's not even counting what it'll cost to start up in Santa Barbara and Eureka."

Cartright looked around. The room was filling up. Now most of the booths were taken and it was two deep at the bar. Through the swinging door he observed several men in business suits waiting for a table. "Looks like this is becoming an in place."

"Damn right. If this keeps up, I'll need a reservation myself! Anyway, you've seen the numbers. It's going to cost a lot more to play the game from here on out. Sometimes I wonder why do I do this. Must be loco or something." He tapped his temple with a finger.

Cartright laughed.

"No, I'm serious," Delgado smiled. "The truth is, it gets in your blood. This may sound weird, but I just can't wait to get to the airport every day, see my people working together, planes coming in, planes going out, everybody humping. I don't know what I'd do if I ever lost that."

Cartright pondered Delgado's remark. How lucky, he thought, to do what you love. How many people can say that? After a moment's daydreaming, Cartright forced himself back to the agenda.

"Frank, let me raise one other point so you can't say we didn't talk about it."

Delgado nodded.

"I want to be sure you're aware, theoretically, it would be possible to take the company public. Right now. Today." Cartright shook his head. "Mind you, I'm not recommending this. In fact, I think it'd be a mistake to do it so soon. But it is an option."

"Yeah, well, don't worry, I'm nowhere near that point. Maybe in a few years I'll let you do your magic and make my fortune. Then I can retire."

Cartright nodded. "No question, down the road it's something to keep an eye on. After this expansion and your name gets around more, it could be a very smart move."

A shout arose from the bar, and the two men looked up to see a flying slam dunk. Good-bye evening news, hello Warriors and Celtics.

Delgado pursed his lips. "I guess it won't be the end of the world, having a partner. As a matter of fact, I've already got a couple of guys interested, right here in town. You know, it's really amazing how people lose their heads when they smell a piece of airline action, even normally sharp businessmen."

Cartright put his napkin on the table. "I have nothing against local people, but what about tying in with one of the big outfits like BellAir? Is that a possibility?"

"*BellAir!* Don't get me started on *that* bunch!" Cartright watched his client struggling for words. Finally Delgado heaved a huge sigh.

"Okay, but don't say I didn't warn you." The waitress was clearing the next booth. Delgado caught her eye and held up an empty Dos Equis bottle and two fingers.

"Sometimes I wonder if those people are as dumb as they seem, but then I think, of course not! How could anybody be? I'm not talking about last night. I mean, who knows what really happened there? What I'm saying, there they are, they run this fantastic operation all over the world, which must take a certain amount of intelligence, but from where I stand, most of the time they don't know their ass from their elbow.

"Think about it. They've been here in Monterey longer than anybody, way longer than me, what a terrific market this is, and what do you suppose they operate? Two flights a day, that's what! Two lousy flights!

"Now don't get me wrong. Last thing I want is anybody coming into my markets, but I ask you, what can those people be thinking of? Even that L.A. trip of theirs, they don't schedule right. I mean, what businessman wants to leave for L.A. at ten-thirty in the morning, for God's sake? What good's half a day when you can get down and back with a good schedule? And they hardly advertise at all, nothing on the TV, almost nothing in the papers."

"They do seem to have problems here," Cartright replied. "Didn't they have a lot of trouble with some outfit in L.A. last year?"

"*They* had trouble! *Dios mio!*" Delgado leaned over the table and pointed his finger at Cartright. "George Steiner is a good friend of mine and those bastards fucked him over. The worst part, he didn't even start it. They came to him!"

Delgado splashed his beer into the glass and watched it foam over the side. "Shit, gimme that napkin."

He inhaled the rest of the froth, then began wiping up the spill. "I'll tell you what really happened. Somebody back in New York decides they want their jets out of southern California. They need them somewhere else. Chicago maybe, or Atlanta. Whatever. So they come to George with this proposition. If he will cover San Diego and Bakersfield for them, feed them traffic at LAX, they will pay him for it. In fact, they will pay him extremely well, is how I heard it."

Delgado's voice rose. "Now George – even compared to us, George is pretty small enchiladas – but still, they tell him he's got to measure up to their so-called standards, that's the deal. Now, that's where he made his big mistake. He adds equipment, a ton of people, new uniforms, gets in *way* over his head. Though I have to admit, they looked very sharp."

Delgado lifted a hand to eye level. "So there he is, up to his eyeballs in debt, but everything is great. George is happy. Mr. BellAir is happy. Except hold on a minute. Is Mr. BellAir really happy? No! It turns out Mr. BellAir is not happy, after all! Four months into the deal, they cancel out on George. Four months! Then they come back in with their jets, just like that! They feed him a bunch of bullshit but what it comes down to is, sorry, George, we changed our mind. It's real important for us to carry the L.A. traffic ourselves again.

"I mean, can you believe that! There's no way anybody can compete with a bunch of jet flights right on top of you so George starts cutting back, but by now the creditors are all over him. Even before he got mixed up with that bunch of sharks, he was extended way too far. Finally he has to shut down the whole operation." Delgado shrugged. "That's it. End of story."

"What happened to him?"

"I dunno. I mean, I really don't know. I tried to call him, but he's not around. I haven't talked to him in a couple of months. Probably back on the sauce. He always had a problem that way, anyhow. The son's trying to get them back up, but the attorneys and all are in it. Shit, I wouldn't give you a peso for their chances."

Delgado shook his head sadly. "See what I mean? Are they bastards, those people back there? Or do they not know what they're doing?" Delgado drained the last of his beer. "But, what the hell. What does it matter? Stupid or mean, it's all the same to us. Either way the little guy gets screwed."

He sat back and folded his hands. "But you know, Will, the strange thing is, us, we work pretty well with BellAir. We give each other a lot of business at SFO, but the only reason it works is they keep their hands off my operation. I am very clear about that. So to answer your question, what I'm saying, sure, I could do more with them, but how can you trust people like that? After what they did to George?" Delgado rubbed his eyes. "I dunno. Sometimes I think I should do more with them. There's one guy in New York, Churchman, I deal with him on San Fran stuff. And their station manager here, we get along all right." Delgado laughed. "He doesn't even know what's happening in that funny farm back there half the time. But I promise you one thing, I will never do a deal with that bunch unless I am guaranteed they can't screw me like they screwed George."

Cartright nodded. "If the other guy wants out, he'll find a way to get out, but we'd set it up so if there's a fight, you're the one who comes out on top."

Delgado was quiet for a moment, then he brightened. "See, there you go! What more can I ask? You're right, counselor, there is no free lunch." He stood up and put on his windbreaker. "But for you, *mi amigo*, there was a free dinner, and you just had it. Let's figure on your showing up about eight-thirty, after we get our first flights out. Ray'll be there, you know my accountant, Ray. These things always look better when the day is fresh and you had a good sleep.

"Come on, I'll drive you to the hotel."

2

No gal made has got a shade on Sweet Georgia Brown,
Two left feet but oh so neat has Sweet Georgia Brown...

A WARM NOVEMBER AFTERNOON outside Stanford University stadium, eucalyptus leaves crackling underfoot, a pickup touch football game in a clearing between rows of parked cars, all accompanied by a Dixieland combo nearby.

"Hey, Dad! Ya see that!"

"Helluva catch, Bobby!" Frank Delgado snapped open a can of Coors.

"Last call," he said, handing one to Tom Barrett, his neighbor and collaborator on this annual trip to the Cal – Stanford "Big Game."

Bobby and older brother Manny were huddling with Dave Barrett, Manny's teammate on the Monterey High varsity. At the far end of the narrow field three other boys awaited the kickoff. The two five-year-old fill-ins, Teresa Delgado and Sue Barrett, were swinging their legs idly from the tailgate of the Delgado family wagon. Mariel Delgado had a bad cold all week, and Doris Barrett gave up her ticket so the girls could keep each other company.

Barrett pulled out his wallet and held it up. "You putting your money where your mouth is this year? Or don't you still have enough?"

"I'll go twenty but I want points."

"No way! This one's too close to call. No points."

"Make it a ten, then."

"You're on!"

Barrett gestured at the boys. "I was just thinking, in a couple of years they could even end up on opposite sides here. I mean, it is possible. Course I never tried to influence Dave toward Cal... well, maybe a little. But they are showing some interest. Now, if he can only get his grades up."

"Stanford's a tough nut to crack. I'm not sure Manny's good enough for a scholarship. Hell, as far as I'm concerned, San Jose State would be just fine."

"They knock off the big schools all the time."

Delgado nodded. "It's funny how different kids are. Manny's so caught up in sports, but Bobby, he couldn't care less about football. For him, music's all that counts."

The crowd was starting to move toward the stadium. A trio of high-school girls swished by, putting an end to the football game. Delgado crushed his empty can. "Time to pack up. Bobby wants to see the bands and all."

"Maybe, maybe not." Barrett shook his head. "These aren't the best seats in the world. But who knows, maybe we'll get some action at our end."

LATE IN THE FOURTH quarter with the score 14–all, California's Golden Bears were driving. Second and eleven at the Stanford twenty, directly in front of Delgado's group. Cal's Rich Campbell dropped back, looking... looking... He drilled a pass to tight end Joe Rose, angling across the end zone. Leaping, Rose came down with the ball but out of bounds. Barrett slumped in his seat.

But wait! The officials confer. The coaches are screaming. Confusion reigns. Finally the referee runs out of the pack. Sorry about that, folks, a little mix-up with the line markings. The catch is good. *Touchdown!*

The partisan crowd roared its disapproval, drowning out the visitors, whose faith in justice had been restored with one happy stroke.

"I told you these were great seats," yelled Barrett. "This game's history!"

Barrett called it right. Stanford's last-minute heroics fell short, and the visitors from the East Bay went home with a tough 21–14 win. Cal's yell leaders paraded around the running track, bearing the prized Axe trophy, theirs until the next meeting of the teams a year hence, as the cheering section next to Delgado set up a chant:

Give 'em the axe, the axe, the axe
Give 'em the axe, the axe, the axe
Give 'em the axe, the axe, the axe
Where?
Right in the neck, the neck, the neck
Right in the neck, the neck, the neck
Right in the neck, the neck, the neck
There!

DELGADO HELD HIS daughter's hand tight as they picked their way down the steep stadium steps. "Helluva game, Tom. Nobody deserved to lose this one."

"Gracious as always in victory, I will agree with you. I'll take my tenner in the car. Too bad the girls weren't here to see it."

The boys were running ahead, darting in and out of the crowd.

"Hey, you guys!" Barrett shouted. "Take it easy!"

Manny was carrying the pregame football while the others ran interference.

"Ah, they're all right. Don't tell me you never did that when you were a kid."

"Never. I wouldn't have dreamed of it."

"Too bad. You really missed out." Delgado smiled. "Every year my dad would take us to see the Seals. After the game, you think that was little Francisco Delgado from Salinas racing around? Hell, no, that was Joe DiMaggio! Back, back, he looks over his shoulder, up against the fence...he makes the catch! The crowd goes wild!" Delgado glanced at Barrett. "See what I mean? You remind me of my father, yelling like that."

Barrett grunted. "I just hope your liability insurance's paid up."

After stowing its paraphernalia, the group piled into the station wagon for the crawl toward the more or less open road. Reaching I-280, the big Olds moved along smartly, threading the crest of the coastal hills, headed for the Los Gatos Gap and the flat farmlands and ocean beyond.

"Hey, Dad, change the station, will you?"

Delgado leaned forward and punched "scan" on the console. KGO's post-game wrap-up gave way to snatches of easy rock, talk radio, heavy metal, and then:

You got to know when to hold 'em,
know when to fold 'em
Know when to walk away
and know when to run...

"Leave it there!"

Delgado glanced around. "All right, but it's going on the back speakers. I've had enough of that song."

"Are we there yet?" A reedy voice drifted up from the backseat.

"About an hour, honey. Manny, see if the girls want a drink or something."

Barrett was leafing through a ragged copy of the *San Francisco Chronicle's* Big Game special edition he'd picked up on the way out of the stadium.

"Well, whaddya know! Frank! Did you see this?"

"See what?"

"There's a guy in here who's with the airlines. BellAir... "

Delgado grabbed the paper and set it on the steering wheel.

"Hey, don't do that! I'll read it to you."

"No problem. In my work you have to steer and read at the same time." Delgado glanced down and scanned the headline. *Big Game Standouts – Where Are They Today?*

"Which one?"

"Hartley. Top right."

Delgado looked again. Picture of a running back in full stride, a ball under his arm. A small inset showed a fortyish man in a suit. The caption – *Phil Hartley, U.C. '58, Vice President – BellAir, New York City.*

"Well, I'll be... " Delgado's head jerked up. In the corner of his eye he'd caught a blue BMW flying by on the right. He was closing fast on a semitrailer. Delgado handed the paper back. "Maybe you're right. Read it to me."

"Good call," Barrett replied, folding it neatly. He read aloud.

Phil Hartley, Second Team All-America in Cal's 1955–
56 season, whose spectacular football career was cut
short by a serious knee injury. Today Phil is in charge
of financial operations for BellAir in New York.

Originally from Manteca, he graduated in business and economics, then went on for his MBA at Harvard and an investment banking career before joining the country's third-largest airline. Phil is married to the former Elaine Dalton and lives in Manhattan.

"So *that's* what happened to him." Barrett looked up from the paper. "That's the outfit had that accident last month, isn't it?"

"You know him, Dad?" asked Manny, leaning over the seat.

"I've heard the name but I didn't realize he was from around here. What year did you get out, Tom?"

"Same year, '58, but I didn't know him personally. The U was a big place, even then. We engineers tended to stick pretty much to ourselves. I remember he was a terrific runner, a real scrappy guy, then he got hurt. That was the last I heard of him."

"Well, well..." Delgado pursed his lips. "This is *very* interesting. I have a lot dealings with those people. What else does it say?"

"That's it. Just more old grad pictures."

The heavy wagon cut through the late afternoon dusk and coastal fog. A few headlights began appearing in the oncoming lanes. Delgado's windshield started to mist over. He set the wipers for intermittent sweep.

> *'Cause ev'ry hand's a winner, and*
> *Ev'ry hand's a loser.*
> *And the best that you can hope for*
> *Is to die in your sleep.*

"WE'RE HOME!" Teresa shouted. "I'm starved!"

Delgado wheeled the station wagon into his driveway. The lights were on in the rambling Spanish-style house in the Monterey hills, just down the road from the airport and his office, which was in a nearby building. For Frank the location was ideal, only a few minutes to commute or, as happened all too often, to plunge into the off-hours crises that befell his complex but lightly staffed business.

"We'll drop our stuff at our place," said Barrett, emerging stiffly from the car. "See you in a few."

Delgado followed the two girls into the house. "Hey there!" he shouted, throwing his arms around his wife, seated at the red-checkered kitchen table with Doris Barrett. "What a game! We had the whole thing right in front of us, too. Say, how's your cold? You look a lot better."

"I think I'll live."

"Where's that champagne we've been saving?" He winked at Doris. "We're good sports, we'll drink to your win. Bobby, take a look in the downstairs fridge, will you? Any calls?"

"Not a thing," Mariel replied. "Everything's quiet."

"I'd better call Ops, see how the day went." As he headed for his basement office, Dave Barrett burst through the door.

"Go Bears!" the boy shouted. "Go Bears!"

Frank cuffed him gently on the ear. "Don't push your luck too far, kid."

In the kitchen, places had been set for the children. Three other young Barretts were charging around the house, making up for missing the game. In the dining room, a candlelit buffet awaited the adults.

"Hi, everybody," said Barrett. "Another great win, Doris!"

"We heard the whole thing. It was wonderful."

"That it was, but it's never the same without you two. I'm putting in for next year's tickets Monday."

Just then Frank bounded into the kitchen, grinning from ear to ear.

"I just got off the phone with Will. Our new planes! The financing came through this afternoon! Now *we've* got something to celebrate, too!"

Barrett worked the cork out. "Glasses. Quick! Here you go Mariel... Doris... Frank."

Delgado raised his glass. "May I propose a toast to our good neighbors, to Tom, especially, for his glorious if undeserved victory in today's game..."

"I choose to ignore that," Barrett responded. "My toast is this. To Frank and Mariel, our best neighbors and their terrific kids, and much luck in your business."

"I accept, with pleasure. What a relief! This deal will set us for the next ten years! *Salud!*"

Mariel set a bowl of spaghetti on the kitchen table.

"Okay, kids, dig in!"

Later that evening, as the adults were relaxing over coffee in the living room, Delgado looked at Barrett. "Tom, where's that paper? The one from the car?"

"It's downstairs, Dad," Bobby answered. "I'll get it."

In a moment the boy returned with the newspaper. Delgado passed it to Mariel. "Look at this! It turns out one of BellAir's head guys is from the Valley. Manteca, in fact. That's near where you lived. What a small world!"

Mariel scanned the article. "Cal '58, so high school '54. That was a little before my time. I sort of remember the name, though. He probably went to Manteca. We played them every year."

"Here, let me see." Doris picked up the paper. "Hmmm... nice looking. Seems to have aged well, compared with present company." Her finger sank into her husband's ample middle. "But we go with what we have, right?"

"Damn straight."

Delgado took the paper back. "I tell you, I can't wait to get hold of that guy! Finally, I've got somebody who'll understand what we do out here. *Damn!* What a terrific surprise!"

3

CHARLIE BELL AND PHILIP HARTLEY stood outside the Lloyd's building in the Old City of London financial district. They had just completed a round of meetings with British and continental insurance companies, underwriters of aviation "risks." Two days in Paris, one in London, the new decade's first business trip.

Bell paused and looked up. A jet was passing overhead at high altitude, its contrail stark against the high blue sky.

"What a crazy business. Your production line's seven miles up, moving nearly the speed of sound. It must look chancy until you know how we do it." Bell looked at his young colleague. "You know, I haven't pulled this kind of duty for years. It felt good being here."

You can say that again, Hartley thought. Early in the game, he had learned how to maneuver Charlie into settings away from the office. Sitting across a desk from the boss was not the way to raise his comfort level, but time away, one-on-one time, that was golden. As much as talent or results, Hartley realized that getting ahead depended on putting Charlie at ease. Well aware of what he was up to, his colleagues would have killed for these opportunities, which he created routinely.

Bell shook his head. "Those people got kind of nervous when we started talking safety, but at least they appreciated how we've tightened up on security since Denver." His face became solemn. "Here it is, January already, and the FBI just identified the damn suitcase. Fat lot of good that'll do! Samsonite hasn't made that model for twenty years. Ticket counter, skycaps, nobody remembers anything about the bastard."

Leaves and scraps of paper swirled and eddied in the street as a breeze sprang up. "Come on. Let's get moving."

They strode along, Hartley easily keeping up despite toting the heavy briefcase that held both men's meeting materials. Bell carried only a thin leather case.

"Phil, I've been meaning to talk to you about something. I guess this is as good a time as any." Bell slowed the pace. "Have you ever noticed how everybody in our outfit's always saying they want to get ahead? That's the way they talk, all the time. Well, as far as I'm concerned, that's a bunch of crap. Most of 'em aren't willing to pay the price, I mean, in terms of your personal life, the family and all. Then there's guys who can't cut it in the first place, but what the hell, there's plenty of jobs to be done. Fifty-five couldn't hold everybody who wants to be there, anyway."

The two men waited for a light, then turned onto a quiet side street of storefront shops and pubs. Bell suddenly stopped.

"All right. Level with me. Where do you fit in? Why'd you come with us? You had a big job, making good money." He stared at Hartley. "What are you really after?"

Hartley thought quickly. Tackle it head-on. That's the only way.

"I want a shot at the top." Hartley looked directly at Bell. "That's the reason I'm here."

Bell eyed him for a moment, then he laughed, a loud, raucous laugh. "Damn it all, that's the spirit! That's what I wanted to hear!"

They started up again, Bell smiling slyly. "All right, my friend, next question. How would you feel about taking over for Wally?"

This one really caught Hartley off guard. His mind raced ahead. Wally... Charlie's old friend, the two of them thick as thieves...

"Come on, come on," Bell prodded, enjoying his companion's discomfort. "Don't tell me that never occurred to you!"

Hartley shook his head. "It'd be a great opportunity, but I don't know how I could put the finance job down, not with everything just getting off the ground."

"I'm talking both jobs," Bell said crisply. "Tell me if *that* makes a difference!"

This time Hartley did not hesitate. "Of course it does."

Bell nodded. "I guess that removes any doubts about your intentions."

Sensing an opening, Hartley looked earnestly at Bell. "Charlie, you give me that chance and back me up, believe me, you won't be disappointed."

"I'd be disappointed if you said anything else." Bell cocked his head. "So, Phil, where'd you get that fire in the belly? Was it the sports? Was that it?"

Hartley avoided Bell's eyes. If it were only that simple, he thought. A flood of memories threatened to break through. Focus, he urged himself. Stay focused.

"Yeah," he replied. "That was it all right."

Bell picked up the pace, swinging his arms. "Okay, that's settled. Now, here's your first assignment. I've known Wally a long time, and he's going to take this very hard. He's a good man. Where do I put him? How do we let him down easy?"

Hartley's confidence surged. "That's exactly what *not* to do! We've got to make a clean break. Give him a good severance, sure, but we can't keep propping up people who aren't doing the job. Not if we're serious about turning the company around."

"That's tough talk."

"Tough? Hey, I feel for Wally, but this is nothing compared to the grief we're in for if we don't clean up our act."

Bell shook his head sadly. "Yeah. And this is just the beginning, too."

"You're damn right. Find the producers, the ones who make things go. Them, we treat like kings. The rest, well, there's no more room for them."

"What you're saying, you probably think you invented it, but you didn't. Hire the best people, work everybody's butt off, that's exactly how I used to run this outfit. Trouble is, it's a helluva lot more complicated these days, forty years of baggage we've got now, all those good people..."

"Unless we start showing a profit, *nobody's* going to have a job. This isn't some kind of welfare agency!"

"You *are* a hard sonofabitch." Bell laughed uneasily. "Let's find a cab. I'm getting cold."

IN THE EARLY DAYS, the panorama from Charlie Bell's office was stunning. Over the years progress had blocked a view line here, trimmed it back there, so only in Bell's memory did the Statue of Liberty still stand behind the World Trade Center towers. At least part of the Verrazano Narrows Bridge was visible, and Bell's eye was inevitably drawn to the parade of aircraft in La Guardia's traffic pattern, nose high, landing gear and flaps down, lights on for visibility. The chief executive's office was warmly furnished in wood and leather, but its real charm was in his photographs, the awards, the airplane models – memorabilia of an airline life.

This particular day, the Monday after Bell's return from London, Helen Foley sat outside Bell's door, presiding at the desk she had occupied for twenty-three years, not counting her six with BellAir in Chicago. Foley was a company fixture. Nothing and nobody passed her desk without her approval. Over the years, many comers had foundered on "Foley's reef," as it was sometimes called, undercut by the large, gray-haired maiden lady whose whim could make access to the chairman difficult or, as on a few celebrated occasions, impossible. However, even this staunch defender of the chairman's prerogative had a handful of favorites she allowed to linger at her desk, recalling times past, prizes gained, chances lost.

This select circle included T. Walter Robertson, earnest, quiet Wally, who for years had pleased her with his genial attentions. Recently, though, she had detected, or, in the vulgarism popular with the younger secretaries, picked up *vibrations* about Wally that were disturbing. Stern, exasperated expressions on his colleagues' faces were part of it, scraps of conversation with an arch and biting edge. All in all, Helen had a terrible suspicion that a trial balloon was drifting through the executive suite with Robertson's name written all over it.

Still, this morning as Robertson approached her desk, the usual thick sheaf of papers pressed against his professorial tweeds, his spirit seemed good. Helen swore by conservative business attire, mentally noting and filing unsound variations along with other signs of unprofessional demeanor. Wally, however, she considered a healthy antidote to the Gucci-come-latelies infiltrating the ranks these days.

"Hel-len, Hel-len," Robertson sang, "keeper of the gate, light of my life."

"Aw, go on with you." She put down the morning's mail, and for a moment the years dropped away. But as she looked more closely at her friend, her smile faded. "How *are* you, Wally? I mean, is everything really all right?"

"Never better," he replied stoutly, but a shadow crossed his face, mirroring the one in her own heart. "Actually, if you must know, we're hanging on for dear life. But one more turn of the wheel, and we'll be back on top."

"I am seeing far too many long faces around here. I'm not used to it."

"Ah, keep your chin up," he said amiably. "We'll pull out of it. We always do."

The buzzer on her desk sounded, and she nodded toward Bell's door. Robertson straightened, making a show of bracing himself. He winked, then went in. Bell was standing at his window wall on the far side of the room.

"Morning, Charlie," Robertson began cheerfully.

Bell nodded, continuing to stare out the window.

"How was the trip? Everything go well?"

"We made our pitch, they listened." Bell turned. "Time will tell if it did any good."

"How did Phil do? This was his first time with that Lloyd's crowd."

"Yeah. Well, actually he knew some of them from before. Oh, he did fine. He really ran the show. I was just window dressing."

"Good, good. Well, when you called I figured you wanted an update on the fleet plan, so I brought along some... "

"No, that's not it." Bell moved toward to the door that opened into his private retreat. "Here, let's go next door."

They entered a sitting room with several comfortable chairs and a long couch. One wall was filled with aviation books and personal mementos. On another, a sliding panel hid a big-screen color television that was seldom used, and behind a wet bar, another door led to a small lavatory and shower.

"Sit down." Bell motioned Robertson onto the couch. "There." He stood beside the chair at Robertson's end of the sofa.

"The inner sanctum." Robertson laughed nervously. "I haven't been in here for years. Hope I'm not in trouble or anything."

Bell averted his old colleague's eyes, struggling for words. "You are in trouble," he finally said. "We're all in trouble." Bell swallowed hard. "Wally, I... I have to let you go."

Robertson's jaw began to work... clenching, releasing. He cleared his throat. "I couldn't have heard you right. You didn't say what...

what I... think you said." His hand trembled as he raised his index finger to his glasses.

"You heard me right," Bell growled.

"But why? What did I do?"

Bell sat down on the couch. "It's nothing you did. It's my own damn fault. I never should have put you in that marketing job. You're over your head. Neither of us saw it, what you were getting into."

"So that's it, is it." Robertson began to perspire. He tugged at his collar. "That's it..."

He looked at Bell's wounded expression in disbelief. "What the hell am I supposed to do? I can't retire, I'm not vested yet. Jesus, I got two more kids to put through college!"

"Don't worry about that," Bell said soothingly. "We'll take care of the money. And we'll make it look like it was your idea. To pursue other interests, something like that."

"Don't give me that crap. That's the same as being canned. Everybody knows that!"

"Listen, you asshole. This is the hardest thing I've ever had to do! Don't make it any harder!"

Bell sighed deeply, then put his hand on the other man's knee. "I'm sorry, old friend. All we've been through together. I didn't mean that."

Tears welled up in Robertson's eyes. "There... there must be *something* I can do here. I have a lot of good years left..."

"You're not going out of here on your knees. I owe you too much to give you some damn mousefart job."

"I could be a consultant. Just for a year or two. That'd work okay..."

Bell shook his head. "It's got to be a clean break. We'll put the best face on it and believe me, we'll make you whole. A lifetime pass for you and your family, enough cash to see you right. Don't worry about that part of it."

Robertson stood. He walked over to a large airplane model on a floor stand, a BellAir 727. He began caressing it, hypnotically. After a moment, when he turned back, he was calm.

"This may sound crazy, Charlie, but I'm... I'm not altogether surprised. You know, it's been rough the last couple of months. Everything caving in, everybody gunning for me." Robertson blinked rapidly. "One time the brakes on the car went out. I was sliding off the road and not a damn thing I could do about it . . . like I was off to the side watching the whole thing."

"Yeah. I guess," Bell said dully. "Have a drink."

"No. I need to get out of here. Clear my head."

"Sure, sure. Take a few days off. Whatever you want."

"You better tell me who knows about this."

"Nobody," Bell answered quickly. "I mean, I talked it over with Scotty. And Arthur Winston."

Robertson frowned. "Scotty I can see, but why Winston?"

"C'mon, Wally. I work for somebody, too. The board, the share-holders. I take it you've heard of them."

Robertson's eyes narrowed. "But that's bullshit! You're in charge. You do what you want around here. You always have. You always will."

Bell paused, then he replied softly. "You know, it never occurred to me until just now, maybe all these years you've been missing something." He nodded his head slowly. "You think you're in the middle, don't you? Well, don't you?"

Robertson looked puzzled.

"Goddamnit, man! Everybody's in the middle. Including me. *Especially* me! Oh, sure, people look at me, it's Bell's company, they say, he even named it after himself. I'd like to be in his shoes, they say, the bastard does whatever the hell he wants!

"For Chrissakes, that's not how it works!" Bell's face was nearly purple. "How many shareholders do we have? Forty thousand? And how many insurance companies and pension funds and fucking banks got their hooks into us? Hell, I even work for the goddamn unions! Everything's backwards! And you have the nerve to say you're in the middle! Well, I am too! More than you've ever been! How could you not see that?"

Robertson picked up his papers. "Time. How much time do I have?"

"Look. We'll go out to lunch tomorrow. This is enough for one day."

"*How much time!* Six months? Two months? *How long,* goddamn it!"

"Sooner than that, I'm afraid."

"Okay, Charlie, you're the boss. Whatever bullshit you may believe, you're the boss." Robertson paused. "And might I ask who you have in mind to replace me?"

"I'm going to give Phil a shot at it, Wally."

A crooked smile flickered across Robertson's face. "That figures, that frigging well figures." He started toward the door, then turned back.

"Tell me. Would it have helped...would it have made any difference if I had talked to you about...about this? Any difference at all?"

"I don't know. How do you talk about this sort of thing?" Bell shook his head grimly. "You people are supposed to read the signals. They're there for a reason. If a person has to be told, well, maybe he doesn't belong here anymore."

Robertson turned abruptly. He stormed past Helen Foley without a glance. The buzzer on her desk rasped one, two, three times. Slowly she rose and walked into Bell's office. He was slumped heavily in a chair next to his window, his head bowed. She forced herself to look at him.

"Charlie..."

"Don't say it, just don't say anything."

"Did you do...what I think you did?"

"Yes," he replied, his voice shaking. "Yes, I did."

"I am so sorry."

Blinking back tears, Bell glanced up, then quickly avoided her look. A high thin overcast was beginning to slide over the sun. Weather was moving in. Bell turned and stared out his window.

"Goddamn it all to hell," he said.

4

I T WAS UNSEASONABLY WARM for March. Puffy clouds slid across the sky on a stiff southwest breeze. Inside the Hartley's silver-blue Mercedes, there was barely a sound, though the speedometer indicated eighty. The Long Island Expressway was nearly deserted this Sunday morning.

Elaine finished skimming the *Times Magazine*. The crossword didn't tempt her. She'd never had the patience for puzzles and games.

"Philip, how much sailing has Roger done?" she asked, putting the paper down.

"A fair amount, I believe. His friend, I have no idea."

"Is this friend his regular?"

"So it seems." Hartley scanned the road. "He went through a messy divorce last year. Says he's sworn off marriage forever."

Good luck, she thought to herself. That's what they all say. She peered out the window, sizing up the day with a practiced eye.

"You know, when I was small, the summers out here were the best times. Daddy's law practice always came first, but for a few weeks every year he let us into his life."

Hartley nodded. Her comment sent his mind spinning back in time. When I was growing up, I didn't have a clue, not a single clue. I must have realized not everybody in the world was frantic about the grocery money or where the rent was coming from, but I don't remember anybody who wasn't.

He glanced across at his wife. Crisp, pretty, totally *appropriate* for every occasion. If I'd met you back then, I wouldn't have known the first thing to say to you. He smiled sardonically. Nor you to me, my sweet.

"I certainly took for granted the nice things we had. It wasn't till later I realized what a price I paid for them."

Hartley frowned. He had no sympathy for her complaint.

At the sign for Oyster Bay he braked and skillfully exited the expressway onto a secondary road. A white wooden church appeared in his windshield. How different, he reflected, this morning and my childhood Sundays. His mind's eye pictured a small boy... brown suit from the Sears Catalog, a hand-ironed white shirt and skinny tie, shoes polished, of course, hair neatly brushed. And his mother in her best dress, on her arm that black leather handbag, her most precious possession, a rare indulgence bought in Indiana for the trek to California. Even then, at his tender age, he knew the two of them were on display, shining examples of the Christian family life, keys to his father's ministry, though of course he didn't come upon the term "marketing" until much later.

His mind drifted. He saw his father towering before him, tall in his pulpit, arms raised over the small congregation, one moment his voice cresting, falling to a whisper the next. And the thrill when his mother walked to the organ and began to play, companion to his father's prayersong. After the service they would preside at the front door of the wood-frame church, greeting parishioners, the Reverend and Mrs. Hartley and their small son, his hair now unkempt from tousling, a willing object in those Sunday morning tableaux.

Unbidden, the arguments returned. Near the end they were frequent, insistent. It's not enough to be a good man, his mother said, as she wept. Ah, his father replied, but consider the lilies of the field. They toil not, neither do they spin. And he remembered his good-night kiss as if it were yesterday, his father bent over the bed, rough beard and sweet wine breath, telling him that he, Philip, was God's gift to the world, His very special gift.

Then, one day, without warning, he was gone. Forever.

For the longest time the boy knew it was his fault. Some unworthiness, some evil inclination of his brought on this calamity, though what it might be, he had no idea. Perhaps the church people held some secret grievance against him, even as they pretended to be friendly. That would explain why the collection plate he passed never came back with enough on it, not nearly enough.

Eventually the boy grew away from his shock and he came to understand he wasn't to blame. The church failed because of hard times, it was said, though later he learned the truth was more complex. Even at its height, the small congregation was barely able to sustain its struggling pastor, and curiously, even in the boom years of the war, his father fell further and further behind. So while the boy's guilt receded, the pain was slow to heal. Long after, his stomach would tighten and cramp at the end of the day, and he could not eat, remembering those terrible sad scenes, and his great loss.

Before the catastrophe, the town's other churches, the Catholic church of Saint Anthony and the United Lutheran, seemed to the boy mere outsized curiosities. But he came to realize how large their grasp on the townspeople loomed in his father's failure, how a few less followers would have meant little to them but much to his father. From that time the boy walked a circuitous path to school, avoiding these impassive reminders of his grief, even as he nurtured the silent rage in his soul. Though he had friends, in those early days there were taunts and fistfights.

As he grew to manhood the bitterness was supplanted by a fierce resolve. Never would Philip Hartley allow himself to be bested as his father had been. Never would his heart's desire suffer the humiliation of defeat. An apt pupil and physically gifted, in his teen-age years Hartley strove mightily to develop himself into a skilled athlete. Coaches and teammates alike were awed by his hours of practice and conditioning. The results spoke for themselves. All-State in three sports.

His objective was a simple one: control. Control of his circumstances, control over those who could help him, control of whatever might interfere with his plan. And achievement would be his strategy. With the playing field his showcase and his stage, he would leave no doubt who was the best, who deserved to lead, who would command. Eventually he discovered he would need some measure of wealth, but for Hartley, money would always be a tool, nothing more. He had no interest in accumulation for its own sake or in the trappings of wealth, except as they might further his ambition.

From that early time, religion played no part in Hartley's life. No formal act of rejection was necessary. The void existed from that day the light of his life was snuffed out. Thus, there was nothing to prevent a shell from growing about the young man, to deflect harm and disappointment. While at college, his mother's death drew the final curtain across the unfulfilled vision of the family Hartley. California, land of promise, land of betrayal.

Despite his lack of religious feeling, as a piece of wood retains its grain after many sandings and layering with paint, so at times Philip

Hartley felt a pang of regret when he passed a church, as on this Sunday morning. From the silence of his German-engineered cocoon he imagined what joyful sounds there were within. This, the pale vestige of youthful ardor.

"What's on your mind, Philip?" Elaine was looking intently at him. "You're a thousand miles away."

Startled, Hartley gazed at the steeple receding in his rear-view mirror. "I guess... I guess I don't remember ever going sailing when I was a kid."

"Well, I must say this a distinct improvement."

She was quiet for a moment. "So. Roger starts tomorrow. That must be a relief."

Her comment brought Hartley back to earth. The everyday challenges and schemes assumed their usual positions in the forefront of his mind.

"That is true." He straightened in his seat. "You know, I was really pleased Charlie went along with me on this. He wanted somebody with airline experience, but we don't need more old baggage. Speaking of that, Wally cleared out last week. He didn't even want a retirement party."

"That's no surprise."

"Too bad he took it that way, but that's how the game is played." Hartley glanced over at Elaine. She was wearing a satisfied, knowing smile.

The car rounded a bend, and the entrance for the Midlothian Yacht Club appeared in the windshield. As they neared the marina the road squeezed down to one lane. Several boats were under repair in the dry-dock, others were having their hulls scrubbed and patched. Most of the slips were occupied, though opening day was still several weeks away. Out on the sound, a few white sails scudded across the horizon.

As Hartley pulled in, a man emerged from a bright red Alfa parked nearby. Roger Bankhead was tall and thin, with a head of bushy brown hair the consistency of steel wool. His dusty Anglo-Afro topped a ruddy face, battleground for an old, lost war against acne. As Hartley opened his door, Bankhead approached, followed by a young woman smartly outfitted in a blue turtleneck, white slacks, and matching boat shoes.

"Hello, Philip, Elaine. I'd like you to meet Joyce Collins."

"So pleased you could join us." Elaine extended her hand. "I hope you're ready for some action. It's really blowing out there."

Bankhead lifted a wicker hamper out of his trunk. "Our contribution to the day."

"With an assist from the local deli," Joyce added.

"Say, she's a beauty!" Bankhead remarked as they approached the Hartleys' slip. "A Catalina, isn't it?"

"The man knows his boats," Elaine observed.

"But why *Hizzoner II*?"

"It's my father's boat. He was a judge."

Elaine led the party aboard. "Roger, you and Joyce take the sail covers off, then we'll hook up the lines. Philip's job is to back us out of here." She smiled. "That's man's work. I do the sailing, the skilled part, that is."

"A zinger!" said Bankhead, glancing at Hartley.

Hartley nodded. "I accept that, but only because she's right."

For the next half-hour, Elaine and her crew scrambled about the deck of *Hizzoner II*. Hartley coaxed the engine to life, and after a brief warm-up eased the boat out of its slip and through the channel into the waters of Cold Spring Harbor, marking the entrance to the Sound. Suddenly the balmy morning gave way to the forecasted stiff breezes.

"We'd better get busy," Elaine shouted. "Time to raise the sails!"

Hartley cut the engine. Now there were only fluttering sails and waves smacking against the hull. A metal fitting clanged a cadence against the mast.

"This is my favorite time in the whole world." Elaine squinted, breathing deeply. "How quiet it is... you can almost see the wind."

A half-hour later the Hartleys' fashionable guest was looking decidedly unwell. "It's too rough for lunch," she gasped. "Isn't it?"

Elaine could barely suppress a smile. "We can hold off."

Bankhead clamped his hands over his ears. "This is invigorating, I must say!"

Suddenly they entered an area of large swells. The boat began to pitch steeply. Joyce's face was now a darker shade of gray, a close match for the sea. Sensing imminent disaster, Elaine decided her test had gone far enough.

"We'll turn back now. Actually," she added brightly, "this gives us a chance to try our new spinnaker!"

Deftly she maneuvered the craft around. Its sails rippled, then suddenly quieted.

"Coming about! Low bridge!" The boom swung as the mainsail again filled. After a few minutes tugging and hauling they managed to raise the spinnaker, and the boat raced ahead.

"Wow! This is really moving!"

HIZZONER II ROCKED gently back and forth in its slip. The marina was alive with activity, though more tinkering and polishing, it seemed, than preparation for braving the elements. Clouds were thickening, and the afternoon showers were rolling in on schedule. As the two women were setting a table on the aft deck, Hartley and Bankhead stood on a nearby knoll, surveying the scene.

"Everything wrapped up at McKinsey?"

"I tied down the last of it yesterday."

"Good. It's time to put all of that behind you." Hartley turned to his new recruit. "Roger, I want to make absolutely sure we have our signals straight. There may be times I'm forced to take us in some direction you don't agree with. You'll have your say, your input, but then we close ranks and go for it with everything we've got. That's what I expect from my people."

Bankhead was puzzled. This is so elementary, why does Philip even need to mention it? "I get the picture," he responded. "If I didn't think we'd work well together, I wouldn't have signed on."

Hartley nodded. "A lot of people around our place have the idea we're running some kind of country club. You'll see what I mean soon enough." He placed a paternal hand on Bankhead's shoulder. "I'm counting on you, Roger. You are a very important part of my team. Come through like I know you will, and believe me, I'll make it very much worth your while."

THE FOLLOWING SATURDAY found Philip Hartley in his office, as usual. During his tenure in Finance, Hartley had become known as a stern taskmaster, insisting that more be done with less, eliminating positions, firing staff and shifting the survivors around. While most of Hartley's fellow officers prided themselves on the size of their empires and bristled at any suggestion of reducing a budget or a head count, Hartley's attitude was just the opposite. BellAir's money man was a cost-cutting messiah, and he meant to set the example himself. This reputation was sending tremors through his new department.

Everyone at the airline recognized that Marketing and Sales was different. It produced *revenue*. Its success could be *measured*. The company's elite sales force cultivated large, important accounts and moved in faster circles than their desk-bound colleagues, who nevertheless absorbed the marketing attitude.

Marketing staff was always the first to adopt a new fashion. For the men, it was longer hair in the sixties, then modish mustaches, sideburns, yellow ties, gold chains. The women favored Magnin's, Bloomies, or Penney's, depending on their sophistication and salary level, with skirt lengths and hairstyles rising and falling in unison, pantsuits and designer boots marching to the current beat.

Shortly before eleven, Hartley appeared outside an office on the fifty-fourth floor, the office of Roger S. Bankhead – Vice President Marketing & Sales, according to the door. The week before, one of the facilities handymen had removed T. Walter Robertson's nameplate, dumping it in a wastebasket while his former staff sullenly looked on. Immediately someone fished it out, saying he'd mail it to Wally.

Bankhead's door was ajar. Hartley pushed it open without knocking and went in.

"Morning, Roger. How're you getting along?"

His new colleague was perched on the edge of his desk. "Off to a good start, I believe."

Bankhead's sports jacket, slacks, and tasseled loafers were accepted Saturday attire. He was already fitting in. Weekends at the Tower represented a curious celebration of duty. Everyone dressed less formally – jeans and sweaters, slacks and jackets – but they pushed hard, trying to salvage part of the day for themselves.

Bankhead swept his hand about the room, which was strewn with moving boxes. "I'm actually a lot better organized than this looks."

"Well, I have something else for your pile." Hartley tossed a sheaf of papers to him. "My speech to that travel agency convention next month. I've marked where I want you to beef it up, particularly the part about our CRS."

"You must be talking about 'Passages,'" Bankhead added with a grin.

"That's right, the new name. Your first major contribution."

"Look out, Sabre and Apollo! How soon do you need my comments?"

"Thursday at the latest. By the way, you ought to plan on coming along yourself. It'll be a good chance to meet a lot of people in one place."

"I was already thinking along those lines."

Just then, Bankhead's secretary poked her head in. "Oh, hello, Mr. Hartley. I hope I'm not interrupting anything important."

As he always did, Hartley stared at the woman. Drawing herself to full height including orange-rinse hair and platform shoes, Rose Markowitz barely nudged five feet. One of the Tower's best-known citizens, there wasn't a company skeleton whose location and story she didn't know. From her neck hung a pair of rhinestone reading glasses, her trademark, on a cord she changed daily to color-coordinate, all resting on an ample bosom packed into sweaters invariably several sizes too tight. Seventeen years in the department, Rose was a flagrant exception to the fashionable affectations of her colleagues. She was an original, an institution, departmental yenta and surrogate mother to the younger secretaries and lower echelons of marketing management.

"I'm taking orders. You people want anything from the deli?"

"Nothing for me," Hartley replied.

"How's their corned beef?" Bankhead asked.

"I won't tell you it's the Carnegie, but it's very good. On dark rye, I'd recommend, and to drink, a cream soda goes well."

"Sounds like you know what you're talking about. Okay, I'll spring for one. With everything."

"We don't have your petty cash set up yet, so . . . "

Bankhead dug into his pocket and extracted a twenty. "Here. Keep the change for next time."

"Right. Next week, for sure we'll get you squared away." At the door she turned, frowning, "Mr. Bankhead, don't you want some help with this mess?"

"Maybe this afternoon, to get rid of these boxes."

"This afternoon, huh," she replied, shaking her head.

"Right. You'll be surprised."

"*That's* for sure."

Hartley stared at the doorway for a moment, then he also turned to leave.

"I'll get a seat on your flight," Bankhead said. "That'll give us a chance to go over things. Oh, by the way, Fritz and I had a good session with those Air Chicago people yesterday. They're ready to bite."

"That still leaves San Francisco. What about that Bay outfit? Any movement yet?"

Bankhead shook his head. "The owner's a real brick, a guy named Delgado. Pete Churchman's been working on him, but he refuses to play ball. He thinks we should bring the guy back here, you know, show him a good time then put the screws to him. We need to make him see we mean business."

Hartley frowned. "I really want to announce that one in Hawaii. So far we have zip on the West Coast and that damned L.A. business just won't go away. We may have to start our own operation out there if this keeps up."

Outside Bankhead's office stood a row of open bays where Marketing's mid-level staff and clerical worked. Directors' and managers' offices were along the window wall, interrupted by open spaces, band-aids for tricking the building's ventilating system, which took the summer off, then coughed up tons of chilled air in December. The company cafeteria was closed weekends, so Rose's Saturday sandwich run was always well patronized. Back from the deli, she made her rounds, dispensing food along with unsolicited but valuable advice.

"Louis, your bagel and cream cheese." She made a sour face. "Whad...a Bermuda onion? You antisocial or something? And who belongs to the chicken salad?"

"Over here. Hey! Don't throw it!"

"Well, you just come here and get it, Mr. Rico Wonderful." She sighed. "Will I never get the respect I deserve?"

"Respect!" shouted the young man, who featured elaborately sculpted hair and a blue and orange Mets sweatshirt.

"So what do you think of your new boss, Rose?" asked a small Black woman from behind a stack of files.

"Shhh! Not so loud! He's just around the corner."

"Go on," Rico demanded. "I'll let you know if he shows."

"Well, you ask what I think. I would say smart but messy."

"I liked how he came around and introduced himself the first day." Marty Samuels, a well-endowed though bookish-looking secretary, unwrapped her sandwich. "He has a nice sense of humor, too."

"He'll need more than that to survive in this place," opined Rico.

"Rose, you heard from Wally?" asked Marty.

"He called the other day. He's doing okay, considering."

"Poor Wally."

"Poor Wally, nothing!" Rico shouted through a mouthful. "Don't kid yourself, he ain't hurting. Those big shots take care of their own."

"Don't knock it," Rose replied. "You should be so lucky."

She could say that, but deep down she felt sorry for Wally. That was no way to end a man's career, so many years with the company, then out the door without even a thank-you. Though in some ways it was a merciful act, cutting him loose, it was so obvious he was drowning in the job. Rose even felt a hollow, guilty satisfaction that she'd spotted it coming. In the last year she had often thought, reflecting on her day as she rode the No. 5 train to Flatbush, Wally wasn't cut out for that job, he couldn't last. Of course, her brash young friend was right. Financially, Wally wouldn't be hurting. But money can't take away that kind of pain.

"Mr. Bankhead seems different from Mr. Hartley," Marty Samuels remarked.

"How do you mean?"

"You know, Mr. Hartley is always so, I don't know, busy or something. Always too busy to be friendly."

"Hartley is a cold fish!" Rico gestured with his sandwich. "I'll tell you something happened the other day. Chuckie and me, a whole month we been killing ourselves on that computer program the man brought over from Finance, right? I must've talked to him three times, maybe four, but see, Chuckie's a *manager*. Me, I'm just a dumb programmer. So the other day we run into Hartley in the elevator.

"'How's it goin', Chuck!' he says. Then he looks at me. 'Hello there,' he says! Get that? '*Hello there!*' Madonn'. That really pissed me off!"

"In Mr. Hartley's defense, if I may," responded Rose, "the man has one of the heaviest jobs in the company, and now two of them since taking over Marketing."

"What you really mean," Rico sneered, "long as you're a big shot you don't have to fit in! C'mon, the man's an outsider! A number cruncher, for Chrissakes! What's he know about marketing? He's not even an airline guy!"

"Hey, he's not my favorite person in the world either, but lighten up! Give the man a chance."

"Same chance they gave Wally?" Rico shot back.

Rose nodded her head, pondering his comment. "You have a point there. You most definitely have a point there."

5

TED ATKINS, BellAir's national marketing director, stubbed out a cigarette, his fourth in a row. "What the devil's keeping that man! The damn reception started half an hour ago!"

"Relax." Harry Tanaka, head of BellAir's public relations for Hawaii, beckoned to the waitress. "Katie! Another mai-tai for Mr. Atkins."

"Okay, Mr. T." The dark-skinned young Hawaiian flashed a brilliant smile.

"Isn't she terrific!" Roger Bankhead stared at the white sarong disappearing around the corner of the bar. "You certainly know the right people."

"It'd be hard not to, I've lived here so long. But I have to admit it's a shock seeing that one all dolled up. She went to grade school with my daughter." He glanced at Bankhead. "Just a little kid with braces, straight as a stick."

Bankhead winced. "I didn't need to hear that."

"Hey, no problem. Everybody's somebody's daughter."

"Or son," grumbled Atkins, fiddling with his straw.

"Or son. Thank you very much, Ted. Somehow that possibility escaped me."

The BellAir group was holding forth in a corner of the Hilton Hawaiian Village poolside bar. Irritated at the delay, Philip Hartley drummed his fingers on the table, wondering why he'd let himself be booked into this hotel in the middle of Waikiki's noisy, pressing tourist crowds. Should have insisted on the Kahala Hilton down the coast, he thought. Quieter. More prestigious.

Casual was the order of the day, light pants and aloha shirts, though Hartley's Hawaiian shirt was much more elaborate, with embroidered detail down the front. In creased white slacks and matching patent-leather loafers, Hartley looked the top dog, exactly as he intended.

Splashes of pool water glinted in the brilliant late afternoon sun. Not far from the low bar wall, thick with vegetation, surf crashed on the white sand beach. Several teenagers in cutoffs and tank tops lounged past, carrying a boom box, leaving frowns in their wake. A pale couple emerged from the hotel's back door, a man with a red, white, and blue BellAir flight bag slung across one arm and an inflated sea monster under the other. His wife toted a plastic shopping bag – *American Society of Travel Agents World Travel Congress, Honolulu, 1980,* it read – both of them in tow behind a tiny girl in a pink bathing suit, drawn forward, irresistibly, down to the beach.

Atkins smirked. "Looks like that bunch just got off the boat."

"Don't knock it, Ted," Tanaka admonished. "These days, every customer counts."

Hartley was flicking his glass with a fingernail, making a dull sound. He looked over at Roger Bankhead. "What's the latest on our Hawaii traffic?"

"Very strong, excellent advance bookings."

"The tour business is real good, too," Atkins added, "and the deal we just cut with this guy Magill, finally we'll be able to cover the Northeast the way we always wanted to."

"What kind of discount do we give those outfits?"

"Typically thirty to fifty percent off full coach."

Hartley frowned. *"Thirty to fifty!* For that, we'd better have an exclusive."

Atkins shook his head. "They deal with everybody. That's what I'm saying. United's had a lock on his East Coast business for years, so this is one terrific move for us."

The waitress reappeared with Atkins' drink. Close behind was a balding, middle-aged man carrying at least three hundred pounds on a fireplug frame, followed by a slim younger man.

"Sorry, Ted." The fat man approached the table. "Got caught in traffic. Hello, Harry."

"Nice of you to join us," said Atkins, humorlessly. "Sidney Magill, Phil Hartley, our senior VP of marketing. And Roger Bankhead, my new boss."

"Gentlemen, a pleasure. My assistant, Randy Martin." He smiled at the blond youth beside him.

"What's your poison?" Tanaka asked.

"Club soda. Been off the sauce for years. What about you, Randy?"

"Oh. . . a glass of chablis."

Atkins swept his hand in a circle. "Another one all around."

Magill carefully lowered his bulk into a chair. As he twisted about, groping for his pants pocket, large wet patches were clearly visible at the armpits of his wilted blue shirt. He pulled out a large kerchief.

"I hear we'll be doing some business together, Mr. Hartley," he said, mopping his face with a flourish.

Hartley's eyes narrowed. "That does seem to be the case."

Listing sideways, Magill shoved the damp handkerchief back in his pocket. His chair tottered, but he righted himself adroitly.

"Ah, Mr. Hartley. I do hope you appreciate that High Horizon Tours will be filling more BellAir seats than ever before. In fact, I dare say we'll be your number-one tour operator to the islands this coming year."

"And even bigger in '82," Atkins added.

"That's right. If the shoe fits, as they say. You have a good product, Mr. Hartley, not spectacular but steady, and I must say, it's a pleasure to deal with people like Ted, good folks, easy to get along with." Magill clapped a handful of macadamia nuts into his mouth, "I understand," he paused to chew, "I understand you're speaking at tomorrow's closing dinner. . ." Hartley watched another handful disappear. "I shall be listening with great interest."

Magill retrieved his handkerchief, this time to wipe his mouth. "You're new to marketing, Mr. Hartley, according to my spies. A finance man, I'm given to believe."

"You might say we're bringing fresh perspective to the sale of our product," Hartley said sourly.

"That is commendable. Very commendable indeed. Every organization must renew itself, and ours is no exception, is it, my boy?" Magill smiled again at his companion, who blushed and looked away.

"When do I see that proposal you people put together?" Hartley said curtly.

A puzzled look came to Atkins' face. "What pro. . . oh, the contract! It'll be on your desk next week."

"Not the 'contract,' the *proposal*!" Hartley glared at Magill. "Ted knows there is no contract until I sign it. That's not even one of our fresh perspectives, Ted, is it?"

Atkins shrank in his chair.

Suddenly Hartley rose. He glanced at Bankhead. "We'll be going. Magill, I look forward to seeing your proposal."

"What about our drinks?" Atkins protested.

"Skip the drinks."

Magill leaned back and tilted his massive head. "I'm sure you'll find our arrangement to be in order, Mr. Hartley, as well as advantageous to all concerned. By the way, be sure to look me up when you come through Chicago. I'd love to show you our city."

"I'll just bet you would," Hartley muttered as he left. Bankhead was at his heels with Tanaka a step behind.

Atkins remained suspended in a crouch, half out of his chair. He fell back heavily. "All right, Sidney, what the fuck's your excuse *this* time?"

"Why, my boy, we were unavoidably detained. I told you that." He winked at his companion. "You know how these things are."

"Okay, Sidney," said Atkins, bolting his drink with one gulp. He stood, raising his hand as if to fend Magill off. "Okay. Just... just stay cool. I'll call you tomorrow."

A smile briefly creased the corpulent face. "Yes, Ted, you do that. That's an excellent idea."

Atkins caught up to Hartley and the others at the elevators. "Phil, what the hell! I know you're the boss, but... "

"Well, what do you know!" Hartley looked around the group. "Ted finally got something right! Too bad he can't remember who's authorized to do what in our company. 'Easy to get along with,' *my ass*! You have that proposal on my desk first thing Monday morning. And I want to know every piece of leverage we have over that fairy. We're going to squeeze him for all he's worth!"

"But we already shook hands," Atkins whined. "I can't go back on a deal."

The elevator doors were opening. "You're a smart guy. Figure it out."

"Aw, c'mon, even if he is, you know... the man's still one of our best customers. I mean, that sort of thing's as offensive to me as it is to you."

"That I doubt."

Atkins paused, then he grinned slyly. "Keep that up and you'll have to fire half our flight attendants. You know what they say, 'hags and fags.'"

Hartley whirled around, his face not an inch from Atkins'. "Don't give me any ideas!" He took a step forward, forcing Atkins back on his heels. A second step, and Atkins began to retreat.

"And you damn well make sure that lardass understands, *nobody* keeps Philip Hartley waiting!"

THE NEXT MORNING'S SCHEDULE called for Hartley and Bankhead to tour the exhibition area of the convention. Everything a travel agent might ever need or want was on display. Exhibits overflowed the hotel's grand ballroom into the corridors. The latest in office automation, slick videotaped travelogues, throngs of costumed salespeople, and of course, pamphlets, pamphlets, pamphlets. Also on display, the conventioneers themselves – the couple with matching powder-blue leisure suits and white shoes, the elderly, leathery-faced gentleman with his string tie, Stetson, dress boots, and purple-rinse wife – all of them diligently stuffing freebies into their *ASTA-1980* shopping bags. With the miniature wooden shoes from KLM, came authentic Lufthansa plastic beer steins, and carp pennants courtesy of the Japan Travel Bureau for Boys' Day in Cedar Rapids and Hartford.

"Let's take a look at our displays." Harry Tanaka was serving as tour guide for the morning. "The first one'll be our model of the CRS system. You can bring up our schedules, fares, seat selection, the whole bit."

Hartley and Bankhead followed Tanaka to a booth outfitted as a travel agency office, where a man was bent over a computer keyboard. Tanaka grasped him by the shoulder, turning him toward his guests.

"Fellows, this is Dave Lapointe. He's our new West Coast rep for Passages."

"Nice setup, Dave," Hartley observed, shaking the man's hand.

"Thanks, Mr. Hartley. This early, it's kind of quiet, but we're seeing a lot of agent interest, tons of leads to follow up. Have a seat. I'll take you through it." For the next fifteen minutes he led the men through the new system.

"Damn impressive," Tanaka observed as they moved away. "Now, our other exhibit features the neighbor islands. Once people see Honolulu, we figure one of the other islands is more likely to bring them back. I trust you slept well, Mr. Hartley."

"No complaints. Incidentally, how much did that room set us back?"

"Oh, it was a comp." Tanaka smiled. "Actually, they'd given you one that wasn't so great, so I got you an upgrade. Nice view of Waikiki, you'll admit. Diamond Head, too, the whole bit."

"I appreciate that, Harry."

"You company officers have a lot on your mind. You should be treated right when you're on the road. Anyway, that's how I see it." They edged through a crowd of onlookers. "Okay, gentlemen, here it is. Just eyeballing it, I'd say this is the best draw in the whole convention."

The second BellAir display was divided into three large booths, each one backdropped by a panoramic photo – Maui, Kauai, and the Big Island, Hawaii. A banner above the exhibit urged people to *FLY BELLAIR TO AMERICA'S PARADISE!*

The first booth held a large replica of the Big Island's twin landmarks, Mauna Kea and Mauna Loa. Shaved ice spread over the peaks suggested winter snow fields. "There's a little freezer element in there, but we have to refresh the ice every couple of hours." Downslope, Kilauea, the island's active volcano, hissed steam and from it poured a simulated river of gold-red lava. "Fire and ice! That's the ticket on the Big Island!"

In the next, a stream of water cascaded down a series of pools, spilling from one to the next, representing the 'Seven Sacred Pools' of Maui's Hana coast. "The natives call this *Ohe'o Gulch,*" Tanaka commented, "but Sacred Pools is a much better marketing name."

Kauai was simple by comparison, a life-sized statue of a *menehune,* one of the Garden Isle's "little people," his hands filled with small souvenir corsages. "We kinda blew the budget with the volcano and waterfall. But the ladies are really scooping up these orchids... "

"Well, what do you think?"

Startled, Hartley turned around. A young woman in a BellAir Hawaiian flight attendant uniform was standing behind him. Her striking looks and direct approach compounded his surprise. She was tall and tanned, with a pert nose and a sprinkling of freckles. Her red-blond hair was tied softly in a chignon. Her uniform, a high-collared sheath in royal blue and white, closer-fitting than airline standard, clung revealingly.

"Shelley Gregory," she said, smiling and extending her hand. "I know who you are. Welcome to Paradise, BellAir style!"

"I'm... very pleased to meet you," Hartley replied, regaining his balance.

"Shelley's one of our best salesmen, Mr. Hartley," said Tanaka. "Actually, in real life she *is* a flight attendant. We have several crews pitching in to help. On their layovers, their own time."

"And this is Tommy Ho," she added. "We're teaming up today."

"*Aloha,* Mr. Hartley." A handsome, young Hawaiian shook Hartley's hand vigorously. His aloha shirt was the same pattern as her dress. "And Mr. Bankhead, nice to meet you. Welcome aboard."

The young woman examined Hartley. "I'm looking forward to your speech. How about a preview?"

Hartley laughed, "I wouldn't want to spoil the surprise."

She turned her lower lip down. "Aw, well, if that's the way you feel about it. But if you're planning to talk the way they do at headquarters, I may need a translation later."

"It's not all that complicated..." Hartley paused, admiring the beautiful young woman. "But I might just have to do a rewrite."

Tanaka interrupted. "Folks, we'd better keep moving. You're on at ten-thirty with the sales reps, then lunch with the Honolulu Chamber."

"No rest for the weary," Hartley shook his head. "Good meeting you two. We appreciate your helping out like this."

"Where I'm from," the young woman replied coyly, "the expression is 'No rest for the *wicked...*'"

They looked intently at each other. Hartley nodded. "You know, maybe you're right. Maybe we're both right."

6

FOR THE CONVENTION FINALE, the hotel's main ballroom was converted into a banquet hall, festooned with balloons and banners. During dessert and coffee, an ASTA vice-president took the podium and droned through his idea of a comedy routine, while Hartley occupied himself making patterns on the tablecloth with his knife. Finally, and from the audience's reaction, not a moment too soon, the comedian wrapped up, and the emcee launched into his introduction of the featured speaker. Hartley took a swallow of water as his cue came at last.

"...the Senior Vice President of Marketing and Finance for BellAir, the free world's third-largest airline, will you please welcome, *Philip Hartley*!"

Smiling, Hartley made his way to the podium. He knew full well the applause, indeed the invitation itself, was due to his position at the airline, and not any achievements of his, for he was not yet widely known in the industry. The waiters were still noisily clearing the tables. They should have finished that first, he thought, annoyed, as he arranged several small cards with his speaking notes.

"Ladies and gentlemen," he began. "*Aloha!* And thank you for your hospitality, for this opportunity to be with you tonight. Though a relative newcomer to the travel industry, I use this ancient greeting, for it calls to mind BellAir's long tradition of service to Hawaii." Along with two other airlines, he thought, which shall go unmentioned.

"Rest assured, BellAir intends to honor its commitment to these islands. We will continue to bring visitors here for their enjoyment and to benefit the economy of this magnificent part of our country." There had been recent rumors of service cutbacks, with BellAir prominently mentioned. "However, as with every business, if we do not move forward, if we do not grow, we perish. Try telling your waiter here tonight, that he may lose his job because of declining air service, thanks to interference from the environmentalists. Ask the skycap at Honolulu International what he thinks about being laid off. Ask the flower growers on Kauai or Lanai's pineapple farmers if they'd like to return to steamships for moving their produce to market." He paused. The room had quieted.

"Think you'd find any takers? You'd better believe you wouldn't!"

The audience began to applaud, many nodding their heads. Good, Hartley thought, I've got them hooked. Now to reel them in.

"Widespread opposition to growth is a major threat, but it's not the only serious problem facing the airlines these days. The implications of high fuel and labor costs also greatly concern us and should worry everyone whose livelihood depends on air service, including yourselves.

"We at BellAir take no delight in high fares when they're accompanied by high costs. Like you, our profits are no better than our margins." He gestured with his hands for emphasis. "And when people can't afford to fly, everyone suffers. If we are forced down that dismal path, the bright promise of deregulation, the expansion of travel opportunities to vast numbers of new passengers will be jeopardized and reregulation assured.

"Let me tell you here and now, and I hope you invite me back and hold me to this promise," Hartley punched out the words, "BellAir is not about to let that happen!"

The crowd burst into applause. Hartley stepped back from the podium. He looked at the BellAir table right below him – Bankhead, Tanaka, other faces from the long day. He caught himself scanning the crowd for Shelley Gregory but couldn't find her in the darkened room. Okay. Time to get personal.

"Now, ladies and gentlemen, I'm going to give you folks an inside look at a few things we have on our drawing board, a sneak preview, if you will. This first one, you are really going to like."

For the next ten minutes Hartley was frequently interrupted by applause as he led the audience through a variety of new and recycled company programs – Passages, travel agent incentives, and more. He was in full stride, preaching from his pulpit of commerce, peering through the cigarette smoke at his anonymous congregation in the darkened room. He had them going. Now for a change of pace.

"At this time, I'm going to let you in on a little secret, and, believe me, I had to twist some arms to let this cat out of the bag here tonight.

In exactly six hours," Hartley pointed at his wristwatch, "at ten o'clock tomorrow New York time, BellAir and the Boeing Company will announce the largest airline order ever for the Boeing 767. This state-of-the-art aircraft will be BellAir's workhorse for years to come, a real passengers' dream. You will love it! So will your customers!

"The 767's cockpit will be so advanced, with video flight displays and computer controls, that our two-pilot crews will easily exceed the current margins of safety we currently enjoy with three pilots. The 767 is designed with two engines, two powerful, quiet, and, so important these days, fuel-efficient engines. Soon we expect to see our 767s flying to Europe, then between the West Coast and Hawaii."

Hartley went on, detailing other programs and schemes, then he glanced at his watch. Time to wind up.

"In a nutshell, here it is, the bottom line. To survive and prosper in the fiercely competitive airline environment, we have to offer a superior product, while at the same time driving down our costs. And to manage this, we must use every possible technological advantage, letting machines do the work of men and helping men to work more efficiently.

"At long last we have thrown off the shackles of big government. As our industry moves forward into a true free-market system, we must sever every tie to the past that cramps creativity and impedes progress.

"In conclusion, ladies and gentlemen, I again wish you *Aloha*! And I offer my thanks for this opportunity to be with you."

Returning to his seat, Hartley sipped a glass of water and looked around. The audience was still applauding, and he stood again and waved, singling out the BellAir table to stand. As the emcee rose for his concluding remarks, Hartley felt warm, excited, flushed with accomplishment. A job well done, a job well received. The crowd swirled around the head table. Several people came up to shake his hand and offer congratulations. Suddenly a strident voice broke in.

"Mr. Hartley! Sam Merriman, *Honolulu Advertiser.* Hey! Mr. Hartley!"

Hartley frowned. This event was closed to the media. That was the clear understanding. PR had prepared a carefully worded statement for release the next day. Hartley looked away, but the short, moon-faced reporter was not to be denied.

"A word, please, Mr. Hartley! Sam Merriman, aviation reporter for the *Honolulu Advertiser*! Have you got a prepared text, a handout?"

"There'll be a release tomorrow." Hartley turned to leave.

"Just a minute! One of your statements. You didn't say you'd be flying West Coast to Hawaii in the 767, did you? In twin-engine equipment?"

Hartley looked for Harry. Nowhere to be seen. Make a note of *that,* he thought angrily. Bowing to the inevitable, he faced the reporter.

"You heard me. That's what I said."

"But that makes no sense! The FAA's so tough on three-engine overwater. What in the world makes you think they'll go along with *two*?"

"Mr. Merriman, our technology is so good, I have full confidence it'll be approved. And if we can do the same job with two engines instead of three or four, that's exactly what we will do. We need to do everything to lower our costs and keep fares down."

"I'm not arguing your economics. I'm talking *safety*! All these years between the West Coast and Hawaii, we've never lost a passenger. What'll you do if both engines quit and you don't have a spare or two?"

Now Hartley was really hot. "Obviously you weren't listening! It won't happen until the FAA approves it! When they do, then it's safe to fly!"

"But *you* run the airline, not the FAA. Bottom line, it's *your call*!"

"And you can damn well bet we'll call it right!" Finally Hartley saw Tanaka and Bankhead approaching the head table. He turned on his heel and started toward them.

"But, Mr. Hartley..."

As the entourage made its way through the thinning crowd, Hartley grabbed Tanaka's arm.

"Who is that asshole? Where does he get off crashing a private meeting?"

"That guy is bad news," said Tanaka sourly. "I don't know why, but he's always been on our case. He's the one reporter we've never been able to get close to. If there's something in the *Advertiser* tomorrow, I'll tell you right now, you won't like it." Tanaka looked around. "Give me a minute. I'll try to straighten him out."

"Don't bother," said Hartley dourly.

"No, the thing is, with that guy there's always distortions, that's how he operates. I'll just talk to him, give him some background..."

"No!" Hartley snapped. "I said it the way it is! If the little prick wants to print it, let him!"

"Okay," Tanaka shrugged. "You're the boss." Suddenly he brightened. "Say, why don't we head upstairs. I have a little celebration put together. I don't know about you, but I've seen enough travel agents for one night."

Roger Bankhead broke in. "Don't worry about it, Philip. We reached the people we wanted. The press packets go out tomorrow. We'll follow through as planned."

"Right," said Tanaka. "Don't let that little shit get to you. It went just perfect."

OUTSIDE THE PARADISE LOUNGE lay the lights of Honolulu. Through one wall of windows, a chain of red and white marked the main highway traversing the city. From the other, the marina at the neighboring Ilikai Hotel could be seen, a black jewel in a sparkling setting. After a short break, the hard-working three-piece combo was reassembling, ready to resume their eclectic mix of Hawaiian songs and pop favorites.

"You did really great, Mr. Hartley," Tommy Ho was saying. "On the way out I heard a lot of compliments."

As Hartley was raising his glass, he felt someone at his shoulder.

"Mind if we join you?"

Hartley caught his breath... Shelley! But how different she looked, hair cascading onto her shoulders. She was wearing a long green silk dress, with a deeply cut halter top. With her was a stunning Asian woman with almond eyes.

"Pull up a chair!" Tanaka extended his hand. "Now the party's complete! What would you girls like? Waiter!"

"This is Bobbie," Shelley said to the table generally. "She's a friend of mine from Pan Am."

"The enemy in our bosom," Roger Bankhead noted. "So to speak, that is."

"May I slide in here?"

"Of course!" As soon as the words were out, Hartley realized he'd been much more enthusiastic than appropriate. Better be more careful. Shelley settled in next to him.

"You said some good things tonight, Mr. Hartley."

"I just told them what we're planning to do, that's all there was to it." He couldn't take his eyes off her.

"Surely things aren't *that* simple, Mr. Hartley. Not with an unruly crowd like us working under you."

"Oh, it isn't so bad. By the way," he said under his breath, "the name's Philip, you can call me that."

"All right. Philip. But what's wrong with Phil? Why can't I call you Phil, Philip?" Her green eyes danced in the light, mocking him, her pendant earrings sparkling.

"It's a long story but not very interesting, I'm afraid. Sure, call me Phil. I answer to that, too."

"*Aloha,* everyone!" Tanaka raised his glass. "To Mr. Hartley, and to his excellent words tonight."

"*Aloha!*"

"Hear, hear!" added Bankhead, careful to brush against the front of the Pan Am flight attendant's dress as he reached across to clink glasses.

In a few minutes the band started up again, this time a rock-'n'-roll set with distinct Hawaiian overtones. Shelley Gregory cradled her glass in her hands, touching the straw to her lips.

"How about it, Phil? Want to give it a try?"

"You mean *out there?*"

"That's where they normally dance," she laughed.

He flushed. Outmaneuvered again.

They joined several other couples on the small floor, already moving to the fast, happy beat.

"This is sort of a test," she said after a few minutes. "I always wondered if a senior executive could handle this stuff."

"Well, how am I doing?"

"Let's see, you get about... about a B-plus."

"I'll take that as a compliment." Hartley smiled. "We don't tend to dwell on it, but some of us were human once."

After the fast set, the band slowed the pace.

> *I found my thrill*
> *on Blueberry Hill*
> *On Blueberry Hill*
> *when I found you...*

"Touch dancing," Shelley murmured, moving closer. "Pretty dumb name, if you ask me."

"Oh, I don't know. I remember when this was big. That dates me I suppose."

She looked up at him. "I'd say you've worn rather well."

He was quiet for a moment. "I'll bet you never heard of Fats Domino," he said wistfully.

"Whoa!" she laughed. "Try me again."

"How about the Platters?"

"Vaguely."

He stared over her shoulder. "I guess. . . I was just thinking. High school, football, cars, you know, that sort of thing."

"And a special girl?"

"Not really. That came later."

He paused, holding Shelley at arm's length. "I like your laugh. You have a way of cutting things down to size."

"Irreverent is the word. My big mouth's got me in trouble more than once. Promise you won't report me to our fearless leader, Mr. Hartley. I mean, Phil."

"Not a chance. You're safe with me."

"Oh, I'm not so sure of that."

They drew closer, their bodies warming each other. Her breasts pressed against him, his hand caressing the smooth of her back. As they moved to the music, he felt himself stirring, growing hard. . .

> *Tho' we're apart,*
> *You're part of me still,*
> *For you were my thrill*
> *on Blueberry Hill.*

"Well, folks, time for a break!"

Annoyed, Hartley looked up, his reverie shattered.

"But stick around! We'll be back with more music for your dancing and listening pleasure."

They held each other for a moment after the music stopped. "Mmmm. . . that was nice," she said, breaking free.

"Who needs music?" Hartley replied. They walked slowly back to the table, Shelley readily accepting his arm around her waist.

What a night, he thought. The speech, this beautiful girl. Suddenly he realized he was scowling. A familiar, nagging thought had presented itself front and center. The last thing I need is to get involved, and with a company inkwell, at that. He stole a glance at Shelley. She was watching him, amusement on her face.

"Nice going, Mr. Hartley," Tommy Ho was nodding his head. "You guys can really handle that old music."

"Careful, don't knock it. I grew up with that old music."

"Hey, just because it's old doesn't mean it's no good!"

"Nice recovery." Hartley pointed at him. "You just saved a very promising career."

The evening went on. They danced and talked, danced some more. Hartley found himself totally enchanted. After a slow, moody set just before midnight, as they were returning to the table Shelley clasped his hand... she pressed something cool and hard into it.

"Don't say anything..." she whispered. "If you want it, it's yours."

Suddenly all Hartley's doubts vanished. He didn't even open his hand. His course was set.

"Half an hour," she whispered, stepping away. "It wouldn't be proper to leave together. Your reputation, you know," she said, smiling.

"You're very beautiful, for a mind reader."

Back at the table she made her adieus, something about a wake-up call for an early flight. Her Pan Am friend, thick-tongued from too many mai-tais, commented loudly what a bullshit outfit BellAir was. She didn't have to report until three in the afternoon.

"Night, all. Thanks for a wonderful evening."

"Be good," Tanaka replied. His eyes followed her as she left the room.

TWENTY MINUTES LATER, after repeated glances at his watch and a show of yawning he hoped wasn't too obvious, Hartley made his excuses and left the bar. With growing excitement he stepped into the elevator, checked Shelley's key for the room number and pushed the button for her floor. A moment later he was at her door. Turning the key, he knocked softly and went in.

"Shelley?"

"And whom did you expect?" Her laugh rippled across the room. She was standing by the window, framed in moonlight. Hartley took her in his arms... she kissed him lightly, then began loosening his tie.

"I wondered if you'd really show."

"I said I would."

"But you don't know me. For all you know, I'm the kiss-and-tell kind."

"I doubt that."

"You're right," she smiled, "Whatever I am, it's not that." She unbuttoned his shirt and stroked his chest.

"I like you, Phil. I really do like you. You deserve the best... and I'm the best there is."

He kissed her and she responded, hard and deep. By now her fingers were undoing his belt. They moved across the room to the bed, their hands and mouths caressing, exploring. For hours they were transported to the heights, abandoned to each other's arms the night long.

HARTLEY REACHED BLINDLY toward the noise, knocking the alarm off the night stand. He slid from the bed and silenced the clock protesting on the floor. The sun was streaming in the uncurtained windows... too bright. He looked around, squinting. Shelley! Where is she? She's gone! Her things are gone!

For several minutes he sat on the edge of the bed, then he stood and stumbled into the bathroom. Looks familiar, he thought, peering into the mirror. No headache... and no regrets. He splashed cold water on his face, then buried it in a towel, luxuriating in the heavy cloth. A vague feeling of discomfort came over him. He had left his clothes on the bedroom floor, at least he was pretty sure he did. But where were they?

Back to the bedroom. By now his eyes had adjusted to the light. No clothes... but he noticed a slip of paper on the dresser. Under the hotel's rainbow logo he read,

> Phil, your suit's in the closet. I hate a sloppy room.
> Off to my flight. That was no joke. Neither was last
> night. Always, Shelley.

Unbelievable! She roars into my life then vanishes, just like that. Too bad, he thought with a pang. But just as well. I have no room for attachments. No time, no room.

Hartley sat quietly on the bed, then reached across and ran his hand over the sheet. In the stillness of the bright room she returned to him, the fragrance of her hair, her soft skin, an urgent, physical presence, then she drifted off. He swallowed hard. There was a hard metallic taste in his mouth. My life, he thought, my self-portrait. A splash of color, one bright moment on the everlasting gray canvas.

He forced his thoughts back to reality. The company. BellAir. Before long, the biggest prize of all. But, he pondered, if not for that, what would it mean? What would anything mean?

My clothes, he suddenly thought. He stepped to the closet and jerked the door open. His suit hung neatly on its hanger, his shoes on the floor. He shook his head and laughed softly to himself.

He dressed quickly. The room key was still in his pocket, nothing missing from his wallet. Money, credit cards, everything in order. Returning to his room the next floor up... make a note of that, he thought, his mind locking onto routine. We're spending way too much on flight attendants if this is how they live. Have to get on Fritz for that. Next, a shower and shave and, his stomach reminded him as he threw on the complimentary terrycloth robe, room service. His flight wasn't until ten-thirty, a small indulgence built into his itinerary to make up for the rigors of the trip. He drank deeply from the espresso he'd ordered as an eye-opener. Not bad, not bad at all.

It was beginning to dawn on Hartley that an occasional night like this could become a most pleasant perk. What was Harry's expression? Our top people deserve to be treated right... yes, that was it, and it was true. Though, of course, discretion is the watchword. Things must be kept in perspective, under control at all times.

He was about to pick up the morning paper still lying on his breakfast tray, to see what that pissant reporter had written about him, when the phone rang. It was Tommy Ho.

"I'm downstairs in the lobby, Mr. Hartley. Ready whenever you are."

"See you in half an hour."

Hartley dressed and, on his way out the door, drank the last of the juice. One of those tropical drinks. Pineapple and passion fruit, guava, maybe, never could tell them apart. Tommy was downstairs, on the ball.

"Man, you were smart to leave early. Mr. Bankhead and I pretty much closed up the place. I just checked on your flight, they say it's on time."

Twenty minutes later they were cruising along the last stretch of freeway before the airport turnoff. Hartley was flipping through the newspaper. On a fast pass he found nothing. Maybe Harry killed the story, after all. Ho looked back over his shoulder.

"Mr. Hartley. Say, I hope you didn't take me wrong last night. I really do like that fifties music. In fact, I even got a bunch of those old records, Bo Diddley, the Big Bopper, some others. I put them on tapes for parties and so on."

Hartley looked up. "I knew you were a man of distinction. Though you were doing your best to hide it."

"Yeah, well, you were doing pretty well, yourself. So tell me, how did you like Shelley? You guys seemed to hit it off real well."

Hartley was caught off guard. "You mean... oh, sure. She's a great dancer, isn't she? I haven't danced that much in years."

"She's terrific, all right, always ready to help out with this and that." He caught Hartley's eyes in the rear-view mirror. "Shelley and Harry are pretty thick. I figured you knew that."

Hartley frowned. "What's *that* supposed to mean?"

"Oh, nothing, really. Just... well, you know, she's one of Harry's girls. At least, that's what everybody calls them."

"Harry's girls?" Hartley leaned forward. *"Harry's girls?"*

Ho looked back to the road.

"There's a lot of important people come through here – senators, prime ministers, that kind of thing. Harry fixes them up, you know, for a good time. You get my drift. Word is, Shelley's the best. She must be, the way people are always falling for her." He turned to look at Hartley. "You can see why. She's great company, full of life. A fantastic person, really."

Hartley's heart sank. His face was suddenly very warm. He stared out the window. The airport was just coming into view.

"Yeah," Hartley said softly. "Fantastic is hardly the word."

7

A S HE WAITED for his client to finish a call, Will Cartright peered out a window through a pair of heavy, military-style binoculars. The modern three-level building that housed Frank Delgado's office was only a block from Monterey Airport, but a large stand of pines blocked Cartright's view of the airfield. On the window next to his elbow, a powerful aviation-band radio gave an occasional squawk of pilot-controller jabber. Defeated by the trees, Cartright trained the glasses west, toward the town of Seaside and the Fort Ord complex. Through the summer haze, he could see Monterey Bay and the shimmering Pacific beyond.

Until the previous year, Frank Delgado had operated out of a cramped office in the terminal building behind Bay's ticket counter, but he finally ran out of room and had to take other space. In truth, the move was highly popular with his airport operations people, who were relieved to be rid of the boss breathing down their necks. And, except for the monthly twinge when he signed the rent check, Delgado was also pleased, for the separation freed him to focus better on the big picture. At least, that was the theory.

Delgado was seated at a small round table next to his cluttered desk. "Right. Right. Talk to you later." He hung up the phone.

Cartright took a seat at the table. "The important thing to remember, Frank, BellAir needs *you* a whole lot more than you need *them.*"

"Yeah. It's strange, isn't it. I hear they're really pissed we didn't fall in line like the others. That outfit in New York signed up last month, and you saw the Air Chicago clipping." Delgado shrugged. "Actually, we don't need all that much. A decent display in their new Res system would go a long way. Then if they move a couple of schedules so we can connect better. But as far as changing our name is concerned, they can forget that. It's not even on the table!"

"The others agreed to that, did they?"

"So I hear." Delgado shook his head. "It makes no sense, Will, absolutely no sense. You work your whole life building up your business, then somebody comes along and you're supposed to drop your name and take on theirs? 'BellAir Commuter'? Just the sound of it makes me want to barf!"

"Maybe they didn't have your options. You've got staying power, good liquidity from your partners and, if I say so myself, a terrific deal on the Metros. Who knows, in a couple of years if you're not careful, you might have a real airline on your hands."

"You know, we just might," said Delgado with a broad grin. He leaned back in his chair, his hands clasped behind his head. "I am really looking forward to this trip. I just know we're going to make out real well. I mean, how can we miss with a local boy back there?"

"You mean Hartley?"

"Yeah. I told you, he's from Manteca."

Cartright frowned. "I don't put any stock in that. He didn't get where he is making deals for old times' sake."

"Sorry, Will, you're wrong there. Valley people stick together. Always have, always will. That's just the way we are."

"Have you talked with him yet?"

"Not yet. I'm kind of waiting to use him as an icebreaker if those other guys give us a hard time." Delgado lowered his eyes. "Actually, I called him a couple of times, but he didn't get back to me. Pete Churchman called me back. I can understand that. He's a busy guy."

Cartright sat back in his chair. "Speaking of partners, I know Fred Bentley's aware of the meeting, but were you able to reach Alexander?"

One of Delgado's new investors was the British actor Frederic Bentley, star of several early aviation films, now retired to 17 Mile Drive, on the peninsula. Ralph Alexander owned a chain of auto-supply stores. Delgado had actually turned down a number of other offers.

"Yeah, I briefed him yesterday. He's on board, too. It'll be easy, I just won't agree to anything until I run it by him and Fred."

"That buys you time, too."

Delgado looked at his watch. "Speaking of that, I'm letting some of our fellas try out the new Metro. Want to come along?"

"How about a ride home?"

"Always thinking!" Delgado put his finger to his head. "Sure, why not? We'll give your seat to somebody important, like a paying customer." He stood up and moved some papers around on his desk. "Let's get the hell out of here. I can't stand this mess anymore."

RESPLENDENT IN BAY AIRLINES' blue and green livery, the gleaming new Metroliner had arrived the night before, Delgado and Marty Barron ferrying it from the factory in Texas.

The curtain separating the Metroliner's cockpit from the cabin was tied back, giving Cartright a clear view of the business end of the airplane. In the left seat, Delgado was speaking into the mike of a earmuff-style headset, looking from the back like a high-tech Mouseketeer. Ed Perry, one of Bay's senior captains, was in the co-pilot's seat beside Delgado. Next to Cartright was Barron, the company's chief pilot, whose task it was to train Bay's crews on the new machine. Behind Cartright sat Stanley Fong, a new pilot-hire. Fong was a scion of one of San Francisco's leading Chinese families, which, according to rumor, was not thrilled with their son's choice of profession.

Out his side window Cartright observed several spectators leaning over the railing on the deck atop the terminal building. The young ramp agent gave the all-clear, tracing a circle with her signaling wand and pointing to the right engine. Delgado pushed a button on his instrument panel, advancing the right thrust lever. The prop begin to turn over... one blade... two... three, then the turbine spun to life with a high-pitched whine that was quickly joined by a muted growl. After checking his instruments, Delgado repeated the process on the left engine. Then, he lifted one earphone and turned to Cartright.

"Notice how smooth this is compared to the 402? And just wait till you see this hummer climb."

Delgado released the brakes and advanced the left throttle, at the same time depressing his right rudder pedal. The plane pivoted and turned to the right. Straightening the nosewheel, he started up the taxiway, which sloped gently toward higher ground. While the plane trundled along, he and Perry completed the takeoff checklist. Their clearance came through as they approached the turnaround area at the end of the taxiway. Delgado pushed hard on his left rudder, turning onto the runway, then smoothly advanced the throttles.

The Metroliner accelerated quickly, its nosewheel tracking precisely the white centerline stripe. Perry placed his hand on the throttle stems, positioning himself to take over instantly, should Delgado fall incapacitated at this critical phase of the flight.

"V1, 80 knots. Vr... V2." Delgado's gentle back pressure on the wheel lifted the nose, and the aircraft leapt from the runway.

"Gear up... Gear up."

"Flaps 15... Flaps 15."

Delgado banked right and began paralleling the coastline. An area of sand dunes, then the firing range at Fort Ord slipped beneath them. Cartright noticed the altimeter. Already passing through 2,000 feet. He checked the vertical speed indicator. It looked like 2,500 feet a minute. *Twenty-five hundred!*

The plane banked left and turned out over the ocean. Delgado pressed a button on the control wheel and his voice came through the cabin speakers.

"They gave us a block of airspace out here to maneuver, but keep your eyeballs peeled for traffic, just in case. We'll level at five thousand and do a couple of steep turns. One to the left first, around that sail-boat down there."

Delgado applied gentle pressure to the control wheel until his wingtip was pointing at a white spot on the water nearly a mile below, then he straightened the wheel and thumbed a switch to trim out the back pressure from the turn. Cartright felt his cheeks sag and his body press heavily into the seat from the "g" forces. He caught sight of the attitude indicator – a 60-degree bank! As they came around through the cool, shady part of the turn, the brilliant sun flared in Cartright's window. Suddenly the plane began jouncing up and down.

"Ha!" Delgado shouted. "We hit our own wake! Let's see if we can hang in for another 360."

A minute later Delgado rolled out on his original heading. Then the engines quieted, and Cartright felt the plane slow and saw its nose rise. The landing gear dropped out, and the flaps began extending from the wings' trailing edge.

"Now a slow turn to the right, around that tanker down there."

The plane whipped through the turn, completing the arc and again ploughing into the wake of its first circle. "When this baby's slowed down, it turns on a dime!"

After a half-hour of maneuvering, Delgado had seen enough. "All right, Ed. Let's see if you can find SFO."

As they crossed the shoreline at Santa Cruz, the coastal hills spread before them. Summer had toasted the grasses and bushes a golden brown, but with the parching heat came the danger of fire. From his perch at six thousand feet, Cartright counted three of the peaks ringing San Francisco Bay. Mt. Hamilton, Lick Observatory at its crest, towered behind the sprawling urban scar that was San Jose. In the distance loomed Mt. Diablo's twin-peak massif, and up the coast, across the Golden Gate, the silhouette of Mt. Tamalpais stood sentry for the City by the Bay.

Passing over the Woodside VOR, a key navigation point for aircraft approaching San Francisco, the Metroliner was cleared for the approach to Runway 28 Left. Keeping his speed up to stay ahead of a 727 bearing down on the same runway, Perry crossed the western span of the San Mateo Bridge, swiftly descending toward the airport.

Five minutes later they were on the ground, taxiing toward the airport's old south terminal and Bay's ramp near the BellAir complex. Perry brought the Metroliner to a stop next to the wing of a BellAir 727 and beside two of Frank's old 402s. Cartright had to admit they looked slow and antiquated compared to the new toy.

"Hell of a job, Ed! Delgado clapped his co-pilot on the shoulder. "You can fly for me anytime." He unsnapped his shoulder harness. "So, how'd you like it, Will?"

"Almost good enough to pay money for," Cartright laughed. "So, we'll be seeing you Tuesday morning."

"Right. At the BellAir gate. Flight 86, I think. Anyway, the 7:45 nonstop." Delgado paused. "Damn! I left your ticket at the office!" He shook his head. "Oh, well. I'll bring it Tuesday."

He grinned at Cartright. "Those people must really want to impress us – positive space first class. None of that standby stuff. It's all fitting together, just like I told you! Stick with me, man. We are going places!"

8

MORNING LAY HEAVY on the city. A languid beige haze blanketed the glass canyons. August in Manhattan, the dog days. As the men passed Saint Patrick's Cathedral, Frank Delgado crossed himself.

"I ought to go in and light a candle."

"Whatever it takes."

They turned onto East 49th Street, then crossed Madison Ave. Nearing Park, Cartright nudged Delgado. "There it is. The BellAir Tower."

Delgado exhaled loudly.

At the entrance, Cartright stepped aside and bowed. "After you, Mr. Stanley."

Delgado laughed. "Thank you, Dr. Livingstone." He pushed his way through the revolving door. "You know, Will, you really know how to keep me loose. That's damn unusual. Most of you attorneys are better at making people uncomfortable."

"Legal Pessimism," Cartright replied. "It's a required course in law school. It works like this. If your client thinks he's in a hole, he feels good when you get him out of it. The bigger the hole, the better he feels. The last thing you want to do is make anything look easy."

"Should you be telling me this?"

"Probably not."

BellAir's entries took up several columns of the lobby directory.

"Here it is. Bankhead. Fifty-four."

A moment later they found themselves in a small foyer. "Marketing and Sales. To the left."

Entering through glass double doors, the men came upon a receptionist deep in phone conversation. She put her hand over the mouthpiece.

"How may I help you?"

"Mr. Delgado and Mr. Cartright to see Mr. Bankhead."

"Is he expecting you?"

"He'd better be," Delgado responded. "We came a long way to see him. We have a nine-thirty appointment."

"May I have your card?"

Delgado fumbled with his wallet. "Will, you got one handy?"

Cartright handed her a card.

"Take a seat. I'll let him know you're here." She glanced at Cartright's card. "And Mr. . . . Del Gatto?

"Delgado."

They stepped into the reception area. "A real Miss Personality, ain't she," Delgado whispered. He began sorting through a pile of reading materials. *Travel Weekly,* an old issue of *Advertising Age,* the morning's *Wall Street Journal.* "Not an airplane magazine in the lot. Well, this is Marketing, after all."

"Ahem!"

A stout woman with flaming orange hair was peering at the men, over a pair of enormous, purple, bejeweled eyeglasses.

"Mr. Cartright?"

"Yes, and Mr. Delgado."

"Very good. Mr. Bankhead will be with you as soon as he can. Would you care to wait here or to step into the conference room where you will be meeting?"

"The conference room," Delgado replied. "We'll wait there."

"Come with me, then. It's back this way."

As they walked along, Delgado touched Cartright on the arm, pointing at the woman's four-inch platform shoes, shaking his head. Halfway down a long corridor, she stopped at a door labeled Conference – 5400 E, reached for a placard marked VACANT, flipped the card over, and slid it back in its frame. Now the room was OCCUPIED.

"In there," she nodded. "There's a pot of coffee, so help your-selves. Anything you need, punch 3211 and ask for Rose, that's me. Dial nine to get out, local calls only. You need long distance, call me and I'll take care of it. Mr. Bankhead shouldn't be too long."

"Thanks, Rose," said Delgado, flashing a smile.

"Don't mention it." She shut the door and was gone. The two men looked at each other and burst out laughing.

Overhead fluorescent lights cast a flat glare about the room, which was small and windowless. A publicity photo of an airplane hung on one wall, a stubby, early-model Boeing 727 in BellAir's old sixties' paint scheme, flying abeam a snow-capped volcanic peak. Most of the opposite wall was filled by a large metal cabinet, next to a plaque with BellAir's winged B logo and a proclamation:

OUR COMPANY'S OBJECTIVES
- *SAFETY! SAFETY! SAFETY!*
- Our Customers: Excellent Service
- Our Employees: Good Pay for Honest Work
- Our Shareholders: Reasonable Profits
- Our Business Partners: Fair Dealing
- Our Communities: Good Citizenship
                                Signed, Charlie Bell

Delgado scowled. "Fair dealing, my ass! I hope they're doing better with the rest of their objectives." He rattled the handle of the cabinet. Locked. Above it a schoolroom clock with a red sweep second hand read 9:48. While Cartright pawed through his briefcase, Delgado poured a mug of coffee.

"You know, that was one weird-looking lady." Delgado set his coffee on the gray Formica and chrome table. He fidgeted with the plastic stirrer, bending it back and forth. "I don't like this having to wait."

Cartright looked up. "Relax! We've got a lot more time than they have."

Twenty more minutes passed. Delgado was on his feet, pacing, whistling low, tuneless sounds. Suddenly the door flew open. In burst a tall, thin man with bushy hair, followed by a sharp-featured woman and another man in a rumpled suit carrying several manila folders.

"Hi! Roger Bankhead! I do apologize, but we just had a scare. Looked for a while like our whole reservations system had crashed." Bankhead caught his breath. "Ah, I forgot. We don't use that word around here. Thought we'd lost all our bookings for the year, but we got them back, thank God."

Delgado nodded. "It's nice to see other people have problems, not just us little outfits."

"Of that I can assure you. Gentlemen, meet Sue Morse, my manager of commuter operations, and Francis Farrell. Francis, here, is one of our top lawyers. He's the reason we spend so little time in jail."

Delgado shook hands. "We've talked on the phone, Miss Morse."

"Yes. You've been dealing with Peter Churchman. He handles the western states for me."

"Right. Pete. He around today?"

"No, he's traveling this week."

Bankhead settled in at the head of the table. Delgado and Cartright chose the side opposite Bankhead's two aides. "Well," Bankhead said, "why don't we begin. First, let me say we've taken a close look at your operation, Mr. Delgado... Frank, and I mean to tell you we are truly impressed. From a shoestring, you've built yourself one neat little empire."

Delgado shook his head. "Empire? That's hardly the word, but we think we run a good operation."

"And you have every right to think that. As you know, Frank, this is a time of great uncertainty in our industry – new start-ups, destructive price competition, and so on, all of which puts one hell of a lot of pressure on us all. Although you've not had much of that out your way. So far," Bankhead added, lifting his eyebrows.

"Now, what we hope to accomplish in these two days is to interest you in an arrangement that will help stabilize BellAir's markets while permitting your airline to grow, in fact, grow much faster than you might have thought possible. Not to mention the opportunity to earn some very handsome returns."

"I'm all ears, Mr. Bankhead." Delgado glanced at Cartright and winked.

"Excellent! Ms. Morse will take over and present our package. Sue?"

The young woman was straight out of the dress-for-success manual – dark blue suit, white oxford-cloth button-down shirt, a bow of red ribbon at the neck.

"Gentlemen," she began in a cultured, professional voice, "what we are about to show you is the BellAir Commuter Airline Program. It has three components."

She leaned forward and raised an index finger. "First, we identify the specific markets you would operate as a replacement for BellAir's service." A second finger went up. "Next, we reach agreement on the number of passengers you would supply us in each market and set your compensation accordingly. Lastly," she lifted finger number three, "you become a full participant in the joint marketing and promotion program we've established for our commuter airlines."

She smiled pleasantly at Delgado, then at Cartright. "In brief, gentlemen, that's the program."

"Sounds simple enough," Delgado observed. "What's the catch?"

"There is no catch, Frank," replied Bankhead affably. "With BellAir, what you see is what you get."

Delgado snorted. "Okay, let's have the rest of it."

Morse went on. "As Roger said, we've studied your operation, Mr. Delgado, and we think you have the type of management style that would fit in nicely. Though we have noticed one shortcoming in your system, in fact, a major shortcoming. You know, of course, what I'm referring to?"

Delgado's eyebrows shot up. "Can't say as I do, Miss Morse. Would you care to enlighten me?"

"San Francisco, Mr. Delgado. San Francisco!"

Delgado nodded. "Well, maybe I better set you people straight. That has been a very conscious decision on our part. Except for our flights that feed you, we stay as far away from that place as we can. It's expensive to do business there, and damn tricky, too. Monterey's what we know best. It's been good to us, so that's why we concentrate everything there."

"But you have to admit, San Francisco is where the passenger volumes are. It's where the action is, and you simply don't have a meaningful presence." Morse tapped the table with her pencil. "Let me ask this. Have you any idea how many passengers BellAir carries every day between SFO and, say, Bakersfield? Or Fresno?"

"No. But I imagine it's quite a few."

"*Quite* a few," she smiled. "And whatever happens, we need to retain those passengers for our long-haul services – Chicago, the East Coast, Honolulu, the Far East. In a nutshell, that is our problem, which is another way of saying that is your opportunity! The traffic count from these small communities doesn't come anywhere near filling a jet aircraft. Thirty passengers in a 130-seat 727 or 737 is rather disappointing to us, but those loads would more than fill your 402s and your new Metroliners. *That's* the point I want you to understand!"

Bankhead glanced at Morse and leaned forward. "Frank, it's a classic win-win situation. We want you to operate BellAir's feeder system in Northern California for us. You take our passengers at SFO, that makes *you* money. You bring the traffic to us at SFO, we put them on our long-hauls, that makes *us* money!"

Bankhead steepled his hands and rested his nose on his fingertips. "Well, what do you think, Frank? How do you like it so far?"

Delgado pushed his chair back from the table. "That's one hell of a tall order. I didn't expect you people were looking at anything that big." He crossed his legs. "Let me get something straight, first. Where do you suggest I would get the equipment for all that flying? My Metros are already committed to our own flying, overcommitted, in fact."

Farrell spoke for the first time. He appeared to be around fifty, a roundish, fleshy-faced man with thick wire-rimmed glasses, black-haired, with a dramatic flush to his cheeks.

"If everything fell into place, Mr. Delgado," he began sonorously, "BellAir would see about assisting you with even more Metroliners. Our finance subsidiary – it's a bank, essentially – would be prepared to offer you very attractive terms."

Delgado frowned. "Okay, say I was interested. Mind you, I'm just saying if. Why in the world would I want to get into this? All it'd mean is twice as many headaches."

"Ah! Now you're wrong, there. Just take a look at these numbers..." Morse traced a column of figures on a computer printout. "Fresno, for example. I see in April we carried 4,844 passengers between Fresno and San Francisco..."

Delgado whistled.

"...and of these, 1,585 were local passengers, which would be yours, free and clear. However many locals you carry, that revenue you keep. The others that continue on from SFO you would hand over to us. We'd target a minimum number of passengers by this time next year and divide the revenue. Exceed the target and you qualify for a bonus."

"And if I don't?"

"Then there are some give-backs."

"Such as?"

"We knock something off the percentage."

"So if things turn down, I get hit a double whammy. Right?"

"The upside is a double payoff! More passengers mean more revenue per passenger."

"That has to appeal to the entrepreneur in you, Frank," Bankhead beamed.

"More like the gambler," he muttered. "So what about your other point, the marketing?"

"Here's where the fun begins." Bankhead folded his hands. "Incidentally, the kind of support we provide our commuter partners, there is absolutely no reason you shouldn't exceed your target in each and every market. Sue?"

"Thanks, Roger. The first order of business is tying our schedules together so they really fit. Peter has briefed me on some difficulties you've had with our New York nonstop..."

"Difficulties?" Delgado interrupted. "It's just your plane leaves before mine can get there. And that's not the only one."

Morse smiled. "Well, it will certainly be in our mutual interest to fix that, won't it? Next, we're talking joint promotions. TV, radio, newspapers and magazines, timetables, frequent flyer mileage – a complete package. We'll feature your destinations in our advertising and bear the lion's share of the expense, and of course, national media coverage is at zero cost to you."

"Come on, don't tell me you're going to promote Fresno on national TV!"

"Actually, there is some of that in our print ads, but what I'm really talking about is this."

She walked to the wall cabinet and inserted a small key. Inside, attached to a corkboard, was a rendering of a Metroliner in BellAir colors, swooping over the Golden Gate Bridge.

"How about *that,* Frank!" Bankhead exclaimed, rising from his chair. He tapped the picture with a metal pointer. "That is *you,* coming into SFO with a full load of passengers. Can't you just picture it? More planes, bigger volumes, more money in your pocket! How does that grab you?"

"Grab me? Grab my wallet, is more like it! Come on, Mr. Bankhead, don't play games. Look what it says on that plane. It says *BellAir Commuter!* Show me where it says Bay Airlines? Nowhere, that's where! I'm sorry, but that is not my airplane."

"You're wrong," Farrell interjected. "Bay Airlines would own that plane. You'd have title to it, subject to our lien, of course, and it would be registered in your name. There's no question it would be your plane."

"Okay, okay," replied Delgado, losing patience. "*I* know that, and *you* know that, but you're telling me a passenger's supposed to know he's on my airline if there's a piece of paper somewhere says I own the damn airplane? *Hell no,* they won't! And what about my ticket counters? What would *those* signs say? And my agents. Whose uniforms would *they* be wearing?"

"Why, BellAir Commuter, of course," Morse replied crisply.

"See! That's exactly what I mean! Pretty soon *even my own people* won't know who they're working for! And the travel agents. What comes up on their screens? Bay Airlines? I doubt that."

"No, but again, that's the way the program works. That's the way it is."

Delgado placed both palms on the table. "Look. Some of what you say makes sense. The schedules, maybe even the San Fran part. But I am not about to let my company's name disappear. I run my company *my way. That's* the way it is!"

He sat back. "Something you people should understand. We've never lost an airplane, but we came damn close last year. One of my best pilots, too. That night his head was somewhere else, I can assure you it was nowhere near the cockpit. Then and there I made a decision. I operate with two-pilot crews, even though you don't have to on the 402. And that hurts. It means one less passenger I can carry. And you want to hear about equipment? I've got equipment on my planes nobody our size has. And maintenance? I pay those guys like it's going out of style!"

Delgado spread his hands wide. "My point is, all this costs me. I won't tell you how thin my margin is, but I'm proud of what I do and I sleep very well at night. And believe me, my sleep is very important to me."

Morse glanced at Bankhead. "I appreciate what you're saying, Mr. Delgado, but look at the bottom line. With the volumes we're talking, you'll cover those costs and you'll do it even better than now. On top of that, a share of federal money for serving these smaller cities for us. You see the advantages, don't you?"

"Miss Morse, the only thing going for me is my reputation. A lot of people trust me. That's *Bay Airlines* they trust. And you're saying I should give that away? For nothing? Come on, that's crazy! I'd have to be out of my mind!"

Delgado rose to his feet and walked over to Bankhead. He stood over him, wagging his finger.

"Okay, Mr. Bankhead, I tell you what. You want to buy my airline? Well, go ahead, make me an offer! Maybe I'll sell the whole damn thing to you. But I'm not about to *give* it away!"

His heart pounding, Delgado stepped to the BellAir Commuter drawing in the cabinet, turning his back on the group. He knew it would come down to this. Bastards! I'll end up like George Steiner if they have their way. Through his rush of adrenaline Delgado sensed Bankhead speaking.

"Frank, I hear what you're saying. We've seen these concerns from our other partners, but they saw the advantages, they came around. You probably know, we have two in our camp and there'll be two more within the month."

Bankhead ran his fingers through his hair. "Perhaps. . . perhaps we should turn to some items we can agree on. Then come back to the tough issues later."

Delgado looked at Cartright, who gave him a nod.

"Sure, sure, let's go that route."

For the next hour they pored over schedule plots, traffic reports, revenue projections – data that would underpin the hypothetical operation. At twelve-twenty Bankhead looked at his watch. It was time to retire to the fifty-fifth floor, there to be joined for lunch by Fritz Mueller. . . and Philip Hartley.

SUBDUED AND ELEGANT, BellAir's executive dining room enjoyed a glorious view of Manhattan's West Side and New Jersey across the Hudson. The place settings were distinctive and expensive – Waterford goblets, gold-plated cutlery, and bone china embossed with BellAir's winged B crest. Filipino waiters in starched white jackets moved about the room silently and deftly, a reminder of the airline's elegant inflight service of years past. Seated between Mueller and Hartley at the large round table, after a few minutes of pleasantries, Delgado could contain himself no longer.

"I hear you're from the valley, Mr. Hartley. You get back there often?"

Hartley put down his napkin. "Not really. There's no reason, no family ties, nothing like that."

"But the university. You must stay in touch there."

"Actually, I did make it to the Big Game last year, first one in years. There was an awards ceremony. I couldn't very well refuse."

"The California Athletic Hall of Fame."

"You've done your homework, Mr. Delgado."

"It's my son. He's up on all these things. He plays high-school ball."

"Oh? What position?"

"Quarterback." Delgado coughed. "Stanford's interested in him."

"I'm impressed. They take only the best at that position."

"Well, right, that's true, but they're giving him a real good look. Yes, I'd say, definitely, he's headed for Stanford." Delgado swallowed. What made me say that?

"You still fly the line, Frank?"

Grateful for the question, Delgado turned to Fritz Mueller. "A couple of trips a week. Gets me away from the damn paperwork. Truth is, I do it for that as much as anything."

"Sounds familiar," Mueller replied. "I gave it up a couple of years ago, but my management people have to keep their hand in." Mueller speared a piece of roast beef. "Well, how did the morning go? Will we be doing business together?"

Have to be careful, Delgado thought. I don't want to come on too strong, but I can't act like a patsy, either.

"To be honest," he began cautiously, "there's a lot more positive features than I expected, but like I told Mr. Bankhead, there's no way I could ever give away my company's identity. Where that leaves us I don't know. That seems to be what you people want."

"We trust you'll see our position, Mr. Delgado," Hartley responded. "We place a very high priority on stabilizing our commuter situation at San Francisco."

"I'm sure you realize how the valley depends on good air service. Being from Manteca yourself, you know what I'm talking about." Delgado nodded with anticipation.

Hartley remained impassive. "I'm afraid I don't remember the place with the same fondness you do, but that's beside the point. We're talking about helping you provide even better service than you do now."

"If it's run from New York, it won't be better. It won't be half as good."

Hartley sat forward. He had a severe expression on his face. "Understand this, Mr. Delgado, BellAir is in a war. But don't for a moment flatter yourself, it's not with people like you. It's the Uniteds and the Americans we are up against, *and we will do whatever is necessary to come out on top.* Even if there are on occasion, shall we say, unfortunate side effects."

Delgado frowned. He felt his ears reddening. He couldn't believe what he had just heard.

"So when the giant sneezes, everyone catches cold," Cartright interjected.

"Well put, Mr. Cartright," Hartley nodded, "very well put."

Fritz Mueller had closed his eyes. He was shaking his head.

"Let me be very clear, Mr. Delgado," Hartley said sternly. "Even if you choose not to come with us, we will keep that traffic. If it means starting our own commuter airline out there, then that's what we will do. Push us that far, you can rest assured we will spread out to other markets. In fact, expanding service out of Monterey would be very high on the list." He shook his head. "What a shame, really. Not only would you miss the chance to join with BellAir, but you'd be going head to head against us. We're not out to damage you, but if you force our hand, that's exactly what will happen."

"So you're threatening me," Delgado said slowly, his eyes narrowing.

Hartley broke a roll apart, placing the pieces on his plate. "Your words, Mr. Delgado, your words. I'm simply being candid. We do what we have to do. That's how we operate around here."

The luncheon continued, chilly and correct. At exactly 1:15 Hartley glanced at his watch and stood up. "If you'll excuse me. I have another meeting." He nodded to Cartright, then turned in Delgado's direction.

"Think over our proposition, Mr. Delgado. Think it over very carefully. It's your call. It's really up to you."

The two men glared at each other for a moment. Delgado did not stand, nor did the men shake hands. After Hartley had left, Fritz Mueller made an attempt to revive the conversation, but after a few lackluster minutes, the luncheon broke up. The working party returned in silence to the conference room.

"The boss comes on kind of strong, doesn't he?" Roger Bankhead observed as they walked in. Still in a state of shock and disbelief, Delgado made no reply.

"This is a very important matter for us, Frank. You need to appreciate what we're up against."

Delgado made a sour face. "If you people are going to insist on that name business, this will be a very short afternoon."

The group arranged itself around the table. Bankhead opened the conversation. "I've been thinking. Maybe there's another way to skin this cat." He turned to Delgado. "How about this. What if we approach the deal as a two-step process. Say we set up the program on schedules and fares, and help you finance the planes. You still operate as Bay Airlines for a year, then we move into the full marketing program."

"You mean commit to the identity point but put off implementation a year?" asked Cartright.

"Right."

"No," said Delgado firmly. "That's the same thing, as far as I'm concerned." He drummed on the table with a pencil. "But how about *this*. Maybe it would play if we leave open whether we go into that second part or just keep on working the same way."

Cartright jumped in. "Even then, we'd need the right to convert to the full program at our discretion. And one year's much too short. We'd need at least five years. Otherwise, we'd be loaded up with so much equipment and debt, we'd be no alternative but to agree at the end of the year."

Delgado nodded. "Right. Good point."

"No way we could go five years," Farrell countered.

"Tell you what," said Bankhead. "Just for the sake of argument, let's think about a two- or three-year test and leave open the 'identity point,' as you put it, for the time being. Why don't we run the numbers on that scenario and see what we have?"

"That sounds reasonable." Cartright glanced at Delgado, who looked relieved. "But no commitments. We'll just make a working assumption we could deal on that basis."

"No commitments is right," said Delgado. "I told you people up front I couldn't agree to anything today even if I wanted to. I've got partners back home, and they're pretty tough customers."

The discussion continued through the afternoon. At about three,

Fritz Mueller poked his head in. "How're we coming in here? Everything signed up?"

"We're getting there," said Bankhead.

Delgado shook his head. "Still miles apart."

"I'm on my way to our maintenance shop at La Guardia, Frank. How about coming along? If we're going to be working together we ought to get acquainted. Who knows, maybe you'll see not all of us have horns and forked tails. Let's see how far Roger and the attorneys can get on their own."

Delgado pushed his chair back. "As a matter of fact, I could use a break. Will, you comfortable with my cutting out for a while?"

"Sure. I just won't agree to anything."

"There's an attorney for you," Mueller laughed. "You and Francis here deserve each other. C'mon, Frank, I'll have you back by six."

THE MORNING AFTER their second day of meetings, Cartright and Delgado found themselves in a BellAir limousine headed for the airport.

"They certainly didn't spare the expense," Cartright remarked. "Nice rooms, nice meals, fancy car."

"Too bad their deal wasn't as good as their hospitality," Delgado said wistfully.

"We got as close as we could, considering."

Delgado looked out the window at the sprawling JFK complex. "Tell me, Will. Am I too hung up on this name business?"

"Not at all. It's too much to give away for an uncertain return." Cartright frowned. "Especially since they still want that commitment up front."

"I'm not about to back down," Delgado said forcefully. "If they won't come around, the hell with 'em! They can piss up a rope for all I care."

A half hour later Delgado and Cartright were relaxing in the first class cabin of a BellAir 747 with champagne and orange juice eye-openers in hand.

"How'd you and that attorney of theirs get along?"

"Farrell? Francis Xavier Farrell? Capable guy, from what I could see. Actually, he's a real character when you get him going. His eighty-seven-year-old mother lives with him. He brought her here from Chicago a few years ago."

"Fritz is damn good, too," Delgado added. "His head's screwed on right. He was being careful, but I could tell he isn't exactly thrilled the way things are going around there. Seems the financial people are sticking it to everybody. Justify this, justify that, that type of thing."

Delgado took a sip of champagne. "I was impressed how they're setting up that commuter operation at La Guardia. Fritz said he wants to visit our shop next time he's out our way, check us out. Can't say I blame him. I'd do the same thing."

"What do you think about Hartley?"

Delgado looked out the window. They were nearing the head of the line for takeoff. "If it wasn't for those other people, we'd have been outta there like a shot after that lunch." He shook his head. "I mean, I've been threatened by experts, but..." His voice trailed off.

"Maybe your expectations were too high."

"If you want to say, 'I told you so,' be my guest. From the valley and he doesn't give a rip about it? That really bothers me." He paused. "Will, who would you say's in charge there?"

"On paper it's Mueller, but Hartley's the man. No question."

Delgado nodded. "And Fritz doesn't know how to handle it, either. Pretty clear, if we get involved, Hartley'll be the one calling the shots." He looked out his window. "Not a real cheery prospect, is it?"

IT WAS SEVEN-THIRTY by the time Delgado reached home. An exhausting day. The long flight from New York, racing to connect with Bay's 4:45 to Monterey, then the fatal mistake, swinging by the office for a quick look in. Damn, he thought, pulling into the driveway, the lawn *still* isn't mowed. Teenagers. Worse than useless.

"Daddy's home! Daddy's home!" Teresa came racing through the grass, throwing her arms around his knees.

"Hiya, honey! It sure is good to see you!"

"'You bring me a present, Daddy?"

Delgado squeezed his daughter. "You women are all alike! Of course I brought you a present. It's in this big bag."

"Oh, can I have it. Please?"

"In a few minutes. Let's go see your mom first." He swept the little girl up with his free hand.

"Hey, Mariel!" he shouted. "Where you at, woman?"

As he walked into the house a familiar aroma hit him. Mexican! What a great wife!

"Sweetheart! How *are* you!" He put the bag down and drew Mariel to him, kissing her hard on the lips. Teresa giggled as the three-way embrace continued. "You miss me?"

"Thought you'd never come back." She held him tight. "Did it go well?"

"Oh, sure," he said, putting Teresa down. "We made progress. Whether enough, remains to be seen. The boys around?"

"Manny's out cruising, Bobby's upstairs. I had to ground him. He got into a fight at school."

"He won, I hope?"

"Won? He broke the other kid's nose, he did so well." She sighed. "And of course Teresa's been sick, she threw up last night. It hasn't exactly been a picnic here."

"Aw, you not feeling good, punkin'? C'mere, give Daddy another hug."

"I'm all right now, Daddy, you're home. Now can I have my present?"

"Later, honey."

"Frank, have you been drinking?"

"Not that much. Just a couple of beers on the flight." He frowned. "We were in first class, so it was free... oh, now that you mention it, I had a little wine, too."

"But you didn't eat, did you?"

"Well, I sorta picked at it. I mean, you have to eat *something* to go with all that wine."

She shook her head, "Aw, Frank, I made a nice dinner, all your favorite things. What am I supposed to do with it?"

"Oh, it won't be wasted. You know me, I'm always hungry for your cooking."

"Come out here. I have to keep an eye on it," she said, walking into the kitchen. She opened the oven and peered in. "So. Tell me about your meetings."

"Well, it turns out this could be a lot bigger deal than I thought. They want us to take over San Francisco for them."

"How exciting! Any new cities?"

"Well, no, not at first, but a whole lot more flying out of San Fran, all their routes up north and in the valley. It's a helluva big commitment. I have to talk to Fred and Alex. I don't know what to think, yet."

"What about the BellAir people?" She wiped her hands on her apron. "What were they like?"

"About what you'd expect. Their operations guy is down to earth, the marketing people, I mean, what can you say? They're fast talkers but they know their stuff. The only one disappointed me was that Hartley."

"Why do you say that?"

"Well, he comes on real heavy-handed. You know, we're the big shots, do things our way or else. He as much as threatened to put me out of business if I didn't play ball with him."

"That's too bad. You were really looking forward to meeting him."

Delgado nodded. "In business sometimes you say things you don't always mean, but what really bugs me, the man has no feeling whatever for anything back here."

"How so?"

"I mean, you'd never know he grew up here, for all it matters to him. I don't know, I guess mostly I'm disappointed I read it wrong. I was hoping I could play up his old loyalties, but it doesn't look like he has any. My mistake."

The phone rang. Delgado picked it up.

"Hello. Yeah, what's up. Shit, you mean nobody's available? Okay, yeah, I'll be right over."

He hung up the phone. "Karen just left. Her daughter's sick. I've got to close up. Sorry." He extended his hands to Mariel but she turned away. He hesitated. "Say, I have an idea. Why don't we go somewhere tomorrow, just the two of us? Get out of here, have some fun for a change. How about it?"

She frowned. "How late will you be?"

"Ten o'clock at the outside...the very latest."

"I'll pack you some dinner."

"Nah, just keep it warm. I'll have it when I get back."

The little girl reappeared in the kitchen, sensing something awry.

"My present, Daddy, where's my present? You promised!"

"It'll have to wait, honey. I don't have time to find it now, I have to go back to work. Anyway, you'll like it a lot better in the morning."

"No I won't, I'll like it better *now*!" She stuck out her lower lip, and her eyes filled with tears. As he drove off, he could hear the child screaming.

9

"A BIG SPENDER! Wine, no less!"

"Skip it, Jessie. Just get us a table."

Vincent Costello leaned across the counter, pulling two twenties from his wallet, which was unaccustomedly full of bills. "A bottle of red, that eight-dollar one. Hell, make it the ten. And a small Coke."

The counter man set a squat, basket-covered bottle with two plastic wine glasses on the cafeteria tray. He pointed to the pick-up station at the end of the counter.

"You're eighty-seven. About ten minutes."

Costello pushed through the crowd around the counter, glancing briefly at the television in the corner. Highlights of the previous Sunday's Bears – Vikings game were on, but they didn't interest him. The women and her son had found a table in the far corner of the smoky room. He placed the tray in front of the boy. "Here you go. A Coke for you. Our number's eighty-seven. Can you remember that?"

The boy nodded.

"Okay, you tell me when they call it."

The boy stared blankly at him. "Where's our pizza, Uncle Vince?"

"That's what I'm *telling* you," he replied sharply. "They're making it now. When they call eighty-seven, it's ready."

"Oh."

Costello took a sip of the chianti, smacking his lips. "Hey, this ain't half bad. Try some."

The woman took a swallow, letting it slide down slowly. "I've been real proud of you," she said, smoothing her sweater and reaching under the table to straighten her skirt. "You haven't missed a day of work, not for a long time. I knew you could do it."

Costello looked at his coarse hands, the stubby, graceless fingers, greasy nails no amount of cleaning could fix. His hands were trembling. He folded and opened them several times, then picked up a knife, testing its dull cutting edge with his thumb, tapping the blade on the plastic tray.

"You're a good drummer, Uncle Vince." The boy giggled and started to tap with his own knife.

"Num-ber eighty-four," a voice droned over the hubbub.

"Numm-ber eigh-ty-four!" The boy counted on his fingers. "Only four more!"

"Three more," the woman corrected. "Eighty-five, eighty-six, eighty-seven."

"Oh boy! Only three more!" He began squirming in his chair.

"Do you need to go?"

The boy wrinkled his nose. "Yeah."

"See that door says 'Men' over there? You can do it yourself, right?"

"Sure! Just watch!"

"And wash your hands," she shouted as he left.

Costello leaned forward. "You should'a got a baby-sitter like I told you," he said under his breath. "I got to *talk* to you."

"I had Jenna, but she couldn't make it. You knew that."

"But it's . . . I mean, how can I talk in front of the kid?"

"Why can't you, Vinnie?" she frowned. "Why not? Is it bad news?"

"Naw, it's good news, but . . . " he lowered his eyes. "I got to go away for a while . . . "

The woman's face darkened. "What do you mean, go away!"

"I can't tell you nothing, except when this is over we'll have more money than we know what to do with."

"You're not in trouble?"

"No, nothin' like that, but I got to leave tomorrow. Could be a coupl'a weeks, that's all I can say."

"You better not be thinkin' of skippin' out," she said sharply.

"Would I be telling you this if I was? You got to trust me, I need some time to pull this deal together."

"But what about your job?"

He looked at the table. "I quit today."

The woman's jaw dropped open. "You quit!"

"I mean, I didn't really quit, I took a leave of absence." He nodded. "Believe me, pretty soon I won't have to put up with that bullshit no more."

"You sure you ain't connin' me?" Her eyes filled with tears. "You'll be back..."

"Yeah, yeah, don't worry about nothin'." He glanced furtively around the room. "Listen, we might have to move. Maybe someplace warm like Florida. But you get one thing straight. Anybody comes nosing around, you say *nothin'*. Tell them I'm working out of town on a job, say I'll be back in a coupl'a weeks. *That's all!* You got that?"

"Yeah, but... I'm scared," she said, putting her hand in his.

"Just don't worry. It'll be okay."

She sighed. "What's keeping Eddie? Will you go check?"

Just then, the little boy emerged from the restroom, wiping his hands on his pants. "They call eighty-seven yet?"

Costello got to his feet. "Let's see what's goin' on." He took the boy's hand and they walked to the counter. "How you doin' on eighty-seven?"

"Just came out. Large with extra cheese, right?"

"That's us." Costello looked down at the boy. "Can you carry it by yourself?"

"Sure thing, Uncle Vince!" The boy gripped the greasy cardboard platter with both hands. "It's easy."

"Lemme keep a hand on it, just in case."

"Yum," said the boy as he carried the platter to the table, steadied by the man.

NEXT MORNING, Costello awoke to the sound of a muffled alarm. It took a minute to locate the clock under the pile of clothes where he'd put it to avoid waking Jessie and the boy. Four-thirty. He dressed in the dim light from the bathroom door opened a crack, pulled on a sports shirt and slacks, and packed his suit in a bag with the bare essentials. This would be a day for moving fast. He laced on his well-worn blue Nikes. They were in case he ended up on foot. Jesus, he thought, this is not going to be a snap. There could be real trouble. His checked sports coat was last. It would be raw outside, this early.

Costello's suitcase lay on the covers beside the hump formed by the woman's feet. Ten years of a life with the airline. Not much to show for it, he thought. If only I hadn't got in so deep with that gambling. I held those damn sharks off best I could, paid back a hundred here, a couple hundred there, but it was never enough, and now they are really closing in, making threats that'd be funny except this time they aren't kidding. If only I hadn't come out of the war hurting so bad, so screwed-up. If only... if only...

He forced his mind back to the task. Have to think positive. No more bad thoughts. Of all days, not today. He lifted the open suitcase and carried it to the front room. A truck rumbled past, setting the windowpanes chattering. Heels clacked on the sidewalk... the city going to work. A shaft of light between the curtains... never did get them to fit. What a crummy place. Whatever happens, I'm never coming back here. It'll be tricky sending for them. This time the cops'll put two and two together, they'll be watching her like a hawk.

Costello opened his wallet and looked in. Phony Mastercard and driver's license, some stranger's picture, long hair and a mustache, matching the disguise in the suitcase. In a few months, my own'll look like that. The new Vince Costello... Raymond E. Marsh, the license said. He fingered the other IDs, the Brenner IDs with the red crew cut and little beard he'd use today, then toss. Today, Thomas Brenner, but tonight, tomorrow, and forever, good old Ray Marsh.

Costello thought about putting on the Brenner beard and hair, but a shudder went through him. Later. Do it later in the car. Suicide, is what this is, I'm killing the only me there's ever been for thirty-nine years. The IDs shook in his hands. A whole year, no letup, every minute looking over my shoulder, scared shitless. If only I can get through today, then away, out to the coast, start a new life, live like a normal human being... whatever that is.

Marsh... Brenner... he thought of the scumbag who made the phony IDs. Miserable crook, but what could I do? You can't just walk into Marshall Field's and order that sort of thing. Wallet full of bills, eight hundred bucks. Every cent I own, but there'll be a lot more in a couple hours. He felt around the side pocket of the suitcase for the loaded .38 Special. Just in case. Today is a one-way street. Do it right and make tracks or go out feet first. Nothing less. Can't let myself be caught. Couldn't stand that.

Costello zipped the suitcase shut and buckled the strap. He looked at the cheap brown briefcase he'd bought the year before, for carrying the money. It *never* should've taken this long! That goddamned explosion did it... his heart sank every time he thought of it. But I covered my tracks pretty good. They were on the hunt, but I'm still here, walking around. He looked in the bedroom one last time... the woman curled up in the bed, sheet strung on a rope screening the kid sleeping on his little cot. Costello swallowed hard. Who'm I kidding. I'll never see them again.

He stepped onto the landing. The apartment door shut with a click. Down the stairs and into the chilly half-light of the hour before daybreak. Across the street the big Pontiac, the one Thomas Brenner rented yesterday from Hertz. Forty-eight bucks a day. Damn steep, but I better have the extra horses, depending. He checked the dummy Illinois plates, Land of Lincoln, AGE 322. Fucking crook really pissed me off, but I'll give him this, he knew his business. Costello opened the door and placed the suitcase on the front seat with the pocket holding the .38 facing him. He zipped the other side pocket to double-check... ticket for Raymond E. Marsh, St. Louis to L.A., a roundtrip so they won't get suspicious.

Go over it one more time. After the pick-up, be sure nobody's tailing me, then down to Midway, *fast*! It's a ghost town, no flights to speak of anymore. Steer clear of O'Hare. They'll have that covered like a glove. Dump the Pontiac, pick up another rental, plain economy type from one of those cheap outfits. Drive all night, back roads, old state routes, but stay off the Interstate. Then tomorrow, the first TWA flight for the coast.

The car started easily. Costello turned on the wipers to clear the overnight dew. Releasing the parking brake, he eased away from the curb. By the time they figure out there's no bomb, I'll be long gone, melting into a new life. A chill cut through Costello... or on a slab in a morgue somewhere. Stomach's jumping around, but I better eat something. Won't be no time later.

For the first time that day, he smiled. The plan's good, very good. All's I have to do now is make it work.

IN THE OFFICE at his usual time, 7:15, Fritz Mueller was immediately immersed in his day. Mid-morning, his private line rang. He tore the receiver off the hook. Not many people had that number, and they didn't use it to pass the time of day.

"Mueller!" he barked.

"Fritz! George here! We got a live one! Same bastard as 159!"

"Good Christ!" Mueller tugged hard at his collar. "What is it *this* time?"

"Hard to tell. It's another bomb threat, but the guy won't talk until we hand over a pile of cash. Two mil, he wants."

"How do you know it's the same guy?"

"Take my word for it."

Mueller slammed down the phone and stared at his calendar. A year to the day! His heart was pounding. The sonofabitch has finally surfaced! He smashed his fist into the palm of his hand. This is the day I nail that cocksucker! He rushed from his office taking the back stairs two at a time. Nine thirty-five EST. The war room was already swarming.

"The call came in ten minutes ago," O'Brien began. "It's Chicago again, but the guy upgraded his act this time. He called from a pay phone in the Hyatt near O'Hare."

Mueller looked around the room – the usual faces. Philip Hartley and Ben Peterson were also sitting in. O'Brien motioned toward the speakerphone.

"Mark, go ahead." His security manager, Maginnis, was on the line from a conference room in BellAir's Chicago office. "Run it again."

"Hold on, I'm rewinding the tape."

O'Brien nodded at Mueller. "We didn't get the first part of the call on tape. It took the res agent a minute to figure out what he had. Here's how it started." He consulted a small notebook. "First the guy says, 'I'll bet you know who I am. It was me that planted the bomb on 159.' " O'Brien paused. "Okay, here's where we pick it up. Ready, Mark?"

"Ready."

A recorder whirred for several seconds. ". . . and if you don't think it was me," a muffled voice began, "listen. It was in a brown Samsonite and I made the call from outside a 7-Eleven, that one on York Road. You got another one today." The words began to pour out, the strain in the voice obvious. "I gave it to this guy. He's on one of your flights. He doesn't know what's going on, he doesn't know it's a bomb."

Then came a long pause. Mueller leaned forward, intent.

"Anybody gets hurt, it's your fault. I never wanted to hurt nobody."

Another pause. "Now, listen close. I'm only going to say this once. I want two million in fifties, packs of a hundred. Got that? The 7-Eleven in Park Ridge, corner of Cumberland and Touhy. Leave it in a briefcase at twelve o'clock. There's a phone booth outside the store. Stick it in the bushes behind the phone.

"I'm warning you, don't play games and don't try to follow me. Everything's cool, I call you back at one-thirty and tell you what flight it's on and what to do. You'll have exactly an hour before it goes off. Try anything funny, you don't get no call. That's all there is to it. You people were lucky last time. I promise you, this time it'll be a lot worse."

There was a click, and the line went dead.

O'Brien stood. "They're questioning everybody at the hotel, but it'll be a miracle if anybody saw the guy. The place is packed this time of day."

"You're convinced it's the same guy?" Mueller asked.

The FBI agent, Andreozzi, spoke up from his downtown office. "No doubt at all. The suitcase and the call, nobody knows those details."

O'Brien added, "We've sent a car for the res agent who talked to him last time, see if she can ID the voice. She's at home with a baby. But it's the same guy all right, Fritz. Absolutely no question."

Hartley shook his head. "So he was after the money, all along. What a cool customer, sitting back and waiting all this time."

"Yeah, but he's nervous, you can tell," said Andreozzi.

"Where's the flight originate?" Mueller asked.

"He didn't say, but it's a safe bet it's O'Hare. That's where it was last time, and there he is again. Anyway, how's he going to arm the device unless he's there to give it to his pigeon? No question, it's O'Hare."

"He could have a partner somewhere else," Ben Peterson, the company lawyer, suggested.

"Possible," said Andreozzi, "but everything points to him being a loner. It did last time, still does."

Mueller moved to take charge. "All right," he said, clipping his words, "we should'a caught this one at security, but with this bastard, we can't take any chances. Here's the plan. First thing, we hand-search everybody coming through security, open all packages, the works. I'm talking *systemwide*, in case he has somebody working with him. We can't rule that out altogether."

"But that'll back us up for days!" Joe Thompson, the O'Hare station manager, shouted.

"Thompson, you asshole, how would you like me to cancel *all* your departures! And I'm warning you, I may do just that!" Mueller exhaled. "Next. We evacuate every terminal systemwide and run everybody back through security. Hand-search all the carry-ons. Same deal. The device could be past security in a sterile area already. No way to know."

Thompson groaned again.

Mueller turned to an assistant. "Chuck, find out how many flights are airborne and won't land until after two-thirty Chicago time. We can rule out anything scheduled in before that. Everything else we need to get on the ground pronto and evacuate all passengers. Carry-ons go to a remote area." He turned to O'Brien. "You people covered the demand yet?"

"Yeah. We have no choice except play along with the guy."

"Until we get the call," Andreozzi added. "Then we move in."

"Real money or fake?" Mueller asked.

"Real currency, marked, special serial numbers," replied Andreozzi. "In fact, we'd better get on that fast. It'll take a while to put it together."

Hartley spoke up. "I'll call Continental Bank in Chicago. We have an arrangement with them."

"What about the tail?" Mueller demanded.

"We're taking care of that," replied Andreozzi, "along with the drop."

"Be *very* careful with the tail," Mueller said grimly. "Scare him off and we're dead meat."

"He doesn't sound too experienced," said Andreozzi. "We'll get our best men on it, a couple of different teams. There'll be a tracking device in the case to be on the safe side. We'll pick the bastard up soon as he makes the call, don't worry about that."

Mueller turned to Peterson. "Now the big question. Do we shut down O'Hare for the duration, or do we not? What's your advice, counselor?"

Peterson paused, drawing on his pipe. "If we don't shut it down and the thing goes sideways, we'd have some exposure on that account. In fact, depending on how it turns out, we'll be criticized for not putting everything on the ground systemwide, anyway. But you're entitled to use judgment. You've outlined a reasonable plan. There's a good chance it's only a bluff, anyway."

Mueller's eyes narrowed. "I think I agree with you, but I'm not sure what the hell you're saying. Forget the legalese. In plain English. Do I shut O'Hare down or not?"

The lawyer reddened. "It's a business decision. What I'm saying, based on the facts as we know them, we can defend it even if you keep O'Hare operating."

"I see. Other opinions?"

Hartley slid forward in his chair. "There's a whole other side to this. You shut O'Hare down, it'll cost us a ton of money – revenue lost to other airlines, aircraft out of position, crew expense, the ripple effect on the whole system. I'd use the leeway Ben's giving us and keep it open. It's worth the risk."

"Thank you," Mueller replied acidly, pulling the microphone over. "Joe, you're going to put a total clamp on O'Hare. Absolutely nothing takes off until I say so. Get hold of United and the others so they know what they're in for if they take any of our passengers. And make sure the airport manager knows what we're doing."

There was a stunned silence. O'Brien finally spoke. "Mark, get with Thompson and the airport manager right away. We got our employees to consider, too."

Hartley was shaking his head. "Damn it, Fritz, I don't believe this! Ben gives us some running room and you *ignore* him!"

Mueller looked calmly at Hartley. "You may very well be right, Phil, and I say that in all sincerity. But there is one minor difference. Your opinion, you're entitled to. Mine, they *pay* me for!"

He stood up, putting an end to the meeting. "Now, goddamnit, get to work! *Let's put that cocksucker where he belongs!*"

VINCENT COSTELLO CRUISED THE STREETS west of Chicago, a street map open on the seat beside him. He'd scouted the area the week before but needed to see it again. . . can't take the chance of getting lost. His watch said eleven-forty. Give them a few minutes to make the drop. Half an hour to kill, angling down toward the pick-up.

Still in Niles... right on Greenwood, a dozen more blocks. He thought of the woman and the boy. A lot of laughs, they'd had, but it'd been rough lately, real rough. He rubbed his eyes... what's past is past. Concentrate. *Concentrate!* Think it through again. After the pick-up, make tracks for the Kennedy, loop around the city, then a straight shot to Midway for the car switch. Pretty close now... like to drive by, but I better not. Got to figure they're doing what I said. He shuddered. They damn well *better* be.

THE VETERAN FBI AGENT, Larose, was on his day off, but the usual griping and complaining aside, he was pleased they'd called him in on a big job like this. He stared at the briefcase in the back seat of the blue Chevy.

"Thirty years in the Bureau and never have I been this close to so much dough."

The driver, a young agent with close-cropped black hair, put his arm on the seat back and looked around at Larose. "Kind of makes you see why people do stupid things."

The radio came alive. "Sweeney, this is Control. Where are you guys?"

Sweeney, next to the driver, picked up the mike. "Where we're supposed to be. Down the block from the 7-Eleven. The phone's right where he said, bushes and all."

"What's the surveillance situation like?"

"Could be better." Sweeney peered out the windshield. "Too wide open for my liking, no trees to speak of."

"Way it goes. Call us after the drop."

Sweeney glanced back to Larose and gave him a sign. Larose nodded, then the agent leaned forward and dialed in a different channel. "This is Car One," he announced. "We're activating the homer now. Radio check, all units."

"Two's here. We have you in sight down the street, also the pick-up point. Loud and clear on the signal."

In sequence the four other FBI vehicles reported in. So far, so good. Larose looked at his watch... it's show time. He took a deep breath and opened the door, stepping gingerly onto the sidewalk. The brief-case tugged at his arm. Funny, he'd never given a thought to how heavy money was. Larose shut the door and started for the phone booth. Normal pace... casually looking around... no sign of any-thing unusual. No sign of anything at all. Mid-day in a normal American neighborhood.

As he approached the 7-Eleven, two teenage girls emerged, suck-ing on straws sticking out of their soft-drink cups. Jumbo size. They passed him, right in front of the phone booth. After giving them some space, Larose stooped down and carefully set the briefcase in the low bushes, then retraced his steps to the Chevy. As soon as he settled in, the driver pulled slowly from the curb.

"We just made the drop," Sweeney said into his mike. "Car Three, come up and take our position. We're going around the block to Cumberland."

"Okay. We're on our way."

"Two has the area covered. Let you know when the suspect shows."

AT EXACTLY THREE PAST TWELVE, Vincent Costello wheeled around the corner. Leaving the car running at the curb, he crossed to the phone booth and peered into the bushes, then reached down. There it is! The leather handle was cool to his touch. Costello's heart pounded as he retraced his steps to the car. Damn, it's heavy! He set the case on the seat and opened it.

My God! Will you look at that!

Costello riffled through a few packets of bills, then he shoved his hand to the bottom of the case. No newspapers or anything, it's the real thing. I'll count one pack... his hands were shaking... just one pack. I know they're watching but they better not try to follow me. Fifty, sixty... ninety, a hundred. Should be four hundred of them. There better be. Stay cool... can't count 'em all now. Do it later. Time to get the fuck out of here.

"ATTENTION ALL UNITS. He just picked up the drop. The vehicle is a black 1980 Grand Am, license plate Illinois AGE 322. He's still in front of the store, south side of Touhy, facing east."

"Control, here. We'll run a make on the plate."

"The suspect is about five-ten, medium build, short reddish hair and a light-colored beard. Wearing blue slacks and a checked sports coat with aviator sunglasses. He appears to be the only occupant of the vehicle. We have several clear photos."

"What's he doing now?"

"Not sure... he's got his head down. Probably checking out the briefcase."

"Not in any hurry, is he?"

"He will be soon enough. Okay, okay, he's looking around. Now he's pulling out, he's going around the corner southbound on Cumberland. All yours, Car One!"

"Roger," replied Sweeney. "He just passed us."

"Don't let him spot your tail! *That's critical!*"

"Thanks, grandma. All right, he's going over the overpass. *Hey!*" Suddenly the Pontiac turned onto an expressway on-ramp. "He's taking the Kennedy!"

"Car Six, copy. We're moving out."

"He's all yours. We'll follow at a distance."

"Okay, Six just picked him up. Black Grand Am, Illinois AGE 322, single male occupant in the vehicle."

"That's our pigeon. You picking up the homer okay?"

"Like a charm."

"Car One here. We're behind you. Good luck!"

COSTELLO LOOKED at the speedometer... sixty-five. Careful... careful... keep it down. He peered in the rear-view mirror. That blue Chevy, the one on Cumberland... not there any more. VW van and a black Ford, a red Volvo further back. His head was clear. I am so *focused!* Better than... I can't remember when. So many bad times, bad years... that fuckup with 159. Could it be, he thought excitedly, could it be something of mine is finally coming out right?

He reached across and caressed the bills, neat little paper band around each pack. Automatically, he started counting... five packs... six... seven... He looked up. Can't do that and drive, both. At least they didn't try to stiff me.

Rear-view mirror... no Volvo, but the van and that black Ford, still there. Maybe nothing, but I better keep an eye on them. Coming to the Edens merge... speed up a little, see what they do. He crossed into the left lane and hit the gas... 70... 75... 80. The Ford's staying right up with me. Shit! Slow down, ease into the right lane, see what happens. As Costello slowed, the black Ford sped by in the far left lane. Couldn't get a good look... couple of guys. Probably imagining things. They don't want to lose a planeload of people. *That* I know for a fact.

Heavy traffic... lot of trucks. Passing over Addison, Costello looked across at the drab tenements. Billboards and factories, old buildings, advertising on the walls, one right after the other. Spanish signs... that's okay, those people been here a long time, they paid their dues. Through a break between buildings he glimpsed a block with Vietnamese signs... groceries, restaurant. Man, that really pisses me off, those buggers moving right in like they owned the place. After all the trouble they caused. Fucked me up but good!

Costello looked around. The Ford's gone but... what's this? A few cars back. That blue Chevy. He strained at the mirror. Can't be sure, but it looks like that one was behind me on Cumberland. *Christ!* Are those bastards tailing me after all?

A sign for the Eisenhower... half a mile. His mind raced... if that's really them I better get off, shake them downtown. Got to change the plan, just in case. I'm a sitting duck out here. He looked at his watch. Twelve-fifty. Still half an hour before they get suspicious... I'm safe as long as they think I'm going to make that call.

That's it! Shake them off, then drop the car in front of some hotel, grab a cab for Midway. Just as good! Better!

"THINK HE SPOTTED US?" said Sweeney, riding shotgun in the Chevy.

"Dunno. He's speeding up again... give him space. "Hey! *Watch it!* He's taking the Eisenhower! He's heading for downtown!"

"Then so are we. Hold on!"

"Attention all units! The suspect is turning eastbound onto the Eisenhower! Car One is pursuing!"

"Don't let him see you! He's got to make that call!"

"Yeah, but we can't *lose* him!"

"All units, the suspect is now on Congress, repeat, he is proceeding down Congress. He has just turned left onto Michigan. *What the hell!!*"

"This is Control! What is going on!"

"*Jesus!* There's a Chicago PD on his tail!"

Lights flashing, a blue and white police cruiser suddenly shot in front of the FBI car.

"That dumb bastard ran the light at State! They're trying to pull him over!"

"Man! *Look at him go!*"

"Keep up with 'em!"

"We ought to have flashers!"

"No shit, Einstein!"

"All units. One is proceeding north on Lake Shore Drive. The suspect ran a light. A Chicago PD unit is now pursuing at high speed! It looks like the operation's blown!"

The Pontiac was weaving in and out of traffic. Lights flashing and siren wailing, the police cruiser was gaining on it fast.

COSTELLO CROUCHED over the wheel. *Damn red light!* I didn't even *see* it! *Jesus God!* I got to *shake him!* Right behind me! Got to! I *got to!*

Round that bend... narrow curve... get over the bridge then hook back. He looked ahead. Oh no, another light! Can't stop! I got to bust through! Costello accelerated in front of a pickup crossing on the green. *Jesus! That was close!* He looked in the mirror. The cop car! Where is it? What the hell's goin' on! Wha...! Holy shit! They rammed the pickup!

Costello pounded the steering wheel. *They rammed the pickup!* Instinctively he floored the pedal, his eyes still glued to the rearview mirror. The intersection... cars all over the place! Jesus! Can't even *see* it for the dust! Yes! The cop car... it's on the sidewalk! He peered again... *it's on its top! It's upside down on its top!* Costello threw his head back and roared.

"*I made it!*" he screamed. "*I MADE IT!*"

Just then he looked ahead. What the...! *Construction! Barricades! Christ!* Got to get around them! *I GOT TO GET AROUND!*

Costello hit the brakes and wrenched the wheel to the left with all his strength. His back wheels shuddered and gave way. He started sliding sideways. Turn it. *The other way! Straighten it out!*

JESUS! I'M LOSING IT!

Sideswiping a concrete abutment, the Pontiac shot across the road, smashing head-on through the wooden barrier as if it were cardboard. The car rocked crazily onto two wheels. Wood and glass flew everywhere. Costello slammed forward into the steering wheel, snapping it off. The jagged post cracked through his ribs, plunging deep into his chest. His head whipped forward against the windshield.

"God... oh, God... "

A sound came to Costello from far away. He tried to move toward it, but a dark red wave rose up and engulfed him.

Unconscious his life's last few seconds, Vincent Costello was spared the sight of his car vaulting the guard rail. It soared through the air and, with a graceful quarter-roll, buried itself, and him, in the river below.

THE FBI CAR careened into a cloud of dust and skidded to a stop. Larose and Sweeney leapt out as a motorcycle patrolman who had given chase ran up on foot. Two black teenagers were already there.

"Man, didja see that car!"

"It flipped! Just like on TV!"

"Beat it, you kids!" the cop yelled. "Get outta here!"

In the dark water, a field of bubbles centered a widening pool of froth. As the cop ran back to his bike, he nearly collided with Larose.

"FBI!" Larose shouted, shoving his badge into the patrolman's face.

The cop slowly straightened. "So this is *your* mess!" His voice was hard.

"Damnit! You people! This is FBI business!"

The patrolman put down his mike. Smoldering, he stared at Larose. "I don't give a fuck if it's the second coming of Christ! There's a friend of mine in that wreck back there!"

Larose stopped, considering his options. "Okay, okay. Let's get on with it."

While the patrolman made his call, Larose picked his way through the debris. He and his colleagues looked down in disbelief.

The cop returned. "I got the divers coming," he said, coolly. "No big rush, I would say. Ain't nobody gettin' out of there alive."

Gloomily, Larose stared at the dark, roiling water.

"At least there's a briefcase you can salvage for us."

"DEAD! WHADDYA MEAN *HE'S DEAD!"* O'Brien's face was purple. "I don't *believe* this shit! Our man just drove into the Chicago River!"

"What the fuck happened!"

"Seems like he panicked and ran for it."

"The tail! He picked up your goddamn tail!"

"No, no! The stupid bastard ran a light! The Chicago PD took off after him! He went through a bunch of construction barriers like they weren't even there. *Goddamnit!* We had this whole thing set up so perfect!"

"What the hell do we do now?"

"We stay calm!" Fritz Mueller shouted, smashing his fist on the table.

"But if he wasn't bluffing..."

"Then we have one helluva problem, don't we?" Mueller glared at Hartley. "Keep O'Hare open, huh?" he snarled.

Hartley began to reply but thought the better of it.

O'Brien leaned wearily over the speakerphone. "Mark, get downtown right away. Find out who that bastard is! Don't even wait for them to fish him out!"

THE LARGE CLOCK in the war room indicated 3:25 New York time. Every few seconds, Fritz Mueller's gaze strayed to the wall. "A few more minutes..." he prayed. "Just give me a few more minutes..."

Suddenly, the speakerphone came alive. "George. Mark here. We've ID'd the guy. You people better be sitting down." He paused for effect. "He was one of ours. A mechanic, name of Costello."

"Jesus Christ," Mueller replied softly. "I was afraid of that."

"We pulled his personnel file. In fact, I'm looking at his picture right now. Vincent Robert Costello. Based at O'Hare."

"The bastard," said Mueller, "the goddamn, lousy, rotten bastard. How could anybody do this to the company!"

"Seems like he was an erratic individual. History of minor trouble, mouthing off, company discipline a couple of times, that kind of thing. Bunch of unexcused absences. His skills look okay, even some good reports. Appears he was wounded in Vietnam... just a guess but maybe that's important. We're getting hold of his supervisors, trying to fill out the picture."

"We better get our shit together," Mueller said to Milt Collins. "The media'll have a field day with this one."

"FBI's searching his place right now. He was living with some woman on the South Side. They reached her at work. She went bananas. First indication, she didn't know anything about it."

"Anything to tie him into 159?"

"There's no doubt in our mind," Maginnis responded. "We'll see what they find at the house."

"What a mess," said Mueller gloomily, his jaw clenched. "I don't believe this. One of our own people."

They watched the clock tick away. At four, Mueller said quietly, "That's it. We're safe."

Everyone at the table was drained. No smiles, no congratulations, no applause.

Mueller got to his feet. He looked disdainfully at Hartley. "I'd better go break it to Charlie." He shook his head sadly. "This's really going to hit him hard. Absolutely unbelievable. One of our own people."

PART THREE

Power Settings

1

B Y THE THIRTIES, when Charlie Bell was getting started, the airlines were a familiar part of American life, though not yet widely patronized. The frequent flyers of that day were the celebrities – movie stars, politicians, sports figures. Unfortunately, however, all too often those big names found themselves in the same headline that reported another disaster for the fledgling airline industry.

Hoping to improve their daredevil, barnstormer image, some airlines began outfitting their pilots in ship-captains' garb – shirts and ties, epaulets, peaked caps. "Captain," they were to be addressed, and "First Officer," if you please. For a while this contrived image outran reality, but in time the message sank in. Not surprisingly, pilots soon began demanding pay and treatment in keeping with their new status, and trade unions started organizing on airline properties.

From its inception, the National Mediation Board, the federal agency responsible for airline labor issues, was committed to collective bargaining as the best way to promote labor accord. However, there existed a contrary view: in the heartfelt words of Charlie Bell, "the goddamn board can't find its ass, even with both hands."

Before 1978, airlines couldn't initiate service between any two cities on their own, for yet another arm of the federal government, the Civil Aeronautics Board, blocked the way. The CAB's job was to guard against "excess competition," and it offered market protection in return for service on marginal or unprofitable routes. Also, the CAB was supposed to keep airline fares high enough for a reasonable rate of return; nevertheless, profitability eluded many carriers, which ended up as merger fodder.

This elaborate regulatory scheme meant pay increases were routinely passed along to customers as higher fares, so in time airline wage levels were among the highest in American industry. Pay for union craftsmen and blue-collar workers provided upward pressure on middle-management salaries, and the pilots' lofty compensation pulled everyone up. Pilots tended to justify their salary demands in the name of safety. After all, what passenger in his right mind would quibble about the size of a captain's wallet as together they threaded their way through a line of thunderheads? A mechanic's estrangement might put the quality of his work at risk, as well. So airline managements tended to treat these vital performers quite well. High pay meant good morale, which promoted safety. At least, so went the formula.

For the most part, BellAir's relationships with its employees over the years had been positive. Its people were among the industry's best paid and most productive, within the rigid job classifications and work rules of their union contracts. But how long this bonhomie would last after 1978 was anybody's guess. Fare wars sparked by new nonunion carriers were conspiring with high fuel costs and the carriers' anxiety about unfilled seats to create an industrial tinderbox. While his ties with individual employees remained healthy, for the most part, Charlie Bell's relationship with BellAir's unions were, as he described them, "poor to wretched." Many of Bell's senior staff had risen through union ranks and were inclined to try and work things out amicably, but change was in the wind. Typified by Philip Hartley, the new breed of younger officers was intent on eliminating all opposition to their gospel of cost-efficiency.

In the early days, the company's union leadership had resented Bell's paternalism as an encroachment on their turf. But BellAir's expansion so stretched and weakened the airline's social ties that the unions' programs of sociability found fertile ground as management withdrew from involvement in the everyday lives of its employees. The recent, incessant pressure to control costs meant that anything outside the airline's "real business" was of little interest to management, which fell back on a cycle of contrived events, notably summer picnics and official Christmas parties. Sports still promoted fellowship, but the company softball leagues and golf and bowling teams couldn't reach nearly enough employees and their families to stem the unraveling of BellAir's social fabric.

The airline's contract with its mechanics and ramp workers expired in 1979, and the two sides had been negotiating for over a year with no agreement on the gut issues – the size of a wage increase (as the International Association of Machinists saw it) or the length of the wage freeze (the company's position) – along with BellAir's demand to cross-utilize employees in a variety of jobs. Though its term had run, under federal law the old contract was still in force. Before the union was permitted to strike or the company could unilaterally impose its working conditions, thirty days had to pass from the time the Mediation Board released the parties from their obligations to bargain in good faith.

Marv Fox, BellAir's long-time industrial relations VP, had used every trick in his book to persuade the board to start this "thirty-day clock" right after the summer so it would run out during the fall, a slow time for the airline. The machinists' union was stalling, aiming for the Christmas season, when the airline would be vulnerable to a strike. Finally, in mid-November, Fox had something to report, though much too late to do any good.

"Our release," he said dourly, waving a telexed message at his assistant, J. Marshall Smith.

"About time," Smith replied, not bothering to look up.

Fox and Smith were oil and water. They rarely agreed on anything, in fact, usually looked for reasons not to. The old hand, Fox had first signed on with BellAir as a mechanic, then rose to shop steward before crossing to management's side of the table. Flabby jowls and a plodding mien were the cover for this brilliant tactician who enjoyed an immense reputation in labor-management circles.

New to the airlines, Smith was small, intense, in his late thirties. After attending a southern divinity school he switched to a business degree, later completing one year of law studies. To hear Smith tell it, this diverse background qualified him as an expert on both morality and law, a paradox that was not lost on those who worked with him.

A short, small-boned man, Smith wore his dirty blond hair parted in the center and slicked straight back, framing a narrow face whose lines converged at the tip of a long, sharp nose. A dramatic overbite and a weak chin led to a variety of unflattering nicknames, for he was not well liked. BellAir's labor team, for instance, was known in company circles as "The Fox and Rat Show."

Burdened with an overly literal mind and having no sense of humor, Smith still hadn't figured out why, a few weeks after he joined the airline, mousetraps began appearing under his desk. The first one, he discovered when it snapped against his shoe as he settled in one morning. A few days later, a second trap. Smith complained, but the janitor on his floor assured him that the building was not infested, nor did he have any idea what was going on. Smith's solution was to crawl the area on all fours at the start of each day. Effective, but not calculated to improve his reputation.

Many found Smith's sanctimony irritating, particularly disliking his thick Southern drawl, but in his own way, Marshall Smith was a talented man. After his short law school stint, he landed a job with an upstate New York chemical company, and several years later his star flashed across the national scene when he engineered the end to a long, bitter strike, breaking the union in the process. He even published an article about his exploit. It wasn't widely known, but Philip Hartley was responsible for Smith's being at BellAir. Hartley was the investment banker for the conglomerate that owned the troubled chemical manufacturer, and after joining BellAir, he pressed for Smith's hiring. Thus, J. Marshall Smith became a charter member of the aggressive young coterie Hartley was quietly assembling at the airline.

As soon as he received the Mediation Board's telex, Fox called a meeting. Charlie Bell was there, of course, as well as Hartley, Fritz Mueller, Marshall Smith, and Ben Peterson. Dave Axelrod, head of Maintenance, was on a speakerphone from Chicago.

Hartley surveyed the group as it gathered in Bell's office. He and Smith had been promoting a tough line in the negotiations, but as the talks dragged on, with a concession here, an informal trade there, he saw nothing but trouble. Now Hartley doubted even his minimum gains could be achieved. He was sorely disappointed by his colleagues' lack of resolve to take a strike, if it came to that.

Fox sat ponderously in his chair, hunched over his folded arms. "Gentlemen," he began, "we're down to nut-cutting time. You are well aware, the union continues to demand a twenty-five percent wage increase over three years. They've come down to fifteen percent for the rampers but haven't budged otherwise. We're still at seven point five."

"Ridiculous!" Fritz Mueller shook his head. "Bag smashers making fifty thou a year! Most management people don't make half that!"

"Unfortunately, it's the nature of the beast," Hartley observed. "It will squeeze everything out of you it can."

At his desk across the room, Bell had been shuffling through an in-box full of papers. Hartley's remark caught his attention. "Phil's right. That IAM doesn't want to be partners. Pay and security's all those assholes care about. Never stop to think, where's the security if we have to lay them all off!" Bell pushed his paperwork aside. "Marv, what's your gut tell you? You think they'll really walk this time?"

"It all comes down to the National IAM. The national loves chaos. The more the better, far as they're concerned."

"What about the pilots and flight attendants? They still on board?"

"The pilots won't go out," Fox replied. "The IAM didn't raise a finger for them the last time around. No love lost there. Flight attendants? You can never tell with them. Good thing we have that no-strike clause." He glanced at Ben Peterson, the company counsel.

"That's right," Peterson nodded. "Sympathy strikes aren't permitted under their contract, though frankly the language isn't as clear as I'd like."

"Frankly, my ass," muttered Fox. "It damn well better be clear."

"Anyway," Peterson added, "what stew's going to cut her own throat for a ramper? Wouldn't make any sense."

Bell leaned forward. "If the mechanics do go out, what's that do to our operation?"

Mueller consulted a sheet of paper. "Best case, first day we'd operate ninety percent of our trips. It'd stabilize around seventy-five after a month. If it went that long, that is."

"Not a chance," Bell snorted. "You're way the hell high."

Mueller shoved the paper at Bell. "See for yourself!"

With Bell jumping in and out, the discussion went on nearly an hour. Finally a decision was made. It was decided they would hang tough, definitely hang tough, but at the same time, be flexible. At the conclusion of the meeting, Fox was authorized to go to ten percent. Hartley closed his eyes. Just as he'd feared, backsliding was the name of the game. As the others chatted, collecting papers, Hartley cleared his throat loudly.

"There's one more thing, Marv." Everyone turned around. "The Street is watching this one very closely," Hartley said soberly. "There's absolutely no way we can go over ten percent. I hope that's understood."

Mueller looked at Hartley sideways. "Making promises to your old cronies, are you?"

"I told them we're going to hang tough, like we said we would." Hartley smiled. "They want to see what we're made of."

"So don't we all," Fox replied with a grunt.

MORE THAN A THOUSAND bodies were packed into the auditorium on a chilly Chicago evening. St. Philomena's parish in the Chicago suburb of Des Plaines, bordering O'Hare Airport on the north. BellAir employees, wives, and husbands jammed the aisles, standees blocked the exits. The beat cop was busy looking the other way... hey, these are good people, working people, some of them friends of mine. Let the fire marshal do his own dirty work. Outside, a pack of youngsters tore through the schoolyard.

The mood was apprehensive as one speaker after another rattled on. Artie Mathews, a BellAir mechanic and vice president of Local 458, had just managed to compress the story of a year-long negotiating ordeal into forty-five minutes and was fielding questions. At the rear, the late-arriving Henry Kowalski sat with several other mechanics.

"Sure rather be at the Stadium," Henry observed, referring to a watering hole where he and the boys often stopped for a cold one on the way home.

"They should'a had food for us," replied Matty Driscoll, an older mechanic.

Henry looked around, taking in the scene. Everybody who wasn't on swing shift seemed to be in the room. There was a burst of applause. A tall, rawboned man was making his way to the podium. This was Otis Jastrow, representative of the national IAM. Jastrow never worked for BellAir, but years ago he'd been a United mechanic before taking up union business full-time. Jastrow had come a long way. He was one of the select few who set national union policy on airline issues.

Pleased at the overwhelming turnout, Jastrow began. "Brothers... and sisters. We mustn't forget our sisters." The comment drew laughter and a few boos.

"You all know why we're here. Never before in its history has the American labor movement faced such a powerful, insidious threat as it does today!"

Jastrow's strike program had been set back by the discovery that an IAM man was responsible for Flight 159 and the lives of two of the brotherhood. Initially, he thought he might profit from Vincent Costello's illness, use it as an example of management's lack of concern for its workers, but he quickly abandoned that idea in the face of a membership unanimous in its condemnation of Costello. Even those who knew the man personally and had some sympathy for his plight were reluctant to say so. Jastrow worked quickly to rebuild support for the tough line. Now it was all coming to a head.

Jastrow was warming to the task. "What a shameful spectacle, our own government backing away from its responsibility to the American worker, and you better believe it's only going to get worse with Reagan in the White House. And here, right here at this airline, we have a greedy management squeezing hard as it can, trying to pressure us into giving up our hard-earned rights. Now I ask you, are we going to sit still and let that happen?"

"No!" A faint echo from the crowd.

"Come *on!* I can't *hear* you!"

"No!" they replied, somewhat louder.

"Jesus spare me. Let's go outside, Matty. I need a smoke. Hold onto our seats," Henry Kowalski told the mechanic next to him. "We'll be back."

They pushed through the crowd and stepped outside. "At least out here you can breathe," he said, lighting up. There was another roar from the crowd. "I just don't believe this bullshit. It's worse than high school!"

"Henry, the man's good, real good. He'll get the strike vote, and he'll know what to do with it, too."

"But it's so dumb."

"Hey, Otis knows how to work a crowd. I've watched him do it for years."

"You know him?" asked Henry.

Driscoll nodded. "I was on the executive board for the local one time. Thing is, management hates Jastrow's guts, they always held it against him he never worked for us. Then, naturally, they get on Artie's case because he does. No company loyalty, is what they tell him. You can't win with management. There's just no way."

Henry took a deep drag on his cigarette. He looked at the glowing tip. The statue of the saint gazed mournfully across the line of parked cars.

"You think we'll really go out?"

"I dunno. I'd say no, but management's really dug in this time. Business being so shitty, they're not about to give us a pay increase, not if they can help it. They probably figure this time they got less to lose."

"I can't even make it as it is. No way I could go without a paycheck."

"Who could?"

"A strike'd kill the holidays," Henry observed. "I just can't see them letting that happen."

"Maybe not, but I say if there's any givebacks, it should be the rampers. Those assholes been riding our back too long."

The men ground their butts on the sidewalk and headed back to the hall, pushing through the massed bodies.

"Aw shit, somebody took our seats."

"I'd rather stand, anyway."

From the rear, the men had an unobstructed view of the union boss. Step by step he was working the crowd to fever pitch. Jastrow was mopping his forehead, speaking softly.

"I'm not going to ask you to vote tonight. That's tomorrow. No, this here isn't an official ballot, we just want to stick our finger in the air, see which way the wind's blowin'."

Jastrow was gathering speed and force. "You heard the issues, you know the company's position, you know where your union stands." He raised his huge hands above his head. "You folks aren't going to tie our hands behind our back! *Of course not!* You're gonna give us what we need to finish off this job, *once and for all!* So I say to you, if this company won't come around, will you support a strike? Are you with us, boys? *Boys! Are you with us?*"

The answer thundered through the building. They stood and cheered, whooping and hollering and clapping each other on the back. Jastrow smiled, nodding his head and wiping his brow. Artie Mathews returned to the platform and raised Jastrow's hand in a victory salute.

"Looks like it's a go," said Kowalski sullenly. "The company'll come around, though. You'll see. They'll come around."

The crowd straggled to its feet and started for the exits. "Ever been through one of these?" Driscoll asked.

Kowalski shook his head.

"I remember the last one, '66, it was. I tell you, it gets damn lean when the excitement wears off. It's a real pisser when there's nothin' left in the checkbook and the wife's bitchin' about what you got her into." He looked at Kowalski soberly. "Your wife got a job, Henry?"

"Nah, she's at home with the kids."

Driscoll smiled. "Mine's had one for years. Tell yours to get one. This week. You're going to need it."

MONDAY, DECEMBER 15, was the deadline, midnight Chicago time. Predictably, not until the weekend did negotiations get serious. Each side took a suite of rooms at the O'Hare Sheraton, neutral turf, and Kirshner, the mediator from Washington, shuttled between the two camps, carrying proposals, cajoling, twisting arms. As midnight approached, no agreement was in sight. With their strike vote the union's leaders had rolled the dice, for if the membership had turned them down, their bargaining position would have been gravely undermined. Instead, they'd won, and won big.

The issues were narrowed. Over Hartley's strenuous objections, the company was now offering the mechanics a twelve percent wage increase over three years, half that for the rampers. The union was still at twenty-five and fifteen. Thus BellAir and the IAM were girding themselves for the strike that few on either side wanted.

The company had made arrangements with independent repair shops around their system and spent countless hours screening replacement workers. Former mechanics now in management ranks took refresher courses. Others were run through training for hauling bags, cleaning aircraft, and other less-skilled jobs. BellAir's managers had met one-on-one with thousands of mechanics, counseling them to stay on the job, applying pressure. The union screamed unlawful interference and antiunion activity, but Kirshner refused to intervene. Inspectors from the FAA were in constant contact, critiquing management's plans for operating if the strike occurred.

For the union's part, picket signs were printed, assembled, and stacked in a storeroom at its Chicago headquarters. BOYCOTT BEL-LAIR – UNFAIR TO WORKERS, they said, and IAM LOCAL 458 – LOCKED OUT. There was a heated argument about NONUNION = UNSAFE, Mathews and others feeling that one went too far, even if they believed it personally. But Otis Jastrow prevailed, so into the stack it went. A large number of signs were set aside for O'Hare and downtown Chicago locations, with the rest boxed and shipped, disguised as company freight for hauling free to every city on the airline's system.

The media was alerted. Two networks had aired feature reports, the union supplying fact sheets and a schedule of rallies in the major cities, while the company postured with backgrounders and briefing papers. The pilots and flight attendants were coming under intense pressure from both sides, but the smart money was betting they wouldn't walk. As a precaution, Ben Peterson and his litigation team from the prestigious New York law firm of Merritt & Carruthers had their papers drawn and were ready to head into U.S. District Court for a temporary restraining order to cut them short if they did.

Some harassment and vandalism had occurred, though no aircraft sabotage yet. Keenly aware of the threat, Fritz Mueller had stepped up security around the system. Aircraft parked outside at night were being patrolled, but everybody knew this precaution was at best a leaky sieve. A determined insider could easily slip a bolt or rock inside an engine cowl with nobody the wiser until the engine was run up. With luck, the damage would be discovered before takeoff with passengers and crew aboard. Mueller was realistic enough not to confuse his hope that even the most red-hot mechanic wouldn't do anything that stupid, with the fact that in the past it had happened. The specter of Flight 159 eliminated any temptation to overconfidence.

The week before, one outspoken mechanic had stood up in a strike meeting at JFK and challenged the union leadership for not going along with the company's last offer, and he continued his badmouthing that night on the job. Retribution was swift and sure. Reporting to work next afternoon, he discovered his toolbox filled with Elmer's glue, his gear unserviceable, much of it wrecked. Wearily, he left the hangar at dawn. His car was resting on its rims, its tires slashed.

The same thing happened in San Francisco and Denver. Around the system a number of windshields were smashed. Sugar was found in the gas tanks of several company vehicles, and there was a rash of flat tires at O'Hare's maintenance parking lot, before tacks were found strewn on the pavement in management's reserved area. At great expense the company readied a new security system with temporary ID cards for workers who remained on the job, to prevent strikers from filtering back to disrupt operations, or worse.

On the evening of the fifteenth, Hartley and Mueller were holed up in Charlie Bell's office for what promised to be an all-nighter, along with Ben Peterson, Marshall Smith, and the airline's public relations chief, Milt Wilcox. A speakerphone stood on Bell's table with an open line to Marv Fox and the company's negotiating team at the Chicago hotel. BellAir's war room had been activated. Contingency planning and security were being directed from there.

Bell's office was a disaster, coffee cups everywhere, a pile of half-eaten sandwiches on a tray, wastebaskets overflowing. The night janitor peered in, but someone waved him off. Helen Foley thought of making a sweep through, but she had no time – she'd been typing ten hours straight for Ben Peterson's overstressed legal staff.

At 11:30 New York time, Marv Fox called in.

"We've run out the string, Charlie," he said wearily. "Kirshner says he has a deal if we go up to fifteen percent with an escalator. Otherwise, we've got a strike on our hands. No question in my mind."

Bell was standing in the corner, gazing out the window. "How many mechanics would hang in with us?" he shouted across the room at the speakerphone.

Dave Axelrod replied from Chicago. "No more than ten percent. A few more here or there, nobody to speak of in San Fran or Seattle."

"Mah people've done a ton of interviews and screenin' for new mechanics and rampers," Marshall Smith interjected, a smug look on his face. "There's no need to deal with strikers. Give me three weeks to a month, ah'll get rid of a good third of them."

Mueller looked at Smith distastefully. "What about our no-strike clause, Marv?" he bellowed into the speakerphone.

"Kirshner says he can sell it if we come up to fifteen on the pay."

Bell turned to Hartley. "Phil, what's the cost to us if we make this deal?"

"At what percent?"

"Fifteen."

"I was afraid you'd say that." Hartley examined a table of numbers. "About twenty-five mil a year. That compares to the *zero* increase we started with."

"That is one hunk of change," Smith observed.

Hartley nodded. "And a rotten message to send the pilots for next time."

Mueller slapped his hand on the table. "Make the deal. That's my vote."

"I agree," said Axelrod. Marshall Smith eyed Hartley but said nothing.

"Is there a consensus for fifteen?" Bell asked.

Hartley stared at the table. The battle was lost. He had already turned his attention elsewhere. "I don't like it," he said crisply, "but count me in. I'm on board, whatever decision you make."

"Well, I'll tell you fellas," Bell said, a resigned look on his face, "we have to be realistic. If this was September like we wanted, I'd favor holding the line with Phil. Trouble is, the timing didn't work out. Those pinko bastards screwed us again, stringing it out like this. Number one, the holidays are coming, and we have a chance to try to salvage the fourth quarter. In my book that's damned important."

He began walking around the conference table. All eyes followed him.

"Number two. Fritz, I don't believe your seventy-five percent. Murphy's law and all, we go out, we won't operate half our flights for a long, long time. That's plain common sense. United, American, some of those new outfits, they'll move right in behind us. It's a new ball game, fellas, no more Mutual Aid. The money comes right out of our pockets and into theirs."

Bell put his hands on the edge of the table and leaned over the speakerphone. "All right, Marv. I hate to do this, but I guess that's what they pay me for. Go to fifteen, but I want that no-strike clause. Don't take no for an answer."

Fox's voice crackled through the speaker. "Let me read that back, be sure I've got it straight."

As Fox was talking, Bell looked around. He saw relief on every face except one. Hartley's brow was furrowed, and he was shaking his head.

"Any more comments?" Bell asked.

No one spoke.

"Okay. That's our final position. If they don't like it, fuck 'em!"

Bell regarded the somber faces. "Gentlemen, gentlemen," he said soothingly, "it's not the end of the world. Any luck, we'll have a great end of the year. Dave's people will be falling all over their fat wallets to make it work. That's not all bad... course it ain't all good, either, but who ever said you'd win 'em all?"

LATE THE NEXT DAY, Philip Hartley received a call. Would he be free to meet Arthur Winston for a drink at the Gotham Club? Would seven be convenient?

After he hung up with Winston's secretary, Hartley called Elaine at her office. She shouldn't count on him for the theater party she had scheduled for that evening. He'd be late, if he made it at all.

"Ed Horn's going to be there, too. He's close to Arthur on the board."

"Don't give it a thought, Philip, I'll make excuses. I wonder what Arthur has in mind. I can't wait to hear. Well, good luck!"

Hartley let his hand linger on the receiver. Elaine, the master tactician. He hadn't expected her to be disappointed, not really, but this constant cheerleading of hers was getting a little old. He'd been thinking about this a lot, lately. It'd be different if they had anything else going, but what else was there?

Suddenly, the thought of Shelley Gregory came to him... she seemed close enough to touch. This was starting to happen regularly. He relaxed for a moment... the images, the sensations of that evening passed in review... but it always ended with that next morning, his humiliation. Yet he knew she would appear to him again.

At six-thirty Hartley emerged from the Tower. He decided to walk the ten blocks in the cool evening air. It was topcoat weather, still very pleasant, considering Christmas was less than two weeks away. As he strode along, he replayed the events of the past few days. He was disappointed how easily Charlie had caved, though not altogether surprised. The strike would have extracted a price in the short run, some disruption and revenue loss, some hard feelings, but since when do you get something for nothing? And though Hartley was critical of Fritz's strike preparations, still, a lot of time, effort, and money had gone into planning and posturing for this fight that, in retrospect, never had a chance to happen.

A white-gloved doorman opened the door. After checking his coat, Hartley spotted the concierge.

"I'm meeting Arthur Winston."

"Yes, sir, in the lounge, if you'd care to step this way."

The concierge ushered Hartley into a high-ceilinged room paneled in dark wood and adorned by gilt-framed portraits of industrialists and bygone naval battles. Tuxedoed waiters glided about as if on well-oiled wheels, servicing the city's business elite as they reposed in soft leather chairs and booths. In the center, several tables were set, but the choice for sociability was the long carved-mahogany bar, a well-used relic of the previous century, for confidentiality, the quiet booths. Hartley was directed to a booth in the far corner that held a commanding view of the entire room. As he approached, Arthur Winston rose.

"Philip! Good of you to join us. You know Ed Horn, of course."

"Yes, how are you, Mr. Horn?"

"Make that Ed. No need to stand on ceremony."

Hartley settled in, observing Horn, sizing the man up. This newest member of BellAir's board was, like Winston, a banker, but cut from very different cloth. Horn was chairman of Great Southeast of Atlanta, one of the country's fastest-growing savings and loans. Bouncing back from an inconvenient antitrust consent decree against the hugely successful freight forwarding firm that was his first venture, Horn diversified, turning his energy to a small S&L where he had been a silent investor. His maverick banking methods soon spawned a network of complex interlocking schemes, and funds began flowing from GSE, as it was now known, into the very high-rises, shopping malls, and tract homes where developers and construction companies quietly controlled by Horn were amassing his second fortune.

Horn looked like a scrapper, short and swarthy, with a broad, flat nose, hooded eyes, and cuffed ears. Word was, he'd been quite an amateur boxer in his youth. To BellAir, Horn brought contacts, a healthy slice of business from his freight forwarding company, and a rough-and-tumble dimension new to the airline's board. Well acquainted with unions, Horn had sparred with the Teamsters much of his life. Hartley thought it interesting that the urbane Winston would sponsor this gritty outsider for the board seat that fell vacant on the recent death of a long-time director.

"Well, Philip," Winston said cheerfully, "I thought we should take advantage of Ed being in town. He's someone you should get to know much better. I'm pleased to say he shares our view about the direction the airline must take."

As Hartley turned to face Horn, he was startled to find himself fixed in a severe stare.

"I won't mince words with you, Phil." Horn was slowly shaking his head from side to side. "I was very, very disappointed to see that deal you people cut with the IAM. You had 'em right where you wanted, then you rolled over. Didn't even put up a fight."

Hartley was shocked. This is *my* line, he thought. *My* position! But his hands were tied. A powerful unwritten code compelled top management to close ranks on important decisions. Hartley ventured weakly, "It came down to taking what we could without blowing the fourth quarter."

"That's horseshit! And you damn well know it!"

Horn continued to glower at the very uncomfortable Hartley. Suddenly he broke into a broad grin. Winston was also smiling.

"Your loyalty is commendable," Winston remarked. "I do admire that in a man. But we must speak candidly here. You may have complete confidence that anything we say will remain in this room."

"I know all about you, Phil," Horn broke in, puffing on his cigar and leaning back in the booth. "In fact I know a whole lot more than you think, and let me say, young man, as far as I'm concerned you're a goddamn breath of fresh air in that organization."

Winston took a sip of his martini. "You should know Charlie has kept me advised all along. I'm well aware you were leading the small camp which was willing to take the strike."

Hartley nodded, feeling immensely better. Confidence restored, he decided to play a card of his own. "In that spirit of candor," he observed, "I have to tell you how disappointed I was in our lack of enthusiasm for the strike. If your top people aren't committed, how can you expect anyone else to be?"

"I agree completely," Horn replied. "I've been through more strikes than I can count, and there's absolutely no way you can keep operating unless everybody's on board. That means from the top down. You have to start early in the game and convince the union you're willing to go the limit."

"This time it was Charlie's call," Winston added, "and in the circumstances, who's to say he wasn't right? Except for Ed and myself and one or two others, the board wasn't prepared for a strike, either.

You're right, Philip. Basically, Charlie's heart wasn't in it, not when it became clear we couldn't get through it before Thanksgiving."

Horn nodded. "If you're going to play tough, you damn well better be sure your board's with you."

"But let's not be gloomy," said Winston. "I prefer to consider this the start of our own personal campaign for the next one." He raised his glass. "Our pilots make much of their leadership qualities. Their turn is next, and Philip and I personally plan to see they set the proper example."

"I'll drink to that," Horn responded.

"Philip, you'll join us for dinner? The kitchen here prepares a fine mixed grill."

"Yes, certainly," Hartley replied, beaming inside.

Winston nodded. "Since we'll be working so closely, we must get to know each other much better."

2

HENRY KOWALSKI leaned forward, straining at his shoelaces. His belt cut into his stomach, and he could feel the rush of blood to his head. This is so dumb, he thought. One of these days I have to do something about this gut. Finally, success. He straightened, breathed deeply, and looked around, drinking in the familiar sights and sounds. It was Friday night following the company's settlement with the IAM.

"Hey, Henry!" A tall, skinny redhead shouted from the scoring table. "You're up!"

"Why'd you do this to me?" Henry complained. "You know I hate to lead off."

"Hey, we go with our best." Red Mulcahy, the Blackhawks' captain, looked at Kowalski searchingly. "I got a feeling about you, Henry. You're going to blow 'em away!"

"I don't know. Lately I haven't been doin' all that great."

"I got confidence. You are hot tonight. You are real hot."

"If you say so," Henry muttered under his breath. He unzipped his bag and lifted out the shiny black ball, turning it over in his hands, testing its heft, admiring its smooth, cool surface.

"C'mon, tiger!"

"Let's go, Henry! Blast 'em!"

He strode to the alley, glancing at his teammates in their black, red, and white shirts. A win meant they'd tie tonight's opponents, the Midway Marauders, for first, then after the Christmas break it was back at it every Friday until summer. Out of the corner of his eye he caught a glimpse of Tiny McNabb, the Marauders' leadoff bowler. Tiny was six-six and could palm a ball with one hand. When he wrapped his huge paw around it, there wasn't much ball left. One time, Henry recalled, they even had to stop play so they could pick up the remains of a pin he'd shattered with one of his supersonic throws.

But Tiny was erratic. Sometimes it seemed like he was showing off more than just laying it in for the score. But when he was hot...

Henry paused at the end of the lane to wipe his hands on a towel. He checked his feet, checked his grip then straight up with the ball, like the pros on TV, out with the left foot and one... swing the ball back, two... slide and *release*... a little twist of the wrist for spin. He slid forward to the foul line, tottering on one foot. Down the polished boards shot the ball, curving sweetly in toward the one-three pocket.

Dead on! A strike!

Henry strutted back to the bench. What a start, he thought. Keep this up, we're invincible! Mulcahy clapped him on the back.

"Helluva ball! Let's see you do it again."

He took a fast gulp from a cup of beer somebody shoved at him and wiped his hands, surveying the next alley as he waited for his ball. Tiny had also nailed his first delivery. Sometimes this game's such a piece of cake, Henry thought, taking his position. Again the set, the swing, the slide.

Aaghh! Terrible!

The ball skidded the length of the alley, six inches from the gutter, didn't break at all. Left with a nasty split, he missed his spare by a mile. Glancing over, he observed the competition knocking off another strike. Jeez, he thought, next time I really better bear down.

Henry flopped down on the bench next to Matty Driscoll, pointing at a banner hanging over the rental shoe counter: *PARK RIDGE BOWLADROME – MERRY CHRISTMAS – BELLAIR EMPLOYEES LEAGUE.*

"Didn't see that on the way in," he remarked, trying to keep the conversation away from his miserable second frame. "When're you up?"

"He put me seventh."

"Huh. You staying around for the eats?"

"Sure. Might as well." The older man lit a cigarette. "The wife's on nights at the hospital. Patty comin'?"

"Yeah, she'll be here later."

"What're they having?"

"I dunno. Italian. Lasagna, I think."

"That reminds me, I gotta pay Red. Driscoll reached into his wallet and pulled out a frayed check. "Got a pen?"

Henry patted his shirt pocket. "Try the counter."

"Ah, th' hell with it. I'll do it later." Driscoll was quiet for a moment.

"Say, I heard that collection turned out okay."

"Over sixteen hundred, they got. But she's not doing too good. She's still all broke up, then there's that kid, too."

"It wasn't Vinnie's, was it?"

"No. Supposedly the father skipped on her." Henry took a drink from his cup. "Somebody said some of the guys wouldn't give anything."

"I heard that, too."

Henry stared into his cup. "That fucking stinks. I just don't understand people sometimes."

"Hell, the man blew up an airplane, killed a couple of our guys. Whaddya expect? Everybody feels terrible to start with, then you find out it's one of our own people? Gives us all a bad name."

He glared at Driscoll, "Don't forget I worked that flight. That could'a been *me* under there when the damn thing blew! Think about *that*! And I tell you something else, it's not all Vinnie's fault he went psycho. Sure, what he did was terrible but there's more to it than that." A roar went up from the crowd around the scoring table.

"Looks like Red hit one," said Driscoll.

Henry crumpled his cup and kicked it under the bench. "What I'm saying, the man needed help and nobody did nothin' for him. Nobody gave a shit, the company, nobody."

"You were a friend of his, weren't you?"

"Nah, nobody was that guy's friend. He didn't have any."

Driscoll ground out his cigarette. "Everybody's got problems but we don't go around blowin' up airplanes and killin' people."

Henry shook his head, exasperated. "Skip it. Sorry I brought it up. I got problems of my own, all these layoffs and everything. You're so senior it's no big deal, but for me it's getting close."

"It's the same old story," Driscoll replied. "Look what happened with our contract. We backed the company down 'cause we stuck together. You ask me, *that* was Vinnie's real problem. You go it alone, you're gonna lose. Every time."

"Hey, Matty! You're up!" Red Mulcahy was waving him on. "Time for a score, old-timer! We need one bad!"

THE FOLLOWING EVENING was witness to a very different gathering. For many Christmases, Charlie and Dee Bell had welcomed the airline's senior officers to their Connecticut home, a hundred-year-old Victorian outside Greenwich on sixteen acres of rolling, wooded land. This evening, the glow of candles in the front windows greeted the Bells' guests as they walked to the gravel turnaround from the parking area below. Against a brooding, overcast sky, smoke drifted up from chimneys at each end of the pitched roof. For nearly a week the Connecticut nights had been in the single digits, and several inches of snow remained from a storm the previous weekend.

Promptly at six o'clock, the Muellers rang the bell, as always the first to arrive. Mueller's preoccupation with on-time performance did not end at the office. If an invitation said six, then, by God, Fritz and Margaret Mueller were there at six, not a minute before, not a minute after. His wife had long ago lost track of the hours she'd logged circling the destination so he could arrive precisely at the appointed time. How she longed, just once in her life, to hear a greeting, any greeting besides, "Make yourselves comfortable. Everybody else should be here soon."

By six-thirty most of the guests had arrived. BellAir's chief pilot, Vern Swensen, checked in and was quickly immersed in a discussion with Clifford Meltzer, the company treasurer, while Swensen's wife went looking for Dee Bell. They had never flown together, Sharon Swensen being many years her junior, but she never missed a chance to talk shop with Dee.

Tonight was Roger Bankhead's first Christmas at the airline. By tradition, Charlie Bell encouraged each senior officer to invite someone from the next level down, partly to somewhat widen the circle, partly as a testing ground. When it came to social gatherings, Bell was careful to keep his hands clean, so any complaints about invitations fell, as did much of his dirty work, to Helen Foley. Tonight, Bankhead and Joyce Collins were Philip Hartley's guests. They were standing in a group with Marianne Keller and Pierre LeClerq. As secretary to the corporation, Marianne Keller was the company's ranking female employee, notably, its only female officer. Monsieur LeClerq, the Escoffier-trained head of the airline's food-services division, was gesturing vehemently as was his wont these days, in protest of the budget cuts that he maintained were compromising his reputation.

General Counsel Ben Peterson and his wife were visiting with Francis Farrell, the three of them warming by the large fireplace in the drawing room. In the far corner Charlie Bell huddled with two regional vice presidents, Bill Dickinson from Chicago and David Hillary, the head of BellAir's Western Region. Dickinson was expounding on the timing of the latest round of layoffs when Bell, overhearing their conversation, interrupted.

"Face it, Bill, there's no way to win. Do it before Christmas and you're a Scrooge. If you wait, they blame you for not telling them sooner."

Ross MacLeod strolled into the room, rubbing his hands vigorously. "Hey, Charlie! What rotgut are you pouring tonight?"

Bell clapped MacLeod on the shoulder. "Well, look what the cat dragged in!"

"It's Glenlivet, sir," replied a nearby waiter.

"Oh, *well*! In *that* case, I'll take one straight up. Second thought, make it a double." He turned back to Bell. "We damn near didn't make the flight. Solid line of cars all the way from the Hill to National. The District's deserted tonight, nobody left but the natives."

"It's dead back there, isn't it," asked Hillary, "until the inauguration?"

"As far as any real work goes, if you'll pardon the expression. We're getting ready for the big show."

Bell frowned. "I see I'm involved in those so-called festivities of yours."

"Damn right! I blocked your calendar three solid days. Did it last summer, to be on the safe side. When you weren't looking."

"I have no choice, I suppose."

"None at all! We have too much invested in this new administration to let you off the hook. For once there's a chance to score some points for the business community. Of course, a lot depends on Reagan's appointments, but I definitely need you around that week. There are a *lot* of people to see."

"I figured as much," Bell grumbled. "Say, where's Annie?" he asked, looking around. "You're not batching it, I hope."

"Over there at the food, with your better half and the Hartleys."

"Well, let's go say hello!"

"You still driving that lemon of yours?" MacLeod asked Bill Dickinson as the group sidled toward the hors d'oeuvres.

Dickinson shook his head. "No, finally got rid of it. I picked up a Seville. Don't know why it took me so long. What're you driving these days?"

"The Continental, but it's coming up on two years. About time for a change."

"Listen to you," Bell growled, "talking about *company cars* as if you were forking out for them yourselves! You better treat that Lincoln nice, Scotty. The way things're going around here you'll be driving it a long, long time."

As they neared the food table, a short, silver-haired woman turned and threw her arms around Bell.

"Charles Duncan Bell! *It's so good to see you!*"

"Hello, Annie," he said, returning the hug warmly. "How is it, every time I see you, you get more beautiful?"

She laughed. "Oh, Charles. You're such a liar."

"And the Hartleys. How are they this evening?" Bell asked, decorously placing his arm around Elaine's shoulder. "Seasons greetings to you, my dear," he said, giving her a peck on the cheek. "I'm happy you could join us."

Elaine smiled. "You have such a lovely home. I so enjoy coming here."

"Why, thank you," Dee replied. "From an expert like you, that's a real compliment. Though we've certainly had enough years to get it right." She turned to Anne MacLeod. "I understand you just had another blessed event."

"Our third. However, still no grandsons."

"Sooner or later." She winked. "Just keep trying. Elaine, you and Philip don't have a family yet, do you?"

"No, but we have a new dog," she replied brightly.

"Oh? What kind?"

"A Llasa-apso. It's Chinese. A lap dog, just right for the city."

"C'mon, you guys, I want to show you something. You too, Phil." Bell put his arm around MacLeod and cut the men out of the pack.

"Didn't I hear the O'Hare mechanics took up a collection for that woman?" Anne MacLeod asked. "That seemed a decent thing to do."

"Decent!" Margaret Mueller leapt to the attack. By now, her

early-arrival blues had been well medicated. "Anne, you must be joking! I was shocked when I heard! I say let the bitch fend for herself!"

"Oh, come on! She had nothing to do with it."

"So what! It's *our* people we should be concerned with, not trash like her – and, oh, by the way, Elaine, what *was* it I heard the other day. Something 'bout that husban' of yours when we had that bomb threat . . . "

"What do you mean?"

Margaret steadied herself against the table. "What I mean is, when Fritz closed O'Hare, it was *your husban'* tried to keep it open." She turned to the other women. "Can you believe, *her husban'* wanted to keep O'Hare open when ever'body *knew* there was a *killer* on the loose!"

"I don't know anything about that," Elaine retorted. "Whatever Philip did, I'm sure he had a good reason."

"I wouldn't be so certain," Margaret sniffed. "In fac', why don't you *ask* your husban' when you're back in your runty little apartment with your runty little dog? Just ask him."

Elaine drew herself up to her full height. "At least I know whose bed to find *my* husband in."

"*Oh!*" Margaret flushed a deep scarlet. "*You bitch!*" Suddenly she rushed from the room, her hand to her mouth.

"Elaine!" Dee Bell shouted. "That was uncalled for!" She stared at the doorway. "I'd . . . better see to Margaret. She's just not herself tonight."

In the far corner of the room, Vern Swensen and another invited guest, J. Marshall Smith, BellAir's acting vice president of personnel, were chatting with Mueller and David Axelrod.

"At least this year we can close the book on 159," Swensen was saying. "I remember standing here last Christmas when we didn't have a clue."

Mueller frowned. "It really bugs me we didn't catch that bastard alive. I wanted to make an example of him."

"Ah can assure you there was no sympathy for him in the rank and file," Smith observed.

Swensen shook his head. "Don't be so sure, Marshall. I've heard talk to the effect maybe we should have spotted the problem earlier and got rid of the guy. Or at least found him some help."

"Found him some help! This is not some funny farm we're runnin' around here!"

Dave Axelrod leapt in. "Vern's got a point. We talked to a lot of mechanics who knew the guy. Seems he was a pretty good man, but then he got real strange, real withdrawn. It's still a puzzle."

Mueller traded his glass for a refill. "I've been thinking, isn't there some way we could do a better job identifying people with problems like that, people that could hurt us? Sort of an early warning system. Maybe some kind of psychological testing."

"You are talking big bucks," Smith countered, "and legal problems as well. Not to mention the unions."

Mueller thought for a moment. "I think it's time to take a look. Tell you what, Marshall, you come up with a plan. We don't have enough jobs to go around as it is. Might as well start weeding out the weak sisters."

"Ah'll get right on it," Smith said unenthusiastically, glancing around the room. The lawyers were still clustered together, now at the buffet table. Smith pursed his lips. "Did you-all notice how Francis is unaccompanied tonight? Once again."

Mueller snorted. "Don't forget, his name is Farrell. He can't be much more than fifty. For an Irishman, he's still underage."

"Well, now, ah'm not so sure that's all there is to it." Smith nodded in Farrell's direction. "Just watch him a minute. See how he stands on one leg like that, and the way he holds his cigarette with his wrist kind of limp-like? Now, what does that say to you?"

"What are you babbling about, Marshall?" Mueller asked severely.

"Course ah don't know for a fact, but you ask me, ah'd say that man is queer as a three-dollar bill."

Mueller exploded. "Nobody did ask you! I've worked with Francis a bunch of years and I have no complaints at all. He always does a helluva job for us."

"Ah'm not talkin' about his work. Fact is, some of his type can be very good workers. You mean you've never noticed the way he talks, that little lisp of his? It fits the pattern to a T."

Swensen nodded. "Now that you mention it, I always thought Francis was, well, a little... different. Mind you, I've no complaints about his work either, but my people, well, some of them're uncomfortable around him. Know what I mean?"

"Like you don't want to bend over with him standin' behind you."

"Goddamnit!" Mueller sputtered. "You don't know what the hell you're talking about! I don't know what the man is, but whatever it is, he doesn't flaunt it like some of those creeps."

"That may be," Smith said soberly. "But ah tell you, gentlemen, if ah had my way, we would hire no more of that homo type into the company, and we'd get rid of the ones we already have. Shee-it! If we're ever going to get this company movin' again, surely the basic values have to count for something! No, there is no way we can tolerate that type person with their strange ideas and filthy practices."

"That flight attendant group has more than a few pretty boys in it," Swensen added. "Some of my captains don't feature *that* at all. There've even been situations where they've turned down meals. I've been concerned one of these days it could get ugly."

"Enough of that bullshit. We have ways of dealing with that sort of thing before it gets out of hand," said Mueller.

"So to speak," Smith smirked. "And don't forget the ladies! They're no better."

Swensen frowned. "I don't know, the idea of that doesn't bother me as much. I'm not sure why. Anyway, it's not as obvious."

"Say what you will, Vern," Smith went on solemnly. "Ah can assure you, it's just as unnatural in the ahs of God."

COFFEE AND DESSERT finished, Charlie Bell rose to his feet. Dee winced as Fritz Mueller whacked his crystal goblet with a spoon for quiet.

"I won't take much of your time," Bell began, "but no gathering would be complete without my interrupting it some. As is our custom, in a few minutes we'll repair to the front room for cordials, but first let me say how pleased I am you're all here with your lovely ladies or, in the case of Marianne, her husband Larry. Except for Stan Morita, who had a commitment that kept him in Hong Kong, we're all here tonight, the senior officer corps of BellAir, the finest airline in the world!"

"Hear! Hear!" Fritz Mueller shouted as everyone applauded.

"I'll ask for a moment of silence for the comrade we lost this past year, Bill Templeton, my right hand in Personnel for so long, who passed away in August. God rest his soul."

The group quieted and bowed their heads. "And let us also remember our two Denver employees, Rodriguez and Jensen, victims of that cowardly attack by one... " Bell's voice broke, "by one of our own people." He took a deep breath. "Some things I will never understand... or forgive."

Bell paused, sipping from a glass of water. "Tonight, we are pleased to have several newcomers joining us. Marshall Smith, and his lovely wife June, they're with us for the first time, and Roger Bankhead is accompanied by his... friend, Joyce Collins. It's good to have you here."

Bell looked around, observing the rich table, the satisfied faces. A portrait of success. "Now, I don't want to talk business here tonight. No, this is our time for fellowship and holiday cheer. But as I look around, I can't help think how this house, in fact, everything we have, Dee and I, has come to us because of the airline. And those of you who've been with us for some time, it's the same thing. It's all thanks to our combined efforts and hard work.

"But the point, my point, it would be a mistake to think that all this company is, is the sum of our financial accomplishments. It's a lot more than that." He paused and waggled his finger. "One *hell* of a lot more! The places we serve, those thirty thousand passengers who count on us every day, our buildings and equipment, whether you're talking about the Tower or a twenty-year-old tug or a new 767. But most of all it's our *people,* all pulling together in the same direction. You here in this room, the people on the front line, those like Bill Templeton who have gone before us, and the youngsters who will follow.

"In its simplest terms, we have a sacred trust to maintain. Never forget that! You should remind yourself of that every day. I know I do."

Bell looked at his colleagues, silent, attentive. "I won't kid you. This has been a rough year. In the red again, that's three in a row. Fortunately, we have plenty of reserve strength, thanks to the good years behind us, but we will need every bit of it to meet the challenges of the People Expresses and the New York Airs."

Bell's voice took on a sharp edge. He pumped his fist in the air. "Price-cutters, that's what they are! Cream-skimming bandits! A disgrace to the industry, paying starvation wages like they do, and believe me, they'll get away with it, too, long as there's people who're willing to work for peanuts. And here *we* are, trying to treat our employees right, we were able to reach a decent settlement just the other day, and what happens? We have to lay people off! That is not true competition, not with the deck stacked against you like that!

"Unfortunately," he said with a sarcastic smile, "unfortunately, that type of outfit has their following, folks who don't care about trivial little things like quality and service and, yes, let's not be afraid to say it, the *safety factor* that comes from experience, from not cutting corners!"

Bell's eyes narrowed. He leaned against the table and surveyed his guests. "Now. One more thing. This really gets under my skin. I've heard some snickering around the Tower about our friends and rivals down the street at Pan American. Some people actually thought it was funny they had to sell off their building this year, and rumor has it the hotels are next. God only knows where it'll all end. Well, let me tell you straight out, that is a lousy, rotten attitude! I don't care for it at all, not one little bit! Sure, we'll take their passengers. If we don't, somebody else will. But it makes me very sad to see a great airline coming apart like that, and anybody with a half a brain, it should make them feel bad, too.

"Having said all that, I want to tell you, sure as I'm standing here tonight, whatever happens, the BellAir Tower will never be sold." Bell paused, a glint in his eye. "But keep an eye out for some other changes in the new year."

Bell smiled, observing the puzzled faces and the murmurs. "Well, that's enough of my mouthing off. Just let me wish you a very Merry Christmas and say how proud I am of you and what you've accomplished. Now let's all go out and make 1981 a year we can really celebrate!"

THE OVERCAST was breaking, and patches of dark sky were starting to appear. The last guest had left, and the household staff was clearing away the aftermath when Charlie and Dee stepped outside for a breath of air. The snow crunched under their feet as they started up the path behind the house, toward the barn and higher ground. A mass of clouds drifted off, unveiling the bright moon, the ice moon.

"Care to walk the loop with me?" Charlie asked.

Dee stuffed her hands into the pockets of her down jacket. "What delicious air tonight." Their collie, Agatha Christie Bell, circled behind them on the path, then trotted ahead. "No chance of getting lost with her around," she laughed.

Beyond the barn was a clearing and at the edge of the woods, a path.

"How'd you think it went?" he asked.

"Everyone seemed in good spirits, considering the kind of year it's been." She was quiet for a moment. "One thing bothered me, though. How come you never once mentioned Wally?"

"Well...I figured I had enough hard things to say without getting into that."

"Strange, isn't it, you talk about Bill Templeton, but not Wally. He's become a nonperson."

"Oh, no," Bell replied, startled. "That's not true, not true at all!"

"But if you can't talk about him, it's like he never existed."

"Aw, you're making too much of it. It's just... well, we need to get on with things. In this business you've got to look ahead, not behind."

"When it suits you, you look behind," she sniffed.

Charlie stopped and took her gloved hand, looking at her intently. "You're right. In fact, I've been doing too much of that, lately. What you say about Wally, though, we have to heal the wound, let nature take its course."

They continued up the path. "You threw them for a loop at the end," she remarked. "Everyone except Phil. I was watching him. He seemed to take it in stride."

"You don't like him, do you?"

"Personally? No, I don't like him. I don't trust him. He's too wrapped up in himself."

"Hey, that's not fair. Look at us, for God's sake! Like I said, we've done very well and it wasn't by accident, that's for damn sure."

"Have you forgotten that part about the 'sacred trust'?"

Bell harrumphed, picking up the pace. They neared the top of the hill and stopped to look back at the lights of the house, shimmering through the skeletal trees. Dee hunched her shoulders and pressed her arms close to her sides, chilly despite the warm clothing. "What I mean, Hartley is...he sees the airline as a tool for his ambitions. It doesn't mean a whit to him, only what he can get out of it."

She linked her arm in his. "With us it was different. All those good things happened because you put the airline first. That's what you said tonight, and you were right."

"I don't remember you talking like that when we didn't have two nickels to rub together."

"But we always knew, somehow we'd survive. You had such energy, such drive. Most of all, you were creating something, making something out of nothing."

"We were lucky, getting in on the ground floor like that. Hell, these days all I'm doing is hanging around, way past retirement." He shook his head. "But you're wrong about Phil. He's a pushy bastard, all right, but that's what we need. Those young turks are beating us to death. We need a fighter to go up against them."

"Being a fighter doesn't mean he can hold things together." She pulled away from him and jabbed at the snow with her toe. "I'm sorry, you're just plain wrong. And that wife of his is no better, either."

"Good grief! Now what's the matter with *her*? She's certainly attractive and intelligent."

Dee snorted. "That woman is every bit as conniving as he is! She's just more clever about it. You should have seen the way she lit into Margaret tonight. A person who's been around as long as Margaret deserves some respect, even if she acts like a jerk sometimes."

"Poor Margaret," he said sadly. "She's in for a rough time of it. I'd hate to have to live with her when everybody sees Phil taking over." He sighed. "Well, at least I made Fritz executive VP."

"So you went through with it," she observed coldly.

"Yeah, it's done. The board'll act on it next week. I never saw Fritz so mad, but I finally calmed him down. We need him to hang in a couple more years until Phil gets his feet on the ground. But Fritz is a real pro, he'll make it work."

"You are making a very bad mistake. Fritz is no saint, but he's a good, loyal man and you're just throwing him a bone."

He started to protest.

"No, that's exactly what you're doing! For once in your life I wish you'd listen to me!"

"Look, I'm still running the show. If things don't work out I can always change it."

"Oh, is that so? You forget sometimes things take on a life of their own."

"Goddamnit! Enough of this! That's the way it is! Let this be the *end* of it!"

"You're as pigheaded as ever, Charlie Bell! There is no fool like an old fool! Finish your walk alone!"

She turned on her heel and stomped down the path, her flashlight beam bobbing up and down. The dog ran back and forth, unsure which of her masters to follow. Whining softly, she returned to Charlie.

"Well, Aggie, I guess it's just you and me." They started toward the top of the hill. Trouble is, he mused, Dee's got a point. But I had to do something. He reached down and patted the dog.

"Not the first time I went out on a limb, is it?" he said aloud. The dog nuzzled Bell's hand. "Tell you what, Aggie, let's go back. We'll make Dee a nice cup of tea. That'll show her what we think of her."

"WHADDYA THINK the directors'll do?"

"Something big, I'll bet. Christmas presents for management. They've been so good all year!"

Rose Markowitz and her associates were trudging back from lunch.

"Hey! Something's on the bulletin board!"

"My God! It's Hartley! They made him *president*!"

"President!" Marty Samuels put her hand to her mouth. *"You got to be kidding!"*

"Says so right here. President of the airline and the holding company both!"

"And a member of the board! *Whoa!* Look at me! What a big cheese *I* am!"

"And Fritz is executive VP. That's a new job, right?"

"A bunch of bullshit is what that is! He's been doing that job for years."

"What else... let's see, Meltzer's finance VP. That's okay."

"Yeah, he's all right. That makes sense."

"And look at this, will you! Roger Bankhead, senior vice president of marketing! Jeez, Rose! You are moving up in the world!"

"Rose. Level with me. You knew about this."

"I had a hunch."

"Aw, c'mon."

"So I had a *hunch*. I mean, if Hartley's moving up, who else could it be?"

"You knew about Hartley, *too*!"

"Hey, it's not like it was some big *secret*! It was all over this place the last couple of weeks. They leaked it to see if anybody'd jump out a window. "

"And nobody did."

"Apparently not."

"Maybe Fritz?"

"That comes later."

"Rose, don't con me . . . you're moving to Fifty-five."

"I don't know. He hasn't said anything."

"But you have a hunch?"

"Yeah . . . I think so."

"Aw, Rose, that's great! Congratulations!" Marty threw her arms around her friend and hugged her. "Let's have a party! Right now!"

"Can I kiss your ring, Rose?"

"Sorry, wrong religion."

By now a crowd had gathered in front of the bulletin board.

"*Hartley! Holy shit!* They jumped Hartley over Fritz!"

"C'mon, Hartley's okay," said a man on the edge of the crowd. "About time somebody kicked ass around here."

"But he don't know diddly about running an airline!"

"How could we do worse than we're doing now?"

"Rico! Looka this! Charlie's leaving!"

"Leaving? I don't believe it!"

"Says so right there."

"No way. Lemme see."

Rico pointed to the notice. "Read it again, dummy. Charlie ain't leaving. He's still CEO and chairman!"

"What's that mean?"

"What it means, meatball, it means he's still the boss. All's this is, it's a fancy way to give Hartley a tryout. Don't worry, the boss is around. He's still in charge."

MUCH LATER that day, Hartley's office phone rang. It was Arthur Winston.

"I was hoping I'd catch you before you left. I trust I'm not interrupting anything important."

"No, not at all." He motioned his secretary to leave and shut the door. "I'm starting to clear the decks here."

"Good, good. Philip, I just wanted to call and offer my congratulations. Sorry I had to rush off right after the meeting."

"I certainly appreciate the board's confidence," said Hartley, sailing an empty folder toward his wastebasket, "and all you've done for me."

"I'm sure it won't be misplaced. Wait a minute . . . " There was a pause on the line. "Yes, here it is. I'm looking at that full-page ad for People Express in today's *Times*. Philip, we can't even come close to those discounts of theirs! I tell you, this is a very, very grave matter."

"Arthur, let me assure you, I'll be examining absolutely everything. As far as I'm concerned, nothing is sacred, nothing at all." Hartley cradled the phone on his shoulder. "While I have you on the phone, let me try an idea on you."

He leaned back and put his feet on his desk. "The way Charlie's been handling these layoffs is frustrating as hell to me. He's just creeping up on a problem that needs to be attacked head-on. But, of course, that's not his style. Arthur, I want to make an all-out offensive on costs. Starting right at the top. A full-scale program, highest visibility."

"Go on."

"I want every single person in this company down on his knees at night, giving thanks he still has a job. And putting out two hundred percent to keep it!"

"That has a nice ring to it," Winston replied. "In fact, I'd say you're right on the mark. Let's plan on lunch next week. How does Tuesday sound to you?"

"Tuesday's fine."

"Very well. Twelve-thirty, the usual place."

Hartley hung up the phone. What a day. What a satisfying day. The recognition is coming. Finally. Setbacks, all those years grinding away in the trenches, it is finally coming. He thought of Elaine . . . what was the emotion she conjured up in him? Certainly not love. Gratitude? A rather thin gruel. Then, as she so often did these days,

Shelley Gregory intruded on his thoughts. Maybe, he mused, maybe the time has come to take that step.

Hartley looked at the litter on his desk, the files on the floor. Today begins the winnowing. In a few months there will be nothing left that doesn't fit the new BellAir. . . and Philip Hartley. Hartley's face hardened. From now on, he thought grimly, from now on this is how we operate. This is how we will run things, no matter who likes it and who doesn't. And that includes Mr. Charlie Bell.

3

"YOU HEARD the one about the CEO in the men's room?"
Francis Farrell shook the water from his hands. Roger
Bankhead rolled his eyes. "Not again!"
"Go on, go on," Frank Delgado shouted over the whine of the
hand dryer.

"Well, these three guys are in this executive men's room, the one
all the company bigwigs use. One of them, it's his first time at headquarters and is he impressed! Real towels, brass fixtures." Farrell
looked around, "much more elegant than these. Anyway, they're
standing there taking a leak when the new guy pipes up. 'So this is
where all the big pricks hang out!' he says."

Delgado laughed. "That's good, Francis! Damn good!"

"Wait. There's more."

Bankhead was still shaking his head.

"Well, who happens to be on the crapper but the CEO. Suddenly
the door opens and there he is, the old man himself. He's holding his
pants up with one hand. 'All right!' he yells, 'who said that! I want to
know who said that!'

"Naturally, everybody looks at the new guy. *'You're fired! Out!'*
He cans the guy right on the spot! Conduct unbecoming an employee,
they called it."

"You'd think a captain of industry might be a little more flexible,"
Delgado observed.

Bankhead shrugged. "Standards must be maintained."

"Appearances, at least," Farrell countered.

Returning to Will Cartright's office, Delgado fell in with
Bankhead. "I tell you, Roger, there were times I didn't think this deal
had a chance. After that session in New York I figured it was dead in
the water. Which wouldn't have bothered me a bit."

"It was a difficult birth," Bankhead replied. "Here it is the middle of February, and we started, when, last August?"

Farrell overtook them. "But what a brilliant solution! Frank wants five years and we want one, so we end up with three. The old split-the-baby routine works every time."

Delgado frowned. "What really happened, you people finally figured out I meant what I said about not giving away my company's name."

"Hell, we saw that right away," Bankhead retorted. "But I had to get you understand what we're up against with United and American. Well, somehow, it turned out all right. Where it matters to you, it's your name in the res system, everywhere else you show up as BellAir Commuter."

"True. Who the hell's going to ask for us in Arkansas, anyway?"

Bankhead nodded. "You know, this is the first time we've used a decal instead of repainting the whole plane. I hope you appreciate this deal was not easy to pull off. I had to push hard to get it approved."

Delgado glowed inside. This sign that he had bested Hartley made him feel immensely better.

The men filed into Cartright's conference room. A secretary was sorting papers on a long table.

"Here's a souvenir for you." Cartright handed Bankhead a fountain pen inscribed with his law firm's name. "These are for very special occasions."

Delgado turned his pen over in his hand. "I bet I know who's paying for this little gadget."

For the next few minutes, Delgado and Bankhead slowly circled the table, pausing at each stack of papers to affix their signatures.

"That should about do it," Cartright announced. "Now, I hope you'll join me for a celebration."

Delgado let out a big sigh. "I'll take a rain check, fellas. The wife and I are heading up to wine country. Going to escape the rat race for a few days."

Cartright laughed. "C'mon, Frank, you can't put it down. You'll be checking in every half hour."

"Not this time. The neighbors are looking after the kids, and my office knows where to reach me." He paused. "Well, maybe once a day."

"What a guy!" Cartright retorted. "Meantime, Francis and I'll be slaving over your airplane deal BellAir has so generously agreed to finance."

"Better nail it down quick, too, if we're going to make One July."

"Okay, let's wrap it up," said Cartright. "You're staying the weekend, Francis?"

Farrell smiled. "I have an old friend here, somebody I don't get to see nearly enough. The timing couldn't be better."

"HEY, THIS IS NICE!" Delgado exclaimed as he slipped behind the wheel of the big white Buick.

"Nothing but the best." Mariel returned Frank's kiss and slid to the passenger's side. "Try to guess the rate."

"Twenty-five bucks a day. That's what they always give us."

"No," she said proudly. *"Seventeen!"*

"That is incredible! I should have you should do *all* our negotiating!"

She sat back and closed her eyes. "Such a pretty flight. I'm glad I didn't drive all the way up here."

"Yeah. That would've been a lousy way to start our vacation."

"We haven't been anywhere without the kids for so long." There was a wistful look in her eyes.

"I can't even remember the last time."

"Tahoe. It's been almost two years."

"That long? Jeez... we gotta do better than that." Delgado started the car. "Ready?"

"I wish you'd let me know where we're going. I didn't know what to tell the Barretts."

"No way! This is a surprise! Don't worry, they can get hold of us if they have to."

They headed steeply down California Street toward the financial district, past the Bank of America Building's jagged mountain motif, past stolid greystones common to all cities, between glass and metal shafts that had risen some years before to block San Francisco's long sunwashed vistas, the gentle pastels that once graced this most Mediterranean of all American skylines.

After turning right, at the top of Sansome Street they paused for a light, then turned onto Broadway, mad and moody avenue of Kerouac and Ginsberg and Ferlinghetti, folkniks, coffeehouses, City Lights, and the Hungry i. So changed, dominated now by the skin trade and its fantasies, hawked day and night. Through the intersection at Columbus, porous dividing line between North Beach and Chinatown, brimming with new life from Southeast Asia, old Italian pride coalescing with the newcomers' vitality.

Mariel stared straight. "Why did you come through this disgusting area?" she asked, frowning

Delgado looked in the rear-view mirror. "Oh, I don't know. It's so tacky it's kind of interesting."

Exiting the Broadway tunnel, they turned onto Van Ness above automobile row, skirting the Marina before entering the Presidio of the Army and the road leading to the Golden Gate Bridge. The heavy sedan sped toward Marin. Rush hour was early, commuters gaining a head start on the weekend. From the bridge Frank observed the familiar fog bank sitting on the water, farther offshore than usual, it seemed to him, for this time of year. Just north of the bridge they left 101 and began winding down a steep hill.

"I really wish you'd tell me where we're going."

"Not a chance."

From outward appearances, Frank Delgado was a happy man. Today, another piece of the BellAir puzzle had dropped into place. But inside he was jittery and tense. Upping the ante so much, how he would get along with BellAir? Since their New York encounter, he'd had no contact with Hartley, only his underlings. But the thought of that bastard, for that was the word he had settled on to sum up the man, cast a pall over the deal, which was dicey enough to start with. Considering how much he was going into debt, considering the people he'd have to hire and train.

And now Hartley was BellAir's top dog, jumping over Fritz Mueller, the only person back there he felt a real kinship with. As he walked around the table today, writing his name under Roger Bankhead's, he couldn't help thinking of George Steiner.

"Now where is that sign," he said, frowning. "I remember it's pretty hard to spot."

"Isn't that it on the left?" Mariel pointed to a small marker with an arrow. "Alta Mira Hotel – Three Blocks."

"So! You knew after all!"

"I had an idea."

"So much for my great surprise," he said gently.

On the town's narrow main street, they stopped to let an elderly couple cross, then accelerated up the winding road. Soon they spied the tiled roof of the lovely old hotel, a dusty rose structure on a hillside that fell away steeply to the mud flats on which the town of Sausalito was built.

He stole a look at his wife. Her face was aglow.

"What a nice thought, Frank."

The idea came to him a few weeks back. Take a little time, get away from work, the house, the kids. This first stop, the place of their wedding night nearly twenty years ago.

The sun had already disappeared behind the hill in back of the hotel. The air was cooling off fast, but it was still comfortable on the deck. Frank sat in his chair, already on his second gin-and-tonic, hoping that the weather would hold. It had been a very wet winter, but maybe they'd luck out for the weekend.

Mariel watched powerboats cutting white swaths in the sparkling water far below the terrace. Late-afternoon racers rounded a buoy this side of Alcatraz Island, their sails strung out in a long white arc, while across the bay, windows in the East Bay hills were just beginning to mirror the fire of the setting sun.

A waitress appeared, and Frank ordered another round. Mariel held up a small camera she'd taken from her bag.

"Would you take our picture? Just line it up and push the red button. And be sure to get the city in the background." She smoothed her hair as Frank leaned toward her.

"Hope it comes out. I'm not very good with these things."

He put his arm around her shoulder. "Happy?" he asked.

"What do you think?" she replied, smiling.

Delgado looked down the hill. The buzz of a floatplane taking off caught his ear. Mariel followed his eyes to the small white craft gathering speed in the channel.

"That looks like fun. You should try it sometime."

He shook his head, watching the plane lift from the surface of the water. A sad expression came over his face. "There's not enough hours in the day as it is. All that talk about my cutting back . . . you know, I really mean it, but how to do it's been bothering me a lot. With our expansion and all, and now we'll be doing all of BellAir flying up north and in the valley."

"It worries me too. We don't talk to each other anymore, I mean just you and me. It's always work, money, the house, Bobby's braces, there's no end to it. Sometimes I feel like a sponge that's been out in the sun too long. Hard and rough, all dried out."

Frank looked at her, and his face softened. "Well, that has to change, and I think I finally figured out how to do it."

"What's the answer?"

"I'm going to put Marty in charge of the operation, the whole damn thing. It's just too much for me, with everything else that's going on. I'll make one of the other guys chief pilot. Don't know who yet, but this'll give me more time to manage things. And keep BellAir honest." He sipped at his drink. "Hopefully, there'll more time for us. God knows we need it."

"I know you've been worried. Ever since you got involved with that New York crowd." She looked closely at him. "And it's not just the business part, is it?"

"What do you mean?" Delgado replied, startled.

"Something else is bothering you. That Hartley."

Delgado nodded.

"You haven't said much about him."

"I guess I didn't feel like talking about it."

"Well, you are, now."

"I guess." Delgado looked out over the water. The seaplane was circling for altitude, its engine straining. He shook his head. "It makes you wonder, why some people get to the top and others don't. Their operations guy, Mueller. He's as straight as they come, but they passed him over for that... creep."

"That's no reason to get so upset, Frank. Please don't let it get to you." She smiled. "I know you can handle it. You always have."

After a moment, he took her hand and caressed it. "Thanks. I don't know what I'd do without you."

They sat and talked until dark. After dinner they strolled down the hill and prowled the streets of Sausalito, poking into shops, listening to a ragged couple on a fine flute and guitar in the village park. They bought ice cream cones and laughed when Frank's dribbled down his wrist.

"My favorite klutz," Mariel said, handing him a napkin.

Holding hands, they climbed the hill to the hotel as they did on a night long ago. For a moment the heartaches were set aside. They made love passionately, finding each other in a way they no longer thought possible. It was very late before sleep came.

4

"**E**NOUGH**,**" Gene Ashmore muttered. "Enough for one day." BellAir's San Francisco station manager shook the water from his eyeglasses, scraping the lenses with his thumb. Across the airfield it was pouring and blowing, one moment a blinding sheet of water, a fine mist the next.

"Let's get out of here!" shouted Frank Delgado, following Ashmore toward the terminal. Marty Barron and Paul Young, Bay Airline's station manager at SFO, were close behind.

Delgado pulled his blue and green baseball cap tight. A United 747 was approaching over the bay from the north, the bad-weather landing direction. The aircraft kicked up a spray of groundwater as it touched down and the pilot applied his thrust reversers.

"Worst March in years," Ashmore grumbled, leading the way up a flight of ironwork stairs to an area of warm, well-lit offices. He gestured toward a coat rack in the corner of the small conference room. "Stick your things in there."

Ashmore barked a coffee order at a secretary, then unfurled a roll of heavy drafting paper from a long cardboard tube, spreading it across the gray metal table and setting an ashtray at each end to hold it down. The drawing showed a portion of BellAir's ramp area outside the terminal.

"Here's what you guys are using now, the green part." The men bent over the drawing. Ashmore tapped a large red area. "And this is what we were just looking at, your new space."

For the next hour the men pored over the drawings, establishing procedures to handle the huge increase in Bay's SFO activity, marking walkways to channel passengers away from the deadly propellers, positioning Delgado's aircraft so jetblast from BellAir planes wouldn't damage them. Security and a multitude of other problems had to be settled. Finally Ashmore slipped an elastic band around the last drawing and pushed it back in its tube. He stood there for a moment, then backed away from the table.

"I gotta level with you, Frank. You people coming in here creates one helluva problem for me. I've got to scrounge two more parking spaces for my own planes, thanks to you, and I don't know where I'm going to get them."

He slammed the tube into a corner. "You sure got yourselves one sweet deal. New York must've wanted you guys damn bad. I've been station manager here nearly fifteen years. It's a crime, us pulling out of the valley like this, and I don't care who knows it, either. I'm so close to retirement, ain't nothin' they can do to me hasn't been done already."

He leaned against the edge of the table. "Don't get me wrong, it's nothing personal. What you people do, you do well enough, but like I told New York, we are making one big mistake. Those folks in Stockton and Modesto, hell, we grew up together. BellAir goes back more than forty years in the valley, if you count that outfit in Sacramento we merged with before the war. It's those fucking greenhorns back there, always looking to fix stuff that ain't broke. And not just here, either, that shit's going on all over the system."

Ashmore shook his head sadly. "You'll make a ton of money here, Frank. This place is a gold mine, if you work it right."

Delgado bristled. "You seem to forget, I am going way out on a limb for you people. Tripling my operation here overnight? That's a crap shoot any way you slice it!"

"That may be. That's your business."

Delgado looked at his watch. "Paul and Marty'll finish up here. We still need to work out those bugs in the schedule."

Ashmore shook Delgado's hand. "I didn't mean to hammer on you. We'll work it out, no matter what I think about it. You need a ride?"

"I've got Paul's car. Remind me, what time's Fritz due in?"

"Two forty-five. You'll see me out there. I always meet the big shots. Part of the job description."

THREE HOURS LATER, after meeting in the city with the accounting firm Will Cartright was pressing him to hire, Delgado was back on the road, cruising down the Bayshore Freeway toward the airport. Two-fifteen. Running late.

The meeting had been painful. Will was right, he had to admit. Bay had outgrown Ray Rivera, over twenty years his accountant, but the prospect of cutting his old friend loose troubled Delgado. Bay was Ray's biggest client. There had to be some way to keep him involved, though he didn't yet know how. Then there was BellAir looming. For better or worse, it was all coming together.

Delgado pulled into a BellAir parking space behind the terminal, a short walk from the main lobby. A flight information monitor told him what he needed to know: FLIGHT 153 – GATE 29 – ON TIME. Turning the corner of BellAir's long counter he came upon the three ticket agent positions under construction for Bay. A carpenter in white coveralls was on his hands and knees, his head in the hole where the scale for weighing checked baggage would be set.

"This be ready by next week? I got training to do in here."

The workman looked up. "So they tell me." He waved his hand at the construction debris. "Draw your own conclusions."

Delgado quickened his step, clipping his SFIA security badge to his jacket pocket. A uniformed guard waved him around the security checkpoint. Nearing Gate 29 he noticed a line of people filing out of the jetway. Damn, he thought, the flight's already in, but then he spotted Fritz Mueller standing at the check-in podium with Ashmore.

"Hey, Fritz! Welcome to San Francisco!"

"Good to see you again, Frank."

"I forgot, you people knew each other," Ashmore said.

"Yeah, we spent a couple of fun days in New York."

"Peculiar idea of fun," Mueller countered. "But at least we got you over to La Guardia for a reality check."

"And now it's our turn."

Mueller pulled a ticket envelope from his pocket. "By the way, I just found out I can't spend the whole day with you people tomorrow. Seems like they need me in Denver by five. I'll have to cut out around noon. Sorry about that."

Delgado frowned. "That means there won't be time for everything."

Mueller handed his ticket to Ashmore. "Appreciate it if you'd change this for me."

"No problem, chief. Your slightest command is my wish."

"Let's make tracks," Delgado said brusquely. "Since you people happened to be on time today, there's an outside chance we'll make our three-fifteen."

"GREAT MEAL," Mueller remarked as they drove toward the hotel. "I've never had better seafood."

After a tour of Bay's terminal facilities and a quick visit to Delgado's office, the men had stopped for dinner at a quiet restaurant on Cannery Row.

"Those sand dabs are a local specialty. Actually, the airport restaurant does them real well, too. By the way, I was wondering, any chance you like Mexican food?"

"Like it? I'm in trouble if I don't get my Mex fix every couple of weeks!"

"Damn! It's too bad you're cutting out so early tomorrow. There's this little spot I know. Best food in town!"

"You're on. Anytime."

"In fact, next trip, why not stay a few days. You play golf at all?"

Mueller grimaced. "I hack at it when I get the chance. What about you?"

"Never touch the stuff. But I could set you up at Pebble Beach."

"I haven't played that course in years. Sure, I'd like to try it again."

Delgado pulled up in front of the hotel. "As far as tomorrow's concerned, I had to cut the tour down, but you'll see the important parts. We'll start off at the maintenance shop and then get you a ride in our new simulator."

Mueller opened the car door. "Let me be candid, Frank. I like what I've seen so far, but don't take it wrong if I have some suggestions."

"Such as?"

"I dunno. Not much yet. Hell, maybe nothing that amounts to a hill of beans, but the way I see it, our reputation's riding with you people, so I need to be damn sure you touch all the bases, staffing, training, that kind of thing."

"You sound like the FAA."

Mueller laughed. "Never been accused of *that* before!"

Delgado paused a moment. "And I feel like I can level with you, too."

"Right. It goes both ways."

"I mean, I'll be surprised if you don't find some things and if you do, hell, I'll be the first one to thank you for pointing 'em out." Delgado shook his head. "But if all you're talking about is different ways of skinning the same cat, you know, your way and my way, I'm not interested."

"Listen, I'm not going to pick nits. You wouldn't have got this far if you hadn't been doing a lot of things right."

"That may be," Delgado glared at Mueller, "but I seem to remember George Steiner was doing a lot of things right, before he tangled with you people. If you want my opinion, that really stunk, what you did to George!"

"Yeah, well, that was not one of our finest hours, I have to admit."

Delgado was quiet for a moment. He'd been trying to figure out a way to bring up a certain subject. "Fritz," he finally ventured, "I want you to know, there is no way you will do to me what you did to George. Don't even think about it."

Mueller was taken aback. "Why do you say that? We want to work with you. I wouldn't be here, otherwise."

Delgado shook his head. "Roger Bankhead called me yesterday. They want to renegotiate the deal."

"What! That's the first I heard of that!"

"I told him to stuff it. I mean that, too."

Mueller looked puzzled. "There's something wrong there. I'll check it out when I get back."

"What's wrong is they want a bigger share of the revenue. He gave me some song and dance about maybe the passenger loads would be smaller than we all figured. After a while I wasn't even listening. Only thing to do, I turned it over to my lawyer."

Delgado turned to face Mueller. "Fritz, we're a little outfit compared to you, but we do okay. I know how to size people up. Roger and I shook hands over this deal three weeks ago. I trust him. I wouldn't have signed up if I didn't."

"What are you trying to say?"

"What I'm saying, I know who's behind this. It isn't Roger. And it isn't you."

Mueller bristled. "It's a misunderstanding," he said sharply. "There's got to be some explanation for it."

"There's an explanation, all right, but not one I have a lot of respect for."

A flicker of recognition passed across Mueller's face. He put a leg outside the car. "I'll look into it. At this point, that's all I can say."

"Fritz."

Mueller halted.

"One more thing. I got to tell you, after I saw how you run your operation, I feel a lot better about BellAir. That's aside from what I just told you."

"What's *that* supposed to mean?"

"What I mean, I can see it's a tough place to work, trying to keep your mind on things when there's so much bullshit flying around." In over his head, nevertheless, Delgado pressed on. "I was sorry they didn't make you president. You deserved it. So did the company."

"You do what you have to do."

Delgado paused. "So, how's our friend Hartley doing these days?"

Mueller stared at Delgado. He looked very tired. "He's doing fine. He learns fast."

"To me, Hartley seems like a difficult person to get along with."

Mueller turned to face Delgado. "Look, Frank. I wasn't born yesterday. I know where you're going, but I'm not going to let you get there. Leave it alone." He stepped out and shut the car door, then looked back through the open window. "Thanks for the meal. And the company. See you tomorrow."

Delgado reached out, and they shook hands through the window.

"Be sure to remember me to Mr. Hartley."

Mueller laughed and shook his head. "You bastard," he said softly.

5

I T TOOK PHILIP HARTLEY no time at all to see the enormity of the challenge he had taken on. Nineteen eighty-one was shaping up as another unprofitable year, though the red ink would be blamed on the old guard and Charlie Bell, still the very visible chairman. For the time being, the airline's successes would be Hartley's, and its failures someone else's. Soon, though, he would own the bad along with the good.

There were hopeful signs. Fares were firming, aided by serious difficulties being experienced by the new entrants. To the delight of the established carriers, the newcomers were learning the hard way that giving your product away is not a formula for success. And despite having entered the field so far behind, Hartley's new management information system for the airline had leapfrogged the competition with next-generation technologies.

Immersed in his new duties, Hartley quickly came to appreciate how vital Fritz Mueller was to the airline's day-to-day functioning, but despite this recognition, their relationship was little more than a truce. Grievously wounded at being passed over, not a day went by that the older man didn't agonize over the role reversal with his rival, who was handed the job he always wanted and fully expected someday would be his. Then, and Mueller shuddered whenever he walked in his front door, then there was Margaret's incessant yapping.

Hartley's rapport with BellAir's directors – particularly Winston, but also Ed Horn and Harold Nystrom, an elderly hotel magnate – was a great confidence builder as he charted the company's course, positioning himself for the day when Charlie Bell would step down. He had expected Bell to be on him like a glove, but that wasn't the case at all. Bell had given him a surprising amount of running room.

As the first few months sped by, Hartley's natural reserve and aloofness hardened into policy. A tough outer shell was essential, he was convinced, to maintain the perspective and will to make hard decisions. How was it possible to dine at a VP's home one night, knowing he might have to demote or fire the man the next day? The added tension of such familiarity he did not need. So in the first half-year of his presidency, Hartley began to distance himself from those few colleagues whose company he had once sought, including Roger Bankhead.

His relationship with Bankhead was complex, for even as Hartley withdrew personally, he came to depend more and more on the younger man, seeking his advice on a widening range of issues and delegating him important new responsibilities. Although it was never mentioned, they understood that a barrier now stood between them. With this development, Hartley had no unguarded relationships in the company, no real friends.

So as Philip Hartley set his hooks in the BellAir organization, extending his influence and amassing new territory, he found the price steep – a monkish austerity, constant alertness, always wary of potential rivals and threatening coalitions, sensitive to meanings masked by the glib cordiality that marked the company's upper echelon. On the offensive side of the ledger, Hartley kept himself spring-loaded at all times, ready to seize any opportunity to advance his personal agenda.

THE SILVER 747 climbed away from Kennedy Airport, banking toward the Manhattan skyline and a distant sunset. The music swelled to its climax – *Fly BellAir, Our Business Is Taking Care of You* – and the familiar winged B logo flashed on the screen. Then it went blank.

Jack Simpson, BellAir's VP of advertising, pushed several buttons on a console at the table. The videorecorder began rewinding with a gentle whir, a panel slid across the wall-mounted screen, and the ceiling lights came up.

"No question, we are looking at our best coverage ever! A total integrated media campaign!" Simpson banged his fist into his hand. "TV, radio, print, all the prime-time shows, every major sports event! We kick off with the NBA finals in June. Sorry about those radio tapes, but they'll be ready in a few days."

Simpson slipped his reading glasses into his pocket and reached for a slim, oversized leather case. "Last but not least, the newspaper and magazine mockups." He unzipped the case. "They are sen-*sa*-tional, if I say so, myself..."

Hartley nodded at Roger Bankhead.

"Jack," Bankhead broke in, "let's not take the time now. These carry through the same theme, I assume."

"Hey, what else? It's the basic 'Take Care' signature but with those variations we decided on. You know, more upscale people, active vacation scenes, etcetera, etcetera..."

"Thanks for the show," Hartley added. "We'll get back to you."

Simpson frowned. "Sure, fellas, whatever you say. And about those tapes, I really apologize. I'll let you know soon as they come in."

"You do that," Hartley replied, standing up.

Simpson retrieved his video cassette and started for the door.

"Take it easy, fellas." There was a puzzled expression on his face. "I'll talk to you... whenever."

"Oh, and Jack..."

Simpson spun around. "Yes, Phil?"

"Close the door on your way out."

After Simpson had gone, Hartley permitted himself a smile. "When I was a kid, I had a dog. A spaniel." He nodded at the door. "If you know what I mean."

Bankhead laughed.

"Jack's been with the company a long time," Hartley said, sitting back. "Too long, in fact. Charlie brought him in from Sullivan & Carstens in '64. No coincidence they've been our agency ever since."

"Meantime they become rich and famous. We're their largest account by far, a real cash cow."

"Well, it's time to shake up that cozy little arrangement." Hartley drummed on the table with a pencil. "How well do you know the Frankenheimer Agency?"

"People say it has the best creative shop in the business. I've never worked with them personally, though."

Hartley nodded. "You may just get the chance. Don Frankenheimer will be making a presentation Monday. I met with him yesterday to feel him out. Clear your calendar from three on."

Bankhead frowned. He had not been consulted on this contact, clearly within his sphere of responsibility. But, well, let it slide. Philip's the boss. I guess he can talk to anybody he wants to.

"Of course," Bankhead replied without missing a beat. "But if we make a switch, it'll go down real hard with Jack and the other old-timers."

Hartley smiled and nodded. "We'll just leave Jack out of the loop for the time being."

"Two birds with one stone."

"I'll be disappointed if it's only two."

"But what about Charlie? 'Take Care' is his baby."

"'Take Care' is finished, Roger. Dead. I want something new, something that'll whack people across the face. And, for your information, I happen to know some of the board are fed up with our advertising too." Hartley nodded. "Don't be concerned about Charlie. I'll handle him."

As Hartley and Bankhead emerged from the conference room, Fritz Mueller was walking by. "Phil, I need you for a couple of things."

"I'm late for a meeting. It'll wait."

Oh, no it won't, Mister Big Shot, Mueller thought. We'll talk right here, right now. "Just take a minute," he replied curtly. "When you're in L.A. next week, I want you to look in on that commuter outfit we're romancing out there. You know, show the flag, pump them up."

"If I can fit it in. I need to be briefed first."

"Would I let you go anywhere unprepared?" Mueller countered, unsmiling.

"How're we coming with that outfit in San Francisco?" Hartley asked. "What's our start-up date?"

Bankhead interjected. "We're shooting for July 1."

Hartley frowned. "Can't you move it up?"

"We're pushing hard, but I'll take another look," Bankhead replied.

Hartley started to walk away. "Hey," Mueller said, halting Hartley in his tracks. "What is going on there, anyway?" He faced Bankhead. "I was out there yesterday and they said you're trying to change the deal."

Bankhead started to reply, but Hartley cut him off. "We are. Now that they're locked in, I told Roger to start chipping away at those concessions we had to give them. That deal's too rich for my taste."

Mueller shook his head vehemently. "But we can't undermine it, for God's sake! We haven't even got started with them!"

"Fritz," Hartley replied pedantically, "it's not just this deal. It's every deal! I'm talking attitude!" He touched his finger to his forehead. "You've always got to be thinking, what can I do to improve my position? How can I squeeze a little more out? If we don't move forward, we fall back. That's how things work."

"But it's set up perfect, just like we wanted. No way we're going to set the guy off for no reason at all."

Hartley looked at him coldly. "I believe I just gave you a reason." He paused. "So, how did you and the fiery Mexican get along? He seemed like a pop-off to me. I know his type. I grew up around people like that."

"The guy's all right. He runs a good shop, even if they're stretched thinner than I'd like. If you can believe it, he even invited me to stay at his house next time I'm out there."

"Watch that kind of thing. Don't let it affect your judgment."

Mueller bristled. "I don't need your goddamn advice."

"Hey," Hartley replied with a faint smile, "it's nothing personal. This goes for all of us here, myself included."

"Okay, but don't lecture me. I wasn't born yesterday. They'll do a good job. Don't mess with it."

Without a word, Hartley turned and left. His face bright red, Fritz Mueller looked at Roger Bankhead. Bankhead just shrugged.

SEVERAL DAYS LATER, Hartley found himself gazing out the window of a BellAir 727, his head resting against the cool gray plastic of the cabin wall. This was the final leg of the new president's strenuous three-day, nineteen-city swing through BellAir's Western Region. Passing over the Central Sierras, the pilot came on the PA to point out Yosemite Valley directly ahead. The left wing dipped, and Hartley caught a glimpse of Half Dome as the plane turned back on course for San Francisco, his final stop. He sank into the comfortable first class seat, weary from speeches and handshaking, cocktail parties and bag lunches. At the same time, however, he felt curiously exhilarated. He'd been apprehensive about the public-relations aspect of his new job, but for the most part these get-acquainted encounters had been a pleasant surprise.

The plane began to decelerate, and Hartley felt a small change in cabin pressure and a gentle whoosh of air signaling the start of their descent. Old Highway 99 down there. Lost a couple of good friends to that death trap. Ahead lay the interstate's concrete ribbon, threading the western edge of the valley. That's probably Merced, he thought. Can't tell for sure, but if it is... he straightened in his seat and looked out the opposite window... if that's Merced, up the line is Modesto and next, Manteca. Why don't I take a quick look...

As he reached for his seat belt, a flight attendant loomed in front of him. One of the older crop, he thought. Must be pushing fifty. But at least she takes pride in her appearance.

"Mr. Hartley, Mr. Blackwood. Can I get you anything? We'll be landing in a few minutes." She leaned familiarly over the seat back, kneeling on the unoccupied seat in the row ahead. Her name was sewn into her service apron – Sandy Stewart.

"No thanks, Sandy, I'm fine."

"Same here," replied Hartley's seatmate. Perry Blackwood was his young special assistant who had orchestrated the tour. "It's sure been a full week. I'm pleased we didn't see that many long faces among the Charlie Bell loyalists."

"Hey, we're all Charlie Bell loyalists," Hartley replied.

"Sure. But I mean, this is a new beginning. At least that's how I look at it."

"That *is* the way to look at it."

"You handled that Denver crowd very well."

"That one threatened to get ugly, didn't it." One of his Denver meetings had been packed by diehard IAM types who arrived with a long, loud list of gripes, despite the new contract.

Blackwood raised his tray table and locked it. "Your Job Justification Program has its enemies, but nobody can deny it's working. Down nearly two thousand positions since January, and that's not even counting the layoffs. That's remarkable!"

"And we're still way too fat. There's a long way to go before we hit bone."

Hartley looked at his young companion for a moment. "You've been with me how long? Has it been a year?"

"A little more, actually."

Hartley looked out again... should give some thought to Perry's next assignment. The South Bay salt flats were coming up and San

Jose lay just ahead. So much for Manteca. He closed his eyes...
scenes of his boyhood town drifted past. Manteca, Manteca. Why not
take a couple of hours, drive out to the old place, see what it looks
like. Probably wouldn't even recognize it. I wonder if anybody's
still around?

Suddenly Hartley sat up and reached forward for the briefcase at
his feet. He extracted a typed sheet from a manila folder. Arrive SFO
9:15... 9:30–11:30, tour maintenance facility and engine overhaul
shop. Lunch with employees, company cafeteria... 1:30–3:00, meet
with David Hillary and Western Region staff. Now *there's* a possibility. Nothing else until six, cocktails and dinner.

He turned to Blackwood. "Perry, I want you to handle something," he said offhandedly.

"Sure. Just name it."

"See this one-thirty with Hillary?" He pointed to the schedule.
"Cancel it when we get in. Tell him... just say I had to go up to the
city early. I'll see all those people at dinner, anyway."

"Plus a cast of thousands."

"Exactly. And get me a car right after lunch."

"Company car okay?"

Hartley thought for a moment. "No, get me... I want something fun.
Use your imagination. I need to get away for a while, clear my head."

HIS ASSISTANT truly outdid himself. By mid-afternoon, Hartley was
behind the wheel of a white Corvette, cruising the streets of his hometown. His suit coat lay on the seat beside him, his tie was loosened,
sleeves rolled up two turns, just below the elbow. The drive seemed to
take no time at all.

He turned onto Walnut Street... wonder what the old house looks
like. Down Alameda... my block. Same little wood-frame houses...
85... 89... 91. There's the Gradys', but what happened to ours? And
the Merediths'? Gone! Both of them! Then it hit him. A boxy three-
story apartment building set back from the road, straddling the space
where the two houses had been. That's the answer. Wonder how long
it's been there. Sign in the window – Apartment to Let, Inquire Within.
Not in that good repair, either. Jesus! What a long time it's been!

Back toward Yosemite Avenue. The high school... I wonder

what *that* looks like now. Crossing to the other side of town, Hartley found himself trapped behind a yellow school bus. Boys wearing baseball caps pressed their faces against the back window, eyeing the Corvette. Hartley slowed as he approached the high-school buildings. Grassy area in front, that same big tree but there's a new sign. Manteca High School – Home of the Buffaloes! Same old buildings but there's something missing, something important. Of course! The tower on the administration building. It's gone! Wonder what happened to it.

He wheeled into the visitors' parking area. Teenagers carrying backpacks and green and white athletic bags streamed by.

"Hey, mister, how fast'll that 'Vette go?"

Hartley grinned. "Just picked it up today. I haven't really pushed it yet."

A heavily lipsticked girl strolled past, projecting her best fifteen-going-on-twenty-two smile.

"Nice car!" She stroked the top of the tan leather seat, then drifted off.

Hartley stepped out and walked up to the main building, through the double doors and into the familiar lobby. Seems a lot smaller, but brighter. I wonder where... sure, there it is. Against the far wall, the old trophy case. *Three* cases, now! But then, twenty-five years is time for a lot of football. He began walking down the line. The 1980 team... more group photos... 1977, all-state lineman's helmet... 1974, game ball from the league championship game... 1965... 1960. He stopped. The 1954 team picture. My old coach, Asa Williams, stern and erect. Middle row, fourth from the left, a sober Phil Hartley staring out of the picture, a deer trapped in headlights. And that headline from the *Bulletin*... he smiled as he read it again. *Hartley's 3 TDs Lead Buffaloes to Valley Oak Title.* My picture, dragging a Hayward player across the goal line. Kid I played against in college, too... Oregon State, I think. God! Look at that paper... faded and cracked, turned brown already.

"I understand that was a good year."

Startled, Hartley wheeled around. A crewcut man in his early thirties was standing beside him.

"Sure was... it sure was."

"How do you like the display?" The man gestured around the

lobby. "We enlarged the football case last year, thanks to the Booster Club." He stuck out his hand. "Mike Mason's the name."

"Phil Hartley." Hartley sized up the man. "You involved in the athletic program?"

"I teach here. History. Assistant football coach too, in my spare time. So, what brings you in here, Phil?"

Hartley nodded at the display. "I'm into history, too. Ancient history."

Mason bent down, toward the clipping. "Oh, right. I thought I recognized the name. Where're you from now? Don't believe I've seen you around here."

"I'm back East, now. New York."

"What line of work're you in?"

"I'm with the airlines."

"Oh? That's impressive." Mason looked at his watch. "Say, before you leave, stop by the athletic office. I'd like to give you one of last year's souvenir programs." He winked. "Have to make sure you're on our mailing list, too."

Hartley moved over to the baseball case. Then basketball. But he came back to the football display. Football was his first love. Always was.

After strolling around the grounds, he stopped by the athletic department, wrote them a check, then returned to his car. As Hartley accelerated out of the parking lot, he glanced at the school buildings retreating in his rear-view mirror. Suddenly he realized he'd forgotten to ask about the missing admin tower. Oh well, he thought, it'll have to remain a mystery.

One thing left to do. Back out Alameda, over to North Main. A lot more stores than before, but fewer houses. Sadler's Department Store... what do you know, it's still in business. Wonder if old man Sadler still does his vampire routine at Halloween. What a piece of work *he* was, Hartley chuckled. McDonald's on the corner... that's new, for sure. Left on Elm. Ah, there's no way the church would still be there. It was practically falling down when I left for back east, abandoned, the paint flaking, wood rotting, its roof half off.

He looked ahead... over that strand of trees. Is that a steeple? *It is!* But as he neared the building, Hartley shuddered. It's hideous! Somebody painted it purple! Next to the front door, a placard hanging from a post. Ysabel's Restaurant – Fine Food and Drink – 11:30–2:00, 5:30–10. VISA logo in one corner. Hanging below, a toothed Rotary wheel – Every Tuesday at Noon.

Hartley climbed the front steps and tested the door. It opened easily. He hesitated, then walked in. What he saw nearly knocked him over. The outline of the room was familiar, but nothing else. The pews were gone, the pulpit was gone. The room was set with tables and chairs, typical restaurant-style. Overhead, brightly colored piñatas hung from long cords, and straw sombreros adorned the walls, interspersed with travel posters – resort destinations, as best he could make out in the dimly lit interior. The room smelled of cooking. Mexican cooking.

His feet made a dull sound on the wooden floor – new floor, it looked like. He walked to the front where, so many times, his father had conducted the communion service. On that very spot stood a table set for four. Hesitating a moment, Hartley pulled out a chair and sat down. Lacquered table, cut-glass tumblers, cloth napkins in colored rings. Totally out of place. As he sat there, tears came to his eyes, the first time in many years, and the memories flooded back, vivid and powerful. The music... his father... as if it were yesterday.

"I'm sorry, sir, we're closed until five-thirty."

Startled, Hartley looked up. A heavy-set, dark-skinned woman was standing in front of him. Her black hair was tied back with a ribbon, and she wore an apron spotted with food stains. She was wiping her hands on a towel.

"If you'd like to come back then..."

Hartley looked at the woman. He took a deep breath. "That's not why I'm here," he said.

She shook her head. "Then what is it you want?" She spoke with a thick Spanish accent.

"I...I was wondering how long this has been a restaurant."

"I've owned it three years. It was a pizza place before that."

"Are you Ysabel?"

"Ysabel Martinez." She stuck her hand out.

"And you're...?"

"Sorry. Philip Hartley." He stood up and shook her hand.

"What is your interest? Are you a real-estate agent? You're wasting your time if you are. I'm not looking to sell."

Hartley paused. "This was a church once, obviously."

She looked around. "So they say. That was before my time. All I know, it was a real mess before Mario took it over. He was the pizza man. He spent so much fixing it up, he ran out of money." She shrugged. "His loss, my gain. That's life."

"But the people who were here when it was a church..."

"I don't know about the church people. It was a real eyesore, maybe even condemned. You know those signs you see on buildings." She laughed. "I guess God was not good to them."

She put the towel over her arm. "Now, if you don't mind, I've got to get back to my cooking."

Suddenly Hartley felt himself growing angry. This woman. This place. They were a *sacrilege*!

"You ought to be ashamed!" he cried, turning on his heel. He strode to the door, slamming it behind him. The woman just stood there, shaking her head.

SIX-FIFTEEN... already late. The hell with it. Let 'em wait. Hartley walked quickly through the lobby of the St. Francis Hotel, hoping to avoid any more encounters. A few moments later, under a hot shower, he replayed the afternoon's events. Strange... I've totally blanked out the drive back. Less than an hour ago but I can't remember a thing about it! He thought about his encounter in the... restaurant. That woman must have thought I was crazy. It's not her fault. She's just trying to make her way, same as everybody else.

Again, the memories threatened to overcome him. What if my father had been there for me... would I be the same person? He turned the hot water off and stood shivering in the icy stream. Forget that bullshit! Focus. Focus! A thousand people waiting for me. Wanting to know how the game is played.

He stepped from the shower and toweled off violently. I'll tell them how the game is played. You push and shove and scratch because you never know when you have enough. That's how the system works.

There is no way to know when to stop, so you never do.

LATER THAT EVENING, long after dinner and speeches, Hartley and a small group of the officers lingered in a corner of the hotel's piano bar. For the moment, the difficult day was set aside. He felt himself borne aloft on a powerful, kindly wave. His dinner remarks had been warmly received, and now his associates were hanging on their new president's every word.

"A fitting end to your tour, Philip!" Dave Hillary was sitting across from him.

"You had them eating out of your hand."

"No question, Phil. As a speaker you have it all over Charlie."

Hartley sat back in the booth. He was in a magnanimous mood. "Gentlemen, filling Charlie's shoes will be no easy matter. Mark my words, we're in for more hard times. Things are going to get worse before they get better."

"You can be assured of the Western Region's full support," added Hillary unctuously.

Several people in the far corner of the room were getting up and filing through the tables toward the exit. Hartley's eyes narrowed. The last person in the line... Frank Delgado! This makes the day complete, Hartley thought. He turned his face away, but it was too late. Delgado was standing in front of him. Hartley scowled.

"How are you, Delgado... what a surprise seeing you here."

"I come here all the time. You remember Will Cartright."

"Cartright." Hartley rose in his chair and shook Cartright's hand, then perfunctorily offered it to Delgado. He settled back.

"Aren't you going to introduce me to your friends?"

Hartley looked around his table. "Gentlemen, Frank Delgado and Will Cartright. They run Bay Airlines."

Delgado held his hand up. He nodded at Hillary, whom he'd met before.

"I guess this is what's left of your big dinner. Saw it listed on the hotel calendar. We even debated crashing the party," Delgado laughed. "But I thought to myself, I've heard enough tough talk for a while. It gets old real quick."

"I'll be sure you're invited the next time. You never know, you might learn something."

"I already know how you operate, Mr. Hartley." He bent over the table, his face close to Hartley's. "I want you to know," he said under his breath, "I don't appreciate that squeeze play you are trying to pull on me. When I shake hands on a deal, it's a deal. Maybe you've got a few things to learn yourself."

Hartley stiffened. "You're out of order, Delgado."

"That's rich!" Delgado threw his head back and roared. "If that's the best you can come up with..."

Cartright put his arm on Delgado's shoulder. "C'mon. Let's leave these people to themselves."

Delgado nodded. He waved genially at the group. "A pleasure meeting you all. If you hadn't heard, we're working together starting July 1. I look forward to a long and mutually satisfying relationship. See you 'round the airport." He pointed a finger at Hartley. "You too."

After they left, David Hillary leaned toward Hartley. "What the hell was that all about?"

Hartley shook his head. "Nothing. Nothing at all. We have a little disagreement with those people."

"I hope it gets resolved," Hillary said seriously. "We're really counting on them. They're an okay outfit."

"I'm sure we will, one way or the other." Hartley raised his empty glass to his colleagues. "One last round for the hard core."

Hartley signaled the waiter and sat back in the booth. What a day. So many highs and lows. Then, a downer like this at the end. Better get with Roger. We need to be practical... don't want to throw the baby out with the bath water. At least not right away. Hartley looked around. The piano player was singing in a dark, rich baritone...

> *...it's still the same old story,*
> *a fight for love and glory,*
> *A case of do or die!*

Hartley looked through the open doorway into the lobby. Suddenly his heart leapt. *Shelley!*

A flash of green under a fur... a young woman on an older gentleman's arm. The couple paused at the window of a lobby shop. As she turned, Hartley saw her face. It wasn't Shelley... it wasn't even close. He laughed at his foolishness. Who could come close? This has been a day and a half, he thought. Better wrap it up before anything else happens.

The waiter arrived with their drinks. Hartley took his glass and ran his finger around the rim. Shelley. That morning I was pissed... so pissed. But what if she really meant what she said? What if she had more than a... professional interest? There was that note, after all. I even saved it, put it in my pocket. Ripped it up in the car, stuffed it in the bloody ashtray. What was it she said? Something like... it was no joke. No joke, indeed. I wonder... if I called her, what would happen? I wonder. His mouth had a bitter taste. It's been a long day, he thought wearily, a long year, and it's just begun. As he visited with his thoughts, he heard the conversation around him but wanted no part of it.

"Phil, I'd better pack it in..."

Hartley looked up. Dave Hillary's grinning visage was hanging over the table. "...hit the road while I still can. Love to stay but, you know, home and hearth, that sort of thing."

"Oh, yes. Well, fine, Dave. See you next time." Hartley reached across and shook the man's hand, then settled back in the booth. His eyes refocused on his glass, then strayed again to the open door. The piano player sang on...

The world will always welcome lovers,
As time goes by.

6

THE METROLINER circled for landing, descending into the mid-afternoon haze layer above the Central Valley. Peering out his side window, Frank Delgado quickly spotted the problem, the reason he'd dropped everything and hurried to Merced. One of his new Metros lay sprawled across a grassy median, one wingtip in the turf, the other pointed up at a crazy angle. A broad brown swath traced the plane's errant path off the runway after its right landing gear collapsed.

Len Barney, the FAA inspector who had accompanied Delgado and his mechanic on the short flight from San Francisco, was shaking his head. "Nice piece of flying. Damn thoughtful of your fella to clear the runway like that."

Barney's gallows humor had a point, since anything disabling Merced's single runway automatically shut the airport down until the problem could be moved away, scraped off, or otherwise handled.

"I'm sure that's just what he had in mind."

These days, thanks to Bay's rapid expansion and its new flying for BellAir, FAA's regional office assigned to monitor Bay's operation was struggling to keep up. But massive federal budget cuts meant the agency had fewer hands than ever to cope with the growing number of airlines spawned by deregulation. In this summer of '81, Barney's crew was stretched paper-thin.

In a few minutes, Delgado taxied to a stop in front of the small terminal building serving this agricultural community at the western gateway of Yosemite Park. Sam Dennison, the airport manager, was leaning against the fence observing the arrival.

"Seems like the only time we see you is when there's a problem, Frank." A few months before, Dennison and Delgado had been caught up in a stormy community meeting called to protest BellAir's pulling its jets out of Merced, and its replacement by Bay. Tom Costa, Bay's station manager, was with Dennison. The Bay pilot who had been in command of the ill-fated flight was standing next to them, looking like he'd lost his last friend. As Delgado shook hands all around, Costa continued the briefing he'd begun by phone.

"Bottom line, we got a couple of irate passengers, that's about it. Except for the bird."

The pilot was one of Bay's newest captains. "Sorry, Frank," he said, gritting his teeth. "Everything was normal until the touchdown, then over we went."

Delgado put his arm around the pilot's shoulder. "Don't blame yourself. You did everything you could."

The men piled into an airport car and drove out to inspect the stricken Metroliner. Its three-bladed prop had been bent back in a shower of sparks as the plane scraped along the concrete. A wingtip was severely dented and its light shattered. One glance told Delgado it could be worse than it appeared.

"It doesn't look good for the engine," he observed apprehensively.

Delgado's mechanic nodded. "It was still turning a lot of RPMs when the prop hit. That could have thrown a lot of shit into the engine."

"We'll have to tear it down, no question, and that wing spar, it'll have to be looked at, too. If the damn thing's cracked, we're really in for it."

After the claims adjuster arrived in late afternoon for his own look-see, Delgado boarded a flight for Monterey by way of San Francisco. If the wing could pass inspection, with luck, aircraft 377BY would be back in service inside three weeks.

"First impression, I'm not too confident we can nail you for this one," Barney observed. "Sorry about that."

Delgado nodded. "That's the first good news I've had all day. We just can't afford that plane being down. As it is, everything we have's flying sixteen hours a day."

"You people're really going crazy thus summer. Not to mention what you're doing to us. That new flying of yours was the killer. That pushed us over the top."

"I never thought we'd fill all these seats, but our load factor's been running near ninety the whole summer. That is unbelievable!"

Barney gave him a long look. "Before you count all that money, let's get through Monday. If those nitwit controllers walk out like they say, it's going to screw things up royally."

"You don't really think they will, do you?"

"I dunno, but you heard the big boss. If they do, he's going to fire their ass. Trouble is, they don't believe the man because nobody's ever done it before. It's always been kiss and make up."

Delgado nodded. "That Reagan has a habit of doing what he says, sometimes just to prove a point. People forget what he was like when he was governor."

"My feeling, personally, I believe he'll do it. No question he wants to send a damn tough signal to all the unions."

"What'll the agency do if they go out?"

"Washington has a contingency plan. We're supposed to be briefed tomorrow. From what I hear, the idea is to shrink flying all over the country, keep the ATC system from getting so overloaded it breaks down."

"What a mess. Right in the middle of my best year."

"Yeah," Barney replied. "But consider the bright side. Maybe you won't need to fix that bird of yours so quick, after all."

AUGUST 3, 1981, the day thirteen thousand air traffic controllers walked off the job. Still half-asleep, Frank Delgado poked around the shower stall, groping with his foot for the bar of soap he'd dropped. Suddenly he heard a banging on the door.

"Dad! Phone!" It was Bobby. "It's Mr. Cartright! He says it's important!"

"Okay, okay. Tell him to hold his horses."

Quickly Delgado toweled down and, securing a towel around his mid-section, crossed the hall, leaving a trail of water on the carpet.

"Yeah, Will."

"Sorry to call so early, but I just heard from my partner in D.C. The East Coast controllers are out and it's spreading fast. It looks like most of them are staying away."

"Those dumb bastards. They are really going to do it."

"Word is FAA's going to cut the ATC system way back. I'll fill you in as soon as I can. Should be in by seven."

"Right. I'll talk to you then."

Delgado headed straight for the airport, bypassing his office. There, everything seemed normal. The early shift was making ready for the day, even though no flights were scheduled to arrive or depart for a half-hour. Then would come the test. Delgado spotted Marty Barron swigging a large Styrofoam cup of coffee.

"You heard about..."

"...the cutbacks? Yeah, we just got a telex from the commuter airline people in D.C."

"They do that and we are really sunk." Delgado stopped and thought for a moment. "Marty, I want you to set up shop at San Fran today. That's where we'll get hit worst if it happens."

Arriving in San Francisco an hour later, Barron came upon a scene of mass confusion. Most of BellAir's inbound flights were delayed or canceled. Would-be passengers milled around the ticket counter. One agent was cornered by a swarm of angry customers, and another stood atop the ticket counter waving his arms, trying to restore order. The FAA was indeed holding aircraft on the ground, not releasing them into the shrunken traffic control system until a slot opened clear to the destination. Nationwide, everything was backed up. The normally smooth-flowing system had been paralyzed.

Bay's chaos was a smaller version of BellAir's. After a few minutes observing and consulting with Paul Young, Barron reached Delgado.

"It's a real zoo up here, Frank."

"Same here. Things are starting to back up. What did you find out?"

"They don't know how many controllers'll show at Oakland Center, but they're expecting the worst."

"Wonderful. Well, keep me posted."

It would be a rough week for Delgado. Bay's flying was slashed in half, and its load factor fell to forty percent. Instead of nine paying customers for every ten seats, there were less than half as many. On Friday night of that first week, the lights were burning late at Delgado's office. He and his long-time controller, Marie Romero, were awash in paper. The day's *San Francisco Chronicle* lay on the floor. Its headline said it all: *FAA 'Rebuilding' Air Traffic Team – Firings Continue – Strikers Won't Budge.*

Romero looked up from her calculations.

"Unless we see a big improvement, by September you will be spending more than you take in. Just like the old days."

Delgado looked at her unsmilingly.

"I hate to be the bearer of bad news, but my projections show you losing three million in the fourth quarter."

"Nice Christmas present."

"I wouldn't put it exactly that way."

HANDS FOLDED in front of him, Philip Hartley sat at a table in a waterside restaurant in Marina del Rey, up the coast from Los Angeles International Airport, numbly watching the young TGIF crowd at the bar. It had been a terrible week for BellAir, complex and excruciating. Its schedules were an absolute disaster from massive cancellations and delays. However, as the week went along, Hartley decided to throw caution to the wind and take the offensive. He ordered BellAir's less profitable flying canceled, and redirected the airline's focus to its denser, higher-yield markets.

Instantly, tremendous political heat came BellAir's way, as Hartley slashed service into many smaller communities. Scotty MacLeod deflected most of the criticism, though coincidentally, some flights were restored to cities with particularly influential congressmen. After all, as MacLeod argued before an emergency meeting of the House Transportation Subcommittee, the administration itself had created the problem. BellAir was merely reacting to events.

Ironically, the emergency gave Hartley's commuter replacement program a major boost. Even Fritz Mueller was forced to admit what a godsend their junior partners were, delivering passengers to BellAir's hubs so its jets could enjoy decent loads and not be flying around empty, wasting fuel, crew time, and precious ATC slots. In retrospect, Hartley was pleased he'd backed off Delgado, even though the little pop-off still rankled him. Time enough to fix that situation when things settled down.

Weeks before the crisis Hartley had scheduled a trip to Los Angeles to meet with city and Olympic officials concerning BellAir's role in the 1984 Games. Roger Bankhead's sports marketing group was eager to secure endorsement as the "Official Airline of the 1984 Olympics," though to Hartley this would be a mixed blessing, bringing with it a huge cost in free transportation and other consideration. Hartley's Olympic meeting was set for Saturday morning, but the real reason for his trip was only a few minutes away, when he would see Shelley Gregory for the first time since the night in Honolulu. Had it not been for this rendezvous, the stressed-out Hartley would have stayed at his post in New York and let Bankhead handle the Olympics. But here he was.

Hartley looked out the window at a forest of swaying masts. They reminded him of Elaine. He felt a pang of what? Regret? But it passed quickly.

The twentyish crowd was lively and casual. Predominately white jeans and T-shirts with graphic designs, mostly, it seemed, promoting various brands of beer. In his dark business suit and white shirt, Hartley felt very uncomfortable. The restaurant was Shelley's choice, a standard business lunch place that obviously changed stripes in the evening.

Hartley checked his watch again. She was late. He thought back several weeks to his phone call. He still couldn't read her reaction. Surprise, that figured, but as the conversation went on he sensed a strain in her voice, even hostility. He laughed quietly. Tonight may see an Olympic record for brief reacquaintances. It was beginning to dawn on him that he had been stood up, but finally, at the crowded entrance, looking around, there she was.

He made his way over to her.

"Phil! Hi!"

Her smile put him at ease. She was very pretty, in close-fitting powder-blue slacks and a bulky Irish sweater that, to his disappointment, did nothing at all for her figure. Something else was different, too... her hair. It was in a short bob and she wore little makeup. She looked younger, much less sophisticated than he remembered. He led her through the massed bodies.

"Sorry I'm late. The traffic was just awful. I'm really embarrassed, I only live five minutes from here."

She looked up at him as he held her chair. "How have you been?"

"Fine, fine. And you're looking great." Her face seemed thinner than the last time. Maybe it's the lighting. Or the sweater.

"A lot of water under the bridge," she observed. "So what's the protocol? Do I call you *el presidente*? What's it like to be a president, anyway?"

"Oh come on, you don't want to hear about that."

"No, really, I do. After all, I am one of your subjects, aren't I?"

He flushed. "That's not exactly what we call them. At least not to their face."

She settled into her chair. "So, how is it? You know, running the whole show."

"Oh, it's okay. You can never put it down, though."

"Just okay? That's a surprise. I had the impression it was number one on your list."

"True, these things don't just happen by accident."

"I'll bet they don't."

Hartley was dismayed. What a very peculiar conversation. He decided to fall back on a sure thing. "Well, then, how about a drink?" He summoned a waitress over. "What'll it be?"

"You order for me," Shelley responded. Observing his blank expression, she shook her head. "Oh, forget it." She turned to the waitress. "I'll have a gimlet."

"A gimlet it is," Hartley repeated, "and another Stoli here."

Shelley was quiet for a moment. She picked up a napkin and began shredding it into small pieces. "I guess... I just thought you might remember," she said softly.

"Remember what?" Hartley asked, puzzled.

She stared at him, frowning. "Never mind." She reached into her purse for a pack of cigarettes and a disposable plastic lighter. He didn't recall her smoking.

"Listen, Phil," she blew a cloud of smoke to the side, "tell me, why did you call? I really can't figure it out. Is it because you're a big shot now? You're setting up a girl in every port, is that it?"

"No, no! It's not that at all!" He felt his face growing warm. "I just thought... I've thought a lot about you and I wondered, you know, how you might be... getting on."

She laughed bitterly, "I must say, I fear for our happy company if that's how fast you can make a decision. What's it been, anyway, nearly two years?" She stared at him. "Oh, *I get it!* You were expecting *me* to call *you!*"

"Of course not! Why would you do a thing like that?"

The waitress set down their drinks. Shelley's eyes were filling with tears. "You have the nerve to ask me that? I suppose that night didn't mean anything to you. Just one of many, that's all it was."

By now Hartley was a deep shade of red. "You're hardly in a position to lecture me about *that* sort of thing."

She began to cry. Hartley tugged at his collar. People at nearby tables were looking at them. She pulled out a handkerchief and wiped her eyes.

"I guess I had that one coming," she said, blowing her nose. "I'm acting like an idiot. I...I've had kind of a tough time of it lately. Though I don't suppose it's been any picnic for you, either."

"No, as a matter of fact it hasn't." He leaned across the table. "Listen to me. When I said I missed you, I really meant it. I don't know why I didn't call you sooner. I nearly did a lot of times, but it... it isn't what you said, not at all."

"I have to admit I gave up on you. I figured it was pretty dumb to think you'd call, just because I wanted you to."

Hartley took her hand. "Let's start over again. Shelley, what do you say?"

She smiled and lowered her eyes. "Well, not from the *very* beginning," she replied softly. "We already began once. Remember?"

PART FOUR

Fortune and
Men's Eyes

1

S EVERAL MONTHS passed. BellAir rebounded strongly from the controllers' strike, and as Philip Hartley had dared to hope, Shelley Gregory took a prominent place in his life. Prominent, that is, as schedules and decorum would permit.

One day in early 1982, Hartley found himself in a most unfamiliar setting. Mares' tails backlit in a brilliant blue sky, wind dusting the scrub brush with snow – it was springtime in West Texas. As soon as he stepped from the pickup truck, Hartley's eyes began to sting and he started blinking rapidly.

According to locals, every year this time, the top few inches of Arizona blow through – that is, whatever doesn't stick to New Mexico on the way. The week before, Hartley had been fitted for contacts, and they were complaining mightily about the glare and grit. It wouldn't have been a crime to be seen with eyeglasses for the first time in his forty-four years, but such middle-aged baggage didn't fit the vigorous, youthful image that BellAir's new leader meant to project. Damn! he thought, fishing in his parka for his sunglasses, what a miserable place!

"Well, fellas, in a coupl'a weeks this'll *all be yours*!" A strident voice broke Hartley's self-absorption. "Beautiful country, ain't it!"

"Yeah," Hartley muttered. "It's really something."

"About as far from New York as you can get." Roger Bankhead was stamping his feet to stay warm, raising little puffs of snow.

His eyes protected, Hartley surveyed the barren scene. It was impressive, he had to admit, in a bleak sort of way. Oil rigs, giant metal grasshoppers nodding in their sleepy mechanical dance, sucking black gold from the earth, ribbons of pipeline converging on a distant tank farm and pumping station. His would-be business partner, Len Garrison, was still waving his arms.

"It really pains me to part with this, fellas. Over there's where I brought in my first well." He pointed to a derrick a hundred yards off. "Nineteen and forty-eight, it was, an' the ole gal's still puttin' out. But I'm sure you boys'll take good care of her."

An idea of Bankhead's had brought them to this desolate spot. At first the plan seemed too bizarre to take seriously, but the more Hartley thought about it, the more sense it made. At a dollar-ten a gallon, jet fuel represented a full quarter of BellAir's expenses. Every penny swing altered the company's annual results by five million dollars. That was bad enough, but then there were the uncertainties of supply, since OPEC's oil embargo proved America's hydrocarbon society vulnerable to events beyond its borders and, to its chagrin, beyond its control. If the Middle East boiled over again, supply interruptions could devastate those airlines that weren't prepared. In the free market the race is to the fit, Hartley knew, the crown to the bold.

Bankhead's idea was exquisitely simple. BellAir should control its own fuel supply. Not all of it, of course, not even most of its needs, but enough to lessen its dependency on costly "spot markets" where the airline was forced to turn when other sources faltered. Warming to Bankhead's suggestion, Hartley told BellAir's fuel buyer, Campy Campanella, to check it out. Ultimately the trail led here, to Garrison.

Len Garrison was a wildcatter who'd made his fortune in the Permian Basin of West Texas. Campanella had learned that he was thinking of cutting back. Recently remarried, he wanted more time to enjoy the fruits of his labors. With Hartley's backing, Campanella made Garrison a proposition. BellAir would buy a major part of his holdings, and for an agreed fee he would refine the Jet-A that was BellAir's lifeblood. Thus it transpired, some months after Bankhead sprang his idea, that the three airline executives found themselves on this early spring afternoon in Andrews County, Texas, forty miles northwest of Odessa.

Though Garrison seemed rough around the edges, he was cunning, and not at all intimidated by Easterners or their retinues of bankers and attorneys. The oilman didn't talk much about it, but he held a doctorate in geology from the University of Oklahoma, and in high-stakes wheeling and dealing over the years he'd stripped more than a few Wall Streeters down to their socks. Garrison's own advisors in Midland and New York were the best that money, a whole lot of money, could buy.

"Seen enough, or you want to drive around some more?" Garrison removed a well-worn Stetson and mopped his face with a blue and white kerchief. He was a ruggedly handsome man of sixty, with an shock of unruly steel-gray hair, a straight nose, and a jutting jaw.

"Let's show them that refinery on One-Fifteen," Campanella said, consulting his map. By now he was intimately familiar with Garrison's facilities. "It's on our way back to the airport, anyway."

The men clambered into Garrison's stretched pickup, sinking into the sheepskin-covered seats. He adjusted his world-class sound system, and, accompanied by Hank Williams, they roared off toward the refinery. After a brief stop at this facility, which would process much of BellAir's crude, Garrison radioed ahead to Odessa, where his Gulfstream jet was poised to fly the men to Dallas, BellAir's nearest online city. Later that afternoon, after onboard drinks and hors d'oeuvres, they set down at DFW for a connection with BellAir's six-forty flight to New York.

"You fellas got yourself quite a deal, if I do say so," Garrison remarked as they shook hands at the door of his plane. "Fact, the more I think about it, I'm afraid you took advantage of this ole country boy."

Campanella put his head back and roared. "Yeah, right! Ever since I met you, I've had one hand on my wallet. Sometimes both!"

"Good doing business with you," Hartley added. "We shouldn't have any trouble getting this deal through our board."

"I don't envy you there, Phil. Never had much truck with boards myself. Just got this puny little one, my brother and my lawyer, coupl'a sidekicks. Don't make much use of it, but when I say jump, by golly, they want to know how high!"

"I'm not quite to that point," Hartley smiled. "Maybe next year."

After running the gauntlet of BellAir's local management who had turned out for the boss, Hartley and Bankhead were relaxing in the stretch 727 as it was readied for departure. The lower-ranking Campanella was squeezed into a middle seat in coach. A last-minute paying customer bumped him from the first class ride he'd been looking forward to all day.

Hartley was idly leafing through the airline's inflight magazine. "I've been thinking about who should head this fuel operation of ours."

This puzzled Bankhead. He had assumed the new subsidiary would automatically slide under Fritz Mueller's box in the organization chart. Campanella reported to Mueller, and Fritz styled himself something of a fuel expert.

"As a matter of fact, Roger, I've made a decision. You're going to run it. Along with everything else you're doing, of course."

"I'm flattered," Bankhead replied after recovering from his surprise. "But what about Fritz?"

"I need somebody I can really trust on this one." Hartley frowned. "You'd better believe a lot of people are going to try and make us look bad. Fritz's been bitching and moaning ever since we first surfaced the idea. Wait'll he finds out he won't even be running it."

"But we need him on board to make it work. I mean, I hear what you're saying, but I'm not sure it's the best way to go."

Hartley smiled. Refreshing, Bankhead's candor. "Don't worry about Fritz. At this point in his life we have him so tied up he has no choice. There's still two years before he's fully vested, and he's not a wealthy man. He'll come around."

He slapped Bankhead's knee. "Roger Bankhead, President of BellAir Resources! Bet you never thought you'd be in the oil business, did you, pardner!" The jetway and terminal were receding as the plane pushed back for departure. "It's going to be a fast ride, Roger. Hang on tight!"

As they took off, Bankhead returned to his magazine. He stared at it but was unable to concentrate. Should be grateful but, I don't know... for some reason Phil's not thinking things through the way he ought to. We'd be up shit's creek without Fritz. *Why not* just let him run the damn thing? I don't need it. What's the point?

FOR OVER TWENTY MINUTES, J. Marshall Smith had been cooling his heels outside Hartley's office. Since ascending to his vice-presidency (acting), Smith seemed to have mellowed. His opinions were more discreet, and it was noted that his taste in clothing had improved. Gone were the shiny polyester suits, the gold-buckle loafers and ankle-length brown socks, their place taken by dark worsteds and Brooks Brothers button-downs. These days, even Smith's longish hair was neatly trimmed. No more moss behind this good old boy's ears. The transformation amused Smith's fellow officers no end. Invited onto the front step of their exclusive club, Smith was trying so hard to make it inside. Though they saw his efforts as mechanical and inept, such emulation was gratifying, another vote for the BellAir corporate style, their chosen way.

Recent appearances aside, however, the soul of J. Marshall Smith still burned with fervor. His mission was unchanged: to exorcise evil from the body corporate wherever it was to be found. If anything, from his position of greater influence, wider vistas now opened to him, calling for redoubled efforts, although, by the same token, greater cleverness and subtlety.

"He's free, Marshall, go on in."

Hartley's secretary, Valerie Wood, gestured toward the closed door. Smith quickly gathered his thick stack of folders. Hartley was at his desk, signing correspondence. Routinely, he invited guests to join him at his conference table, but this time he chose to preside at the more formal setting of his desk. While Hartley was favorably disposed toward Smith – he had hired and promoted him, after all – J. Marshall had a way of getting under his skin. Occasionally he needed to be put in his place. Today, four feet of solid oak and a chair several inches lower than Hartley's would set the right tone. Smith sat quietly with his hands folded as Hartley finished a letter and tossed it in his out-box.

"Well, Marshall, what's on your mind?"

"It's about our drug program, Philip." Smith pulled a blue-jacketed sheaf of papers from one of his folders and handed it across the desk.

"'Eliminating Substance Abuse in the BellAir Workplace'," Hartley read aloud. "Catchy title."

"That's true, but what we're actually goin' to call it, is 'Corporate Leadership to Eliminate All Narcotics.' C-L-E-A-N! Tell me *that's* not one terrific name!"

Hartley tapped the thick document. "Twenty-five words or less, what's in here?"

Smith opened his copy to the first page. "Basically there's three elements. The heart of it's the random testing, and that's for all employees, not just pilots, but mechanics, ramp workers, reservationists, the whole bit..."

"Officers?" Hartley asked, raising his eyebrows.

Smith smiled. "Well, no. You have to draw the line somewhere. There's other ways of gettin' at that. Now, this next part has to do with discipline. We've got new regulations and procedures, and ah can tell you, we mean to deal *very severely* with anyone who abuses the company's trust. Finally, there's the educational part, the videos and speakers and so on. We'll be working with rehab centers around the system, but ah must stress, *one chance* is all anybody gets." He drew a finger across his throat. "Mess up twice and they've had it."

For the next fifteen minutes Hartley questioned Smith closely. What did the unions think? How did Smith intend to pitch it to the workforce? Finally, Hartley closed his folder. "What does Legal say about this?"

Smith grinned. "Ah haven't run it by them yet. Figured ah'd stand a better chance getting their okay if you're for it."

"All right, Marshall." Hartley leaned forward. "Let's put our cards on the table. This thing is going to be dynamite, especially the random testing. The unions'll beat us to death with the privacy issue. You appreciate that, I'm sure."

"Oh, that's absolutely right, no question about it."

"There are only a certain number of hot potatoes I can carry at one time, and it happens I've got a fistful about now. So, what I'm saying, *you're* carrying the ball on this one. I can't afford to be out in front." Hartley looked down at Smith and smiled. "It's your baby, Marshall. If it flies, you get the credit."

"And if it doesn't?" Smith asked.

Hartley spread his hands. "Then I make full use of my wiggle room."

Smith paused, then a broad grin crossed his face. "Well, ah guess that's what you're payin' me for."

Hartley nodded. "I believe we understand each other."

Smith reached for the rest of his folders on the floor. "You know, another reason we need to score big here, ah got another program in the works that'll make this one look like kids' stuff."

"Oh?"

"Well, you know how ah feel about that so-called gay rights business. Ah tell you, it's gettin' clearer every day, the scourge those people have been asking for will soon be visited upon them."

"You mean AIDS?" Hartley responded.

"Yes, indeed," Smith replied, his voice rising. "That's *exactly* what ah mean. Can you imagine those people, acting in the most heinous way while they actually laugh at god-fearin' folk and the Christian values we know ain't easy, but who ever said they were supposed to be?"

Smith snorted "Faggots! It's about time they get the retribution they deserve! And there's something else, too. It's goin' to cost us a fortune in health benefits if we don't start doing something right now. Ah have to believe there's going to be a big reaction to this AIDS business, ah mean, who in their right mind'll want to associate with scum like that? It's a problem, all right, but ah see it as an opportunity! When we see our customers and employees turnin' on these pre-verts, finally we'll have a handle to fire their ass out of the company!"

Hartley listened in silence, thinking... Shelley. He grimaced. Her former "clientele." Who knows what she might have been exposed to. Too hard to deal with, too hard. Have to go on from here... hope for the best.

He pointed to Smith's report. "This is dangerous ground, Marshall. Don't do a thing without my specific approval." He nodded toward the door. "Now I have to kick you out, I need to get ready for a directors' meeting."

As he searched the desk for his board folder, Hartley reflected on his visitor. Something of a loose cannon... have to keep a close rein on him. But that enthusiasm is valuable. You need somebody you can trust with the dirty jobs. Hartley shook his head. There are plenty of those around here.

SOME HOURS LATER, Philip Hartley had finished his presentation to BellAir's directors on the Garrison deal. Technically, management could have proceeded on its own, but Hartley wanted the board's backing for this novel venture, such a departure from BellAir's normal line of business. Actually, Charlie had insisted on running it by the board, but if Hartley and Arthur Winston had the votes counted right, the proposal would pass easily.

Initially, Bell opposed the idea. First and foremost an airline man, over the years he had spurned many opportunities to delve into other businesses. Particularly now, with the airline trying to recover from its long slump, Bell's reaction was predictable. It's a bad idea. Stick to what we do best. If we ever figure out how to run an airline right, he lectured Hartley, there'll be time for other adventures. Maybe.

But as Bell listened, his position softened, especially after Hartley explained how the company would not be sharing in the risks of oil exploration. BellAir Resources would acquire only proven reserves, the exact amount in any particular well subject to some variation, of course, but overall, predictable enough.

From the outset Arthur Winston was a strong supporter, commending Hartley on his initiative. With Cliff Meltzer, Winston devised a complex financing scheme that avoided any need to dip into the company's cash reserves. Winston's backing counted heavily with Bell. He respected Arthur's acumen, and in Charlie's view, it was not a drawback that Winston's bank, as usual, stood to profit. Bell had to chuckle...Arthur's made a lot of money on us, but he always returns good value. Though once in a while I have to deal him and his bank out, just to remind him who's boss.

In the meeting room the four top company officers, inside directors, were spotted around the table among the other seven board members. In theory, those outside directors were supposed to be distant enough from the airline's day-to-day business to provide objective, independent counsel to the corporation and its shareholders. However, it wasn't that simple. Important ties inclined them to identify with company management, for fundamentally they owed their places on the board to Charlie and his inner circle who presented them to the shareholders for election. Then too, there were the perks – free travel benefits and generous directors' fees, $35,000 and expenses for four annual meetings. Each year, a BellAir director and his spouse could count on trips to Paris or Madrid, London, San Francisco, Hong Kong. For the out-of-towners, New York itself was an attraction. For some reason, absenteeism always increased when Detroit or Cleveland hosted the meetings.

There were other business relationships as well. Ed Horn's freight forwarder did substantial business with the airline. Martin Byrnes' catering firm provisioned BellAir's flights in a number of cities, supplementing the airline's own kitchens, to the chagrin of Chef LeClerq. The elegant and reserved Harold Nystrom's hotel chain had joint-ventured with BellAir for years on tour packages worldwide and held contracts for flight crew accommodations. And of course, Arthur Winston himself, so closely aligned with the airline as its lead banker.

Today, Marianne Keller's briefing package included a thorough analysis of the Garrison acquisition, prepared by Bankhead under Hartley's supervision. Ordinarily, key directors were lobbied in advance by Charlie Bell on controversial issues to ensure the vote came out right, but this time Bell had been notably inactive. He neither called, nor met, nor twisted any arms, for deep down, he still did not welcome Hartley's innovative proposal and accorded it only lukewarm support.

In the end, Bell allowed the plan to go forward, but he decided to let Winston intercede with the board. Charlie was surprised when he heard Phil was making some calls, himself. Well, it's his idea, he thought, I guess he should take responsibility for selling it. In the board meeting Bell spoke briefly for the proposal but took great pains to point out the downside aspects, making Hartley squirm in his seat as he did.

When the roll was called the vote stood at nine for, including Bell, Hartley, of course, and Ben Peterson. Winston abstained because of his bank's financial interest in the deal. Only one director, Fritz Mueller, voted against. Bell wasn't surprised. Over the years Fritz had vehemently opposed all diversions from the airline's core business. Charlie knew Fritz was enraged at being dealt out of the new organization, feeling it was just another nail in the coffin for him. That issue, Charlie debated at length with Hartley, but again he decided not to override his protégé's judgment. How can I test him if I don't let him live with his mistakes, Bell reasoned. Within limits, of course.

Ironically, Mueller himself was responsible for Bell's coming around. Charlie knew, for all his grousing, Fritz would continue to hang in, loyal foot soldier that he was. So when Bell received Marianne Keller's tally and asked that the vote be made unanimous, as he always did on important issues, he looked down the table at Mueller. His old colleague just shrugged.

Thus, with the stroke of a pen, Philip Hartley was in the oil business.

The meeting ended at three-thirty. After accepting congratulations, Hartley excused himself to catch BellAir's late afternoon flight for Los Angeles. He'd built enough business into the trip for respectability and to mollify Elaine, who, it turned out, mentioned something about weekend plans of her own. Hartley's excitement grew as he envisioned the two days he and Shelley would spend together, the longest time yet they would have to themselves. He was looking forward to seeing her new condo. The apartment had become impossible, with the ever-present risk of discovery by her flight attendant roommates. Now they could see each other more often, while maintaining the all-important facade of appearances. The expense to him was certainly tolerable, a modest down payment, a monthly contribution.

These golden moments they stole were theirs and theirs alone. There could be no other way.

2

O N A FRIDAY afternoon in early May, Frank Delgado stopped off in Palo Alto to watch son Manny in Stanford's spring football scrimmage. Hope springs eternal, even for fathers of third-team quarterbacks. Delgado's next stop would be San Francisco Airport, and the last, an overnight visit with his sister in the Mission District, positioning him for an unusual Saturday meeting at Will Cartright's office.

As Delgado passed through airport security, he noted with annoyance that the so-called moving sidewalk was again down for repairs. Swimming against a flood of humanity – a couple of BellAir widebodies must have just arrived – he reached Bay's holdroom, finding it jammed with passengers waiting for their flights.

Clustered behind a podium serving his two gates were the flight information boards. Bay 2610 to Sacramento and Stockton, a 4:50 departure, ON TIME...2833 for Fresno and Bakersfield, ON TIME, 4:55...2666, due in from Monterey at 5:05, then turning and departing for Monterey and Santa Barbara. And this was just the late afternoon rush. The airline would see many more arrivals and departures before it shut down around ten.

Delgado looked around, invigorated by the lively scene. After the controllers walked out the previous August, it had been a long way back for Bay, but they'd had a terrific Christmas and since then things had been gangbusters. Unfortunately, not so for the fired controllers. Most of them were still on the street, hoping somehow to get their jobs back. Just the other day he'd heard that another friend, a former controller at Monterey tower, lost his house to the bank.

Several of them were now working for him on the ramp, but there was no way he could match their controller pay, not even close. A lot of second thoughts in that crowd, throwing good jobs away, high-school graduates making thirty-five, forty thou a year. Why they did it was beyond him.

"Frank!" Paul Young greeted Delgado. "Didn't know you were coming up today."

"Just happened to be in the neighborhood. Have to keep you guys honest. If it isn't too late, that is."

"Hey, it's never too late. So what brings you to town?"

Delgado thought for a moment. Can't let the cat out of the bag yet. They'll hear about it soon enough. "Oh, a little of this, a little of that, stopped in on Manny's spring practice, visiting my sister in the city. That sort of thing."

"How's he doing down there, anyway?"

"He looked damn good today. I tell you, if he keeps throwing the ball like that, he'll see some serious action this fall."

"Must be tough playing behind Elway. Has he figured out what he wants to do with his life?"

"Next to being a first-round draft choice?" Delgado laughed. "I don't know. With those courses he's taking, he could do about anything. He's even been talking law school."

Young grimaced. "You'd set another attorney loose in the world, would you?"

"Sorry. I forgot you've had a snootful of that lately. Your divorce final yet?"

"Next week, knock on wood. By the way, yesterday I had another call from your friend and mine, BellAir's own Peter Churchman."

Delgado frowned. "I told him not to call you. You don't have to take that crap from him."

"This one wasn't so bad, but they never miss a chance to stick the needle in."

"Damn! It's not like we aren't doing everything we can to keep up."

"At least their people here are okay." Young scanned the crowded waiting area. "They see us busting our ass. It's those idiots in corporate that don't know what end is up."

Delgado bristled. Mention of the BellAir brass always put him in mind of Philip Hartley. "I get a couple of calls every week myself." he said sourly.

"But what can they really do?"

"Well, that's the point. A lot of bluff, is all it is. There's no way they're going to bring their jets back in the valley, and I dare them to tell me who could do the job half as good as we are. We are doing one helluva job for them, considering our volumes."

The pager on Young's belt beeped. He switched it off and walked over to the check-in podium, reaching inside for a phone. A moment later he hung up.

"Message from your office," he said, handing Delgado a slip of paper. "Some guy named Mike Webb wants you to call him. Two-one-four area code."

"Huh. He's with American." Delgado looked at his watch. "I wonder what he wants."

"Oh, probably nothing at all. They just want to buy the company or something. Use my office. You'll want privacy for an important call like that."

Delgado looked at Young curiously. "Full of laughs today, aren't you?"

THE SCENT OF FRESH COFFEE greeted Delgado as he walked into Will Cartright's reception area. A secretary was arranging a platter of doughnuts.

"Help yourself, Mr. Delgado," she said cheerfully as he passed by, heading for the conference room. His new accountant, Bert Robbins, was already there, talking with a man he had never seen before. From the underwriting firm, he surmised. Cartright was right behind him.

"Morning, Frank." Cartright gestured at the newcomer. "Meet Russ Connolly from Drexel."

A slightly built man with wispy blond hair reached across the table. "A pleasure, Mr. Delgado, a real pleasure."

"Same here. Hi, Bert, how the hell are you?"

"Good, Frank, for this early on a Saturday."

"Have a fat pill, everybody," Cartright said, nodding at the doughnuts and taking his place at the head of the table. "Well, let's get started. We've got a lot to cover. As you all know, our purpose today is to map out the program to take Bay Airlines public."

He looked at Delgado, who was rolling a pencil between his

thumb and forefinger. "Frank and I have talked a lot about this, and we believe the time is right to take the big step. The company's in a very strong market position statewide..."

"Actually," Delgado interjected, "with the national exposure we get from BellAir, we're starting to be known all over the country."

Connolly made a note on a yellow pad. "Interesting. We might want to think about expanding our sales effort for the initial offering." He nodded at Delgado. "We'll talk about that later, Frank."

The accountant handed out several spreadsheets. "This details the plan for the use of funds from the offering. Paying down Bay's debt is a big part of it, but this'll also provide capital for some of Frank's other moves, particularly the additional Metros and improving his maintenance facilities."

"Right now the market looks good," Connolly added. "The analysts expect airlines to make a move this summer. Our people in New York are especially bullish on smaller carriers with solid ties to the majors, like yours with BellAir, Frank."

Cartright consulted his notes. "Our first cut has the initial offering at 1.8 million shares. Frank, that means your shares would represent about fifty-five percent of the total outstanding, after all is said and done."

"And you're guaranteeing me that's enough to keep control of the company," Delgado responded, solemnly.

"For all practical purposes that's right. Counting your partners' shares and what we'll set aside for employees, you'll have almost seventy percent in friendly hands."

Delgado turned to Connolly. "So how much do you think we can raise?"

"Of course, we'll have a better idea when we get closer in," Connolly replied, "but let's assume we go out at ten dollars a share..."

Delgado whistled.

Connolly nodded. "Actually, it could go higher, based on some recent deals, but assuming ten bucks, after the underwriting discount and..."

Delgado interrupted, "The what?"

"That's a polite way of saying, 'Russ's fee,'" Cartright explained.

"As I was saying," Connolly continued, "after the 'expenses of the issue,' let me put it that way, Bay would stand to clear on the order of $16 to $18 million."

Delgado swallowed hard. "You really believe we'll do *that*?"

"Absolutely. Unless things fall apart between now and then. You won't do worse, you could do a lot better."

"Now, looking at it from your personal standpoint," Cartright continued, "if the stock were to end up trading around the offering price, you'll be a wealthy man. On paper, at least."

"I'll believe that when I see it," Delgado grinned wryly. "What happens if I want to sell some of it?"

Connolly responded. "Well, that's where we have to be careful. Sell too much and you depress the value. People tend to get nervous if they think the key man's bailing out. Actually, we'll have to insist that you not sell for some time after the offering. That's standard practice."

"The SEC restrictions on insider selling, you and I'll need to spend some time on those," said Cartright. "But more to the point, you don't want to reduce your control stake. That's what would happen if you sold any appreciable amount."

"Yeah, that's true. So, what you're telling me, I'm rich but I can't get my hands on any of it."

"It's not quite *that* bad," said Robbins. "You know what they say, rich or poor, it's good to have money."

"Okay, let's move ahead. We don't have a lot of time to pull this together, considering how complicated it is." Cartright passed out a long sheet of paper. "Here's a flow chart showing who has to do what and by when. We'll start at the top."

For several hours, the men pored over the details of the deal. Slightly expanding their circle of confidants, they would meet again in ten days, then often over the next two months. Robbins and Connolly departed about four, and a short time later Cartright escorted his client to the elevator.

"I had a very interesting call yesterday." Delgado paused. "This guy from American called me, their marketing VP in Dallas."

"Oh?"

"'Turns out, they're doing a big review of the West Coast, particularly San Fran and L.A. You know, except for east-west they don't have a hell of a lot going out here. He wants to talk to us about working with them. Like we do with BellAir, except in L.A., too."

"That's all well and good, but you have a year and a half left on the BellAir contract."

Delgado looked at Cartright intently. "What if I wanted to break the contract? I'm at the point of thinking it isn't worth all the shit we take from that bunch." And it'd give me a way of sticking it to Hartley, he thought.

"The agreement is very tight. You'll remember we wanted it that way for our protection. Of course, if you had cause, say, if they weren't keeping some important part of the bargain, then we could try something. What do you really have in mind?"

"I dunno. . .American's a damn fine outfit. Thing is, if we don't do it, they'll go with somebody else. If they're really serious, that is."

"But if you tie in with them, BellAir would have to find somebody to replace you. Either way, that's competition. What's their time frame?"

"He was vague on that, but he wants to talk in the next couple of weeks."

Cartright was shaking his head. "Be very careful, Frank. Don't say or do anything we'd have to disclose in the stock offering. We sure as hell don't want anything in there about potential competition, nothing beyond the usual generalities." Cartright paused. "Something else, too, what Russ was saying, a good part of Bay's value in the market comes from your deal with BellAir. That helps your story tremendously. The next three months is no time to be messing around with that."

"Yeah," Delgado replied, "I see that, but it pisses me off the way they keep trying to put the screws to us. Maybe we could say they violated the contract in spirit?" He shrugged. "Well, anyway, take a look when you get a chance."

"What makes you think American'd be any better than BellAir?"

"I don't know for a fact they would."

"It may be a case of the devil you know and the devil you don't," Cartright added soberly.

"The devil part I won't argue with, that's for sure."

3

THE THURSDAY evening before the Memorial Day weekend, Philip Hartley was the last person in his office as was commonly the case. As the hands of his clock reached nine, he set aside his reports and papers and rested, quietly observing the lights of Manhattan. Rarely did he take time to look at the city, much less see it. This evening, as usual, Philip Hartley's mind was on debentures and deadlines, fuel costs, labor problems, and the myriad of corporate concerns for which he was responsible, though, admittedly, by his own choice. Then, there was his personal life.

Hartley stepped to the built-in wet bar and poured himself a large drink. Pleasantly warmed by the first sip and with the city at his feet, he allowed his mind to roam. Shelley...Elaine... He took a large swallow. Fidelity isn't the issue. There've been women over the years, brief and discreet, the excitement of the chase, the conquest. Though until now, I never wanted more from any of them. Traveling all the time, too busy to join in Elaine's endless socializing...she's taken lovers herself, I'm convinced of it. One dark-haired stockbroker at the yacht club especially comes to mind.

The emotional ties have loosened so much. I often fantasize, would I have married her if I had it to do over again? At first, there was that strong attraction, but things cooled so quickly. So disappointing. But in terms of my career, the answer is yes. No question. In that department she's more than I could have hoped for, encouraging, prodding, sometimes even offering surprisingly sound business advice. And her father's influence in the early years, that alone was worth the price of admission, the doors he opened for me.

Still, after twelve years, what's left? A hollow aftertaste, the feeling that all along she's been promoting herself, not my interests, nor ours, whatever *that* might mean, manipulating me as she does everyone else. We used to talk about having a family. She always was the one to cut such conversations short. Hartley laughed bitterly to himself...we haven't spoken of that for a long time.

Then there's Shelley. It's impressive, comforting actually, that she seems to want nothing but the simple enjoyment of being together. No hidden agenda...so unusual, these days. If anything, she avoids talking about the airline, even seems to resent my job and the burdens it carries. And she is so willing, so...passionate. He thought of her kiss, her touch. She makes me feel whole, a complete man.

But accustomed as he was to plotting every move, Shelley represented a strange blind spot in Philip Hartley's life. Where she was concerned, he simply could not bring himself to look to the future. She was his only spontaneity. He hadn't the faintest idea how their relationship might resolve itself, if at all. In fact, he harbored the hope it would never change, that as he accepted Elaine's limited though useful offerings, he might continue to enjoy the time he and Shelley stole together.

He was well aware of the risk. As Charlie Bell became more erratic and distant, Hartley sensed he was closing in on the prize, and it was doubly important to maintain his image, the image of the guarded, conservative, professional man. Any slip could be fatal. Take Fritz. Everyone knew of his philandering, and his indiscretions had cost him dearly at the pivotal point of his career. Hartley had no illusions; Fritz certainly would have been Charlie's choice for the top job, if not for his disregard of corporate mores and style. For though Charlie talked a good game, when it came to the company, as Hartley saw it, what mattered was less what you did than how you went about doing it. Plenty of the officers had something going on the side, but they were discreet, the only trace the offhand jokes, the admiring innuendoes within the confidence of the inner circle.

Nor was divorce a way out. The organization frowned on divorce, for it severed social ties that, though seldom lasting and frequently not even cordial, supplied a vital veneer of respectability. Even slight imperfections were resented. The officer in a divorce was a marked man. Clearly, he had failed to manage his domestic life competently. What other flaws might this suggest? An intemperate personality? Some instability that foreshadowed trouble in what really mattered – his department, his division, his region.

Fritz had run afoul of another important precept, for his catting around had gravely embarrassed the long-suffering Margaret. That simply wasn't right. Pain was one thing if kept private, but shame was not acceptable. With this, Hartley agreed. You do not rub a woman's nose in it. Better you make a clean break and take the consequences, though, as he often thought, for me that's not possible. He poured himself another drink. No, that's not in the cards at all.

THE NEXT MORNING, Philip Hartley found himself in the lobby of one of Manhattan's oldest hotels, which, he noted with distaste, looked shabbier every time he saw it. Two seedy bellhops lazed near the front desk, their drab uniforms matching all too well the dusky rose drapes and lobby furniture. A cleaning woman pushed her vacuum across a carpet that was ragged and threadbare in places.

Once a crown jewel of the city, host to presidents and kings, a worthy rival to the Waldorf Astoria and the nearby Plaza, the Park View was no longer an appealing place to visit, much less to stay in. Time was, a flicker of desire on the face of a Park View guest would be enough to summon an attendant instantly, but those days were long past. Hartley frowned, thinking of the so-called banquet he recently attended in the hotel's main ballroom. The food was terrible and the wait staff in the terminal stages of EAS – Eye Avoidance Syndrome – the modern service-industry disease. By the time Hartley trapped a waiter into inspecting his chicken, it was stone cold on the plate, congealed in a puddle of *sauce à l'orange*. Nor was the grudgingly-provided replacement any better.

This day, Hartley was particularly inclined to be critical, because he was about to call on the person responsible for this malaise, his fellow BellAir director, Harold Nystrom. Thanks to Arthur Winston's efforts, Nystrom, well into his seventies, was still the largest single owner of Nystrom International Hotels stock, though barely holding a controlling interest. In recent years, a number of investors, particularly Japanese, were rumored to be interested in NIH, but nothing had ever materialized.

As Hartley approached the elevators, an elderly Black operator peered out, holding the door. Edging into the cab, Hartley noticed the man's hand resting on an automatic control panel. Lousy management, he thought. Buy good equipment, then pay people not to use it. Suddenly

Hartley felt a tap on his shoulder. It was Winston, several bodies back in the crowded cab. Hartley nodded his greeting, again wondering why he had set up this meeting. When the elevator finally crawled to the penthouse level, it was empty except for Winston and Hartley.

"Here you are, gentlemen. Knock on wood, we'll have the express fixed by the time you're ready to leave."

Winston slipped the man a bill. "Why, thank you, Mr. Winston," he said, tipping his cap. "You gentlemen have a nice day, now, y'hear?"

"I normally give Horace a little something," Winston commented as they crossed the foyer. "I make it a practice to be recognized by the help wherever I go. You never know when it may come in handy."

At an unmarked door Winston rang the bell. "This should be very interesting for you, Philip. A bit out of the ordinary."

A short, wizened Asian man in a tuxedo opened the door. Filipino, Hartley surmised. The man's broad smile featured several gold front teeth.

"Hello, Mr. Winston," the man said, ushering them in. "Please. Mr. Nystrom is expecting you."

"Good morning, Carlos," Winston said, passing his topcoat and hat to the valet. "This is Mr. Hartley."

"How do you do, sir," he replied, leading the men into a large, high-ceilinged room.

Hartley looked around, shaking his head. Scattered about the room, in no discernible order whatever, was a wildly mismatched collection of trophies, furniture, and other *objets d'art* from Harold Nystrom's world travels. African masks, Chinese pottery, and – Hartley's eye was drawn to what must have been intended as the focal point of the room – the head and shoulders of a huge Bengal tiger. Across the room, two large double doors were open to the summer morning. A tall figure stood silhouetted against a thin curtain. As Hartley and Winston entered, Harold Nystrom turned and advanced toward them.

"Gentlemen, gentlemen, how good of you to come!" He grasped Hartley's hand. "Philip, I don't believe I've had the pleasure of entertaining you in my home before. Come, let me show you the view." Nystrom guided Hartley onto a small balcony. "Have you ever seen the likes of this?"

Central Park, an island of green, lay at their feet. "The lake is over there," Nystrom said, pointing. "Cleopatra's Needle, too, though this time of year you can't see it for the leaves."

After a few minutes admiring the view, the two men went back inside. The valet was pouring coffee from a silver urn. Winston was picking through a basket of croissants. "We've had many fine times here, Harold," he said, looking up.

"Indeed we have. Philip, I'll have you know we made quite a four-some, until my Marguerite passed away. And how is Catherine? Over that bug she had, I trust?"

"Oh, yes, back on her feet, busy as ever."

"Give her my best." Nystrom gestured at a sofa. "Why don't we sit over here."

He covered the distance in several long strides. Well over six feet tall, large-framed, with an angular face and a thick shock of white hair combed straight back, Nystrom's bearing bespoke his Nordic roots. Occasionally they had encountered each other on BellAir business, but now, as fellow directors, Hartley saw Nystrom regularly. Everyone knew the story of the Nystrom family's arrival from Sweden in the twenties, how Nystrom's father found work at the Park View and stayed on, rising to assistant manager to be far surpassed, however, by the son.

Early in his career the junior Nystrom happened to make the acquaintance of another rising star, the young Arthur Winston, who became his financial advisor and close friend. By this time, Nystrom was sporting a beautiful wife, a Parisian model, and together they were much in demand in Manhattan social circles. Backed by Winston, Nystrom's firm began to take over one distressed landmark hotel after another in cities across the country, restoring many of these treasures of more luxurious times. After the war came overseas expansion, and in 1952 he achieved his lifelong ambition by acquiring the Park View, where his immigrant father had toiled and he had spent his youth.

But now, as they made small talk, Hartley was struck how little remained of the man's vaunted fire and energy. He was convinced that this accounted for the sorry state of Nystrom's empire, which once had such a commanding position in the industry. As the pleasantries wound down, Hartley selected a straight-backed chair, declining Nystrom's proffer of the overstuffed sofa. Winston began.

"Philip, I thought it appropriate to let you in on some conversations Harold and I have recently had." He glanced at Nystrom. "Actually, we've been mulling over this idea for some time. To be candid, it comes too soon after our company's oil venture for my taste, but certain...events make it timely for consideration."

Winston took a sip of coffee, balancing the delicate china cup on its saucer. "We have here a rare opportunity, a chance for BellAir to acquire Nystrom International Hotels, and to do so on extraordinarily favorable terms."

Stunned, Hartley stared at Winston.

"As you know, several of our competitors are already in the hotel business. To me, it makes great sense to think of BellAir moving in that direction as well."

Hartley put his cup down, searching for the deft response, the right tone. "I'm sure the idea has merit, but, as you suggest, timing would be a problem, given our situation. I'd even venture to say, impossible."

Nystrom's face fell, but Winston was unfazed.

"I anticipated this would come as a surprise, Philip, but let me give you some perspective. You know I've advised Harold for many years, so I'm in a position to know the value of his company and, my goodness," Winston leaned forward, "the land they own in Tokyo and Hong Kong alone, it's simply phenomenal! Undervalued by a factor of ten! Not to mention London and, of course, their great properties in this country."

"I'll give you some background, too," Nystrom broke in, "if you promise to keep it confidential." His eyes met Hartley's, then slid away. "It's not a question *whether* I'm going to sell. It's a matter of *when.*"

Winston glanced sharply at Nystrom. "The difficulty is, if Harold's intentions became known, this could bring on other bids, and even with his personal stake, he'd be hard-pressed to block a sale if, let us say, another party offered somewhat more than BellAir might be disposed to..."

"But that makes no sense," Hartley interrupted. "Why wouldn't he *want* top dollar?"

The old man smiled. "Frankly, I want to do, or as Arthur says, to *attempt,* a negotiated sale. Oh, I know I could get more if we shopped the hotels around, but I'm well off, money is not my main concern. If it's possible, I want to leave my hotels with people I know and trust, and not, shall we say, to strangers. After all, the hotels have been my whole life."

Winston nodded. "I find myself in a particularly delicate position, since my bank has such substantial involvement with NIH. To satisfy Harold's other investors we'll certainly need a third-party opinion on the reasonableness of any offer from BellAir. And of course, I'd have to remain neutral on our board, at least as far as voting is concerned."

Hartley decided he had better get to the point. The conversation was headed in a dangerous direction.

"With all due respect, Harold," he said firmly, "what could your hotels possibly do for BellAir? We can't get involved in an investment that won't carry itself."

Nystrom started turning red. Winston jumped in. "Philip, I assure you, I wouldn't waste your time if I didn't think this was a fabulous opportunity on a strictly financial basis. True, Harold *could* probably get a higher price by auctioning the chain to the Japanese, but as he mentioned, he is not inclined to do that."

Winston began making little chopping motions with his hands. "My concept is for BellAir to take over NIH, then immediately put certain properties up for sale." He leaned forward. "Let me put it to you this way. If I can prove to you that BellAir comes out ahead, right from the outset, then what would you say to the idea?"

Hartley thought quickly. Arthur's pushing so hard...I can't afford to be completely negative. Better take a look, at least. No harm in that.

"Well, as I say, there are serious questions, but you know me, Arthur. I'm not one to turn down an opportunity."

"Good show! Now, that's the spirit!" Winston smiled. "What we need is the same sort of enterprise you showed with your oil venture. Today, all I want is to introduce the idea. Go back to the office, think it over. Ask yourself, if you had the hotels, what would you make of them? How would they help the airline? Your marketing man, Bankhead, he's discreet, I take it?"

"Certainly."

"Then I suggest you put your heads together. Personally, I think it would make great sense. Take our resort destinations. With Passages so successful, it seems to me we have the tools to capitalize on an airline-hotel combination! Think about conferences. Conferences with thousands of people, all flying BellAir!"

Hartley shook his head, admiring Winston's tenacity. "All right, Arthur. It doesn't cost anything to look."

"Excellent! Now, you'll be in town this coming week?"

"I'm planning to."

Winston patted a folder Hartley hadn't noticed before. "We'll meet again after you go over these figures Harold and I have pulled together. If you don't like what you see, we'll just forget the whole thing and no hard feelings. But if you do, then we'll plan on approaching Charlie and the board."

"You haven't spoken to Charlie yet?" Hartley asked, surprised.

Winston smiled. "I know how Mr. Bell will react, particularly given my relationship with Harold. No, Philip, if we go ahead, it's your show. So you see, it's essential for you to truly believe in the idea yourself."

The men set a date for the following week to touch base. In strictest secrecy, Hartley would have Roger Bankhead start analyzing the upside potential. What if, instead of their current arm's-length arrangements, BellAir could meld the hotel's marketing with its own? And he'd have Cliff Meltzer tear into Nystrom's analysis. Together, this would show how the two companies might help each other or, depending on how the numbers fell, the opposite.

After Hartley left, the two men continued to talk. "I appreciate your breaking the ice," Nystrom said, as they sat on his balcony. Winston sipped tea. Nystrom had nearly finished the day's second martini.

"It's my job, Harold, just doing my job." Winston gazed over the tranquil scene. Something has to give, he thought, and soon. "Philip's smart. He won't have to look very far to see what a mess your financials are. And that's not half the story, is it?"

Nystrom avoided Winston's eyes. "I only wish they didn't have to... pore over everything. But if they must, they must."

Winston stared at Nystrom's empty glass. What a waste, what a terrible waste. He never did recover from losing Marguerite...that's when the slide started, when be began to find his comfort in a glass. To Winston, the hotel chain's troubles were due far more to Harold's inattention rather than any thrusts from the Hyatts and Marriotts, formidable as those competitors were. NIH had been well-positioned to move ahead and prosper, but Harold frittered away the opportunities. Lifelong friends though they were, in recent years there had been many sharp words between them. Finally, sadly, Winston came to the conclusion, everything considered, Nystrom had to go. And, as always, foremost among the things to be considered was the Bank of Manhattan's stake.

For the last few months Winston had wrestled with his dilemma. If he encouraged the Japanese contacts – and he knew they could be brought along and an attractive deal made – he stood to lose his bank's highly profitable relationship with NIH. Not right away, certainly, but over time the Japanese could be expected to shift lines of business to their own banks, which were already aggressively competing in the American economy. On the other hand, NIH was losing ground fast, so Winston had to move quickly to shore it up and maintain, ideally even improve, his bank's position. The past year, NIH's cash position had worsened dramatically, and bankruptcy was no longer out of the question.

As Winston was shaving one morning, it came to him. With BellAir, he could cover all the bases, though Charlie Bell would be a problem. He would have to work around Bell very carefully. That's where Philip Hartley came in.

Nystrom poured himself another martini. "Arthur, what was it you said 'bout those Japs? They 'proach us again?"

Winston looked at his old friend with pity. . .and disgust. "I may have embellished the story just a bit for Philip. Actually, there is a group of investors looking, but so far, only for a specific Manhattan property."

"I see, I see. Well, I'm not innerested in that. But you're sure they don' want the whole company?"

"No." Winston gazed out over the park, his thin lips pursed. "There's nothing like that to speak of at this time."

ROGER BANKHEAD'S enthusiasm was predictable. More product to sell! The two travel giants feeding each other, with Passages the glue binding it all together. The possibilities were limitless. Joint frequent flyer and frequent guest programs, tour packages, the chance to lure hotel guests away from BellAir's airline competitors, the whole enterprise designed to funnel passengers to BellAir's increasingly crowded planes. Also no surprise, Cliff Meltzer was far less sanguine. Between the lines, what *he* found were steep borrowing costs, deferred maintenance and negative cash flow. But even with his unease, Meltzer offered a qualified "yes" to the plan, provided BellAir's cost of purchase was kept at rock bottom and several hotels sold immediately.

Winston's pressure weighed heavily on Hartley. The older man's experienced judgment deserved serious consideration, but what really mattered was his mentor's patronage. After much soul-searching, Hartley was able to persuade himself that the acquisition deserved to be made. The very factors creating risk also presented a unique opportunity, one that could be made to work, possibly spectacularly. The number they settled on was $345 million, subject to approval by both boards. Once again, the clever Winston devised a financing scheme to shield BellAir from the immediate sting of the acquisition, though Hartley was well aware they would have to turn the hotel operation around in very short order.

As a rule, Hartley wasn't reluctant to approach Charlie Bell with unsettling news, particularly when the problem could be laid at somebody else's door, but this one was different. It was his alone. For tactical reasons, Bell had been kept in the dark, but now, several weeks after the Park View meeting, Hartley sat quietly on the boss's couch, his briefing completed, waiting for Bell's reaction. After a long silence, Bell rose from his chair and started pacing next to his corner window. To Hartley this was a good sign. Charlie did this when he was thinking hard. At least he's coming to grips with the idea. Finally, Bell stopped.

"You may not know this," Bell began matter-of-factly, "but hotels are not a new idea around here. I probably never told you, but I had a feeler from Eddie Carlson about Western Hotels years ago, before he linked up with United." Bell chuckled. "As far as Harold's concerned, I even had a few talks with that rummy, but they never amounted to anything, and you know why? It never made any sense!"

Now Bell was standing directly in front of Hartley. "So tell me, what is it that makes it so good this time? Can you answer me that?"

Hartley placed his hands on his knees and looked up. "There's a huge difference. For the first time ever, we have the tools to make it work! With our computer tie-ins, we'll be able to sell each other like you could never do before. It's got terrific revenue potential, and that's not even counting the tax benefits..."

"Tax benefits, you say! *Tax benefits!* Good God, where have you been? Who needs a shelter if there ain't no rain!"

"No, be serious," Hartley replied. "We'll sell the tax credits, just like with our planes. You saw the projections. Everything's factored in."

Bell waved at the red "Confidential" envelope lying on his desk. "I didn't even bother to read that shit! When's it supposed to turn profitable, you say? Two years out? Jesus, who's to say we'll even *be* here in two years! Take on a bunch of falling down buildings and a debt load that won't quit? In a business we know nothing about? No sir! Not on your life!"

Hartley said coldly, "If I didn't think it would improve our position, I wouldn't be recommending it!"

"Recommending it! *You're* recommending it! May I remind you how much we're planning to spend on new planes alone this year! Two and a half billion dollars, in case you'd forgotten! That's *two-point-five billion!* If that isn't enough to keep us all awake at night I don't know what is."

Hartley struggled with his composure as Bell rolled on. "You haven't discovered this yet, my young friend, but around here you need to convince a lot of people before anything gets done. The day you start thinking you're really in charge is the day you start losing it." Bell spread his arms. "Take the pilots. We got a negotiation coming up, our biggest negotiation in forty years, and you want to tell them you just signed up to buy a bunch of fucking *hotels*!" He laughed caustically. "They'll frigging nail you to the cross! They'll say you're draining money away from our main job, and attention, too. And you know what? They'll be right! One hundred percent right!

"What about the people we still got out on furlough? And that pay cut we forced on management? How're you going to explain half a billion to *them*! Listen, Phil, I didn't fight you on that Garrison business." Bell was trying to speak slowly and calmly. "Okay? I didn't fight you. I went along with that, but *Nystrom*! Christ, I didn't bring you in the company to waste your time on stupid gimmicks like this!"

"Charlie, listen to me..." Hartley stood up.

"*No!* You listen to *me!*" He wagged his finger at Hartley.

"In this business you've got to think *airline*! When you get up in the morning it's *airline*! When you go to bed at night, it's *airline*! *Nothing else!* You say you want to run this company? Well then, fucking *run* it! Not something *else*! When you get a handle on that, we can talk. Not before!" Bell paused, out of breath.

Hartley tried to collect his thoughts. Slowly Bell walked over to the desk and sat down. Now he was smiling, shaking his head.

"Phil, I'll let you in on a secret," he began in a fatherly tone. "Maybe it'll do you some good. I never felt I was so smart I could spread myself around, not with so many people counting on me to do my job right. And I doubt you can do it, either. Sure as hell not 'til you get a lot more experience. No, there's no way we should do this. Let Harold peddle his junk to somebody else. We don't want it. I don't even want it getting out we *considered* it. Don't waste another minute on this stupid idea. I'll talk to Arthur myself. I see his fine hand in this one up to the elbow." He looked at Hartley gently. "Now, is that all?"

Hartley felt like a schoolboy who'd just had his ears boxed. "Don't ignore this, Charlie. It's not going away."

Bell frowned. He looked over the reading glasses he had just slipped on.

"And just what does that mean? 'It's not going away.'"

"Arthur's on board! And we're going to the executive committee next week." Hartley pointed to the red envelope. "It'll be best for all concerned if you take this seriously."

Bell's eyes narrowed. "Arthur's on board. Is that so? And who *else* is 'on board', may I ask? His lackey Horn? Who else, goddamnit? *Who else!*" Bell's palms were flattened on the desk...the veins in his temples were bulging. Never had Hartley seen him this angry.

Hartley stiffened. "Arthur and Horn...and Nystrom. Nobody else. Yet." He shook his head, "I'm sorry, Charlie. That's the way it is. For the good of the company we're going ahead on this. Read the report. Everything's in there."

"For the good of the company? For the company, you say? Bullshit! For the good of Phil Hartley!" Bell slumped in his chair, a wild look on his face. "So it is true, after all. You really would go against me. It's all lined up. First the executive committee, then you're on your way."

"You told me to use my judgment. Goddamnit, that's what I'm doing! And I'll tell you something else. I will sell it to the board! Read the damn report!"

Speechless, Bell stared at his protégé...but it wasn't Hartley he saw standing there, it was Dee. Dee and her angry warnings. A great sadness came over him.

"Get your ass out of here," he said softly. "We have nothing more to say to each other."

4

PHILIP HARTLEY and Arthur Winston sat in a quiet corner of BellAir's Skymaster Club at Honolulu International Airport. It was Friday of the week following Hartley's confrontation with Charlie Bell. The two men had just flown in from BellAir Industries' July board meeting on the island of Maui. Most of the directors and their wives were staying the weekend or longer, but for Hartley and Winston it was back to New York to set in motion the complex machinery for BellAir's purchase of Nystrom International Hotels. In the stormiest session in the company's history, by a slim majority the board had authorized the acquisition.

Winston nursed a scotch and soda while awaiting his flight, which wouldn't board for another hour. Hartley was watching carp swimming in a landscaped pool outside the glass wall next to his chair. He fidgeted with a damp paper napkin, twisting it into a ring one way, then the other, until it began to shred. Winston observed Hartley's jaw muscles working. His young colleague was obviously reliving Charlie Bell's bitter remarks in the meeting. After losing on the very close vote, Bell stunned everyone by taking the unprecedented action of adjourning the meeting, condemning the hotel proposal and its sponsors in the strongest language.

"I know what you're going through," Winston counseled. "But we have to put it behind us."

Hartley wadded his napkin into a ball and fired it at a waste-basket in the corner. "I didn't think he'd take it so personally," he said gloomily.

"That was unfortunate," Winston responded, "but predictable. He's resisted this sort of thing for years. But there's more to it than that. We're seeing a different Charlie Bell, these days. He's not the same man he was, even a few years ago."

"What do you mean?"

"He's lost his confidence, his resiliency. Deep down, he doesn't want to be out front anymore."

"I won't repeat some of the things he said to me the last few days. I knew he'd be against it, but I thought he'd come around eventually."

"People with power don't 'come around.' Everyone's supposed to close ranks with *them*. Obviously, Charlie thought he could carry the day as he always has, until now, that is. Do you realize, he didn't even discuss the hotel proposal with Ed Horn or me? Or with Harold? That is not smart, not smart at all. Take it as a lesson, Philip. Anything as important as this, a CEO simply must go to bat for his position, even with those in the other camp – in fact, especially with those in the other camp. You can stand only a certain number of face-downs like this." Winston sipped his drink. "If I may say so, Philip, you've handled yourself in a most statesmanlike manner, and don't think that has been lost on the directors."

Hartley picked up his glass and stared at the soggy lime wedge floating in a watery Bloody Mary mix. Normally Winston's remark would have cheered him, but he was truly troubled by the spectacle Bell had made of himself.

"I just hope we can patch things together."

"Don't worry," Winston soothed, "I'll have a little chat with him. The board has made its decision, and whatever the company once was, Mr. Bell works for us. Frankly, I'm more troubled by his attitude on the pilots." A thin smile came to his lips. "I assure you, that IAM fiasco will not be repeated. This time the directors will insist on going all the way. As far as we're concerned, you're calling the shots now. We can't afford to leave anything that important in Charlie's hands. I may mention that to him, too."

"We'll be ready. Count on it." Hartley set his glass down. "The acquisition team meets tomorrow. We'll have to move fast to get our offer ready by next Friday."

"Are you staying over in L.A.?"

"No, I'm on the red eye. I have to attend to some personal business first."

"You're young, stay up all night if you want. I'm past that sort of foolishness."

WHEN HARTLEY landed at LAX he headed for a pay phone. He had called Shelley's number from Honolulu, even tried reaching her through the airline's new inflight phone service, but the line was constantly busy. Waiting for it to be checked, he shifted uneasily from one foot to another. Finally the operator came back on. The line was in working order, she said. Most likely the phone was off the hook.

He'd planned to surprise Shelley with a call, then drop in, but now he was concerned. She wasn't scheduled to fly this week, though at the last minute that could always change. Hartley stopped to think. Less than half an hour to the condo...if she wasn't home he could easily be back for the onestop through O'Hare that left at six.

In a few minutes Hartley was heading north toward Marina del Rey. He quickly reached the modern four-story oceanfront building. S. Gregory, Apt. 401. He pressed the button. No response. Ah, he thought, she's on a trip, probably knocked the phone off the hook by mistake. He opened the security latch with his key and waited pensively as the small elevator crawled to the fourth floor. Down to the corner apartment. Ring the bell...wait. Still no answer.

Hartley unlocked the door. Dark inside, but was that the television he heard? He stepped to the bedroom door, hesitated a moment, then opened it and went in. In the half-light of the television he saw Shelley...fully dressed, sprawled facedown across the bed!

Dangling from its cord, the receiver was making a loud rasping noise. Hartley silenced it, shut off the TV, then opened the blinds. Cautiously, he went over to the bed and sat on the edge. She was breathing regularly...she appeared to be in a deep sleep, though every few breaths she gave a fitful start. He leaned over and touched her face, stroking her cheek lightly.

Thoroughly confused, Hartley looked around. As he did, his elbow knocked something off the nightstand that shattered as it hit the floor. He reached down. It was a small bottle. A piece had broken off, a stem of some sort, and lay amid the pieces of a shattered dish. He got down on his hands and knees...there was some white powder clinging to the carpet amid the shards of glass. He looked at the night table more closely. A burnt-down candle, a small plastic vial. Frowning, he opened the container, shaking its contents into his palm. Pills. Blue pills.

On full alert, Hartley wet his finger and touched it to the white powder, then to his tongue. Suddenly a chill surged through him. He slid up on the bed and reached for Shelley's wrist. Her pulse was strong and regular. He patted her on the cheek.

"Shelley, wake up...wake up!"

She moaned but didn't move. He slapped her soundly across her face. "Wake up, Shelley! *Wake up!*"

Slowly she opened her eyes, blinking them rapidly against the bright sunlight. "Whad're you doing here?" Her words were slurred. "What time is it anyway?"

"What is going on here!" Hartley looked around wildly. "What the hell are you doing with this...this stuff!"

She rolled over onto her back. "Get me some water...I'm really dry."

Hartley stared at her for a moment, then he went to the kitchen, opening the cold water tap full force. His mind was spinning. Jesus! This was when he and Elaine always checked out, when that fun crowd she ran with brought out their chemistry sets. Plenty of people were into that scene. But Shelley! He knew her so well. *It wasn't possible!*

He returned to the bedroom. Now she was half sitting, leaning on one elbow.

"Here," he said, thrusting the glass at her. "Drink this."

She took several long swallows. Water dribbled down her chin, wetting her rumpled blouse. Shakily, she handed the glass back.

"I must look a wreck."

"What the hell are you doing!" Hartley pointed at the floor. "This...*this is cocaine!*"

Her hair was matted. With no makeup she looked pale and drawn. Only two weeks since he'd seen her, but here, now, she looked twenty years older.

"Give me that mirror, will you?" she said, pointing to her dresser, "and the brush." He handed them to her and she inspected her face. "Oh, that is awful!" She gave her hair a few cursory strokes, then put the brush down definitively on the bed.

"Yes, Mr. Hartley, you are right. Yes sir, how right you are. It's cocaine. That's exactly what it is." She looked Hartley in the eyes. "I guess it was bound to happen. Sooner or later I knew you'd find out." She pushed a strand of hair away from her eyes. "Well. We had a pretty good ride while it lasted."

Hartley tried to speak, but no sounds emerged. Finally he blurted, "Shelley...Jesus, how long have you been into...into this! I had no idea!"

She forced a laugh, "That's why a gentleman always calls before he visits a lady."

"Goddamnit, this isn't funny!"

She fell back on her pillow. "Well, what do expect me to say?" Tears welled up in her eyes...now he saw how red and puffy they were. For a long moment she was quiet, then suddenly she turned and hurled herself onto the pillow, shaking the bed with tremendous sobs.

"It's over," she moaned. "It's over. Leave me alone...please leave. I just want to die."

Hartley sighed deeply. He reached down and put his arm around her, caressing the back of her neck. After a few minutes she turned around and looked at him. He put his arms around her. The sobs were coming in little gasps, now. She pressed her face into in his shoulder. They held each other for several minutes. Finally she began to quiet. He stroked her hair and kissed her neck. To his dismay he felt himself hardening. He broke free and shook his head violently. She blinked rapidly, confronting his stare with her own.

"How long, you asked. What about since I was fourteen? Is that long enough for you?"

"You mean, you've been involved with...this sort of thing since *then*?" He waved his arm around the room.

She wiped her eyes on her sleeve. "No, no, no. You work up to this. First it's beer. Parties and beer and booze. And pot. Oh, a whole lot of pot. Then uppers, downers...you know." She pointed to the broken apparatus on the floor. "But this...this's the best thing ever. It's so fast!" She laughed bitterly. "Do you see why I was so...obliging to Mr. Tanaka and his friends. This little hobby of mine doesn't come cheap."

Hartley's face was contorted with pain. "But you seemed so normal! This is incredible! I mean, I never saw any evidence! Nothing! Nothing at all!"

She eyed him menacingly. "My God!" she said, brushing hair away from her eyes. "You're not a man, you're a fucking recording! That mickeymouse drug program your lawyers dreamed up! 'Never saw any evidence!' What bullshit! Have you no idea how clever we are, to keep two lives going? Most people have enough trouble with one!"

Shelley's eyes hardened. "You don't understand. I *am* normal! I have to be damn good to play the game day after day, and believe me, my friend, I am far from the only one." She settled back on the pillow. "I guess you'll have to turn me in now. That's what your program says, isn't it? Snitch on your buddy. Isn't that what comes next?"

"I make the rules," he said softly. "They're my rules. I can do whatever I want with them."

Suddenly she threw her head back and began to laugh. Hartley looked on, befuddled.

"Yes," she said, wiping her eyes, "of course I'm safe. Can't you just see the headline? 'Airline President Turns in Druggie Girlfriend!' Oh, I'm safe, all right."

Hartley reddened but said nothing.

"You were thinking about that. You were thinking about your own skin just then, weren't you? Come on," she taunted. "You were, weren't you!"

Hartley looked at the disheveled woman, at the room strewn with clothes. "It so happens that I care about you...very much."

"You must be some kind of mental case." She shook her head. "Anyway, thanks for the thought."

Hartley forced a smile.

"No, really, I mean it. I'm just so fucking mixed up. I'm two different people. Which one is the real me...it's all too hard."

Hartley looked at her sternly. "You can kick this thing! If you want to, you can!"

The corners of her mouth turned up a little. "Such brave words, and to think you really mean them!" Now her eyes were afire.

"You know nothing, Phil! Not a goddamn thing! You think those words are new to me? A thousand times, I've used them! Ten thousand times! More times than I could ever count!

"You can be clean for weeks...once I went a whole month, but it's always the same. You get feeling sorry for yourself, and you go looking for it. Or it comes looking for you. Believe me, it isn't hard. It's there. I tried, Phil, I have really tried. I point my feet the right way, but it's like a magnet. It is a magnet."

Hartley was staring at her.

"Hey! Don't look at me like that! That's not fair! Don't!" A crooked smile came over her face. "So tell me, Phil, you ever done coke? Well, have you?" She closed her eyes and hugged herself around the shoulders, rocking back and forth on the bed. "No, of course not, not Mister Clean Airline Executive. Very bad for the image!" She opened her eyes and saw his shocked expression. "I'm sorry, but that's the way it is. If you could only crawl inside my head. My God! You have *no idea* how great it feels! I tell you, Phil, I've been higher right here in this room than I'll ever be in one of your 747s."

She closed her eyes again and was quiet. Several moments went by. Hartley thought she had fallen asleep. Finally she raised herself on an elbow and looked at him.

"You know, this is such garbage, what I'm saying," she said resignedly. "Garbage...my life is such garbage. I love doing it, I love how it feels, I love it and I can't stop loving it..."

She began sobbing convulsively.

Hartley took her by the shoulders and shook her. "You *are* going to stop this!" Her head snapped back and forth. "If it's the last thing in this world I do, *You – are – going – to – stop – this!*"

He threw her down on the bed and stood up, looking around wildly, "Now...now...get yourself cleaned up! Damnit! When was the last time you ate anything?"

"Dunno," she replied sullenly.

"Is there any food in this place?"

"I don't remember, exactly."

"Christ! I'll get something into you if I have to cook it myself!"

Shelley looked at him. Suddenly she clamped a hand to her mouth and bolted for the bathroom. She slammed the door behind her. Hartley could hear her fall to her knees before the toilet. He sat on the edge of the bed and slowly ran his hands through his hair. He stared at the closed door, listening to her retching.

5

FRANK DELGADO peered from the window of his van, watching a speck three miles out, over Monterey Bay. Rapidly it grew, curving in toward the airport. It touched down and rolled past. N377BY, the bird that lay broken at Merced the summer before.

"Bay One, cleared to cross Runway Ten Right and Two-four, proceed via Taxiway Charlie to Maintenance."

Delgado accelerated toward the large metal-sided hangar. How far we've come, he thought. Eighteen Metros, more on order, and still the ancient 402s hang on, so valuable and, best of all, they're paid for. Eight hundred fifty employees, too. Keep this up, we'll hit a thousand next year, easy. Nearing the old hangar, a cramped World War II relic, he smiled. At last, finally we'll be able to expand in here. As Delgado stepped from the van, several employees greeted him.

"Congratulations, Frank!" one old-timer said, pumping his hand hard.

A young red-bearded mechanic caught his eye. "Mr. Delgado, we've been wondering what this means for the new-hires. I've only been here since April."

"Makes no difference. C'mon, we'll cover all that in a minute."

Inside, the hangar was decorated with blue, green and white balloons. A banner hanging from a girder told the story: *AUGUST 25, 1982 – BAY AIRLINES GOES PUBLIC!*

For the festive occasion, the long workbenches along the back wall were covered by white linen tablecloths, coldcuts and cheese, salads, rolls, and soft drinks instead of the normal array of tools and parts. Delgado flagged Marie Romero down.

"Tell Will and Bert I'm here. We need to get started."

In a moment Cartright and Robbins appeared from the corner office. "Anything new?" Delgado asked.

"Russ says it's going great," Robbins replied. "Looks like all the shares'll be placed today."

"What are we trading at now?"

"Eleven and a quarter."

"That's real investor interest," Robbins observed.

"You talked to your partners yet?" asked Cartright.

"Oh, sure, first thing." Delgado smiled broadly. "They're out of their minds, especially Alex. Alex's had problems lately. I really have to give the guy credit, the way he hung in with us. A couple of months ago he was saying he needed to get his money out. Thanks, Marie." Delgado cracked open a can of soda. "Let's get going."

He walked over to a floor mike under the banner. As he tapped on it, a loud thud boomed through the nearby speakers.

"Seems to be working," he said, looking around. "Okay. Well, I guess you all know why we're here, it's a..."

WHEEEEKK!!!

"Oh, damn."

Quickly, a mechanic in white coveralls stepped from the crowd and squatted in front of the amplifier. After fiddling for a moment he nodded at Delgado, who tapped the mike again.

"That's better. As I was saying, this is a huge day for us, for you here in Monterey, for our people at the other stations. Today we sold our first Bay Airlines stock ever to the public!"

Delgado smiled as the crowd cheered. "That's exactly how I feel. Now, I won't bore you with all the details, but we want to give you an idea what it means and to thank you for getting the company to the point where we could do this."

Delgado took a sip of soda. "First of all, our stock is called BAY, that's B-A-Y, and it'll be trading on the Pacific Stock Exchange. Remember that, because all of you are owners of the company now and you'll want to follow how we're doing in the *Herald* every morning. I can tell you the stock started out at 10½ today, that's ten dollars and fifty cents a share, and it's already up to eleven dollars and a quarter. So all you shareholders already made some money!"

They began to applaud again, but Delgado held up his hand. "Now, some people have asked, why did we do this? What was wrong with how we were running the business up till now?" He glanced at Cartright. "When I think of all the trouble we went through to make this deal happen, I have to wonder about that, myself. But seriously, we needed to raise money for more expansion and pay off some of the loans we took out the last few years, especially on the Metros. So, you should be happy to hear the company's nearly eighteen million dollars better off than it was yesterday, thanks to what we did today!"

"All that money! What're you going to use it for?" a mechanic shouted from the middle of the crowd.

"Fair enough." Delgado lifted a booklet from the table behind him and held it up for the crowd to see.

"This is called our prospectus. There's a lot of technical stuff in here you can skip, but to answer your question, the money's going for six new Metroliners, and more spare engines and to build up our parts supplies..."

"Right on!"

"All right!"

"...and together with the bond money the airport board promised, in September we'll be breaking ground on our addition to the hangar here. Now, like I was saying, from today on, everybody in the company is an owner. Everybody on the payroll gets a hundred shares of stock right away, plus another hundred for every year you've been with us. This is a special bonus, a thank you for the job you've all done..."

Another loud cheer rang out.

"...and for every three dollars you invest, the company will match it with a dollar of its own. It's all in here," he said, slapping the booklet with his hand. "So take this home, we've got enough copies for everybody.

Delgado looked over the crowd. "You know, for a long time I've been thinking, what could I do to pull us all together, and this is what we came up with. If all of us do our jobs right and, knock on wood, things keep breaking our way, working for Bay Airlines will really pay off for you and your families."

A ramp agent standing in front raised his hand. "Since I'm an owner, what if I want to sell my stock? When can I do that?"

There was a chorus of boos and laughter. The man looked around sheepishly.

"So soon, Ernie?" Delgado tapped his watch. "You've had it what, six hours?"

The agent shrugged. "I'm not saying I will. Just seems like something I ought to know."

"That's all right. It's a good question. The answer is, some of us, like me, Marty Barron, the other officers, there are a lot of restrictions on our selling. I don't understand half of them myself, but for everybody else there's no restrictions, unless you happen to know some inside information about the company. Will, come on up here, help me out."

"What about taxes?" someone else shouted.

"Better get up here, too, Bert."

For the next half-hour a lively discussion ranged back and forth, questions about the stock offering, complaints about Styrofoam drink cups cracked in their packing cases, comments on how the arrangement with BellAir was, or, as several agents suggested in no uncertain terms, was not working. Delgado was about to wrap up when a uniformed pilot at the rear of the crowd raised his hand.

"Frank, some of us just got a letter from ALPA. What's your position if they try to organize us like they did a few years ago?"

Suddenly the room hushed. This was a sore point. During the pilot union's last organizing effort, harsh words were exchanged. Undercurrents of bad feeling still swirled around several Bay pilots who had led the attempt. Delgado scratched his head.

"You know, Mark, I heard there might be something going on along those lines, but to tell the truth, this is the first I've heard about any letter."

He threw another look at Cartright. "My counsel will probably shoot me for saying this, but I feel you're entitled to know where I stand. My position was then and it still is, we don't need ALPA, we don't need *any* union on the property. It's one thing if you have the type management that doesn't try to deal with situations, but that isn't the case here. At least I hope it isn't! If it was, I expect I'd hear about it pretty quick. See, the problem with the union, they're always looking for issues. It's no different from any politician that's running for something. They dwell on problems instead of pitching in to solve them. The bigger they make the problems out to be, the better they like it.

"Think about it! All of you are owners! Just ask yourselves, can we do a better job working together, or do we need outsiders coming in and telling us how to run our operation? That's my position."

"Yes!" Delgado pointed to a woman ticket agent at the rear of the crowd. She was holding up a prospectus. "It says here you own three million, three hundred thousand shares." Somebody let out a long whistle. "I want to know, what entitles you to so many shares compared with everybody else, when we're the ones working our butts off for the passengers, day in and day out."

The crowd began to mutter. An agent standing nearby told her to cool it.

"Marge..." Delgado paused before responding. "Marge, did I ever make any secret about my stake in the company?"

The woman shook her head.

"Of course not. It'd be different if it was some dark secret, but everybody knows how we got started, and you old-timers surely remember the lean days. It was Mariel and me and our mortgage that kept this outfit going and paid the gas bills. Damnit, that's how we met the payroll a lot of times, too. I guess I just feel this is a fair payback, and if anybody thinks different, you're entitled to your opinion. But hell, if we hadn't done that, there'd be no Bay Airlines today. You'd all be working somewhere else, and just ask yourselves, would it be nearly as interesting or well-paying a job?"

Delgado went on softly. "Last thing I want is to minimize how important you all are. I mean, that's why we wanted everybody to be an owner. But I will say this," Delgado pointed his finger at the audience. "Anybody who thinks I'm about to sell my shares and take a hike, you got another think coming. First of all, legally I couldn't do it even if I wanted to. But you know this is my life, this company. Ask Mariel. She'll tell you the company's our fourth kid, and she makes me feel bad because sometimes I act like it's the most important one."

Delgado looked around. "I guess that's it. Thank you all for coming, now let's get back to work!"

Cartright came up to him. "That was good, Frank. You handled that woman very well."

Delgado shook his head. "That one's always complaining about something, but you know, I'm not the least bit embarrassed. These people, they've all got a good job, good benefits, medical insurance, passes. Why complain? It makes no sense!"

"Now that the offering's behind us, I guess it's safe to ask. Where do things stand with American?"

"I'm going to turn them down. Even with all the crap BellAir gives us, the fact is we're doing better than we ever have. Like you said once, sometimes the devil you know is better."

By now the day shift was straggling in, most of them ticket agents and rampers from the terminal across the field. They were in a jovial mood, the day's work done, many of them looking forward to a weekend off. The grapevine had already picked up Delgado's message, so this session went more quickly. As he neared the end of his comments, Delgado was handed a note, which he read to his audience. On its first day of trading Bay's stock had gained a full dollar.

The meeting over, the employees took their leave, except for the front office staff who had volunteered to help with the cleanup. The swing shift was already hard at it, well before the leftovers were packaged for a homeless shelter in downtown Monterey. A 402 with an engine problem was being wheeled in, and the avionics people were troubleshooting a Metroliner's autopilot. After dispatching Cartright and Robbins on a flight to San Francisco, Delgado drove back across the field. He climbed the stairs to the terminal's upper level and stepped out into the parking area. Mariel was waiting by the curb.

"How did the meetings go?" she asked.

He leaned over and kissed her. "Real well. Couldn't be better. We sure have a great bunch of people working for us. Did you hear, we closed at eleven and a half?"

"How wonderful!" She looked at him seriously, "I hope now you'll back off like you said. You promised. Remember?"

"Maybe we should take a week and go somewhere."

"I'd love to stretch out on a beach, just soak up the sun!"

They headed for downtown and a favorite restaurant in one of the older hotels, off the beaten path. After dinner, over coffee, he took out an envelope and a pen and began scribbling.

"What are you doing?"

"Oh, I just wanted to see how much we made today, with the stock and all."

She put her hand on his. "Let's don't talk about it anymore. Enough to know, it's more than we ever thought we'd make in this crazy business."

He put his ballpoint pen down with a flourish. "Okay. You're right.

Like Will said, we can't sell anything now but maybe in a couple of months. I'd sure like to get that Stanford loan off our backs."

"And the second mortgage."

"That too. This sure isn't the way I was taught you make money. You get a paycheck every week and save a little if you're lucky. That's how we've been living all these years."

"Tell me about it."

The waiter appeared with coffee. Delgado sipped his quietly. Mariel looked at him. It was obvious something was troubling him. After a moment he put his cup down.

"I have to tell you something. I decided to turn American down. I called them today."

"You're staying with BellAir!" she said, dismayed.

He nodded. "The devil I know."

Mariel frowned. Suddenly she looked very tired, and worried. "The way you feel about that Hartley, how can you stand working with them anymore?"

"I have to. I can't afford to make any big changes right now." He shook his head. "I still can't understand how they could put a robot like that guy in charge. You know, I liked American, I really did. If I had the whole thing to do over, I would have gone with them."

"But it's not healthy. . .you'll make yourself sick."

He sat rigidly in his chair. "I am not about to give in to that guy," he said severely. "He is *not* going to get the best of me."

6

A CHIME SOUNDED. Philip Hartley set the nearly empty scotch glass on his latest copy of *Barron's*. Into the kitchen, cooking dish out of the microwave, off with the plastic cover. He stood back, comparing the stroganoff and noodle mix against the picture on the package. Close enough. Salad on a plate, leftover rolls warmed in the oven, a bottle of Bordeaux breathing half an hour.

He switched on the small television in the eating nook, flipping through the channels with his remote control. There it is, Mets and Cardinals from Shea, one of the last games of the season. "Wait 'til next year" time, again. He poured a glass of wine. He took one sip, then another.

Such a treat, a rare night alone, though the solitude seemed to set his troubles in sharp relief. Things were worse between Elaine and him. Shelley's rehabilitation was a huge emotional drain. Not that Elaine minded his inattentiveness, for increasingly their interests traced separate courses, touching at times but more often floating free. At least we're growing apart together, he thought, no profound regrets, either side.

End of the first, closeup of Dave Kingman sailing his helmet toward the dugout after a called third strike. Next, a beach scene, tans and bikinis plus lite beer equals good times, fun in the sun. Flash to a familiar face, some former athlete. . .forget the name, bragging about his underarms. Ultimate dry. Good for him. . .I needed to know that. Just as the field reappeared, the phone rang. Hartley glared at it, then picked it up. It was Shelley.

"Shelley! Where are you?"

"At home. I get home this afternoon."

"Are you all right?"

"Never felt better. Except for the ten pounds I gained."

"There is one thing," he said gently. "You shouldn't call me here. It's too risky."

"Risky," she laughed. "I could tell you a few things about risk. Listen, I wanted to tell you I appreciate everything you did, getting me into that treatment center, the leave of absence and all. Some of the people there, you wouldn't believe. Wait until I tell you about it."

There was an awkward pause. "When are you coming out?" she asked.

"I was just thinking about that. Maybe next weekend. Maybe we could drive down to Baja or something."

He closed his eyes, picturing that pitiful scene in her apartment he'd replayed a thousand times. He shook his head...try to be positive.

"This time I'm going to beat this thing, once and for all. I'm really going to do it."

"That's the spirit!" He twisted the cord around his finger. "Is anybody there with you?"

"Janie's coming over. She's going to stay here awhile." Janie French was a neighbor from her old apartment building, a bank teller, with no connections to BellAir. Hartley had met her. She knew of their liaison, but she was reliable, could be trusted.

"Tell you what, let's count on it. A week from Friday."

"Well, I'll get off. I suppose you have a lot of things to do."

"No, that's okay." He rubbed his forehead. "You know, the hell with it, if you need something, just call me here."

"Don't worry, I would anyway. Call me tomorrow?"

"Sure thing. Take care of yourself, Shel."

"I will. Love you."

Hartley pressed his forehead against the wall. He hung up the phone in slow motion, Shelley's words echoing in his mind. He shook his head and took a deep breath. There's my meal, untouched. He refilled his glass to the brim and walked back to the living room, dropping heavily into his soft chair. He shook his head slowly. Everything had been going so well...I sure got more than I bargained for. Best thing would be to drop her, right now. But even then, there's no guarantee it wouldn't all come out.

He stared through his window at the dusky twilight, the scene he and Elaine had shared so many times. I can't just drop her. That could really set her back, then Jesus! Who knows what could happen?

Maybe we can ride it through. I *do* care for her, that's a fact. He couldn't help smiling...she's like nobody else I ever met.

Wallowing low in the water, a barge was passing up-river behind two tugs. That treatment didn't come cheap. Six weeks, thirty thousand bucks, but it's not so much the money. Keeping it quiet, that was the tough part. She sure as hell couldn't be in the company program. Hartley smiled bitterly... *my* program, mine and Marshall's. And now he's pushing that AIDS business. There's no end to that man's ideas. He'd hang us all if I didn't slow him down. Already have a bunch of lawsuits on the drug program.

Hartley shuddered. I'm in so deep. Have to see it through. No choice. Damn! I had better get out there! Make sure things don't come off the track, make sure everything's under control.

THE PHONE was ringing as Hartley arrived at his office the next morning. Helen Foley on the line. Charlie wanted him, on the double! Hartley frowned. What could be so urgent?

He walked toward Bell's office, reviewing what the two of them had going. Since Bell's blowup, the need to work together had thawed relations somewhat. Over Bell's objections, the purchase of NIH went forward, and BellAir Industries now owned nearly a hundred percent of its stock. As the legal machinery gathered the loose ends, an interim team headed by the ubiquitous Bankhead was busily integrating the two companies' marketing programs, and the search was underway for a hotel company president to replace the old one that Hartley had already fired. For Bell, though, it was strictly hands-off. He ordered Hartley not to spend a penny of airline money on the hotels, to trouble him with major developments only.

As soon as he opened the door Bell attacked.

"What the hell is this!"

In Bell's hand was a sheaf of yellow paper, the *Aviation Daily*, bible of the airline industry. He was waving it back and forth above his head.

"This interview! What the Christ are you doing, saying things like this!"

Hartley nodded. Now he knew. Today's lead article summarized his remarks to a group of industry analysts, influential Wall Street experts who reported on the airlines. It paid to keep these gurus informed. Their recommendations could make or break a stock's performance. Hartley opened his mouth to reply, but Bell cut him off, whacking the paper with his hand.

"Here we are, negotiations barely started, and already the company in the person of Philip Hartley is playing to the galleries. This business about welcoming a pilot strike! What is it with you? You got a death wish or something?"

Hartley gathered himself. "We are using the media, all the tools. This time it won't be the good old boys cutting a deal in the back room!"

"Good old boys, my ass! You're so fucking smart, you can't even get it right! Demanding a pay cut? It's an *hours increase!* That we can sell! There's no way we'll get a pay cut! This is pure bullshit!" he screamed, throwing the paper down.

"We need a pay cut and we're going to get a pay cut!" Hartley looked at Bell defiantly. "Everybody's behind it including the board! Everybody but you!"

"The board! The board doesn't know squat about running an airline, and what's more, it's none of their goddamn business! They'll go the direction I point them in, like they always do!"

Like with the hotels, Hartley thought.

Bell's face softened. "Look, Phil, we've been through a lot together. It's thanks to me you're where you are. I appreciate what you're trying to do, but you got to be realistic. This company's not bankrupt or anything close to it, thank God," he rapped on his desk. "Nobody's going to agree to a pay cut unless we're down for the count, least of all the pilots. You know that. And I am not about to screw up forty years of good relations for something we can get a different way."

Hartley shook his head. "We've got to get our costs down. The Street wants a cut. Management took one last year. The pilots can, too."

"Come on, cutting management's one thing. What's a secretary going to say, for Chrissakes, or a goddamn station manager? But do you seriously believe the union'll give money back when we've still got some in the bank? Wise up, my young friend, that's not how it works!" Bell's voice quavered. "And don't you dare talk to me about raising capital, not after you just pissed away half a billion of our money on those fleabag hotels."

"Damn it, you know we put no money into the hotel deal!"

"Maybe not yet, but check with me in six months." Bell glowered. "You know, Phil, for such a smart guy, sometimes you're too smart for your own good."

He pointed to the newspaper. "You're way out on a limb here, and I'm not going to help you off it, either. You'll back down. If somebody doesn't saw you off first."

Hartley stood up. "Is that all?"

"Isn't that enough!"

Bell watched Hartley storm out the door. A great sadness came over him. He slouched in his chair, nervous, uneasy. Things were flying out of control. That hotel deal...clever how he did it, and who's to say? Maybe he can pull it off. But what a terrible risk. Already, mutterings in the pilot ranks. No coincidence, that visit last week from my old friend, Joe Hennessey, the ALPA rep and that new fellow...what's his name? Jarvis. Fine looking boy, that Jarvis.

He walked to his window. I won't give Phil the satisfaction of knowing it, Arthur either, but I argued with those guys, even made the case for the hotels, best I could, though I don't believe a word of it. But a pay cut? And force a strike? The absolute last resort. You don't make enemies of people you need as friends.

He looked down at his table. A copy of *Newsweek* lay open to a BellAir ad. Full page, color, a terraced hillside overlooking a white sand beach...young couple on a balcony, he's tanned and fit, the girl's in a beach robe, thrown open to show off her swimsuit. C'mon, call a spade a spade, her boobs. Very modern. Very modern but it isn't mine. Why'd I ever let them kill "Take Care"?

And Winston! Now Bell's heart was beating fast. Imagine! *Him* warning *me!* Warning *me* I'd better get with the program! Who's he think he is, anyway! Bell smiled grimly. He's a candidate for the trash can, that's what he is. Old Arthur's finally got too big for his goddamn pinstriped pants. But...that board meeting. He shook his head glumly...got to admit I was out of line, there. At least I sent a bottle around to everybody, apologizing...well, sort of. That'll fix everything. Bell gazed at the skyline.

Phil...Phil...what has got into him? I thought he had more common sense. Didn't even talk to me about the hotel deal until the damn thing was done. His eyes lit on the newspaper. And that miserable speech! Where do I find out about it, but in the fucking *Daily*! He picked up the paper and scanned it again, his anger rising. This one I can't let go by. I got to do something about it. Right now!

"Helen!" Bell shouted into the intercom.

"Yes, Mr. B."

"Tom Morrison! Get him for me right away!"

"Will do."

He put the paper down. We go back a long way, Tommy and me. That company history he did . . . a free-lancer he was, before he went with the *Times* and became a big shot. He's somebody a person can trust. And I've got more than a few Morrison IOUs.

"Mr. Morrison on the line."

Bell picked up the phone. "Tommy!"

"Hello, you old goat," the reporter grunted. "Long time no see. What's up?"

"I was wondering, you free for lunch?"

"Ah, lemme check . . . sure, sure. Twelve-thirty?"

Bell looked at his watch. It was only eleven-fifteen. "How about earlier? I need to get out of this place."

"Oho! One of *those* days! Sure, let me get this piece of drek out of the typewriter. This on the record or you just want to drink?"

"Bring your goddamn notebook."

"Wings Club. Half an hour. Say, your boy wonder's all over the *Daily* again. He's a real pistol, isn't he?"

Bell deliberated before answering. "That's exactly what I want to talk about."

7

To los angeles and back, so pushed for time he could stay only one night, Hartley was catching breakfast on the run. Standing over the kitchen table, he'd just flipped through the sports pages. Won't be much business news, he thought, not on Monday.

Suddenly Hartley jumped, spilling his coffee on the paper. Charlie! And the headline! *What Direction BellAir? The Chairman Speaks.*

Goddamn that Milt! He's supposed to brief me ahead! The byline...Tom Morrison. That figures. Charlie's old crony. Hartley sat down and began to read.

> Asked what he considers the industry's most pressing problems, Bell, never an enthusiastic supporter of deregulation and in recent years an increasingly vocal critic, lashed out against what he called "wildcatter airlines undercutting prices and skimming profits."

Fluff. Nothing new. Hartley ran his eye down the column... "BellAir's profit picture...looking forward to turning the corner in '83...new markets..." Nothing there, either, thank God. "As to the upcoming pilot negotiations..." Okay. Here we go.

> ...Bell admitted that talks with the ALPA unit representing BellAir's five thousand pilots will be crucial. "We need to reduce our costs, and we'll do it by being more productive," Bell said. "We're going to increase the hours our pilots fly while holding the line on wages."

Hartley's eyes narrowed. *Son of a bitch...*

> Commenting about the proposed cut in pilot pay recently announced by BellAir's President, Philip Hartley, to a group of investment analysts, Bell replied, "From my experience that sort of thing is impossible except maybe where you have a failing company, which we are not. In fact, we're planning to restore last year's management pay cut as soon as we can."

The toaster popped. Hartley gripped the paper tighter.

> Asked whether the company would take a strike to achieve its objectives as Hartley had indicated, Bell replied, "No, I don't expect that will be necessary." He went on, "Sometimes our young tigers let their enthusiasm get out of hand. We mean to work this thing out with the pilots. We always have, no reason we can't this time."

Hartley threw the paper down. *"Christ! What is that man doing!"*

He grabbed the phone and punched the cab company button on his speed dial. Goddamn Charlie just cut us off at the knees!

"451 East 52nd Street," he shouted. "Five minutes *sharp!*"

He slammed down the receiver and rushed into the bedroom, picking a tie off the rack. Elaine was in the shower.

"I'm leaving!" he yelled.

"Is everything all right?"

Is everything all right! he thought, struggling into his jacket. Is *anything* all right! What a stupid dumbass stunt! What the hell is *wrong* with that man! He rushed to the front door, but then he paused, his hand on the knob. This is bad, all right. So bad. Could it be, this time Charlie Bell has finally gone too far? It might just be, he's finally gone over the edge.

Excited, suddenly feeling much better, he decided to take the stairs. He sprinted down the seven flights, two steps at a time – just for the hell of it!

"MR. HARTLEY!" Valerie was frantic. "The phone's going crazy! What is going *on*?"

Hartley didn't break stride. "Get me Arthur Winston."

"He called a few minutes ago. Said he tried to reach you at home."

A pile of message slips was stacked next to his phone. Winston's was on top. Seven-fifty... *Urgent!* A moment later he was put through. He'd never heard Arthur so angry.

"This time Mister Bell has done it!" Winston shouted. "He goes against the express direction of the board and what's more, holds us up to ridicule! We cannot tolerate this behavior any longer! It's nothing short of scandalous!"

"We'd better start repairing the damage," Hartley replied, "and damn quick."

"I'm afraid words won't be enough this time. It seems we'll be putting our little plan into motion sooner than anticipated."

Hartley's heart leapt. Winston spoke rapidly. "I want an emergency board meeting. If Charlie won't call it, I'll do it myself. Ed was just beside himself! Martin Byrnes, too, and we can always count on Harold. First he cuts short our meeting and now this! He's finally lost his grip!" Hartley sat back in his chair as Winston raged on. "We'll set the meeting for Wednesday. You'd better plan on getting together with us tonight."

"I'll clear my calendar."

"Good man. We'll need to tie everything down. This may get ugly."

SURPRISINGLY, Charlie didn't oppose the meeting, but when Marianne Keller asked him about the agenda, Bell told her to call Winston, it was his show. Winston's agenda was innocuous enough. "Review of Current Policy," he worded it, but as the directors assembled they knew more was in the offing. Winston had called each outside director personally, reaffirming the tough negotiating line they'd endorsed and talking plainly about Bell. Touching all the bases, he messengered a copy of the company's articles of incorporation and bylaws for review by his personal attorney. Based on that reading, Winston was satisfied he had the authority to do what needed to be done.

Following his instincts, Ben Peterson smelled big trouble and tried to warn Bell, but he just laughed it off. "Nothing to worry about," he said. "We've been there before."

At 1:45 on a warm September afternoon, they assembled in the directors' conference room. Harold Nystrom was off in a corner with Bill Clevenger of the Southhampton Clevengers – family money so old, no one cared that it was first acquired in retailing. Stanley Harper, the insurance executive from Philadelphia who affected polka-dot bow ties and summer straw hats, was staring out a window, alone. Despite the apparent congeniality, tension filled the room.

Two o'clock passed. No Bell, no Mueller. Annoyed, Winston drummed on the table. Bell had assured him he would cooperate, in fact, said he welcomed the chance to clear the air. Though Winston knew he could act without him, he had a hunch Charlie's presence would play into his hands. Two-ten. Winston was about to call the meeting to order when the men appeared at the door from Bell's private office. Suddenly the room fell silent.

Bell seemed relaxed, as if nothing were amiss. He greeted Ed Horn and exchanged a pleasantry with Louise Boyd, the former Carter cabinet member now president of a Michigan university, the only woman or Black on the airline's board. Mueller was grave and unsmiling as he took his seat. Bell stood at his accustomed position at the head of the conference table and signaled for everyone to be seated. There was a certain amount of shuffling, the table being too small for the number of chairs jammed around it when there was a full house. In her customary position next to Bell sat Marianne Keller, secretary to the board.

Still standing, Bell began in a strong voice. "This meeting is called to order." He glanced at the short agenda. "Now, I notice we're supposed to be talking here about a policy review." He smiled and glanced around the room. "'Policy review?' Come on. I know why Arthur wanted this meeting, and so do you."

He glared at Winston opposite him at the far end of the table, then at Hartley, seated in the center. "A certain difference of opinion is healthy, and God knows we've had our share over the years, good lively discussion going back and forth, but in the end we always find a way to close ranks and do the right thing for the airline.

"The last few months we've taken several major steps that have been controversial, no question. Buying the oil business, then going ahead with those hotels." A sour look came over his face. "You know how I feel about the hotels, probably always will, but I can tell you we already have a task force setting about making it work. And, incidentally..." Bell took a sip of water, "you all got my letter but I want to tell you personally, I realize last time I made a mistake. I was so mad, to be honest, I was afraid I'd say something I'd be sorry for, so it seemed best to just cut it short." Bell smiled. "Then again, maybe it wasn't so smart. I don't know.

"Well, anyway, here we are, and we need to talk about the pilot negotiations that're just starting. Let me say first, I'm not altogether opposed to a strike. Some of you may think I am, but I'm not. Not that I'd welcome the disruption and all, a man'd be a fool to wish that on the company." Bell raised his finger for emphasis. "But if it's worth it, if it's necessary to get something we truly need, then, so be it. And if it comes to that, we have to be prepared. You can't go into battle half-cocked, any more than you'd take off without enough fuel. So I'm all for preparation." Bell glanced at Hartley. "I even put Phil in charge of gearing us up, if that ever becomes necessary.

"So I say, you got to be firm and you got to have the muscle and the will to back it up." Bell's eyes narrowed. Suddenly he brought his hand down on the table, hard. "But you have to be intelligent about it! And it is not smart to come on all uppity and belligerent before you even get started with the other side!"

He shook his head, a rueful smile on his face. "Listen to me, will you? 'The other side!' You've even got *me* saying it!"

Bell took a deep breath. "Goddamn it all, this is just not right! These are our own pilots! Come down on them like a ton of bricks – why, we'd play right into the union's hands. And all those fence-sitters out there who haven't made up their minds, you're going to lose them too, and you'll never win 'em back."

He placed his hands on the table and leaned forward. "Now, one last thing, then you all get to say your piece. I realize our opening position calls for a salary cut, but let's face it, we're going to come off that position, and damn quick, too. You're living in some kind of dream world if you think that'd ever sell. We don't need to paint ourselves into any corners," Bell smiled grimly. "Given our experience, we'll manage that without half trying."

Bell gestured at the group. "That's all I have to say. Who wants a shot at it. Arthur?"

Winston looked at Bell. You had to admire the man, he thought, he can be a real charmer when he tries. While Bell was speaking, Winston had observed the other directors. Several were smiling and nodding. But not enough of them, by his count.

"Ladies and gentlemen," Winston began, "our chairman put his finger on the issue, but he removed it much too quickly. The issue is, when the board makes a decision do we pull together to make it work? Or do we go our separate ways, promoting our own personal agendas?" Winston paused for emphasis. "We simply cannot appear to be divided, much less actually *be* divided, on a matter of such import. And that, unfortunately, is exactly the position we find ourselves in.

"That piece in the *Times*. Charlie, I want to believe, I truly want to believe you were misquoted. I pray you will tell us that you were misquoted. If so, I ask you to put out a release to that effect, immediately. I'm sure you all saw yesterday's *Journal*. It asks, correctly, I'm sorry to say, what is going on in this company. One day our president states a policy, a few days later the chairman contradicts and ridicules him. 'Disarray!' That term appears several times in the article.

"I can't count the calls I've had. A 'crisis of confidence' is how the *Journal* described it. And our stock price! Off four dollars since Monday! Ladies and gentlemen, we are down to twenty-four dollars a share! That is under book value!" Winston smiled wanly and shook his head. "It's a crisis of confidence, all right. Even more, it's a crisis of leadership!"

At the opposite side of the table Horn raised his hand. "Yes, Ed."

Horn stood up. "I happen to be on speaking terms with some people in the union movement. Still." This drew a few nervous laughs. "The fact is, today BellAir is a laughingstock. The best show in years, they're saying. Even before we start our negotiations, the word is ALPA's got it in the bag, and you know what? They do! Unless we do something about it!" Horn sat down and folded his arms. "That's all."

Winston turned to Bell. "What is the real story about that interview? Can you enlighten us?"

Bell was quiet for a moment, then began speaking softly. "You want the real story? Well, the real story is, I had a chance to set the record straight and that's exactly what I did." He sat ramrod straight in his chair. "You people need to understand something. This board has no business whatsoever messing around in a union negotiation, not unless I ask you. Your expression of support for taking a tough line was just that, an expression. I never asked for it. If I remember right, it was your idea, Arthur. I told you then what I thought of it, and I'm telling you again. Second, like I said in the article, Phil went too far in that speech of his, but we've been over that, just him and me, in private, man to man."

Hartley closed his eyes.

"The real story?" A crooked smile came to Bell's lips. "I was doing union deals before some of you were born, and, goddamnit, I know what I'm doing! When I need you to put the squeeze on somebody, I'll tell you! That's what we pay you people for!" He slammed his fist on the table. "*But do not tell me how to run my airline!*"

The directors looked at each other, appalled by the outburst.

"Charlie," Harold Nystrom broke in, "I must say it was highly irresponsible for you to embarrass our president and the company. A well-run organization keeps its dirty linen to itself."

"Dirty linen!" Bell leaned over the table. "Well, I guess you know about dirty linen! There hasn't been a clean tablecloth in one of your fleabags in ten years! And now I got all of it to wash. Throw it out's more like it, none of it's any good, need all new stuff, they tell me…"

"*Now, that's uncalled for!*" Nystrom screamed, leaping to his feet.

At that the room erupted. "Gentlemen! Please! *Gentlemen!*" Winston struggled to be heard over the din. "Philip, have you anything to add?" he shouted.

Calmly, Hartley shook his head.

Winston paused to let the chaos settle. He glanced at Horn who nodded. "Then, I move that the board go into executive session and ask Mr. Bell and Mr. Hartley to excuse themselves, so we might discuss certain personnel matters."

"Second," Horn said loudly.

"All in favor…"

"Wait a minute!" Fritz Mueller cried. "*What the hell are you trying to pull!* There's nothing like this on the agenda! You've got to give *notice*!"

"That's not so." Winston looked at Ben Peterson. "Ben will confirm that."

Peterson avoided Mueller's eyes. "The agenda's a guideline," he said glumly. "The board isn't limited by it, not if everybody's present."

Mueller was still sputtering.

"You'll have your chance in a moment," said Winston, moving ahead. "All in favor?"

Six hands shot up.

"Opposed?"

Mueller and Boyd raised their hands.

"Ben?"

"Abstain."

"Philip?"

"Abstain."

"Very well. Charlie?"

Bell shoved his chair back from the table. "Fuck you, Arthur!" he shouted, stomping across the room. At his office door he turned back, looking about wildly.

"Go ahead! Play your goddamn games! *I'll have no part of it!*" Then the door slammed shut.

The directors were silent, stunned. Winston went on calmly, "I believe the motion is carried." He nodded at Hartley, who stood and left. "Marianne, you are excused also. We'll let you know when we need you."

Hartley went directly to his office, telling Valerie not to disturb him for anything but a call from the meeting. Bell had already left the building. He returned before long and locked himself in his office.

For the next two hours shouting could be heard inside the room. Terrified, Helen Foley sorely wanted to put her ear to the door, but decorum won out. At precisely four-fifteen the doors opened, and several directors emerged, looking for empty offices to make calls. Others headed for the restrooms. Arthur Winston approached Helen's desk, smiling serenely. Never before had she seen him without his jacket.

"Will you ask Charlie and Philip to rejoin us at four-thirty? And tell Milt Collins to stand by. We'll be needing a press release."

At four-thirty the doors closed again, this time with Bell and Hartley inside. Winston looked around the table.

"This has been a most difficult afternoon. However, I trust we will be able to close ranks and go on from here."

Winston looked directly at Bell, the man he had worked with for so many years. "Charlie, it is my unpleasant duty to ask for your resignation as chairman and chief executive officer of the airline and the holding company."

Bell's mouth dropped open.

"After full consideration the board has determined that you no longer have its confidence at this critical time for our company."

Slowly Bell got to his feet, looking around, searching every face. No one could meet his eyes. Mueller was holding his head in his hands. Hartley stared straight ahead, impassively. Bell began speaking in a husky voice.

"This is a joke. This has to be a joke. You people can't do this. I made you all. I made you all, I made this *company*..." The veins in his head looked like they would burst.

Winston replied sternly, "Charlie, take your seat. Please! This is difficult for all of us. I assure you we can indeed do this. Isn't that so, counselor?" Winston turned to Peterson.

"You can ask for anything you want," he replied grimly.

"You're asking me to *quit*?" Bell roared. *"There's no goddamn way in hell I'll quit! I'll throw you out of here before I'll quit!* Get people in here I can trust. Secret session, *ha*! I suppose you *voted* on this too, didn't you? I want to know right now. Who's man enough to stand up..."

"Don't make this any harder than it already is," Winston pleaded.

"Watch it, Arthur! You're the first one to go! You and that Judas over there!" He glared at Hartley. "Get out! *Both of you! Get out!*"

Winston's eyes became slits. He spoke slowly and deliberately.

"Mr. Bell. There is something you don't seem to understand. If you don't go gracefully, the board has voted to replace you! Now, will you please..."

"Replace me! You can't replace me! Ben! They can't do that! *Tell them they can't!"*

Peterson shook his head. "I'm afraid they can," he mumbled. "They can't fire you as a director, though."

Bell's hands were shaking and he was breathing fast.

"I'll see you burn in hell first!" he snarled, turning and bolting from the room.

Again the meeting exploded. The directors dissolved into angry groups, one surrounding Mueller, the other with Peterson and Boyd shouting at its center. They were only three who had stood with Charlie Bell. Winston signaled for the door. As it swung open Marianne Keller looked in fearfully. He beckoned for her, then handed over a scrap of paper with his tally of the board's decision. She looked at it and burst into tears.

"Damnit, woman!" Winston snapped. "Pull yourself together!"

She crumpled the paper and threw it at Winston's feet, then rushed from the room.

With a sour expression Winston looked around. "Philip, come here," he shouted.

He extended his hand as Hartley approached. "It's a pity it had to happen this way, but this would have been yours sooner or later, anyway. Get Milt in here. We need to put out a release."

8

THE FIRING OF CHARLIE BELL rocked the industry. The news reports were blunt about the event, Bell flat-out rejecting the sugar-coating offered by Arthur Winston. Thus, the last great airline pioneer was gone, driven from the scene.

Although in late '82 there still were frontiers, many of the post-deregulation innovators were either gone or feeling serious heat. United, American, BellAir, the titans, were throwing their weight around in earnest, and the TWAs, Deltas, and Northwests were beginning to flex their mid-sized muscles. Several spectacular failures and old-fashioned mergers had fueled the trend to consolidation, and there was even speculation that the airlines' attractive cash flows might make them takeover bait for outsiders. These days BellAir was looking like a survivor, at times even flashing a winner's form.

The new chairman allowed no vacuum to form. Within days, Bell's belongings were boxed and gone. Helen Foley called to say that an office had been set aside, a smallish room where Bell could come and go as he pleased. Hartley pondered whether it would be wise for Bell to be seen around but decided this courtesy was a low-risk way to bolster his own acceptance. His calculation proved correct when the unrepentant Bell sent word – everything was to be shipped to his home. Never again would he set foot in that place. Past retirement age herself, Helen Foley agreed to stay on only long enough to service Bell's correspondence and screen his calls, and generally aid the transition.

These were the events that brought two men in BellAir jackets to the Bells' house on a wet afternoon in late September. Charlie was out, invited for a day of duck hunting at a neighbor's private reserve on the Connecticut shore.

"I'm Tom McNally, Mrs. Bell." The older of the two stood at the front door, company cap in hand and wearing a mournful expression.

"I...uh...we all want you to know how sorry we are what happened."

She smiled. "I appreciate your saying that."

"Charlie has a lot of friends. I mean a lot of friends! Everybody's really broke up about it. He's not here, you say?"

"No, he won't be back for a couple of hours."

The man frowned. "Well, be sure to say hello for me. McNally's the name. Building Maintenance. He'll know me." The man clamped his hat on his head. "Where do you want this stuff?"

"Around back would be best."

McNally walked to the end of the porch and peered around the corner.

"Sure, we can handle that."

Forty-five minutes later the unloading was finished. As he worked, the silent partner overcame his shyness, venturing a few words with the airline's grand old lady, of whom he'd heard so many stories. Wrapping up the job, he was folding the sheets Dee had spread on the floor.

"Sorry we made such a mess," he said, looking at the mud spattered on the wall. "If you have a rag or something..."

"We raised three boys here. You get used to a certain amount of mud." She gestured toward the kitchen. "I made some coffee. Would you have a cup?"

McNally shook his head. "They got us on a tight schedule today, ma'am."

"Well, take some with you, at least. How do you like it?"

"Sugar and milk, if you have it," said the younger man.

"If I *have* it! When was the last time a flight attendant ran out of sugar and milk?" She began opening and shutting cabinet doors. "How-*ever*...it looks like we're out of paper cups. Here," she said, stretching for two winged B mugs, "we'll use these. Just leave them with Miss Foley, she'll get them back to us."

"Even better," McNally replied brightly, "I'll leave them on top of Charlie's desk in the little office. He can use them when he's in there."

Dee's face darkened. "That could be a long time, the way he's feeling."

"He *better* come around! The place isn't the same without him." He dug into his pants pocket. "Here," he said, holding up a key on a string. "I almost forgot. This is for his new office."

She took the key. "Thank you for coming by...and for the kind words."

"Remember, it's McNally, Building Maintenance. He'll know me. I been with him since '57."

She stood at the back porch watching them maneuver his truck out of the tight space. With a crunch of tires on the wet gravel, they drove off.

A few minutes later Dee heard a sound at the back door. "Charlie?" she called.

"None other." Bell stood in the doorway, soaking wet, puddles forming on the floor at his feet.

"You're back so soon!"

"Well, as you can see," he pointed to his slicker, which he'd hung dripping from a hook, "it was a bit damp. At least I got a couple of mallards. They'll clean them for us at the club."

"They brought your things up from the office. One of them particularly asked for you, Tom McNally."

"Oh, sure...funny old guy."

"There was a nice young man with him. He reminded me of Chip," she said, referring to their youngest son.

Bell took off his boots and waterproof pants, and stood there in his stocking feet. He sneezed.

"I hope you didn't catch something," she scolded.

"No, I'm okay." He padded across the kitchen in his damp socks and opened the door to their back room, which was piled high with boxes of all sizes. Bell scanned the room quickly.

"Where's my leather chair?" he shouted. "And my desk! It's not here!"

"I told Helen to keep them. You can use them when you go in."

"*Damnit,* I wanted everything *here!* I'm not going back, Dee. I *told* you that!"

She looked at him sadly. "Just give it a little time. Please... for me?"

"Oh, all right," he muttered. "If it makes you feel better."

He gazed slowly around the room. "So this is what a career comes down to. One room, not even full, at that. Not all that impressive, is it?"

"If I thought you really believed that, I'd be worried," she replied, looking at his forlorn expression.

"What makes you think I don't?"

She took a deep breath. "We'll start on this next week," she said crisply. "You decide what you want in your study, the rest we'll leave here. The boys can move it to the cellar."

Weeks passed. The nights turned chilly and many days were overcast. Bell's depression deepened, and Dee, normally so positive, became edgy and short-tempered. Even without the trauma, she knew it would be hard having Charlie around so much. She'd always heard how difficult a husband's retirement could be on the household, but she had badly underestimated. Charlie's mood swings were very tough to deal with. One morning he'd wake bright and cheerful, full of plans and projects, other days he didn't rise until noon, then just hung around in his bathrobe and slippers, unshaven and unkempt. She recalled her own convalescence several years back, but she searched her memory without solace, for her own stretches of depression had never been as pronounced or persistent. He was even resisting plans for the family Christmas gathering. "Why don't we just go to a restaurant," he complained.

He was up to two packs a day again. More than once Dee observed cigarettes burning in different ashtrays, and to her alarm the dry hacking cough that marked his heaviest smoking had returned. His outdoor activity now amounted to walking the dog and raking leaves, with an occasional drive in the country. Charlie had never watched much television, in fact he took pride ridiculing the "vast wasteland" as friends would rave over this or that new show. But now he sat for hours changing channels, playing with the remote control, though rarely pausing to watch anything all the way through.

Only once did he venture into Manhattan, taking the train for lunch with Fritz. He returned exhausted and exasperated. "How anybody can stand that is beyond me," he grumbled. "And it wasn't even rush hour!"

Twice weekly he opened the mail Helen Foley sent by messenger, but correspondence went unanswered and calls forwarded to the new line Dee had installed in his study backed up on the answering machine. Requests for interviews and speeches were ignored.

One night Dee awoke trembling, drenched with perspiration. In her dream Charlie became smaller and smaller until, finally, he disappeared altogether. The next morning at breakfast she was horrified when she looked at him, how thin and disheveled he had become. The course he was on, the specter in that dream was no illusion. She stopped by the church they, that is, she, attended, for a frank talk with the minister, who recommended a psychiatrist in downtown Greenwich. The family doctor agreed but urged her to have Charlie see him first for a checkup and a chat. The reaction was predictable.

"Me! See a shrink! You must be out of your mind!"

He did consent to an appointment with Dr. Read, the family physician.

One day in early November, a particularly gray and blustery afternoon, Charlie was sitting in front of the television. He had just paused on an Italian soccer match when Dee burst into the living room.

"I just had a great idea!"

"And what might that be?"

"We're going on a trip!"

"Just like that," he parroted, "we're going on a trip."

Undeterred, she emptied a large envelope onto the coffee table. "I picked these up from the travel agency." A street map of London fell out, and a Great Britain travel guide and several brochures.

"Here's the plan," she said brightly, sitting down beside him. "We fly to London, stay a few days, see some plays, then drive to the Lake District and up to Scotland." She paused. "Well, what do you think?"

He pursed his lips. "The weather'll be rotten this time of year."

"No worse than here. C'mon, it'll be good for us! What do you say? We certainly have the time."

"That's for damn sure."

His laugh warmed her. "I couldn't believe it, but *The Mousetrap*'s still playing at that same place we saw it...what, twenty years ago! Wouldn't it be fun to go again?"

"Actually, I could look in on Bill Taylor. I'd love to hear what British Airways is up to these days."

"They said we could use that flat of theirs."

"You know, I think you have a winner." Charlie unfolded the travel guide. "We'll write to Angus, too." Angus McIntyre was a cousin in Glasgow.

She smiled. "Not write, *call!* I want to go *next week!* What do you say? Will you set it up?"

"Damn right, I will!" He clicked off the television. "On one condition. We use our Pan Am pass, or I'll get one from Bill. I'm not going to fly on us."

"It's a shame you feel that way," she replied softly, "but. . .I guess that'll take time."

Bell traced his finger over the British Isles map. "Remember that hotel? Where was it, the one with the swans in that little lake?"

"Gloucester," she replied with a smile. She rested her head against his. He reached over and hugged her about the shoulders.

"Great girl! What would I ever do without you?"

THE SCENT OF FRESH LEATHER filled the room. Philip Hartley clasped his hands behind his head and leaned back in his new chair. Late afternoon and he was enjoying a short break before his next commitment. He gazed around his office – his office! – noting the appointments installed by the decorator, one of Elaine's designer colleagues. No faded black and white photographs, no more aviators staring into space, one foot on the wheel of some ancient biplane. All gone. Hartley's only concession to the trade was a large BellAir 747 model on a floor stand, consigned to a corner of the room.

The office was clean and modern, in Scandinavian light wood, a stark contrast to his predecessor's dark walnut. Hartley's eye was drawn to the centerpiece, a de Kooning directly across from his desk. All day he had been half-watching it. . .something was wrong. He focused on it carefully. . .I knew it! Slants down to the right. He shook his head. Damn thing wouldn't look any different upside down. He straightened the painting, then stepped to his long window wall and stood there, hands on his hips.

I'm here! I made it!

Ideally, it wouldn't have happened this way. Still, a clean break has a lot of advantages. I've learned a lot from Charlie. I owe him. The right time, when things blow over, I'll give him a call, let him know I appreciate what he did.

However, as Hartley luxuriated in his success, Bell's parting shot returned to darken the moment. Judas. He called me a *Judas*. That was *way* below the belt. The plain fact is, he'd lost it. He couldn't cut it anymore, but if it weren't for his tendency to self-destruct, he'd still be here.

Hartley leaned forward and fingered his desk calendar. Cliff Meltzer at 4:30 – "Preliminary November Results." That's at least an hour, then a reception for some retiring assistant VP. Like to skip that one, but I can't...have to stay in touch. He closed his eyes, replaying his meeting with Marshall Smith just concluded. You have to admire how the man keeps plugging away.

With Bell out of the way, management's position had stiffened on its demand for a twenty percent cut in pilot pay. The pilots were still committed to a substantial increase. Both sides were laying back, waiting for the Mediation Board to start the thirty-day clock. Mid-January, no sooner, no later, was Hartley's very specific instruction to Smith.

Hartley had signed off on Smith's plan for screening and training replacement pilots and extending conditional job offers. The process had to start this early for the company to be ready when the whistle blew. Smith's replacement program would send BellAir's pilots into orbit, but so much the better, as far as Hartley was concerned. This time there'll be no mistake about our intentions.

As for the others, it was very unlikely the mechanics would back ALPA, since the pilots blew them off two years earlier and the language in the new IAM contract barring sympathy strikes was very explicit, one of the few "wins" the company gained in that ordeal. The flight attendants were a different story. Always unpredictable, nobody knew what direction they might go.

AFTER LEAVING HARTLEY, Marshall Smith proceeded through the executive suite to his office two floors below. He always chose this route so he could show his face around Fifty-five, to the people who mattered and to their influential secretaries. He wanted it *noticed* that he spent time with the chairman. As Smith approached the stairwell exit, he observed a gathering around Helen Foley's desk. Hidden away in this remote corner, Charlie Bell's tiny office was dark, as usual. Smith sidled up to the group and peered in to see what was happening. Just as he did, a secretary turning to leave bumped into him. She jumped back, startled.

"Oh, Mr. Smith! I didn't see you."

"What's goin' on, Judy?"

"Nothing you'd be interested in, Marshall," admonished Rose Markowitz.

With Smith's arrival, the group began to break up. As the bodies parted, Helen Foley was left glaring at Smith. She held him, in fact, all of Hartley's henchmen, personally responsible for Charlie's demise.

"You ask what's happening? Charlie and Dee are having a fabulous time in London, that's what's happening!" She waved a postcard at Smith, a picture of Buckingham Palace. "Perhaps you would care to read it," she said acidly.

"No, ah don't have time." Smith glanced at the card. "Ah see. The changin' of the guard. A timely sentiment," he smirked. "Very timely, indeed."

Several days later another card arrived, addressed to Fritz Mueller, this one showing a flock of sheep on a green hillside. After reading it, Mueller's secretary brought it in.

"Well, they made it to the Cotswolds. Dee says they're having a really nice time."

"When was that sent?" Mueller snapped. The secretary looked at him blankly. "The card! When was it sent!"

She turned the card over, looking for the postmark. "It's hard to make out but...it looks like November fifth. Gee, the mail is slow, that was over a week ago."

She handed the card to Mueller on top of a stack of mail. "What's wrong?" she asked, puzzled.

"Dee just called. They've been back since Tuesday."

"You're kidding! Why?"

"I dunno. She said he cut the trip short, had enough driving or some foolish reason. She had to cancel the whole Scotland trip. Damn! That's the part he was looking forward to the most!"

For a moment Mueller was silent. Then he grimaced and ripped the card into pieces, flinging them across the room.

CHARLIE BELL leaned on his rake. Early December. He'd waited long enough. By now every leaf that meant to come down was down. Strong winds had swept through the night before, and persistent gusts kept scattering the piles he gathered so laboriously. Aggie was no help, tearing from one stack to another. He started to yell at her but held up. What the hell, somebody around here might as well enjoy them-selves. He clapped his hands...temp must be in the low teens. Suddenly he cocked his head and looked up. A 737 was passing over, the sound of its engines crackling through the cold, dense air, so thick you could cut it with a knife. He shaded his eyes...can't quite make it out. Could be one of ours.

"Ours," he thought morosely. They even took that away from me. All those years a plane passing over made me feel so alive...happy memories, a thousand projects needing my attention. Now, nothing. Just hollow inside. Nothing left.

Now I know what they mean by a heavy heart, he sighed. Same as on that trip. Dee was so mad...pissed is more like it. Ah, I shouldn't have done it, but I was so antsy. Just couldn't sit in that damn car any-more, three straight days of rain. Had to get back, thought maybe it was time to get into things again.

Bell placed his rake down and walked back to the house, holding the storm door open for the dog. He removed his red and black checked jacket and hung it on the peg in the back entry, putting his cap over it. Something cooking, he thought...smells like stew. Aggie's slurping the water dish. Reminds me, I'm thirsty. Maybe a beer would go good. He looked at his watch...three-thirty. Still a little early but that's okay, it's Saturday. He stopped, then shook his head sadly. They're all Saturdays now.

He walked into the kitchen. Dee was standing at the stove, stirring a pot.

"The mail came," she announced. "It's on the hall table."

He cracked open a can. "Anything interesting?"

"Your package from Helen."

A moment later he returned, holding up a small square envelope, squinting at it knowledgeably. "And this, no doubt, is our invitation to the company Christmas party."

"Have you changed your mind?" Dee said, not looking up.

"I don't know...it's just too soon. I need to ease back into things. Let them have their fun this year."

"If we don't go, you'll be letting a lot of people down again."

He put the papers down, a wounded look on his face. "Again? *Again*, is it?"

She looked at him, "I'm sorry...I..."

His face became very sad. "That's all right...you're right, Dee, I screwed up. I lost my head. Still don't know what came over me. He paused. "You *were* right, all along, you know."

"What do you mean?"

"About Hartley. You were right. I was wrong. Now I know."

"Well, what's done is done," she replied brusquely. "You need to keep busy. That's what Dr. Boland says, too."

"Ah, that quack. Nuttier'n a fruitcake himself. I'm never going back to him!" He took another sip of beer.

"But he did have a point."

"Yeah, yeah...I suppose." Bell sat down at the kitchen table. He began sliding the beer can across the smooth surface, from one hand to the other. "You know, I was thinking, maybe I should get together with a few people. Fritz, a couple others. But I just can't go this year. Next year for sure. Okay?"

"Okay," she replied, wiping her hands on her apron, "whatever you say. But let's make a start on those cartons. Two months now, you've just been looking at them. Maybe you'll feel more like working if we get your study set up."

"Yeah, you're right," Bell replied. "I shouldn't just go on moping around here. It's not fair to you."

"Fair to me, nothing!" she replied. "I've put up with you all these years, haven't I?"

She smiled, but inside, she was in turmoil. His agitation, his despair carried a whole new, unsettling dimension. Mercurial, Charlie had always been, at times even cavalier, but his sharp edge seemed to help him function and it moved the people around him. But now...now there was no focus at all, no outlet. Everything was directed inward. His eyes told a story she dared not face.

"Sure," she heard him mumbling. "Good idea, good idea. Don't do anything special on my account, though..."

9

A SIGN FLASHED BY. Long Island Expressway – Queens Midtown Tunnel – 5 mi. Bell glanced at the dashboard: 12-17 – 5:56 p.m. Damn! I can't do anything right! But...well, I never drive in here, plus it's dark. Ah, that's bullshit. I should've reacted faster. Dumb, turning toward La Guardia, the exact wrong way. They'll understand, though, they'll wait. He pressed harder on the accelerator. The Cadillac sped toward Manhattan. Good friends, Scotty and Fritz, the kind that stick with you no matter what. Doing 70...I better pick it up a little more. They won't be in any hurry to get to that goddamn party. They'll wait. I'm sure they'll wait.

In a few minutes Bell wheeled down an off-ramp and angled toward Grand Central Station and the Wings Club. He swerved to a stop at the curb, ignoring the No Parking sign as he hurried into the lobby. Exiting on the eighteenth floor, he skirted the wall of familiar pictures...his own face went by in a blur...and rushed into the bar.

"Hey!" Fritz Mueller clapped Bell on the shoulder. "We'd given you up for lost."

"Sorry I'm late, fellas. I...had a little trouble on the road." Bell signaled the bartender. "Glenlivet. A double, on the rocks. And a fill-up for these two drunks."

He stood back, admiring their tuxedos. "Fancy, very fancy." He fingered MacLeod's red tartan vest. "Where are the ladies? Don't tell me you guys are stag tonight."

"Yeah, right," Mueller said wryly. "That'll be the day."

"They're over at the Park View." MacLeod wrinkled his nose. "Best thing about that place, I don't have to drive anywhere."

"We haven't had the Christmas party at that dump in years," Bell snapped.

"Things have changed," Mueller rolled his eyes. "There are plans. My *God*, are there plans! You should see the budget." He downed the last of his drink. "We were right, Charlie. It's a fucking disaster. Talk about pouring money down a rathole!"

The waiter arrived. Bell touched his glass to the others. "Well...cheers!"

"Here's looking at you!"

"Up yours!"

They fell quiet as the two men scrutinized Bell. "You're looking fit," MacLeod finally ventured.

Bell lit a cigarette. "Some days are better than others. I don't know...I really miss you guys."

"Sure as hell is different without you," Mueller replied.

"Back on those, are you," MacLeod scolded.

"Ah, just a few a day. You know, something to keep my hands busy. So, I hear we're having a good fourth quarter."

"That is true," replied Mueller. "The year's shot to hell, but we're going out in style."

Bell rolled his glass back and forth in the palms of his hands. "You know, a couple of weeks ago I was over at La Guardia...just sort of looking around." He stared into the glass. "I'm ashamed to say this, but it made me feel bad to see everything running so well, everybody so busy and all."

MacLeod frowned. "How do you mean?"

"Well, this may sound dumb, but I was sorta thinking when I left, maybe things wouldn't go so good, maybe they'd even fall apart some." Bell laughed bitterly. "That way I'd know I still made a difference."

"You're right!" MacLeod retorted. "That's about the *dumbest* thing I ever heard!"

Mueller glared at MacLeod but held his tongue.

Bell was staring into his glass. "You fellas realize, this is the first Christmas we haven't had the officers up to the house."

"Come on over to the hotel," MacLeod said. "For a few minutes, anyway."

"Nah, I'd just be a fifth wheel." Bell gestured at his dark blue suit. "I'm not even dressed right."

"Come on," MacLeod prodded. "Everybody'd like to see you."

"I know a few who wouldn't. I'm afraid not all my appointments turned out as good as you two." He looked at Mueller. "I'm sorry, Fritz. This can't be easy for you, either."

Mueller shrugged. "Face it. Whatever way you went, you were taking a chance. I'm just an old warhorse, I can take it. Hell, aside from wasting our money and fucking up everything with the pilots, your boy's doing a fine job."

Bell frowned. "What do you mean, with the pilots?"

"Ah...we had a few words today. I told him to can his war-planning shit and get on with making a deal. We're just asking for trouble, operating with a bunch of new-hires like he wants to do. I'm going to nail him at the board meeting next week. Hey, you're still a director, for Chrissakes. Be there! Back me up!"

Bell shook his head. "I wasn't planning to."

"Whaddya mean! You've *got* to be there!"

"I can't show my face around there." Bell's hand trembled as he lit another cigarette. "In fact, I'm thinking of resigning from the board. What's the point? They don't need me anymore."

The men talked a few more minutes, then Mueller set his glass down. "Well, time to do it. We can pick up a cab outside."

"No, no," Bell protested, "I'll give you a ride. My car's right in front. Here, I'll get this." Bell signaled the waiter, who produced a leather folder with the check.

"No, this one's on me," said MacLeod, snatching it away. "Rather, the company."

At the street, Bell's Cadillac sat squarely in the red zone. But there was no ticket. "You sure live dangerous, don't you?" MacLeod commented.

Confused, Bell looked around. "I didn't even notice..."

They started uptown, toward the Park View, Bell staring straight ahead, silent.

"Annie'll be real disappointed not to see you tonight. Why don't we set a date for you and Dee to come down to D.C.? Think about the first weekend in January."

"Maybe that would be good," Bell replied.

They drove along in awkward silence for a few minutes. Mueller leaned forward. "Say, I was wondering, you guys heard anything about Francis?"

"Farrell?" MacLeod asked.

"Yeah. He's been on medical leave. Saw him yesterday, first time in a while. Damn, does he look terrible! He's lost so much weight you wouldn't even know it was him."

"What's the matter?"

"Some kind of a nerve thing, he said, but I dunno…"

"What'd the medical report say?" Bell asked.

"Well, that's the strange thing. Doc Alberts said he hasn't been in, didn't even know he was sick. He must be going to his own doctor."

"That *is* strange," Bell replied. "The officers always go through Doc. That's our policy."

Mueller shook his head, "I've got a bad feeling about this one. I hope I'm wrong, but with all the talk about AIDS these days…"

"Not Francis!" said MacLeod. "You've got to be kidding!"

"I hope so but…I dunno."

Bell stared straight ahead. "The poor bastard. You wouldn't wish that on anybody…"

They turned a corner. Just ahead lay the Park View. Bell drew alongside a line of cars and double-parked. Under the front canopy men and women in evening dress were milling about.

"Take it easy, Charlie." MacLeod reached across and shook his hand. "Plan on D.C. I'll call you about it."

Bell peered out the windshield at the brilliantly lit scene. "I don't know. I'm not sure…I may need a little more time."

"Well, whatever you say. Just let us know when you're up for it."

"So long," said Mueller, cuffing him on the shoulder. "I'll give you a call, we'll have lunch next week."

"Yeah, that would be good. Take care, you guys."

Bell watched for a long moment as Mueller and MacLeod waded into the colorful crowd to an enthusiastic greeting. His eyes were moist as he pulled out into the street.

SLOWLY, BELL DROVE along Central Park South. Stopped at Madison for a long light, he leaned over the steering wheel and closed his eyes, replaying the festive scene at the hotel. Suddenly a horn blasted from behind. Bell looked up. The light was green.

"Asshole," he muttered, blinded by headlights in the rear-view mirror. Bastard has his high beams on, too.

Nearing Park Avenue…the Queensboro Bridge. Bell paused. Traffic coming up fast…suddenly he racked the wheel over and accelerated down Park. Soon the Tower's familiar outline appeared in his windshield. Bell rolled to the curb, then stopped, gazing at the entrance. His heart was pounding.

He sat for several minutes, huddled in his heavy black topcoat. With the engine off, his feet soon became cold. Unbuckling his seat belt, he reached across to the glove compartment and removed a small, heavy object wrapped in a scarf and slipped it in his pocket. Setting the hand brake, he opened the door and stepped awkwardly into the street. As he had done so many times, Charlie Bell crossed the broad plaza to the building. His building.

He nodded at the mammoth Calder metalwork brooding beside the fountain. In the summer the water sparkled with life, hundreds of people perching on the cement rim with their sandwiches and drinks. Tonight it was drained and still. At the front door, Bell's key card made a loud rasp, and he pushed open the door. His heels clacked on the marble floor as he strode across the lobby. At the noise, the security guard looked up.

"Can I help...why, Mr. Bell! What are you doin' here this hour?"

"Evening, Lowell. How come you're not at the party?"

The man clasped Bell's hand. He was tall and powerfully built, the far side of middle-aged. A lamp, the only bright spot in the spacious lobby, lit his ebony face with long vertical shadows. Behind the curved counter that formed his station, a bank of small blue-screened television monitors displayed locations around the building. On his desk a copy of the *Daily News* lay open to the crossword puzzle.

"'Fraid not, Mr. Bell," the guard answered. "Somebody's got to look after this place."

"That's too bad, Lowell. You and your wife cut a fine figure on the dance floor."

The man beamed. "I'll tell her that! She'll be pleased as punch!"

But his smile quickly vanished. "Fact is, Mr. Bell, a hundred bucks is a lot of bread this time of year, then naturally, the wife would have to do some shopping. Wouldn't do to be seen in last year's outfit. You know how it is, it adds up mighty fast."

"You mean they're *charging* people!"

"It's part of the economy move, is what they say." The man paused for a moment. "Mr. Bell, remember last year, you asked us to take a cut? Well, nobody liked doing that...I mean, you'd need to have your head examined. But people figured, if Mr. Bell says it has to be done, well then, it has to be done. But this new crowd..." he shook his head, "maybe I'm out of line saying this, but they are small people, if you ask me. Real small!"

Bell winced. Suddenly he doubled over with a deep, hacking cough.

"Here, I'll get you some water, Mr. Bell."

"No," he gasped, fighting for breath, "just...give me a minute."

The guard rooted around his desk for a cup. "Sit down here. I'll get some for you."

Bell shook his head. He took a handkerchief out and wiped his mouth. The coughing fit had passed. "No, no. I'm...it's all right now."

The guard scrutinized him. "Where're you goin', Mr. Bell? Only ones here this late is Ops."

"I...I'm going up to Fifty-five," Bell replied, his voice soft and chalky. "Just want to look around some."

"Well, I'll sign you in. Your key card'll work the elevator." The guard paused, then began to roar with laughter. "I'm telling you that? You know our security better than anybody!"

"Damn right," Bell responded, clearing his throat. "I put the damn thing in. Sixty-nine it was."

"You did a lot, Mr. Bell. We feel real bad, what happened." He smiled warmly. "Everybody misses you, and that's a fact!"

"It goes both ways, Lowell." Suddenly Bell felt much better. Maybe he should ease back into things a little. Fritz was right, that board meeting *is* important...

"How long'll you be up there, Mr. Bell?"

"I don't know," Bell replied, his voice nearly normal again. "Not too long. Well, good to see you, Lowell."

"Oh, we'll see you on the way out. I ain't going nowhere."

Bell smiled and nodded. He strode to the open elevator, inserted his card and pressed a button. The doors shut smoothly. A moment later, Bell stepped into the reception area on Fifty-five. After a few paces, he stopped and chuckled...old habits run deep. Without thinking, he'd begun to trace the well-worn path to his office.

Noiselessly Bell padded on, across the thick carpet. Rich red and blue. My colors. Those first partners of mine...Chicago. Green and orange, they wanted. *Never* would have worked, *terrible* colors for an airplane! Past a line of desks...secretaries...Mueller, Marianne... all my top people. Here we are, my reception...*the chairman's* reception area. All the doors closed. They would be, this late. Always are after hours except when we have something cooking. He smiled. Many's the night I spent here on my couch.

He stepped up to his door and turned the knob. Locked. Of course. Security. He fumbled in his suit coat pocket for his key ring, holding it up by the BellAir crest. In the dim light the key fell familiarly to his hand and he slid it into the lock. I'll just take a quick look around. Nobody'll ever know...

Bell frowned. He removed the key and pressed it in again, twisting it, forcing it in the slot. He rattled the doorknob furiously. The key won't turn! He stood there open-mouthed. The sonofabitch changed my lock!

His lower lip trembled and his eyes began to smart. There was no cause for that, to change my lock. Suddenly he felt dizzy, lightheaded. He closed his eyes and leaned against the door, his head a dead weight upon his arm. Tears came rushing up...dizzy...he spread his arms, hands clutching for the door. He winced...that pain again...my head...hammering in my head.

Bell's hands slid down. He sank slowly to his knees and let his forehead drop forward against the door. He began to beat his fist against the thick wood. From a distance he could hear himself pounding. The sound resonated dully in his ears.

Hartley. He changed my lock. The sonofabitch changed my lock.

After a time, he couldn't tell how long, Bell's eyes opened. Confused, he reached for the doorknob and pulled himself to his feet. He brushed off his topcoat and turned away. In a trance Charlie Bell began to walk. He walked back through the reception area. Past Legal. Francis Farrell's nameplate...something nagged at his mind. Something wrong there...walking...something bad... walking...can't remember. Where am I going...oh, yes...my office...my new office.

He kept walking until there was nowhere left to walk. At the far corner of Fifty-five, next to the back stairs, no more offices, nothing but that old storage room. That can't be it! But the desk in front...the desk seems very familiar. He cocked his head...there's the picture of Helen and her nieces and, for God's sake, that's the one of Dee and me they took last year at the party. Huh...she never had that out before. He swallowed hard. *In memoriam.*

Bell reached into his coat pocket for the shiny new key, still on its string. He inserted it into the lock. The handle turned easily and he pushed the door open. The room was dark except for a faint light shining through the window. He fumbled for the switch, then lowered his hand and stepped to the window. He craned his neck to look out...he could see nothing except the building next door.

No view, he thought. That figures.

Gradually, Bell's eyes grew accustomed to the dim light, and, as they did, his mind began to clear. Where before, everything was blurry, soft-edged, now it was diamond-hard, diamond-sharp. The room isn't empty after all. There's my old desk and chair in the middle. A desk in the middle of a room, for Chrissakes! And he thinks he can run an airline! Jackass can't even set up an office right!

He placed his hands against the back of the chair, setting it in motion. It rolled forward and bumped against the desk. Bell caressed the soft leather. Cold. It's always cold when I'm here early, before anybody else. He pulled the chair back and sat down, propelling himself toward the desk with his feet. He reached across...couple of old coffee mugs, nothing else.

He tried a drawer. Paper clips, elastic bands, pad of yellow Post-its, gummy back. He leaned forward and folded his hands on the desk. The executive position, he thought bitterly, the wise, all-knowing executive position of the Chairman of the Airline and the Holding Company, both. Sir! His hands were cold, the fingertips icy. He shoved them in his overcoat pockets for warmth. Ah. A violent shudder passed through him. He desperately wanted to remove his hand, but some force kept it there...grasping, releasing...grasping, releasing...

For a long time Charlie Bell sat motionless. Everything was clear, amazingly clear. As he had when he was young, he felt the spin of the earth, the wind and cloud and rain on his face, he heard the song of the sky. But for now, all that mattered was to be still, not to move, not ever to move.

Finally, he sighed and sat back. The leather was warm. Through his topcoat he could feel its warmth, and now the hard mass in his pocket also warmed his hand. Through his window a few lights burned in the building next door, but that was all. There was no view, there was no sky.

Charlie Bell closed his eyes and blinked back the hot tears. What's the point, he said to himself. There is no point, came the reply, if there is no sky. If there is no more sky.

FOR MANY BELLAIR employees it was their first visit to the famous old hotel. As they exchanged tickets for nametags outside the main ballroom, a brass ensemble entertained with Christmas music. The Park View's new management had outdone itself. Nothing was spared. The main ballroom was strung with lights and festooned with fragrant boughs of spruce. Dozens of lavishly-laid buffet tables awaited the airline's eighteen hundred guests. Troubadours in Elizabethan garb strolled through the crowd. Pierre LeClerq, the airline's food genius, stood preening beside his masterpiece, a ten-foot-long 747 sculpted in ice. In their starched white toques, chefs from flight kitchens around BellAir's system presided at each table, supervising the assistants who cut and served, carried and replenished. All in all, a cacophony of joyful sounds and sights, a gorgeous treat for the senses.

At the far end of the room a dance band was already hard at work. Roger Bankhead, the evening's appointed impresario, had decided to go the big band route, with an electric overlay for the younger set. One discordant note. Midway through the evening, he sidled up to Philip Hartley as the chairman was readying his words of greeting.

"Phil, before you get up there, you should know we've had a lot of complaints about the cash bar."

"Such as?"

"People figured the drinks should've been included for their fifty bucks per."

Hartley frowned. "If anybody wants to look at the budget for this thing, be my guest."

"Just a word to the wise," Bankhead said curtly. During the advance planning, Bankhead had argued that the company should absorb the cost as a morale-builder, but Hartley summarily overruled him. At exactly ten-thirty, a fanfare sounded, and Bankhead mounted a low platform to the side of the orchestra.

"Ladies and gentlemen..." he paused to let the crowd to settle down, "ladies and gentlemen, BellAir employees, families and friends. I'm Roger Bankhead, Senior Vice President of Marketing. It has been my most pleasant assignment to organize this elegant and, we hope, enjoyable evening for you. Before I introduce our chairman let me single out several people for special thanks. First of all, George Chartrand, the new general manager of the Park View, and his staff, for their hospitality…"

Standing at the side, Hartley noticed Arthur Winston approaching. "Philip, I need a few words with you."

"Of course, Arthur." He nodded at the podium. "This won't take long." Hartley turned his attention back to Bankhead.

"And without further ado, I'll turn it over to our Chairman and Chief Executive Officer, Philip Hartley!"

Hartley stepped up to the microphone, acknowledging the loud, friendly greeting. A large group formed a semicircle in front of the platform, their eager faces lifted toward him. The crowd was spread out as far as he could see.

"Let me say how very pleased I am to welcome you, this first time as your president and chairman," Hartley began. "I hope you're all enjoying yourselves tonight. For the first time at one of these gatherings, we're privileged to have two members of BellAir's board of directors with us, with their lovely wives. Please welcome Arthur and Catherine Winston," he gestured toward the Winstons on the fringe of the crowd, "and Bill Clevenger and his wife, Pat."

"And I'd like you to say hello to my good right hand, Elaine," Hartley beckoned to the side of the platform where Elaine was standing with a group of officers' wives. She came up to join him and waved at the crowd.

"Now, very briefly, I want to make a special point and personally assure you that our company is moving ahead. Finally, firmly and steadily, *we are moving ahead!* With our acquisition of the hotel company and the way traffic has turned around the last few months, we are on the verge of a great year, the best year we've ever had! If everybody pulls together, 1983 will be the most profitable year in BellAir's history, hands down. But I emphasize, there is no way we can do it without all your efforts, your *extra* efforts. So, as we enjoy this evening and the festive holiday season, let us not forget the important task we have ahead. To work hard and work smart and give our customers the best possible product!

"Now, in conclusion, may I wish you and your families the happiest of holidays."

Loud applause greeted Hartley as he stepped from the platform. He was quickly surrounded by employees coming up to shake his hand and introduce themselves.

"Good job, Phil..."

"We're glad you're with us..."

The band struck up a fast number as Hartley made his way through the crowd of admirers. It was a heady experience, reminiscent of the old days, his days of heroic deeds. Hartley's spirits, already high, were buoyed by the warmth of the reception. It took several minutes to reach the side of the room where Winston and Bankhead were chatting.

"Good remarks, Philip," Bankhead said. "Just right."

"Yes, well done." Winston gestured toward a vacant spot on the edge of the dance floor. "Let's take a minute now...will you excuse us, Roger?"

Bankhead watched as the two men moved away.

"I don't mean to talk shop tonight, Philip, but I read your report on the strike preparations..."

"Yes, the pilot hiring is going very well."

"All to the good. But I must caution you on one thing..."

Winston paused and looked to the podium. The music had come to an abrupt halt. People were milling about in apparent confusion. After an odd hush, the hum of conversation began to rise. Hartley heard someone shouting, heard a woman scream. Then a thud from the loudspeakers. Hartley's head snapped around. Someone was taking the microphone! He craned his neck to see. It's Fritz! What the hell is *he* doing up there?

"Ladies and gentlemen, please! May I have your attention."

The noise was louder than ever.

"I said be quiet!"

Mueller's voice boomed out over the room. The crowd began to settle. Confounded, Hartley looked on.

"I...I don't know how to say this. I just got a call from Ops...something terrible."

There wasn't a sound. Hartley edged closer to the platform. He'd never seen Fritz so grave. I'll bet we lost a plane, Hartley thought. Damnit, he should have told me first.

"This call..."

Mueller took a deep breath. He let it out.

"Charlie's dead."

People looked at each other. What! What did he say? I heard him wrong...he couldn't have said...

"He's dead. He shot himself. Tonight. They just found him in...in the Tower. I don't know what else to tell you except...say a prayer for him. Say a prayer for all of us..."

Mueller stepped down. Instantly he was mobbed. Hartley stood staring at the stage as bodies surged around him. Over the babble a wail went up. This cannot be happening, Hartley thought. He felt very warm. What now? He felt his face flush. What happens now?

An image rose up in him. He tried to fight it off, but it wouldn't be denied. He saw a man falling. The man fell through a window with glass exploding all about him. He seemed to fall for a long time, twisting in the air. Just as he was to hit the ground, Hartley caught a glimpse of his face. Hartley shuddered violently. *He has my face.*

A woman sat sobbing on the floor. Beside her, another woman crouched, her arms about the weeping woman. Hartley looked around the room. People everywhere in small groups reaching out for one another.

Elaine. Mechanically he started walking. Elaine. Several yards away, he spied Arthur Winston. He started for him, then stopped, frozen in place. Winston was staring straight ahead and nodding. It can't be...Hartley looked again. Smiling! *He's smiling!* Winston's eyes were far away. Behind the mask the mind was already at work. A wave of revulsion swept over Hartley. He turned away. Fritz was trying to reach the exit. Hartley began pushing through the crowd toward him. There must be something he could do...should do.

For a long time the guests stayed, then they began to drift off. Unbidden, the musicians replaced the instruments in their cases, the servers started clearing the unused platters, dismantling the festive tables.

One by one they slipped away, the family of Charlie Bell, as he had left them. Into a night with no sky.

PART FIVE

The Tallest Peaks, The Fiercest Winds

1

T HE EMPLOYEE cafeteria was ringed with people looking for seats. Tony Catalano, BellAir's labor law expert, pocketed his change and glanced around the room. His regular table was full. Everybody seemed to be moving at half speed, still recovering from New Year's. Tray in hand, Catalano shuffled ahead.

"There's one." Carol McNulty, a young staff lawyer, pointed across the room. "Over there, with the finance people."

They approached the table. "Room for two more?" Catalano asked.

Harvey Green inched his chair over. "And what are our legal beagles up to today?" the portly accountant asked.

Catalano set his tray down. "Oh, your typical morning. Tied an old lady to the tracks, fed a couple of others to the wolves, you know the drill."

"You been on vacation?"

"I took the week off."

"Go anywhere?"

"No, just stayed around the house." Catalano spotted a newspaper on the table, a *BellAir Flightline* special edition with the photo of Charlie Bell on the front page, bordered in black. "I still don't believe it. You work with somebody all that time. I guess you never know, do you?"

Green nodded. "Only thing I can figure, it must've had something to do with the new crowd. Hartley, Bankhead, and so on."

"I don't follow you."

"It's obvious. They were out to get him." Green smiled grimly. "He couldn't take it, being cut out like that. So something snapped."

Catalano frowned. "I won't dispute you, but it's got to be more than that. Maybe he was sick but nobody knew."

"I don't know, I'm just guessing. But I'll tell you, never in my life will I forget that night at the hotel."

"I skipped it this year. Too rich for my blood." Catalano picked up the paper. In a small box beneath the picture was a small headline: *A Statement from Philip Hartley, Chairman, President and Chief Executive Officer.*

Catalano read aloud. " 'I wish to express the deep regret of the corporation, its directors, and its employees...pay tribute to Charlie Bell's leadership and vision...will be sorely missed...' " He threw the paper down. "Blah, blah, blah...and so on and so forth."

"Hey, what else can the man say?" asked Green. "He has to rally the troops."

"Aren't *you* the cynic," McNulty countered.

"Not at all, I'm a realist. It's part of the formula. It's all for effect."

"Well, he *might* mean it. I mean, how can you tell he *doesn't?*"

Catalano scowled. "If he's got to talk that way, there's no way to know whether he means it or not. This whole discussion is irrelevant."

"Ever since that Hartley walked in our door, I've had a bad feeling about him." Heidi Rosenbaum folded her arms as if to defend herself. She was an older woman, an administrative assistant in Finance. "Always above it all, no time to stop and talk, see how you're doing or anything. That kind of thing gets to you after a while."

"Maybe he's shy," someone ventured.

"Shy! You don't get where he is being shy!"

Catalano picked up the paper again, opening it to an inside page. "Is there anything about...oh, here it is. 'Private services were held in Chicago earlier this week with interment in the family plot in Springfield, Illinois.' I thought there was supposed to be some sort of memorial, too."

"Next week. At Fifth Avenue Presbyterian."

"That part of the formula too, Harvey?" McNulty prodded.

"C'mon, Carol, don't make me out the bad guy. They're just doing what everybody wants." The group fell quiet for a moment. "Not to change the subject or anything," Green looked at Catalano, "but how're your pilot negotiations going?"

Catalano shrugged. "Not well. They're recessed for the holidays. We're still miles apart."

"Think you'll get there?"

"I don't know. And now *this.*" He pointed at the newspaper. "This could make it a lot harder."

"What a mess if they go out."

"Like nothing we've ever seen, that's for sure. But we have our marching orders. Prepare for the worst, is the word, so that's what we're doing."

Just then Green looked up. Ben Peterson and an attractive young woman walked by.

"Who's that?"

"Job candidate," Catalano replied. "I interviewed her this morning. Sharp girl…Columbia Law. Law Review type. Nothing but the best for Legal."

"Better watch out, Carol," Green laughed. "There's competition for you."

"The more the better with all you MCPs around here!"

Rosenbaum winked at her.

"Touch-*ee,* touch-*ee.*" Green took a second look at the thin older man following Peterson and the law student. "Can that be Francis?" Green said under his breath. "My God, he looks terrible!"

"He never looked that good, anyway," Rosenbaum observed.

"That's not funny," Catalano snapped. "The man's been sick. He's only back part-time as it is. A guy works as hard as he does, you know something's wrong."

"Anybody know what's the matter?" she asked, chastened.

Catalano paused. "We don't know. He isn't saying."

THE LONG GRAY limousine slowed for the tolls at the Triborough Bridge. Seated in the backseat between Fritz Mueller and an unusually subdued Margaret, Dee Bell looked out the window, across Randall's Island toward the Bronx. A short stop, then the Bruckner Expressway and home. Home, she thought sadly…how can I call it home anymore?

In the middle seat was her youngest son, Chip, with his wife and eight-year-old daughter. Her other sons and their families followed in the next two limos, with the cortege of company and family friends strung out behind. As the car gathered speed, Dee rested her head on the plush velour seat.

"A beautiful ceremony," Fritz Mueller said, looking at the small, white-haired woman. They had hardly spoken since leaving the memorial service twenty minutes earlier. "You're a real trouper, Dee."

Poor Fritz, she thought, he feels so bad himself, and here he is, trying to cheer me up. "Wasn't Scotty good?" she said, turning to him. "Just the right touch. Charlie loved those stories about the old days." She patted Fritz's hand. "And thank you for your kind words."

"He would have been proud of the boys," said Margaret. "They spoke very well. Fine young men, they are."

I-95 and the New England Thruway. Half an hour more. A small reception, family, a few neighbors, their closest company friends, the MacLeods, the Swensens. Wally Robertson, looking more relaxed in his retirement than he had for years. And not so long ago, *he* was the one we gave up for dead, Dee thought bitterly. Arthur Winston also... and Hartley. A wave of anger swept over her. Hartley and that wife of his. She swallowed hard...*that* will be difficult. They were the beginning of the end and they know it, too. But let them squirm, they'll be more uncomfortable than I will. I have to face them, though, get it off my back. Or else I might never be able to.

"I've never seen a church so packed," Fritz was saying, "all those friends of his."

She stared out the window. "He's home now," she sighed. "Nobody can hurt him anymore."

Out of the corner of his eye Fritz caught her blinking. She touched a handkerchief to her eyes and swallowed hard. "Arthur and Catherine are coming over."

"And the Hartleys?" Mueller asked, knowing the answer.

She nodded. "I have to give him this much, he called me that night. At least he didn't sneak off and hide."

"He damned well should have," interjected Margaret, "and that wife of his! Brassy as ever, with that little smirk."

"Drop it, Margaret," Mueller said wearily. "Leave it alone."

"That's all right." Dee nodded at her friend. "Margaret has a special talent for saying what's on our minds. We could have used more of that all along."

"Well, just watch it," he grumbled. "We don't need any scenes today."

"Don't tell *me* to watch it, Fritz Mueller! I'm perfectly capable of being a lady. Even if I'd rather punch the bitch out!"

Dee chuckled to herself. Margaret's famous mouth. Where will it lead us today? For once, I really don't care. Let her say whatever she wants. She sat back, feeling more composed, if not calm.

"Fritz. I've been thinking. In fact, I've been doing a lot of thinking recently. You know, this company was *my* life, too, not just Charlie's."

"Of course! You're still the first lady of the airline, Dee. Nothing'll ever change that."

"I'll have a lot of time on my hands," and, she thought grimly, a couple of scores to settle. "What if I told you I'm thinking of taking Charlie's place on the board?"

She was staring at him, her eyes glistening. The determined set of her jaw made it clear she was not seeking Mueller's advice, much less his approval. It was a foregone conclusion. "I'm going to take Arthur aside today and have a little chat with him."

Mueller's mind spun. Dee! On the board! What a hell of an idea! Everybody'd be for it, the employees, the officers. Well, not Winston and Hartley, but so much the better. He took her hand. "Are you sure you want to go to all that trouble? You weren't that well yourself, not so long ago."

Dee cut him short, "I have never been more certain of anything in my life."

"Well, if that's how you feel, I'm all for it!" He broke into a big grin. "You can count on me!"

"It just came to me the other day, this is something I have to do. Charlie would have wanted it." She laughed. "You can't be the only one keeping that crowd on the straight and narrow, you know."

Mueller snorted. "Tell me about it!"

"We...I own a considerable amount of stock. I was talking to Ben. He says it's not enough to get me elected but I could cause a lot of trouble if I wanted to, so I'm going to make Arthur a proposition. If they appoint me, I'll be a good little girl and I won't make any waves." She held up her gloved right hand with the fingers crossed. "At least not right away."

"This is the best news I've heard since...since...I don't know when!" He looked darkly at Margaret. "And not a word to anybody, you hear!"

Margaret returned his glare. "You think I'd do anything to foul *this* up?" She threw her head back and roared. "Oh, would I love to be a fly on the wall in that board room! Kick 'em in the balls, Dee! And give them one for me!"

MID-DAY ON THE following Saturday, Philip Hartley burst through the front door into his apartment. "Elaine!" he shouted. "Elaine!"

Dropping his briefcase in the kitchen, he spotted a note next to the phone.

"Meet you at the playground – 12:30."

Hartley looked at his watch – 1:05. "Damn! *Damn* that Winston!"

He stormed into the bedroom, loosening his tie and belt. Pawing through the bureau...tennis shirts, sweatshirts. Damnit, where's that gray one? He kicked off his loafers and laced on his nearly new running shoes. Warmup jacket and pants next. Layering. Gore-Tex gloves and a blue and white toque. New York Giants.

Suited up, ready for the elements, he felt better. He looked at his watch – 1:10. Out the door and down the back stairs. *Damn* that Winston, he muttered again. Bad enough he kept me on the phone half an hour, but what he wanted, that beats everything! Dee Bell! A director! Ridiculous! Asinine!

He strode rapidly along First Avenue then cut back toward the river. Onto the pedestrian bridge over the FDR Drive...cars whizzing past. No letup, not even on a Saturday. Down the other side...stretch out. Feel those hamstrings. He scanned the playground ahead. A few children, small, bright bundles scattered about, covering the horse and the tortoise, dangling from the swings. One of them caught his eye, a tiny red spheroid, gender unclear, sitting alone in the frozen sandbox. How'll that one ever get up, he wondered.

Leaning against the jungle gym, Elaine was doing her stretching exercises. We don't get out like this much anymore. Damned if I'd let Winston foul it up. Finally had to cut the man short. Jesus! What can he be thinking of, to even consider such a dumb idea! But forget it for now.

"Philip! What kept you?"

"Sorry. I had a last-minute call."

"Let's get moving. I'm getting cold."

They began jogging toward the footpath along the river bank. They ran easily, side by side. Elaine, her pale yellow running suit with matching hat and gloves. Have to admit she looks good. Ralph Lauren. Shoot, Hartley thought, I bet we have a thousand bucks tied up in this run. Really ought to get out more...amortize. Amortize! He shook his head, hard. Stop! Leave it alone! *Concentrate!* See the river. Tugboats. Trees. No leaves. Views you hardly ever get. Hartley

glanced around. A faster runner was passing...back of his jacket...
Bank of Manhattan – 1980 Memorial Day 10K Run. Bank of
Manhattan. Winston's bank. *Winston!* He clenched his teeth. *Damnit!*
Is there *no way* to put it down!

"Phil? What's wrong? You look like it was a rotten morning."

"Not to mention being late," he grunted.

"Those things happen."

"That's the least of it."

"What do you mean?"

"Oh nothing. Nothing at all."

They swerved around a young man pushing a pink-cheeked baby
in a stroller. The Queensboro Bridge loomed ahead.

"Just that Arthur's lost his mind, that's all."

"I don't understand."

"Well..." Hartley's words came out choppy as he bounded along
the path, "...turns out...Dee Bell...approached him...for a
seat...on the board."

"You're kidding! She did that?"

He looked over at her, "I don't joke...about things like
that...Elaine. But the topper is...his first...reaction is we...should
go along and...appoint her. I'm going to talk to him on Monday...
can't let that happen."

Elaine slowed her pace. "That's interesting. That is *very* interesting. I assume you can do it."

"Of course I can. But I sure as hell won't!"

Now they were walking. "What's Arthur's reasoning?"

"He doesn't want her there, either, but he says it's better to keep
an eye on her instead of letting her roll around like a loose cannon."
They stopped at a bench. Elaine sat down and he followed suit.

"There's some risk, but I can see it. My father has a word for this.
Co-opting, he'd call it. You have to admit, Philip, it would be a nice
gesture to the old guard. Symbolic."

"That's just the point! Think how she could screw things up. All
that support but minus Charlie's mistakes to carry around."

"But if she's willing to play ball...I should think it'd be a plus for
you if people see she's on your side."

"She'll never be on my side!" he replied brusquely. "Don't kid
yourself! It's a lousy idea."

"She's a reminder to you. That's what you're really saying."

"A reminder? Of what?"

"Of Charlie's death, of course."

Hartley paused. "But that makes no sense. I mean, it wasn't my fault, what he did. It wasn't anybody's fault. He couldn't take the pressure. He just cracked. That's all there was to it."

She laughed humorlessly. "Oh, I wouldn't be so sure."

"What do you mean?"

"Look. You had a plan, you and Arthur. You did what you had to do. Surely you have some responsibility for what comes after."

"Responsibility? For him killing himself? Come on, don't be ridiculous!"

"Of course you didn't mean it to happen but it was a risk you ran...we ran. When you think about it," she continued placidly, it was one of the most likely possibilities. Plain as the nose on your face, actually. I mean, I'm part of this, too, but at least I admit it. Really, Philip, ever since he blew up over those hotels, anybody could see he wasn't stable any more."

They were silent for a long time. Finally he exhaled deeply. "This is one heavy trip you're laying on me."

"Philip, you amaze me! You knew damn well if you forced Charlie out, it could kill him." She shrugged her shoulders. "He could have had a heart attack, for God's sake. So he made a dramatic gesture. What's the difference? One way or the other, he's just as dead." She looked at him sternly. "What you need is to get a grip. How does it affect your position? What does it mean for *us*!"

Hartley spread his arms on the back of the bench. "Yeah, I guess. I guess I know I had a piece of it. I can't get his face out of my head... even at night, sometimes. I almost feel like... like it was me pulled the trigger..." He squeezed his eyes closed, then opened them and looked at her. "Was is it worth that? Can you tell me it was really worth that?"

"I don't believe this! What do you think we've been working for all these years?"

Hartley looked out over the river. "You never let up. Not for a single fucking minute."

Instantly she was on her feet, staring down at him. "You worry me, Philip, you really do. I'm beginning to think you don't have the guts to handle your own success! In fact, do you know what I really think? When the chips are down, you're nothing but a little boy still kicking a ball around!"

She walked a few paces, then turned. "Don't expect everybody to fall down and kiss your feet like Charlie Bell! If you're lucky, maybe you'll get some respect, and damnit, that's plenty! Find your loving somewhere else!"

He watched her disappear, jogging up the footpath. For a long time he sat on the bench, the taste of ashes in his mouth.

2

NEW CARPETING and drapes gave the Park View lobby a badly needed facelift. In fact, refurbished in royal blue and maroon it looked almost elegant. Damn well it should, Philip Hartley observed as he climbed the stairs to the mezzanine level. A $290,000 budget item ought to make some difference.

The hotel's occupancy rate was up, even after a steep boost in room rates, and the new president he'd lured away from Hilton was stepping out smartly, sewing up a prime property in Cancun and negotiating for another outside San Juan. It was all coming together. Damn pilots bitch and moan about diverting funds, but my plan is *working*. And that's the story I'll be telling this morning.

In a few minutes he would be briefing the securities analysts who reported on the airlines. Many of them he knew personally from his investment banking days. He was pleased at the deference they accorded him, a former colleague, one of their own, now holding a lofty position in the glamorous industry they followed for a living. However, today might be different. The session was scheduled at his request on short notice, to deal with apparent confusion on the Street and in the media following Charlie's demise, also to allay concerns about management's grasp on the situation at the airline.

A month into 1983, BellAir was continuing to post strong traffic results, but its yield had dropped precipitously, thanks to Pan Am's $99 fares, which BellAir was forced to match in several key markets. Before that disconcerting move, Hartley and his crew thought they had a chance of breaking even in the first quarter, which would have been remarkable, since the first three months were traditionally soft for the airlines. That was out the window now. And after an initial uptick following Hartley's appointment, BellAir's stock had settled back and was again trading in the low twenties, below book value, a matter of serious concern. But if he could generate some enthusiasm, motivate these market makers to change their recommendations on BEL from "hold" to "buy," the buying that invariably followed would surely push the stock up.

For BellAir to escape the doldrums, its stock price needed to be near thirty by late spring, then it would be poised for a real boost from the company's second- and third-quarter earnings, which Hartley expected to be excellent. These days, so much depended on quarterly earnings. Everyone knew this short-term perspective was highly artificial. Nevertheless it was vital, because that's how the Street operated. Disappoint the experts too often and you were asking for trouble. Hartley had a good feeling about 1983, assuming, of course, the pilot deal went well. If it didn't, all bets were off. That would be a different story altogether.

"Looks like you're a real draw," Cliff Meltzer remarked, sizing up the crowd. It was the first time in anyone's memory that such a meeting had been held in the Park View. Hartley had insisted on hosting it here to show off improvements at the hotel. He'd also stipulated that hotel industry analysts be invited, to learn firsthand about progress in BellAir Industries' Nystrom International Hotels unit.

Mike Greenberg of Merrill Lynch came up to the men who were standing near the coffee urn. "Phil, Cliff, good of you to come."

"Couldn't very well stay away," Meltzer laughed. "After all, it's our meeting."

"We can start anytime. Who's leading off?"

"I have some numbers, then you get to beat up on Phil."

For forty-five minutes, Meltzer took the analysts through BellAir's 1982 results, year-to-dates and trends for 1983, then after a round of questions it was Hartley's turn. Hartley decided to let Meltzer's remarks stand without embellishment, since they were more ample than usual, so after making a short presentation of his own, he invited questions. In his pocket he had a list of points to make if they weren't raised by the audience.

Greenberg was first on his feet. "Mr. Hartley, what can you tell us about the pilot negotiations? And that 'B-scale' proposal you announced last week. What's your thinking there?"

No surprise. This was a hot topic. It had been controversial even within his staff, when Marshall Smith first sprang the idea.

"First of all," Hartley replied, "it's a 'two-tier' wage scale. We prefer that to 'A-scale, B-scale.' To answer your question, we're making progress, though we're nowhere near agreement..."

"But won't the two tiers make it a lot harder to reach agreement?"

Hartley shook his head. "We see it as an alternative. If the pilots don't like the twenty percent cut that's already on the table, they can go with the ten percent in this plan. In that case, all future new-hires would come in at the lower scale, which is a full thirty-five percent below current levels."

"What kind of response have you had?"

"It's too early to tell, but let me emphasize a point Cliff made. We intend to grow BellAir substantially over the next few years, on the order of ten to fifteen percent annually. That's a gigantic commitment! The problem is, some of our competitors have much lower costs, so they can undercut us. Can? They do it, every day! You see, the beauty of this two-tiered approach is, it allows us to finance our growth with lower wages as we bring on new people."

Greenberg pressed on. "But that'll pit one person against another, won't it? I mean, two people in the cockpit doing essentially the same job but paid nowhere near the same? That's bound to cause hard feelings. Some people even say it's a safety issue."

Hartley took a sip of water from a glass on the lectern. "People with different experience and seniority are paid different wages all the time. That happens everywhere, in all kinds of businesses."

Another analyst rose at the side of the room. "What's your outlook for '83 on fuel prices and what results are you seeing from your fuel subsidiary?"

"I'm glad you asked that." Hartley launched into his answer and for the next hour he fielded questions. As twelve o'clock approached, a short, balding man he'd never seen before stood up at the press table.

"Tom Morrison, *New York Times*."

Hartley looked at the man intently. So this is Bell's old crony.

"Let's get back to the pilots, Mr. Hartley. You say you're prepared to take a strike, and you went on at some length about your preparations – new-hires, the training, and so on. Frankly, sir, I find what you say hard to believe. How can BellAir possibly stand the disruption, not just the harm to your market position but the long-term effect on the work force?"

Hartley felt his neck warming, but he resisted the urge to lash out. "Mr. Morrison, you will be doing BellAir and its pilots a real disservice if you underestimate our resolve. We have an obligation to return value to the shareholders who put their money into our business, and we cannot do that unless we're able to compete. I understand we may have to accept a certain amount of turnover and hard feelings. We don't welcome it, but if it comes to that, then so be it."

"Come on," Morrison said impatiently. "That widows-and-orphans talk is a bit much. You know as well as I do, it's the institutions – the banks, the big pension funds, and so on – that really call the shots, same as any other major corporation. The way your stock's performed the last couple of years, they must feel you're a helluva drag on their portfolios."

Hartley glared at the reporter...like to grab him and break him in two. Slow down, calm down. He took another sip of water. "If you'll trouble yourself with the facts, you'll find BellAir is as widely held as any other company in the industry. We're interested in *all* our stockholders, not just the large ones."

"ALPA says you're trying to break the union. What do you say to that?"

Hartley shook his head in disgust. I'm not going to take that bait. He began collecting his papers on the rostrum.

"Thank you very much..."

"One more question, please." A woman standing in back. "American is rumored to be interested in buying some of its commuter partners. What's BellAir's position?"

"Under the right circumstances, I wouldn't rule it out."

"Do you have any current plans..."

"If you'll excuse me..."

"Mr. Hartley..."

He started for the door. "Sorry."

"...would you comment on Mrs. Bell's appointment to the BellAir board?"

Hartley froze. "I assume you saw our announcement."

"Yes, but..."

Hartley fixed his gaze at a point on the back wall, over the questioner's head.

"We regard Mrs. Bell as a valued addition to our board, providing continuity with her husband's tradition, and as a tribute to his memory. What more is there to say?"

LATER THAT WEEK, a special meeting of BellAir's board was called to deal with business left from the December session canceled because of Bell's death. Hartley's two-tiered wage proposal spawned a heated discussion, Fritz Mueller opposing it so violently that at one point Hartley asked him whose side he was on, the company or the pilots. Surprisingly, even Ed Horn voiced skepticism.

"It's ingenious," Horn told the group. "But my gut tells me we're overreaching on this one."

However, with Winston's support, the board backed Hartley's decision to hold firm against the union, while expressing serious concern about lost revenue in the event of a strike, considering the immense difficulty of coming back in time to salvage the summer. Again Mueller bucked Hartley, contending they should just close the doors if the pilots struck and not try to operate, as he put it, "a patchwork operation with crews off the street." As expected, the board supported Hartley on this issue as well, but with reservations. So while Hartley had his go-ahead, it was a caution signal rather than the solid green he had sought.

After the meeting adjourned, Hartley asked Arthur Winston to step into his office. He buzzed Valerie and told her to hold his calls.

"Arthur, I was very disappointed with Ed today. I thought he was on board with our two-tier proposal."

"He is, Philip," Winston replied. "He simply wants the board to have the benefit of his thoughts. It's not a clear-cut issue, after all. There are arguments on both sides."

"Well, I certainly hope you're for it."

"I am, and I said as much." Winston looked pensive. "Ed made a good point, though. The two-tier goes further than we need, though it may turn out to be a useful tactical move. After the dust settles, our original offer may look better by comparison. We shall see."

Hartley smiled. "It certainly sent national ALPA into orbit. If nothing else we got *their* attention."

"Yes, and a very emotional reaction, too. So, we meet with the union Monday?"

Hartley looked at a message slip. "Apparently it's on for Saturday. At their request." He crumpled the paper. "Marshall thinks we'll get our release about the twenty-fifth. That's what he's been hearing from the Mediation Board."

Winston frowned. "In retrospect, I wonder if it was wise for you to put Smith in charge of this negotiation. He's never handled anything this important before."

"Don't worry, Arthur, he'll get everything out of it there is to get."

"Only a thought. With Marv's experience, it might be he'd sense the deal point better."

Hartley was beginning to feel maligned. "Marshall has plenty of experience," he said wearily, "and he has my full confidence." He stood and poured a glass of ice water from a decanter, motioning at Winston.

"No," Winston replied, looking at his watch. "I should be on my way. Well, was Mrs. Bell compliant enough for you today?"

Hartley sat down on the arm of the sofa. They had been over this ground many times before. "I still think it was a mistake."

"Look at it this way. For a small price, you made a lot of friends in the company. A magnanimous act, is what it was."

Hartley smiled. "That's hardly the fact, Arthur."

"It's all in what people believe. In any event, she didn't participate much today."

"She didn't have to. Damn Fritz said enough for ten people. I tell you, that man is really getting on my nerves. Safety this, safety that. These days he's so damned conservative it's a wonder we ever get a plane in the air."

Winston chuckled, "The trouble is, you don't have an alternative, not for the time being. I don't believe in indispensable men, but Fritz comes close as anyone we have, wouldn't you say?"

"That may be, but if he keeps this up he's going to panic the board."

"Much better that he say his piece..."

"But he *says* his piece, every day, day in and day out! What bugs me is there's absolutely no need to involve the board in all that training and hiring business. It's a waste of the directors' time, and I don't appreciate his questioning decisions that've already been made."

"That's where I disagree, Philip. No, let me amend that. In a normal situation it might be too nitpicky, but with us heading for a showdown, as CEO you ought to be looking for ways to overcommunicate with the board, if there is such a thing."

Winston stood up. "Difficult as Fritz is, he is doing you a big favor. At a time like this, it's better the directors know more rather than less. The last thing you need is for them to feel uninformed, especially if things don't go according to plan, which is always a possibility. Well, time to move on." He reached for his topcoat and hat lying across the couch, then folded the coat neatly over his arm.

"Here's some advice from an old hand, Philip. Don't take everything so personally. Lighten up! We've a long way to go before this one's over."

As soon as Winston had left, Hartley jabbed his intercom.

"Get Mueller up here, right away! And don't take no for an answer!"

SEVERAL DAYS LATER, Frank Delgado's phone rang at his Monterey office. It was Will Cartright.

"Frank, did you see today's *Journal*?"

"Not yet."

"There's a very interesting item on page eighteen. Seems BellAir just bought a controlling interest in some commuter outfit in Dallas that used to work with Braniff."

"You mean Mesquite?" Delgado asked.

"That's the one."

"Well, what do you know. That *is* interesting."

"What do you think they're up to?"

"American and them are both trying to pick off Braniff's Dallas traffic, but this is new. They always swore they wouldn't get into an ownership situation with the commuters, 'least that's what they told me."

"Just passing the word along."

"I know those guys at Mesquite. Let me give them a call, see what's going on. I wonder..."

"What did you say?"

"It's probably nothing..." Delgado paused. "The other day Fred Bentley called me, said some broker approached him, asked if he wanted to sell his stock."

"I see. A private sale. What was his answer, I hope?"

"The right one. He told them to stuff it."

"Good. What'd they offer him?"

"Three bucks over market. Seventeen."

Cartright whistled.

"You know, I was kind of curious about our volume last week. You think something might be going on?"

"I don't know. Let me sniff around, see what I can find out. Who was the broker?"

"I don't remember. Some outfit I never heard of."

"You mind if I call him?"

"No, go ahead."

A half hour later Delgado's phone rang again.

"Fred said it was Davies in L.A. that called him. The name mean anything to you?"

Delgado sucked on a pencil. "Never heard of them."

"Take my word, in takeover circles they are very well-known, if not respected. They have a reputation of fronting for the big players, meaning you can't find out who's really buying until they want you to."

"Can they do that?"

"Until they get to five percent. Then, according to the SEC, the company's supposed to be notified, though even then, I say supposed to be. But here's the payoff. Fred told me your other partner received the same call on Monday."

"Alexander? From this Davies outfit?"

"You sitting down? Alexander sold them a big block."

"Jesus!" Delgado exclaimed.

"Right. Somebody's building a stake. They may want to take a run at you."

"But I'm still safe, right?"

"Correct, but you end up with an uninvited partner holding a big block. It could be an irritant."

"You think it's BellAir?"

"I wouldn't bet against it. Take a look at that article. They're in that ball game now."

"Hartley again."

"And nothing holding him back, now that Bell's gone."

Delgado stabbed the pencil at his desk, snapping it in two. "Shit," he said softly, closing his eyes.

3

"KEN. COME ON IN." Fritz Mueller took Ken Jarvis's coat and ushered him into the living room. Vern Swensen had arrived a half-hour earlier so he and Mueller could get their signals straight. BellAir's flight-operations chief stuck out his hand.

"How're you holding up?"

Jarvis smiled wearily. "About as well as can be expected."

"Make yourself comfortable. I'll grab some coffee." Mueller disappeared in the direction of the kitchen.

Jarvis looked around. "Quite a spread."

"Not exactly my style, but it's, well, it's impressive, all right."

"I'm surprised he lives in something that looks like this."

"It's mostly his wife's doing," Swensen replied.

Jarvis walked around the room, testing each designer chair, all upholstered in gray-blue, matching the full-length drapes that prevented any natural light from entering. He was patting the armrests of a plush easy chair when Mueller reappeared.

"God, don't sit on that! Damn stuff cost a fortune and you can't even use it! Here, try this one." He pointed at a small, stiff-looking sofa. "It's no prize, but at least it's better than that piece of shit.

"Here you go," he said, placing a coffee mug on a coaster. He waved his arm around the room. "Sorry about this. I'm having some work done in my study. Nobody ever sees this."

The men settled in, Jarvis and Swensen at opposite ends of the sofa and Mueller in a chair facing them. Mueller examined the young pilot...one of my very best. Jarvis had come in for special commendation as the First Officer on Flight 159, and Mueller was keeping an eye on him for bigger things – quietly, of course, since right now he was so wrapped up with the union. Nine years with the company, before that the air force, heavy equipment, B-52s in Vietnam, the works. The kid had guts, Mueller knew that. Progressing nicely, too, captaining a 727. But these days, Jarvis was in a different hot seat as chairman of ALPA's Master Executive Council at BellAir.

The sides were dug in and negotiations had broken off. With the thirty-day clock at the halfway point, unless somebody flinched, by the end of February Ken Jarvis would lead the pilots out on the strike that could cripple the company. After the small talk wound down, Mueller settled back.

"Gentlemen," he began, "I'd like to see if we can't call off this dumb business and get back to the job we're paid to do. The normal channels are sorta blocked and I thought maybe it'd help if we batted things around, man to man, just the three of us. How about it, Ken? What do you think?"

"I wish it were that easy." He shifted uneasily. "I don't think you understand how far things have gone. The guys are really stoked. In fact, I'd have to do a ton of explaining if they even knew I was here."

"Ken's right," Swensen observed. "I've never seen them this riled up, not in my thirty years. It's almost like they *want* to go out just to teach the company a lesson."

"Then let's get right to the point," Mueller retorted. "Tell me what you need to take back, and no bullshit, it's too late for that. Exactly what do you need to make something happen?"

Jarvis shook his head. "What I'm saying, it's not just the lunatic fringe. A lot of solid guys are pissed at the chairman and that idiot Smith. The company's position is bad enough, but to think you'd even consider firing us and operating with new-hires! That really sent them over the top."

"It's not firing," Swensen noted. "It's replacement."

"C'mon, Vern, don't play games! If the company gets away with this, we'll end up on the street. Sure, you say we'll have a job, but there'll be people on furlough for years."

Mueller nodded in agreement. "It's not like the old days, kiss and make up and get your back pay in the settlement. This is a new crowd, and what's more, they've got the board behind them."

"Most of the guys don't believe it."

"They better believe it! If you do nothing else today, make damn sure they know what they're getting into. This isn't going to blow over."

"Let me ask you," said Jarvis, "does Hartley understand how *we* feel? Or is he counting on us backing down at the last minute?"

"I never know what's going on inside that man's head," Mueller replied grimly. "I won't say he doesn't care, I mean, it'd be stupid not to try and make a deal, but yes, if you push him he'll go the whole nine yards. His pride's wrapped up in this thing. That's what you people have to appreciate."

"You realize what that would do to the airline, don't you?"

Mueller looked at Jarvis sadly. "All too well, all too well. Trouble is, there's people, Hartley, Smith, some of the directors, for them the bottom line is all that matters. They have to find out what the fucking investment community thinks before they take a leak, for Chrissakes. 'Lean and mean!' That's all you hear these days." He snorted. "I like to save a buck as much as the next guy, but we're on the wrong track when you make it number one."

"That is one sick attitude. First they do away with the VP safety, our engineering department's a joke, but you've got enough money to buy a bunch of hotels. Sick, that's what it is. Sick!"

"That is the reality. You can't wish it away. And I'll tell you something else. You and your pilots are just as far off-base when you start thinking *you're* the company!"

"But that's..."

Mueller pointed his finger at the young pilot. "Let me finish! I've *been* there, I know how you guys think! Shit, I was flying the line before you were born! You people're just as arrogant as Hartley and his bunch! How can you not see that?"

Jarvis sat back, looking from Mueller to Swensen. "Can I ask you guys a question? Just between us. We keep it in the room."

Mueller relaxed a little. "Just the three of us. Shoot."

"I...uh, I don't want to come across like a jerk, but you guys, particularly you and Charlie, God rest, when I came on board, this company was really something special. People looked up to management. I mean, when I was in the service, BellAir had the best rep in the whole industry. This is one sharp outfit, they said. Go with them, they'll treat you right. It sounded too good to be true, but when I got here, damned if it wasn't so, and I found out why, too. It was your doing, Fritz, and Charlie's. You and him. You always went the extra mile for the pilots, you knew what we needed to do the job and you went to bat for us."

Jarvis shook his head. "I wasn't raised a union brat. My dad ran a grocery store, for Chrissakes, but I ended up safety officer in my squadron, so it was sort of natural to get on the safety committee here, then they asked me to do some more things. That's how I got into this godforsaken spot I'm in now." He turned to Swensen. "Hell, Vern, you and I worked on a lot of stuff together, we even cleaned up the goddamn manuals. I mean, the union's a damn healthy influence when it comes to safety. No offense, but it makes the fellas feel good that somebody's on their side when management gets its head stuck up its ass. You've got to admit that happens sometimes."

"I never said it didn't," Mueller replied. "Even with all the bullshit, you guys keep us on our toes. But what I'm trying to tell you, times have changed, and a lot of people are going to get hurt if you don't pull in your horns, and damn quick, too."

"Jesus! That's exactly why it's so important for us to hang together!" Jarvis paused. "Look. Here's what I wanted to ask you. Do you really believe you can run a safe operation with that bunch you're running through Personnel? You better look that one square in the face, because that's who'll be flying for you if this thing comes off. What kind of pilot are you going to get for fifteen hundred bucks a month? The bottom of the barrel, that's what! People who couldn't make it anywhere else. Or guys with no experience to speak of."

"Hey, come on." Swensen frowned. "There's plenty of good people out there..."

Jarvis jumped forward on the sofa. "Bullshit, Vern! We know who you're interviewing! Less than two thousand hours? You've got to be kidding! Two months ago you wouldn't give those people the time of day! So what if there are some good ones. What about the others! What the hell's six weeks' training going to do for them when they're on approach to Kai Tak? Hell, you like people looking down at you from a goddamn building on final, what about San Diego? Or National?

"And you'll be moving people into the left seat like it was going out of style. Topside'll be all over you to build back the schedule." He sliced the air with his hands. "I ask you, is this union talk? Do I sound like we're trying to feather our nest? Hell, no! This is your own line! 'BellAir, the world's most experienced airline!' That's your line! How can you guys not see it? How can you live with yourselves? How will you sleep at night?"

Jarvis sat back, exhausted. Mueller and Swensen looked at each other. Mueller replied quietly. "Listen, Ken, I'm in the middle too. My job is to hold things together."

"They don't deserve to be held together!" Jarvis shouted. "Let the goddamn thing fall apart!"

Mueller shook his head. "It's not that easy, my young friend. What I'm trying to get across – with or without you, this airline is going to fly. That's fact number one. Fact number two, somebody's got to be in charge. If I thought anybody else could do it better than me, I'd quit in a minute. That's how bad I feel about this whole frigging business!"

"Ken, I don't believe I heard your answer to Fritz's question," Swensen interjected. "What will it take to make the deal? You must have some wiggle room."

"I only wish I did. You saw the vote. Ninety-four percent turned down your last offer. I can take them out – shit, I have to take them out unless you people come back with something. The ball's in your court."

"If we took that two-tier business off the table..."

Jarvis laughed sarcastically. "Far as we're concerned, that's never been *on* the table! The only thing that did was piss off everybody even more. But okay, say we wanted to negotiate on that, just for argument's sake, which we don't, national ALPA wouldn't let us touch it, not with a ten-foot pole. They're scared to death what'd happen if that ever caught on."

"Goddamn national," Mueller muttered. "All's they care about is how much dues they take in."

"C'mon Fritz, that's not true!"

"That's a lot of it!"

"All right, have it your way, but so what? There's plenty else wrong with the idea. You're trying to split the ranks, setting up the older guys to shit on everybody else. You think that's the way to build a team?"

Mueller was silent for a moment. "Let me ask you direct," he finally said. "Could you sell a ten percent cut if we sweetened the profit sharing? Would that fly?"

Jarvis looked seriously at the older man. "If that's a formal offer, I'll have to take it back..."

"You know it isn't. I don't have that kind of authority."

"If the company wants to make an offer, I'll take it back, but I can tell you straight out, a freeze is the best I can sell. Shit, we said we'll fly more hours for the same money. In anybody's book, that's a pay cut! We're not Braniff. The company's got plenty of cash, and it's having a good first quarter. There's absolutely no way people're going to give money back!"

"I see."

"How about you?" Jarvis asked. "Is the company willing to come our way?"

Mueller replied sadly, "Not this crowd. They're dug in too deep. There're too many people they're beholden to."

Jarvis stood up, a pained expression on his face. "Well, then... I guess there's nothing more to talk about. I'd better be getting back. There's a lot to do before the twenty-eighth."

"I'm sorry."

"So are we, guys. Believe me, so are we."

TWO WEEKS LATER the thirty-day clock was down to its last few ticks. At 10 p.m. Sunday night, February twenty-seventh, Hartley was closeted in his office with Roger Bankhead. Smith and Fox were at the La Guardia Sheraton, where the federal mediator had been knocking heads two straight days. The company's position had moved, from a twenty percent cut to fifteen. The pilots were offering to increase the monthly cap for hours worked to eighty, but were holding firm against any pay cut at all. So the gap remained. Bridging it appeared to be hopeless.

Smith was expounding over the speakerphone. "Ah still can't believe those people'd kiss off their hundred fifty thou and those nice country club homes. They'll come back to us at the last minute. Just wait and see."

"Bullshit!" Fox shouted. "Don't listen to him! I'll bet my next year's pay we'll see pickets tomorrow, and believe me, fellas, you are not going to enjoy this part of the program, not one little bit."

Hartley bristled. "Enjoying it isn't part of our job description, as I recall. Marshall, the new-hires are in position. Right?"

"Right. You know, Philip, at worst it would be a short strike, just a week or two. Those mortgage payments come due very regular, no matter what." Smith could be heard laughing. "Ah do love employees with big mortgages. Them with seconds're even more loyal."

"Well, hang in there," said Hartley. "We're at rock bottom. If there's a deal to be made, it won't come from us." He hung up the phone. "Roger, get down to the war room and keep an eye on things. Make sure Fritz has all the bases covered. You know what I mean."

Bankhead left the room, filled with trepidation. Again Hartley was forcing things. Too far, too fast. Another risk not worth taking.

MARV FOX CALLED it right. Daybreak Monday, pickets began appearing on the East Coast. An hour later the tidal wave rolled into Chicago and the other midwestern stations, then across the Rockies and on to the West Coast. A unique sight, pilots in uniform, some stern and militant but most looking sheepish with their sandwich boards and picket signs.

ALPA ON STRIKE, said the signs, parading back and forth in front of La Guardia and Logan. BELLAIR UNFAIR TO LABOR they read at LAX and Stapleton and Sea-Tac.

They'd come close to a deal, but not close enough for Jarvis and his team to push back the midnight deadline. In the end, as Smith saw his verities vanish, he pleaded for more time. But Hartley gave him nothing to offer, and the pilots did not yield. At eleven forty-five, the cause was given up for lost.

At midnight the word went out, over the news and late-night talk shows, across the union's telephone tree. The strike machine coughed and belched and rumbled to life. Quickly, it gathered momentum. Instead of checking into ready rooms and flight dispatch offices, in the hours of "oh-dark-thirty," BellAir's pilots began showing up at union halls, rented offices, even colleagues' garages for their strike assignments and picket signs.

Most did, that is, though not all, for a small but sizable number reported for work as usual. It would be several days before anyone knew for sure how many would cross the lines, since management was desperately trying to reach crews not scheduled to fly, attempting to bring them in to cover the short-staffed trips. Some of those who worked did so because of company loyalty, others through a fierce individualism that made no space for collective action. Some of the old-timers simply didn't want to jeopardize the size of their retirement benefits.

Management couldn't be confident of its numbers, nor could the union, for in this clash of loyalties no one could tell who would go and who would stay. In some cases an event, perhaps small in the scheme of things, tipped the balance and determined the outcome – something in a flight manager's voice, or a comment from an old flying buddy, or a wife's encouraging or sharp word. As always, the fence-sitters needed more time, just a little more time. They turned off their answering machines and lowered the shades, hoping the situation would resolve itself so they wouldn't have to declare for one side or the other.

But the situation didn't clarify after the first day, or the second, or the third. Desperately, BellAir scrambled to put planes in the air, while the picketers kept on walking. Spouses began appearing about the third day, some pushing baby carriages, others with toddlers in tow. At each picketing location a station wagon or a pickup truck was stationed nearby, with hot coffee and sandwiches for the men and women on the line.

Then there were the others. The mechanics and rampers stayed on the job. It gave them a keen and perverse pleasure to watch the lofty pilots come around on bended knee, and then, for all their trouble, to kiss them off. Getting involved would be bad news, as the mechanics saw it, and few of them walked the lines, not enough to be called even token support.

The flight attendants, however, were a different story. In their ranks there was considerable affinity and support for the pilots. Many of them were married or otherwise involved with the flight crews. ALPA worked long and hard on the AFA leadership, knowing that the attendants were BellAir's weakest link, since the company did not seem well prepared with an alternative if they refused to work. The pilot union believed that if the attendants went out and were able to resist the company's legal maneuvering and economic pressure, this would surely shut the airline down. But in the last analysis the flight attendants weren't convinced there was enough in it for them, either. Though the pilots offered to support AFA's contract negotiations scheduled later in the year, they waffled on a pledge to back a flight attendant strike if it came to that. Who knows, the pilots reasoned, if we can beat the company alone, why give up that costly chip? So the flight attendants worked, though many of them lent moral support by walking the lines on their own time, some in uniform, some carrying ALPA signs, others with homemade signs of their own.

And did the media love it! Heavy public interest meant feverish newsstand sales, top network ratings. Captains in full regalia, caps and gold braid, striped sleeves, trudging up and down with picket signs – this was good for days of front-page photographs and prime-time air. Viewing audiences were captivated by the sight of these professionals, many with six-figure incomes, walking the line like the bluest of blue-collar workers.

Commentators reinforced the public's belief that none of this was real. It had to be a charade. Soon the whole thing would blow over, and these privileged barons of the sky would return to their glamorous megabuck jobs. After all, people asked, what *is* the big deal? A hundred and fifty thousand a year instead of a hundred and twenty-five? Come on! Somehow this distinction was lost on folks making twenty thou in a good year, or pounding the sidewalks looking for work. This elite group's complaints, most people would kill to have.

The union tried hard to push the safety issue, but its words were lost on the media, hence ignored by the man in the street. Editorial support for the pilots was sparse. Several papers took the pilots to task. "Spoiled brats" and "petulant professionals," were among the labels used.

But the heaviest criticism was reserved for the company. At BellAir's doorstep were laid the long terminal lines, the canceled flights, the stranded passengers. Initially, the harried Milt Collins acted as management's spokesman, but as the days wore on, the media clamored for someone with more stature. Irony of ironies, Fritz Mueller was thrust forward, Hartley hoping to capitalize on his nuts-and-bolts orientation and his plain, honest face, to divert attention from the company's financial hemorrhaging. Meanwhile the media, running out of angles, was on the scent of the crew experience issue.

A typical briefing. This one an afternoon session at the New York Hilton, timed for the early news.

"Mr. Mueller, on this fifth day of the strike, what does it look like to you? How many flights are you operating?"

Mueller rubbed his scalp. "Well, in terms of number of trips operated, we're up to thirty percent as of today."

"That's much less than you were counting on."

"We had hoped to be at fifty percent the first week, but right now it looks like that's a ways off. We're shooting for forty by the end of next week."

A reporter from the rear of the room. "Thirty percent! How come you were so far off?"

Mueller was perspiring heavily under the television lights. He looked haggard and grim. "Plain fact is, fewer pilots crossed the lines than we expected. We're adding about a hundred a week from our training program, but if this thing drags out, I'm sure you'll see more of our regular people back to work."

Tom Morrison, in the front row. "The union says that out of five thousand pilots, only about three hundred fifty have crossed the line. In percentage terms that means that over ninety percent are staying out..."

Mueller interrupted him. "That's wrong. We've had four hundred and six come to work so far, and they're all flying. With our new hires, that makes a total of six-eighty."

"Will you comment on the safety aspects?"

Mueller shook his head. "I have no concerns, none at all. I'd have no hesitation putting my own family on any flight. In fact, I just got in from Chicago this morning. Went smooth as a whistle."

"ALPA doesn't think much of your new-hires. They call them young and inexperienced. How do you answer that charge?"

"Tom, you know as well as I do, the union *has* to say that. It's part of the line they're feeding you people. The fact is, we've hired former military pilots with many hours of heavy jet time, and quite a few captains from other airlines." Mueller consulted a slip of paper. "I can tell you, the average age of our new people is thirty-six, and they average thirty-five hundred total hours. I wouldn't call that exactly wet behind the ears, would you?"

"The FAA is monitoring your operation?"

"Damned right! They're on us like a blanket."

A flood of noise surged up at him. He turned his head to hear but couldn't make out anything. "One at a time!" he shouted. "One at a time!" He pointed at a woman at the side of the room and shouted "You. Over there."

"When's your next meeting with the union?"

"Unfortunately, we have none scheduled at this time."

Half an hour later the embattled Mueller picked up his papers and left the room, pursued by several reporters who followed him into the corridor, still baying questions.

As the second week came to a close, the sides had settled into an uneasy stalemate. With a shrunken schedule, the company was operating most of its lucrative international and peak-hour domestic flights, but according to plan, the shorter-haul flying was cut to the bone.

In the West, Bay Airlines added several flights, from San Francisco to Reno, along with Medford and Salem in southern Oregon. Peter Churchman had spent many hours putting the screws to his commuter partners to cover more of BellAir's normal flying. During one of these calls, Frank Delgado took the opportunity to prod Churchman. Was BellAir the mystery buyer of Bay's stock? The market activity was continuing, and Bay's stock was at an all-time high. Delgado was worried.

"Frank, I don't know and if I knew, I couldn't tell you anyway."

Most of Fritz Mueller's flight managers and supervisors had been requalified and were flying the line. He was tempted to go for it himself, but decided he couldn't afford the luxury. With so many management people flying, his support staff was short-handed at the very time that more bodies were needed to keep the complex operation straight.

BellAir's competitors were only too happy to help, rushing into the most profitable markets it left unserved. For the most part, service to outlying areas was handled by BellAir's commuter partners or not at all. Scotty MacLeod's phone rang constantly, calls from irate congressmen and mayors. Why did it take somebody two days and most of his life savings to get from Pierre, South Dakota, or Helena, Montana, to anywhere else? MacLeod's beleaguered staff didn't have enough fingers to plug every hole in the dike, not nearly enough.

Amid the chaos and confusion there was heroism, people going the next extra mile for stranded passengers, unscrambling fouled-up reservations, producing the essential report.

There was even humor, though these days it came with a sharp edge. A few trips remained in BellAir's decimated charter operation, including one gamblers' special to Las Vegas for several Teamster locals out of Detroit. As it happened, parked next to the Teamsters' plane was an identical 707, chartered by the heavily chaperoned Boys and Girls Club of Grosse Point, bound for Disneyland on an early spring break. As BellAir's ground crews readied the two aircraft for departure, the overworked ramp supervisor's attention was momentarily diverted, but no problem, after a delay and some snarled paperwork, away they went.

The first call came at mid-afternoon from Mueller's old drinking buddy, Clyde Stearns, the Las Vegas station manager.

"Fritz! What the fuck is wrong with you people? That Teamster charter..."

"I don't know about any goddamn Teamster charter," Mueller snapped. "What the fuck are you talking about?"

"The damn movie! *Willie Wonka and the Chocolate Factory?* You gotta be kidding! I got a bunch of, what shall I say, extremely disappointed Teamsters on my hands."

"I'll look into it." Mueller had the phone on his shoulder, his hands over his head. "I hesitate to ask. What were they supposed to see?"

"*Debbie Does Dallas.* You know, one of those type flicks."

"Jesus! Who got *that* one!"

"I been wondering about that myself. Take it easy, pal."

It didn't take long for the second shoe to drop. Five minutes into that call, Mueller set the phone down on his desk and stared at it. How did an Episcopal priest come by that kind of language? More to the point, how did he manage to stay in such eloquent form? Mueller was tempted to ask how the kids liked their two minutes with Debbie before the film was cut, but thought the better of it.

Midway through the third week, with sixty more new-hires, Mueller was able to add more flying and the operation crept to thirty-eight percent of normal. Except for a few isolated storm areas, by and large BellAir was benefiting from an unusually dry stretch of March weather, though the extended forecast was calling for a powerful cold front to sweep down across the eastern Great Lakes over the weekend and collide with warm, moist air from the Gulf.

To the company's dismay, attrition among the strikers was practically nil. In a stuffy office near O'Hare, striking pilots manned the phones fifteen hours a day, counseling with their wavering brothers and sisters. This scene was repeated across the system. An ALPA 800 hotline out of Washington was updated daily with taped information and encouragement for the troops.

As the days wore on, the split widened between the workers and the strikers. Bad feelings grew worse. Families were divided, brothers no longer spoke to brothers, best friends came to blows. Several pilots crossing the line were cursed and spat on. A restaurant in Oakland run by one working pilot was defaced, with "SCAB" spray-painted in red letters across the front door. Pilot-owned businesses were picketed. Several pilots were suspended for badmouthing the company in television interviews, and another for a tire-slashing incident when the victim recognized him. There were threatening letters and a rash of late-night phone calls that just happened to coincide with the husband's absence on a trip, leaving the wife and children alone in the house, shaken and in tears.

For the company's part, headquarters had sent thousands of letters advising the strikers of their imminent replacement and warning that nothing but their swift return could guarantee continued work. Depending on the number of new-hires, the letter said, there would be fewer pilot positions available later on. Less senior strikers could find themselves at the end of a very long line since, as Marshall Smith recommended, the company was pledging to keep its new-hires on when the strike was over.

During this time Philip Hartley maintained a low profile, rarely leaving the Tower during the day, sometimes not even at night. BellAir's revenues had fallen precipitously. This was expected, though the shortfall was much worse than planned, since the operation still lagged below forty percent of normal. The climb back was far slower than anyone had anticipated. Several times a day Hartley and Arthur Winston consulted by phone. Winston's patience was wearing thin.

On Thursday afternoon of the third week, a haggard Philip Hartley was alone in his office. He'd slept poorly on his couch the night before, tossing and turning, finally calling it quits at five a.m. and resuming his effort to clear the backlog on his desk. Late in the day, after reviewing the week's figures Hartley had finally decided to make the move Winston was urging and furlough a substantial number of management personnel as well as underused flight attendants and mechanics. He'd just directed Marshall Smith to get it done.

Hartley looked out the window. . . snowing hard. He picked up his phone for the last call of the day, punching Winston's button on his speed dial. Arthur was at home today, a rare day off. Hartley put some papers in his briefcase for his imminent departure, cradling the phone on his shoulder.

"Winston residence."

"Mr. Winston, please."

"One moment." The maid's voice... Hartley tried to picture her but came up blank. Peculiar, he thought. Close as I've worked with Arthur, I've never once been inside his house.

"Arthur Winston here."

"Hello, Arthur."

"Well, good afternoon, Philip. Actually, as I look out the window it's a rather miserable afternoon. What news have you?"

"We're going ahead with the furloughs. I just told Marshall to get on with it."

"Fine, fine."

"The notices'll go out Monday. Twenty percent of management, mostly clerical and support staff. Same for the flight attendants and mechanics."

"What's the impact?"

"About three million a week in payroll. The schedule's building back so slowly it'll be two or three months before we need these people again. That's about thirty million to the good."

"And what about the negotiations?"

Hartley stood up and closed his briefcase. "We heard from Kirshner an hour ago. He's calling us together in D.C. on Tuesday."

"Neutral ground," said Winston.

"If you don't count national ALPA being there."

"Ah, of course. I forgot about that."

"Don't expect anything except head knocking. We've taken so much grief, no way in hell am I going to cave now. The Street still likes what we're doing. They know we have to ride through this tough time."

"Be that as it may. They will appreciate the furloughs. It's a drop in the bucket, but we need to keep reminding them our heart's in the right place."

Hartley noticed another button flashing on his phone...his private line.

"Well, very good," Winston was saying. "I have to go out in this mess in a few minutes. Anything else we should talk about?"

"No. That's it."

"All right, then. I'll talk to you Monday, if not before."

"So long, Arthur."

"Good-bye."

Hartley punched the other button which was still flashing insistently.

"Phil."

It was Mueller. Hartley stiffened. . . something in his voice.

"I got bad news. We just lost a plane."

"Aw, no. What..."

"At Boston. A Seven-three. Went down on takeoff. It's on the shoreline, just missed a neighborhood. It's real bad...exploded on impact. Nobody knows why."

"Jesus...the emergency team, are they... "

"We're calling everybody. I'm heading up there now."

"What about Milt?"

"He's with me. Don't worry, we'll deal with the media. Listen, why don't you go home. We can keep you posted there."

Hartley slumped down heavily in his chair. He put his hand over his eyes.

"I'll stay here. This is where I belong."

4

"Good morning! It's five forty-five and the Boston temperature is twenty-four degrees. Have a nice day!"

Fritz Mueller pushed the receiver back on its base. He rolled over and lay facedown on the bed. What a night. A godforsaken never-to-be-repeated night. A fully packed 737 headed for Chicago. Hundred and twenty-six passengers, six crew. Barely got airborne. Tower saw the whole thing. Happened right in front of them.

For the hundredth time he replayed the horrible scene. Takeoff on Four Left, everything normal, then, three, four hundred feet above the runway, a bank to the left, nose coming up, steeper, steeper until suddenly the plane rolled right and pitched down! Fell off on a wing, just went straight in. Cartwheeled on the wingtip, broke up and exploded. *JESUS!*

Hundred and fifteen dead, the rest in hospitals. Bad shape, most of them. One guy sitting in the rear walked away, not a scratch. Absolute miracle.

Mueller sat up and rubbed his eyes. Sure, it was snowing pretty good. But they de-iced the plane... then what? Then what? As best he could piece it together, it'd been sitting on the taxiway a good half-hour, just inching along, traffic backed up. Maybe... maybe the crew wasn't as sharp as it should have been. That thought made his gut ache. After Air Florida went into the Potomac the winter before, he'd beefed up their cold-weather training but... even if they should have de-iced again, even if it was marginal, *still* they should have been able to power out of it.

That was the lesson of Air Florida. If you're hanging on the edge, damn the engines. Firewall the bastards! They can always be replaced. Not so, people.

A two-man crew. New-hire in the right seat, a commuter pilot they'd just put on the line. Air force man, some heavy jet time, but new to the 737. All perfectly legal, all the i's dotted and t's crossed, but still...only his third week on the equipment. And the captain... Tom Rice. Tommy. Ten years with the company, but *his* first captain's job, moved up from right seat of the 727 during the strike. Mueller shuddered. The chickens are coming home to roost. Are they ever.

Now he was wide awake, turning over The Question. How could it happen, two pilots so new on the equipment? The computer never serves up a pairing like that. And even if it did mess up, his people were trained to catch it. He shook his head bitterly. Fail-safe, my ass!

He had put Vern on it right away – immediate, absolute top priority. If flights had to be canceled, that was too goddamn bad. Fuck Hartley! Fuck him and his fucking financial objectives! Nothing like this would never happen again. Fritz Mueller would see to that.

Of course, Milt would put the best face on it for the media, and good old Fritz would defend the company with the FAA and the National Transportation Safety Board. But deep down, he knew they had screwed up, plain and simple. And because they did, a hundred-plus people paid for it. He wouldn't rest until he found out why, and he would personally hang the sonofabitch responsible. Mueller switched on a lamp and stared at his reflection in the mirror, a great gray hulk in the dim light. A chill went through him. Could be I'm looking at him.

The insane pressure, everybody stretched so thin. All of us have a piece of this one, from Mr. Hartley and Mr. Winston on down, including the goddamn shareholders they're all so fucking afraid of. He punched on the TV. Local news. There it is...jumble of flashing lights, fire trucks, ambulances, police cars, and, sticking up at a crazy angle, a big piece of the tail, our winged B straddling a twisted mass of metal that a few minutes earlier had been the railbed of a commuter train line.

"...a miracle Flight 492 stopped where it did," the studio announcer was intoning. "A hundred yards further and it would have wreaked havoc in the congested Orient Heights neighborhood." The scene shifted to the newscaster on the scene, a round-faced, bespectacled man in a dark topcoat. The animation in his face and voice belied his somber subject. He could have been reporting the St. Patrick's Day parade.

"Eyewitnesses reported the plane's engines screaming to the very last when it dove into the water just off Orient Heights beach, a popular summer recreation area for this largely Italian-American neighborhood of East Boston."

The picture shifted to the main wreckage. . . it was still smoldering when Mueller and his "Go Team" arrived. Bodies were being removed and placed in the heavy plastic bags stored in the back room of every station on the airline's system. Just in case.

"The aircraft's nose section, compressed almost beyond recognition, lies on the beach. . ." Mueller looked. There it was, half-immersed in the patchy ice extending from the shoreline into the dark water. Couple of boats standing by, one a fireboat from the airport.

The camera moved to the center section of the fuselage. "The main part of the plane, foamed and iced over, no more than a skeleton, really, lies across a little playground." Ironically, a lone basketball standard stood there, untouched and erect, surrounded by debris, mocking the end game playing out around it.

"You can see the tail section lying across the commuter-rail tracks. Service to the Orient Heights and Wonderland stations has been halted indefinitely, with buses picking up the slack."

On the perimeter of the chaotic scene, the two- and three-story wooden tenements, well-maintained, some freshly painted. A weeping priest, praying over the charred body of a child. ". . .heroic efforts of firefighters from nearby Engine Company 56 who were first on the scene. . ." A haggard fireman, his face blackened by soot. . . onlookers cordoned off by yellow tape, *Boston Police* in black letters. In the eerie glare of television lights the cop faces chalk-white against the dark night.

The camera panned back to the newscaster pointing along the water's edge. ". . .a temporary morgue has been set up at the municipal skating rink at the far end of the beach. In a related development, investigators from the NTSB arrived from Washington early this evening. We have board member Joseph McDermott here with us. Mr. McDermott, at this point what can you tell us about the investigation?"

A man in a tan raincoat stepped into the picture. "We're looking at everything, of course, but we can't speculate at this early stage about a cause."

"Could it be that snow played a part in the accident?"

"Yes, that certainly could have been a factor."

"And you have recovered the flight data recorder, the so-called black box?"

"It seems to be in good condition, given the severity of the impact, also the cockpit voice recorder, though that suffered some damage. We need to examine everything thoroughly, you understand, before we can piece together what happened here, what went wrong."

"Of course. Thank you."

The reporter turned to the camera. "Reporting live from the scene of today's crash of a BellAir plane at Logan Airport, Jim Gardner, Channel 4 News."

The morning anchorman reappeared. "That, of course, was film from last night, immediately after the disaster at Logan."

The newscaster smiled, then turned thirty degrees in his chair. He continued smoothly. "BellAir has been locked in a bitter dispute with its pilots, waging a desperate battle to keep flying after nearly five thousand of its pilots struck the airline a month ago. We reached an official of the Air Line Pilots Association in Washington. While declining comment about the cause of this accident, he noted that crew inexperience is certainly a possible factor.

"According to Milt Collins, BellAir's Vice President of Public Affairs, the airline is already conducting its own investigation. Mr. Collins told us the company's immediate efforts are to assist the families of the victims and attend to the survivors. Overnight, the toll rose to one hundred sixteen with the death of thirty-four-year-old William Hickey, of Milton, a sales representative for Digital Equipment. Thirteen survivors, including three children, remain in area hospitals, most in critical condition, and two passengers are still unaccounted for.

"We'll have more on this developing story, including interviews with Edward Goldman of Natick, who miraculously escaped injury, and City Councilman Sal DiNunzio of East Boston, who again is calling for restrictions on operations at Logan, in just a moment," the newscaster neatened a stack of papers on his desk, "right after these messages."

Mueller switched off the TV and shuffled into the bathroom. He leaned over the sink. Why'd I ever get into this miserable business? He ran the water cold, splashing it on his face, then filled the sink and stuck his head in until his face began to turn numb. He toweled off vigorously.

There was a breakdown, no question. As he looked at himself in the mirror, Ken Jarvis's words rang in his ears.

"Let it go, Fritz. You'll only hurt people, trying to hold it together."

There was a sinking feeling in the pit of his stomach. Why did he stay on? Why did he fight the good fight... what he thought was the good fight? Was it arrogance? Pride? Were things any better because Fritz Mueller insisted on keeping his hands wrapped around them? He thought of the smoldering, stinking rubble he walked through last night. What could possibly be worse than that?

He turned on the shower and stepped in.

THE FOLLOWING MONDAY, Scotty MacLeod found himself in a large, brightly lit office. A tall Black secretary directed him to a sofa beneath a wall full of certificates and pictures.

"Mr. Kensington's with the administrator. He shouldn't be much longer."

MacLeod set his Styrofoam cup down and started picking through a pile of magazines. Unsettled, he stood again and stepped over to the window wall overlooking Independence Avenue. There, up the street, well below his perch on the FAA building's tenth floor, was the Air and Space Museum. With a start, the memory of his last visit came flooding back to him. He blinked rapidly, then looked away...God, how he missed Charlie.

MacLeod was completely exhausted. Losing a plane was always terrible. They'd had their share, but none for almost ten years if you didn't count 159, an all-time record for the airline. In this business you glory in the win streaks, but you dread the day the law of averages catches up. This one was so hard to deal with. It all came back to the strike. He'd handled hundreds of calls from the Hill – senators, representatives, staff aides, most of them he knew on a better-than-first-name basis. Invariably the calls began the same...a slight hesitation, the proper distance and decorum as with a death in the family, but soon they got to the point. Settle with the pilots, Scotty...insinuating that the company, *he,* had been to blame. Make your deal and close ranks, or else. Already, several congressmen were demanding that the transportation department look into BellAir's fitness to operate.

Some of the critics were opportunists trolling for an issue, but MacLeod was concerned that a number of the Hill's best people were arraying themselves against BellAir. They were coming under tremendous heat themselves. They'd all heard from the unions, particularly ALPA, which was pushing the line that unsafe conditions prevailed at the airline. The freshman congressman whose district included the crash site was particularly harsh, no doubt reflecting the fears of many of his constituents.

Damn! MacLeod pounded his fist in his hand. If it had to happen, why did it have to be a *new crew*!

Early reports from the NTSB were focusing on a buildup of snow on the wings, though nobody believed that would have been enough by itself. Then, as the investigators sorted through the wreckage, they found something very peculiar. The flap position indicator in the cockpit was correct for takeoff – fifteen degrees – but the wing flaps were actually in the one-degree position, four settings less than normal! So, was it pilot error? Or was it not? Did the crew try to correct a mistake but too late? Were they misled by an errant cockpit indicator? The Boeing rep was heatedly denying any mechanical failure, but behind the headlines he was digging in and cooperating like everyone else.

Hearing the door, MacLeod turned. A short man with white crew-cut hair covering a bullet-shaped head was advancing toward him.

"Scotty!" The man seized MacLeod's hand in a powerful grip. "Sorry to bring you over under these circumstances."

MacLeod had known Dave Kensington twenty-plus years. Since leaving the Strategic Air Command as a brigadier general, Kensington had shuttled between senior positions with West Coast airframe manufacturers and top-level government appointments. For the past two years he had been the respected deputy administrator, number-two man at the FAA.

"Sit down, Scotty." Kensington pointed to the couch. Frowning, he took a seat next to MacLeod. "I hope you appreciate, you people have dealt the agency one tough hand to play."

"I wouldn't exactly call ours a winner."

"I have no doubt of that." Kensington sat forward with an intense and alert expression, hands on his knees. "I'll level with you, Scotty.

We're coming under tremendous pressure to shut your airline down."
MacLeod's mouth fell open. "Don't think for a minute I'm pulling
your chain. We are giving the most serious consideration to suspending your certificate on an emergency basis."

"What!" MacLeod sat bolt upright. "You can't do that, Dave!
There's no cause for that! It's never been done!"

Kensington smiled. "Now, Scotty, that's three different things you
just said, and you're oh-for-three. Sure we've done it, plenty of times,
though not on such a large scale, I'll grant. Let's face it, just between us
girls, you people fucked up. And what's coming out leads us to think it
could happen again. Personally, that's what gives me heartburn."

"How can you say that! The board's damn investigation has
hardly begun!"

"We have our people on this, and we have our own responsibilities.
Like I said, maybe this isn't just an isolated case. Maybe that jury-
rigged operation of yours just can't stand the pressure you people're
putting on it."

MacLeod shook his head. "Since Thursday afternoon we've taken
our procedures apart, stem to stern, no holds barred. The minute this
happened we started, and we didn't need the FAA telling us to do it.
Whatever gaps there were, we have already plugged, I can assure
you." He sat back and folded his arms. "Sounds like I'd better put
together a briefing for you on a hurry-up basis."

"That'd be an excellent idea," Kensington replied. His face
relaxed. "Look, nobody *wants* to shut you down. That'd create a
whole other set of problems for us, maybe even worse ones, but we've
got to do something, so whatever you have to say you'd damn well
better say it. The administrator's comfort level on this thing is about
zero and sinking fast. You know we've got budget hearings coming up
next week. Last thing we need is to look like we're sitting on our ass
not doing anything."

MacLeod smiled wanly. "We've known each other a long time. I
simply cannot believe you'd cave in to that kind of pressure. Not for
one minute do I believe that."

"You know how this town works, you know it even better than
me. For every idiot senator who's got himself on TV with this thing, a
dozen have called me or visited one-on-one. Forget the pop-offs, I'm
talking good people. I'll protect you guys to a point, but if there's a

scalp to be served, you can bet it won't be mine or the administrator's. Personally, I believe you screwed up. So whatever you've got, you better get it to me, pronto."

"Well, if we did screw up, you're in it with us," MacLeod replied sullenly. "Shoot, your people have been all over us. You approved our contingency plan for the strike, for Chrissakes!"

Kensington stiffened. "I am really disappointed in you. Sure, we'll get our knuckles rapped, but when it comes down to it, it's your responsibility we're talking about! You invited those passengers on board, not the Agency. You didn't have to do it. You people could be flipping hamburgers for a living, but better or worse, you're in the airline business. That is your choice!"

Chastened, MacLeod nodded. "Yeah, yeah...I hear you. I know that. How much time do I have?"

"I don't know, exactly. One day? Two? Two at the outside. Depends on a lot of things."

"Soon as I can pull the people together we'll set it up. It's a good story, Dave. Trust me."

"I can't hardly wait."

WHILE MACLEOD WAS CONTENDING with the FAA, across town another meeting was taking place. Despite the media attention and political pressure, ALPA's leadership didn't believe the FAA would really shut BellAir down. That would be unprecedented, suspending a major airline's right to operate. Despite pressure from ALPA's congressional allies to do just that, absent compelling reasons the Reagan administration would be loath to intervene and tip the negotiating balance to the union. That would be lose-lose politics at its worst, a tacit admission that one of the government's most visible agencies had failed in its oversight mission, perhaps even providing a spur for airline reregulation, which a growing number of Democrats were already on record as favoring. Then there was BellAir's service coverage, already stretched thin because of its slimmed-down sched-ules. Complaints about that would become even more strident if the airline were shut down altogether by government fiat.

Something more was needed to close BellAir down, and that's where the flight attendants came in. Since the loss of Flight 492, Ken

Jarvis had detected a significant shift in their attitude toward joining with the pilots. And by this time the pilots were ready to promise the Association of Flight Attendants just about anything.

"But how do we know you'll follow through?" Susan Bigelow, Jarvis's AFA counterpart faced him over a table at ALPA head-quarters. "What kind of assurance can we give our membership?"

"I can't put it in writing," Jarvis replied. "You'll have to take our word on it."

"But that makes no sense!" Gene Stephens, Bigelow's BellAir colleague and first vice president of the AFA local, scratched his head. "Think about it. We help you get a great contract, you guys are heroes, it is hard to believe you'd throw it all over for us in less than a year. I'm sorry, I find that very unconvincing."

Barry Arkin, ALPA's attorney, stepped in. "Susan, you need to pre-sent your demands to the company now, when you go out. Then your contract'll get wrapped up at the same time as ours, in the same settle-ment. See? You come with us, and we'll really have them by the shorts."

"We were thinking along those lines, too. That's the only way it could work. But what about the IAM?"

"Not a chance," said Jarvis. "Jastrow's still pissed at us. But if we have you, we don't need them."

"Susan, what's the real story?" asked Bob Feldon, a national ALPA official. "Are your people ready to go out?"

Stephens jumped in. "Since Boston our people are jittery, I mean, *real* jittery. People have lost confidence in management. Some of them are just plain scared. They don't want to fly without the regular crews."

"Which will be never, if we don't hang together." Jarvis looked directly at Bigelow. "How fast can you set it up? Can we shoot for Friday?"

"I'll see. I'll have to talk to my leadership," she answered nervously. "We'll give it a try."

"Right on!" Jarvis reached across and gave his new ally a high-five.

WELL INTO THE INVESTIGATION, the NTSB staff was focusing on a combination of factors. Buildup of wet snow, possibly heavier, because of wind direction, on the left wing than the right, though there was considerable doubt this alone could have caused the plane to fall off on a wing as it did. Also, failure of the flaps to be deployed in takeoff position, for whatever reason, human or mechanical. They hadn't commented on the crew's experience, only to say they were looking into it. However, that issue was coming in for major media comment.

As promised, Scotty MacLeod orchestrated a meeting with Kensington and the FAA administrator. Fritz Mueller was persuasive on the steps the airline had taken after the accident. MacLeod continued to work the Hill long and hard, rallying his supporters. portraying the disastrous results if the airline were shut down. In the end, as the union expected and the company prayed, the FAA did not suspend BellAir's certificate. Instead, it assigned more inspectors to monitor the airline's operation and decided to let its normal procedures operate. The FAA would await the results of its investigation. No doubt a substantial fine would be levied. That and the accompanying publicity would serve as punishment for whatever deficiencies and violations were found.

MacLeod's news was greeted with a huge sigh of relief by Fritz Mueller. Even Hartley, intent on weeding out Charlie Bell cronies around the company, had to agree that Scotty pulled this one out of the fire for them. However, the unions were ready with fresh fuel.

On the Thursday afternoon following the ALPA meeting, Philip Hartley was pacing the floor in his office.

"You're certain, Marshall? You are absolutely certain?"

"Yes, sir, ah'm sure," replied a highly agitated Marshall Smith, seated in front of Hartley with his hands folded meekly. "Karen confirmed it. The vote was eighty-seven percent for a strike, except they're calling it an advisory ballot."

"Who's Karen?"

"Karen Bates. She's a flight attendant. Used to be a secretary in marketing. She, shall we say, keeps us informed about what's goin' on in the union."

"But the AFA hasn't even approached us. What the hell's their game?"

"This whole thing is weird," replied Marv Fox. "The leadership isn't talking and like Marshall said, they're not calling it a vote. An 'expression of personal opinion' is what it is, supposedly."

"But that's bullshit!"

"Absolutely. But whatever you call it, it's set to go tomorrow morning. That's the word."

Hartley turned to Ben Peterson. "Are you people ready?"

"Almost. We'll be ready by the morning, if we need to…"

"I mean now!" Hartley barked. "Get into court! Get us an order! If they go out we'll be screwed! Even if the court sends them back!"

"'Trouble is, Phil, they haven't done anything yet except take a vote, and they're not even calling it a vote. Until they actually walk out, the company hasn't been damaged, and unless and until you're damaged, odds are a court won't be inclined to act. Sometimes you have to put up with a certain amount of grief before you can enforce your rights."

"Your logic is truly impressive."

"Anyway," Peterson went on, "we want the best possible story to put in front of the court. Some disruption would be absolute proof of what they're up to, whatever they may be calling it. Unfortunately, the theatrics do matter."

"The best possible story? You said this case is a slam dunk!"

The attorney shook his head. "There is no such thing in this business, not with the human element. Depends on the judge you draw, depends how he looks at it, sometimes it depends what he had for breakfast."

"That is *not* what you've been telling us!" Hartley shouted.

Peterson wagged his finger at Hartley. Since Charlie's death the company counsel had become much more outspoken, frequently abandoning the cautious posture that had characterized his climb up the corporate ladder and had been the key to his staying power.

"Not so!" Peterson shot back. "What I said, the law favors our side, but it depends how a particular judge applies it to the particular facts at hand. We have good contract language and bargaining history. How it actually comes out, I can only give it my best call."

"God damn it! You lawyers really piss me off! I'm paying you for results, not 'on the one hand this, on the other hand that!'"

"In my experience," Smith snickered, "this kind of thing could just drag on until a trial on the merits or somebody gives in. Management, most likely, since we're the ones shut down and bleedin'."

"Is Marshall right? Could they stay out until there's a trial?"

Peterson glared at Smith. "What I'm saying, at the district court level anything can happen. Chances are it won't, though to be candid, there's no case in this circuit on our exact facts. It's a matter of probabilities."

"You mean guesses!"

"Educated predictions. I'll go that far."

Hartley shook his fist at Peterson. "Counselor, you'll be going a whole lot farther if this doesn't come out my way!"

THE NEXT DAY almost all of BellAir's flight attendants stayed home. Those who called, called in sick. By 7 a.m., many were walking the lines with the pilots. Their signs avoided any reference to AFA or the term 'strike.' SUPPORT BELLAIR PILOTS, they said. And THIS FLIGHT ATTENDANT VOTES WITH HER FEET.

The effect was devastating. Nearly all the airline's flights had to be canceled. You could count on one hand how many trips management crews got in the air. Now, almost all the pilots who had crossed the lines earlier absented themselves, including many of the new-hires.

Shortly before nine, Peterson and Amory Johnstone, the top litigator from New York's white-shoe Merritt law firm, walked into the Manhattan courtroom of federal judge Simon Rivkin, followed by their retinue of bag-toting associates. Going in, the attorneys were already displeased.

"Worst possible judge we could have drawn. Carter appointee...so far left he's off the map...social conscience, they say. Social conscience, my ass..."

Ninety minutes later, the doors opened. Barry Arkin and Susan Bigelow emerged all smiles, gesturing and talking. Peterson, Johnstone, and the bag-carriers trailed behind. Ashen-faced, Peterson elbowed through a crowd of reporters to a bank of phones. He flopped down in a booth and pressed the door shut, punching in Hartley's private number. Hartley answered the phone himself.

"Hate to tell you this. We didn't get the restraining order."

"Goddamnit! Why not?"

"We drew Judge Rivkin...couldn't have done worse. You know, the big Democrat DA from Queens. He went on the theory there wasn't enough likelihood we'd win at trial. Pure bullshit, but that's where we stand."

"And for your next act?"

Peterson could feel the chill through the phone. "The preliminary injunction hearing's set for Tuesday," he answered. "We'll have to live with it until then."

"What do you mean! We've got to appeal!"

"This isn't an appealable order. I mean, we can always file an appeal, but it'd be a total waste of time and money."

Silence on the other end. "Well, come on back. We'd better figure out where we go from here."

Peterson hung up the phone. As he pushed the door open he spotted Milt Collins outside the courtroom door, holding forth for the media. What the hell does *he* have to say, Peterson thought. We haven't the faintest idea ourselves. He cut Johnstone and Tony Catalano out of the pack with a hand signal.

"Bad start," Peterson said glumly. "The boss is not pleased."

"And not a good sign, either," Johnstone commented. "In some ways this one should have been relatively easy to win. Well, we'll saddle the union with a bond the size of Manhattan Island if they take the next trick, too."

"Don't say that!" Peterson shouted. "Don't even think that!" He waved disgustedly at the Merritt lawyers. "Get rid of that crowd. I want them out of my sight."

The following Tuesday, Judge Rivkin heard the arguments, asked for witnesses on matters of factual proof, and reserved judgment to study the opposing presentations and briefs. He didn't rule from the bench, as Peterson and Johnstone thought he might. As they left the courtroom, the two lawyers speculated. Perhaps he needs more time to understand the subtleties of our case, not just give a knee-jerk, pro-union reaction. He might want to fashion a strong opinion to support the company and put the strikers back. Maybe. Maybe not.

Two days later, Peterson's phone rang. "Mr. Peterson, please hold for Mr. Johnstone." In a moment Johnstone was on the line.

"Well, Ben, we're oh-for-two."

"Jesus..." Peterson put his hand over his forehead.

"We just heard from the clerk. Rivkin ruled for the union. I have a messenger picking up the order. He wrote a sixteen-page opinion. Remarkable!"

"Cut the crap, Amory! What's the bottom line?"

"I won't know till I study it, of course, but I gather he said the sympathy strike issue wasn't part of our contract, said we never even bargained over it."

"That's outrageous! Marv's affidavit made that perfectly clear! He was there when the damn thing was negotiated! That's what he said on the stand!"

"You're preaching to the converted, Ben, but unfortunately Rivkin didn't buy it. The hearing on the bond is tomorrow afternoon. We'll file a notice of appeal, of course."

"I need to talk to my client. You may be dealing with another general counsel, the way this thing's going." Peterson laughed bitterly. "How about converting this mess to a contingent fee?"

"Be serious, Ben. Call me after you read the opinion."

The opinion was duly read and the client duly advised. Predictably, the client went into orbit. Peterson was not fired, at least not yet. The notice of expedited appeal was filed and the hearing set by the Second Circuit for three weeks hence.

BellAir was shut down. For Hartley and his disconsolate management team, altogether, completely, shut down.

5

APRIL'S TRAFFIC came and went. As BellAir's crews walked the lines, the competition feasted. With everyone waiting for the Second Circuit's decision, the Mediation Board insisted on bringing the warring sides together one more time, so they met, but only briefly and to no avail. The pilots seemed more interested in healing the split in their own ranks than finding common ground with management, and the flight attendants, euphoric over the outcome in their litigation, were in no mood to back down.

Behind the scenes, Mueller and Vern Swensen were in quiet, earnest contact with the dissidents, meeting with the pilot leadership several times a week, as Smith and Fox did with the flight attendants. Scotty MacLeod continued to fend off the politicians whose constituents' air service was suffering.

"Lean on the unions," was MacLeod's line. "Get the board to knock heads. We're ready to deal."

Across BellAir's system, aircraft lay idle, protective covers fitted to engine inlets and other openings, lavatories drained, batteries disconnected, doors secured. All but a few station personnel were furloughed for the duration, as well as many office staff and mid-level management. In state unemployment offices, business was booming, some locations even setting up a special BellAir window. After the third week, Hartley cut the salary of everyone still on the payroll by half, with another twenty-five percent targeted for mid-May. Although he made much of the fact that everyone participated, the secretary slashed to eight or nine thousand looked none too kindly on Hartley and his top officers who still drew their six figures, even after the cuts.

The mood in the Tower was grim and getting worse. A siege mentality had set in. Day after day, employees gathered at the bulletin boards, hoping for some sign of breakthrough, but there was no good news. There was no news at all.

These days Hartley was rarely seen. He had taken to entering the Tower by the side security door, then riding his private elevator directly to Fifty-five. Several times a day he and Arthur Winston conferred by phone. Winston pulled no punches. The financial community was demanding that BellAir finish what it started, and do it fast. The company's infrequent public statements came by way of Milt Collins.

In California, Bay's traffic from BellAir had completely dried up, of course. Although Frank Delgado moved quickly to minimize the damage, patching together deals with United, American, and other airlines at SFO, he was carrying fewer people, and it was costing him a lot more time, trouble, and money to do it. He was working eighteen-hour days, trying to juggle everything, and still it wasn't enough.

Two weeks into BellAir's shutdown, Delgado couldn't contain himself any longer. He'd had a frustrating day, wrangling on the phone all morning with United. His deal with them seemed to be unraveling. He searched his Rolodex for BellAir's New York number and determinedly punched it in. When the switchboard picked up, he asked for Hartley.

A couple of times in the past, fed up with BellAir's machinations, he had tried to reach Hartley, but he'd never been able to get through. He didn't expect any better luck this time, but at least he'd leave a message and a piece of his mind with it. To his astonishment, Hartley picked up the phone himself. As it turned out, Valerie was out ill and her replacement was on a break.

"This is Frank Delgado."

Hartley was also having a bad day, nothing new.

"I'm busy. I'll have Peter Churchman get back to you."

"No, no. I don't want to talk to Pete. I want to talk to you."

"We don't have anything to discuss. Call Churchman."

Hartley began to press the disconnect button and lower the phone.

"...want you to know I'm holding you personally responsible..." he heard Delgado saying. Hartley put the phone back to his ear.

"...if you people didn't act so high and mighty, you wouldn't be shut down. This never should have happened."

"Delgado…"

"Thanks to you, my business has gone to hell. We had a deal, but I'll tell you something, if you don't get your shit together in a hurry, you'll have to find somebody else."

"Don't think I haven't considered that."

And I'm warning you, keep your hands off my company. I know what you're up to."

"You don't know what you're talking about."

"Oh, don't I? I know you're buying up our stock."

"We're doing nothing of the kind."

There was a pause on the line. "You're a fucking disaster, Hartley. You wreck everything you touch! Keep your hands off us!"

This time Hartley did hang up. For a moment, he sat with his hands folded on the desk, breathing heavily. Suddenly he raised his fist and slammed it on the desk.

"That goddamn little pop-off!"

He reached for the phone and punched Cliff Meltzer's number. Meltzer answered.

"How much Bay stock do we have?" Hartley shouted.

"Five percent. Davies probably has some more squirreled away, but you don't want to know that. Why do you ask?"

"Call Davies and tell them to step up the buying."

Meltzer paused. "Do you really want to do that? The publicity is what I'm thinking of. Any more and we have to file with the SEC, technically, at least. Why not wait until we get back flying?"

Hartley thought for a moment. There was sense to what Cliff said.

"Okay. Have them buy as much as they can and still keep it quiet. Tell them I expect them to earn their money this time." He shook his head grimly. "When we're back up, I am going to stick it to our little amigo."

WILL CARTRIGHT was floored when his client told him about the shouting match with Hartley. The next day, Cartright was on a plane for Monterey, his mission to cool Delgado down. After a long and difficult session, Frank finally conceded that he'd let his temper get the best of him. They decided that Cartright should set up a meeting with

Roger Bankhead to smooth things over. At Bankhead's level. No contact with Hartley, no apology of any kind.

Besides damage control, it also seemed a good time to have a go at straightening out some of the problems Bay had been experiencing with its large partner before they shut down. Frank's decision was bolstered by a call from United, backing off their demand to up their share of joint revenues and putting the temporary arrangement back on a solid footing.

Delgado hoped the prospect of BellAir's SFO commuter partner snuggling up to one of their biggest competitors might provide a goad to BellAir. Will was right. Difficult as it was, he had to put this Hartley business aside. With Cartright's encouragement, Delgado even decided to have his emissary explore a contract extension, possibly even a couple more years if BellAir would agree to more favorable terms. But he didn't want to show his face in New York. Will would go it alone.

His first morning in New York, after a flurry of diplomacy, Cartright felt he was making good progress. However, there were several disconcerting elements. A mood of gloom and intrigue unprecedented in Cartright's experience pervaded the Tower. Everyone seemed to be looking over his shoulder. Then, there was Francis Farrell's absence.

Dealing with a less-experienced lawyer slowed their progress somewhat, but beyond the purely business aspect, Cartright missed Farrell's irreverent humor, which could be counted on to lighten these arduous, often acrimonious sessions. During a mid-morning break, Cartright cornered the stand-in, Carol McNulty, and asked about Farrell.

"He's home. He got out of the hospital last week."

"When's he expected back at work?"

"We don't know. It... from what I hear, it's pretty serious."

Cartright frowned. "Last time we talked he said they were handling it with medication. He made it sound routine."

"I don't think it's as simple as that."

Peter Churchman was hovering at the edge of the conversation. "Let's get back at it," he said abruptly. "We have a lot to cover."

At the lunch break, Cartright intercepted McNulty at the elevator. "Why did Peter react like that? What's going on around here?"

She glanced around. "You want the truth? If you can forget where you heard it?"

Cartright nodded, puzzled.

She spoke softly. "The fact is, Francis has become an embarrass-ment to certain people around here."

"What are you saying?"

"What I'm saying, nobody knows for sure, but the word is, he has AIDS. And it's pretty far along."

This stopped Cartright in his tracks. "That is unbelievable!"

"Isn't it. It's also too bad people around this place can't deal with anything. Listen," she said, drawing Cartright aside, "I know for a fact he's been cut off. Nothing's ever said, you understand, but it doesn't go well for people to be, well, to be known for associating with him."

Cartright stiffened. "Your company's hang-ups are no concern of mine. Get me his number. I'll call him before I leave."

"Of course. I didn't mean it that way." She smiled grimly. "I know he'd appreciate hearing from you."

Cartright swallowed hard. Francis. The poor devil.

THE RED-BRICK APARTMENT building was situated in a block of identical, well-maintained row houses on the Upper West Side, south of the Columbia campus. After pushing the "Farrell" button, Cartright bent toward the intercom.

"Yes?" a woman's voice crackled, a tinny facsimile of the voice he had encountered on the phone. "Please, who is it?"

"It's Will Cartright, Mrs. Farrell."

"Will Cartright?"

"I called this morning. I'm the lawyer from San Francisco. Francis's friend."

"Oh, yes. Well, you should come up, then, shouldn't you."

Cartright waited impatiently as the elevator crawled to the fifth floor. Down a long corridor. The door to 5-D was open a few inches, and Cartright knocked lightly. No response. Putting his eye to the crack, he cried, "Hello!"

As he began to push the door open, it slammed in his face and he heard the security chain sliding free. The door opened and a tiny, white-haired woman stood before him.

"Mr. Cartright...oh, of course. I remember you now. We

spoke on the phone yesterday. Come in, Francis will be so happy to see you."

The woman's faded house dress covered a blocky, undefined figure. A fine hairnet was drawn back so severely that it stretched her skin paper-thin at the temples, revealing delicate bluish veins and lifting the corners of her eyes to produce an almost Asian effect. But her eyes sparkled, dark and alert, precious jewels in an antique setting. Nearly ninety and still going strong, Cartright observed, recalling Francis's stories about her.

"Francis was *so* pleased to hear you were coming." She smiled, wiping her hands on an apron. She put her finger to her lips. "You know," she whispered, "he has his good days and his bad days. You're lucky. This is one of the good days." She beckoned him into the room. "He is *so* looking forward to this. Please, this way."

She crossed the sitting room with a soft shuffle, looking back over her shoulder as she approached a half-open door. "He really brightened up when I told him you were coming over. Right away he knew who you were!"

Apprehensive, Cartright took a deep breath and followed her into a large, sunny bedroom. At once an overpowering medicinal odor assaulted him. There, next to the neatly made bed, a figure was sunk in an armchair that overwhelmed his slight frame. The window behind was so bright that Cartright had a hard time making out Farrell's face. He stepped cautiously around the bed and reached for the hand extended to him. He was startled how bony it felt, how feeble the grip.

"Hello, Will." Farrell's raspy greeting grated on Cartright's ears. "Don't mind me if I don't get up."

"Francis. It's...good to see you."

Farrell smiled. "You always were a rotten liar, counselor."

Cartright had tried to steel himself against the worst, but as his eyes adjusted to the light, he was overcome. This slight apparition, lost in an overstuffed chair, bore no resemblance whatever to the vigorous, jocular man he had known. Farrell's eyes had withdrawn into their sockets, and his once-abundant black hair was wispy, slicked back as if glued against the skull. A stalk of a neck poked up through a shirt collar several sizes too large.

"...a lousy liar," Farrell repeated. "I could always tell when you were putting me on." He laughed, and for the first time Cartright noticed the teeth. Huge, oversized, dominating the shrunken, sallow face.

"I'm sorry you've had to...go through this," Cartright said, searching for words.

"Not half as sorry as I am." Farrell tried to laugh but instead began coughing, a deep, rheumy cough that went on and on. He reached across and pulled several tissues from a box beside his chair and held them to his mouth. After a moment he composed himself. Farrell glanced at Cartright, then averted his eyes again.

"Just *look* at me, Will, what a sight I am..." A smile briefly appeared. "Imagine. Most days I can't even get dressed by myself."

Cartright looked around the room uncomfortably. "Can I get anything for you...for that cough, I mean?"

"Not really. It comes and goes. I'm sorry, Will, I don't mean to depress you. I guess...I guess I've sort of lost the knack of being around people. Not very good company anymore..."

Cartright noticed Farrell gazing over his shoulder at the doorway. Cartright turned. Mrs. Farrell was standing there quietly, taking everything in.

"I'll leave you two alone now. I know you want to visit with your friend. Mr. Cartright, would you take a cup of tea?"

"No thanks. I'm fine."

"You boys just let me know if you need anything," she said, leaving the room.

Farrell raised himself onto his elbows to sit taller in the chair. "Well, now," he said brightly. "What news from the outside world? From what I read, my employer is still on strike."

"Yes," Cartright said. "I gather there's no end in sight."

"Couldn't happen to a nicer bunch. You know, the last one, '65, I think, maybe '66, I don't remember...hated it! Hated every minute. It rained every day, and of course I was assigned to the ramp, schlepping bags. A most miserable experience, though from what I hear, this one is much worse."

"There are plenty of long faces in the Tower, I'll tell you."

"So I understand. I do stay in touch, you know, in my own way. And once in a while somebody calls or comes by, though not very often." He smiled. "Say, *it's so good to see you*, Will! You can't imagine how happy I am you're here!"

Cartright racked his brain...there must be something cheerful I can contribute. After a moment's silence, he caught himself staring, this time drawn to the enormous teeth. Farrell pressed a tissue to his mouth. "You know," he said in a muffled tone, "about the only good thing about this thing is, it's not catching. Not like this, I mean." He closed his eyes, "Don't stay if you don't want to. I won't be offended."

"Don't worry about it, Francis," Cartright replied. "I've known people who've...had AIDS."

"Caught you!" Farrell fixed Cartright in a fierce stare. "What you mean, you knew people who *died* of AIDS! That *is* what you meant, isn't it? Don't bullshit me."

"There was this young fellow from my law office...but others, I don't know... "

"They will, just like I will." Farrell reached for a glass. "Get me some water, please. I'm very dry. It's the medication. There," he pointed with the glass. "Use the bathroom so you don't get my mother started again."

Cartright filled the glass and brought it back. "It's true, you know," Farrell said between swallows. "They don't give me much longer."

"Have you been...very uncomfortable?"

"I could tell you all about it...but as our advertising people say, you had to be there to believe it. But you know," Farrell brightened, "I got some new medicine the other day, one of those experimental drugs. It really makes me groggy, though. What else it's doing I couldn't begin to tell you. Everybody asks about the pain, but the hardest thing to deal with isn't the pain, it's the people. Or should I say, the *lack* of people."

Farrell's face became very sad. "One day you're surrounded by friends, the next day it's like you're already dead. I guess as far as they're concerned I *am* dead. Business friendships – *piss on 'em!* As the business goes, so goes the friendship! I learned *that* in spades. Did I ever!"

He closed his eyes. Cartright watched as the mouth worked silently...he was trying to swallow. Finally he opened his eyes and smiled. "You know, in some ways I can see their side of it. Listen to me, Will, still the lawyer, arguing both sides. Actually, it's a very simple dynamic. They're scared. Everybody in that company is scared.

If they're not scared about me, they're scared about a hundred other things. Their job, the strike, even before the strike they were scared. They're scared if they shake my hand, they'll die, for God's sake, and they're scared that word'll get back if they come to see me. But what else is new? If I've learned anything, it's this." He held up a finger. "How useful fear is to those people. Companies don't love. They don't even care. Fear is what holds that place together. Fear is the tie that binds!"

Farrell began to cough again and struggled to fight it off.

"Hartley, Smith, that whole crowd," he rasped. "Jesus, Will, it's so funny. I've got them tied up in knots! On the one hand they're worried I'll come back to work. But then, they're afraid I'll embarrass them by dying. Just find a rug and sweep me under it, pretend I never existed. That's what they'd *really* like to do!" Farrell pointed to the bureau across from the bed. "All those years of good work, of *faithful service*, as they say. Look in there, you'll find my service pins. The last one's twenty-five years, five diamond chips it has..."

Farrell shook his head. "Still and all, it would be nice if more people came by." Again he raised himself in his chair. "So tell me. How's young *Ms*. McNulty doing? I hear she took over my commuter business."

Cartright smiled. "She's easy, Francis. Nowhere near the fighter you are."

Farrell nodded.

"And I met your general counsel for the first time."

"Old Ben? Ben the survivor?" Farrell laughed again. "You know, his heart's in the right place, I knew he was for me. He just couldn't bring himself to say so. Very careful Ben is, very discreet. That's what it takes to hang in there, year after year. Among the many people who didn't visit, he was prominent."

Cartright heard a sound at the door and turned. Mrs. Farrell again.

"Mr. Cartright, I'm making a nice cup of tea for you." Cartright looked at Farrell, who shrugged. "Will you take milk and sugar?"

"Yes, that's fine." Cartright smiled as she padded from the room.

Farrell went on. "Like I said, that's the way things are in a big company, running scared, I mean. Thing is, when you get to a certain level, all you know is what people *want* you to know. Take Hartley. In a way, I feel sorry for him. Most of the time he hasn't the *slightest idea* what's really going on, not a *clue*! All he knows is what somebody's telling him he ought to know, somebody who's kissing ass, trying to look good. Not that it matters. A nice, quietly running machine with no problems. That's all those people care about."

Cartright observed. "I'll tell you somebody who doesn't think very highly of Mr. Hartley. My client. It's almost irrational how Frank reacts to that man."

"He's not alone."

Cartright paused. "By the way, you haven't heard about somebody buying Bay's stock on the q.t., have you?"

"Will! I am *shocked*! Now, could I tell you, even if I knew?" He nodded and winked. "But don't bet against it, if you follow me."

"Thanks," Cartright replied. "That's what I needed to know."

Mrs. Farrell was at the door again. "Now, don't get up, Mr. Cartright, I'm bringing your tea, fixed just the way you like it. Careful, now," she cautioned, handing him a cup and saucer, "it's very hot. That's how we take it, isn't it, Francis?" She went over to her son and fluffed up his pillow. "Is there anything you want? A glass of juice, maybe?"

"No, Ma," he responded. "I'm fine."

"All right. Well, I'll check back in a little while, then."

Farrell's expression became serious. "You know, Will, the last couple of years in that place was really discouraging. I hope it didn't show too much. It's so different compared to what it used to be. These days, all they're interested in is how far can they push the limits, what's the chance of getting caught, what happens if they are."

"Don't think they're the only ones," replied Cartright. "I'm seeing more of that all the time, the kind of pressure everybody's under."

"Your client seems to hold the line pretty well against that crap."

"Hey, don't assume it's easy. Frank doesn't have the kind of resources you people do. That makes it tougher when things aren't going well."

"No, no, that's not what I'm talking about. What I mean, if ever there was a business where you've got to be honest with yourself, even *encourage* people to speak up when they see something going wrong, this is it. What worries me, people are so concerned about covering their ass...it's a disaster waiting to happen. Not right away, maybe, but sooner or later it's bound to catch up with you. You want to hear my theory on all this?"

Cartright nodded.

"In my book, it's all in the signals from the top. Take Charlie Bell. Where it mattered he had very good instincts. Like Frank, if I read him right."

"That crash in Boston, do you think..." Cartright said, his words trailing off.

Farrell looked at him intently, "I have no doubt they were cutting corners. At the least, they were pushing the limits too far." He gestured at the bathroom. "More water."

Cartright brought the refill and Farrell gulped it down. He wiped his mouth. "You know, I haven't had a good talk in so long!" He put the glass down. "One thing makes me feel bad, though. Here I am knocking Hartley and his crowd, but when you come right down to it, I'm no better than they are."

"What's *that* supposed to mean?"

"I've thought about this a lot, lately. You see, I've spent my whole life denying what I am...who I am. To everybody, even to myself. Then, when I finally figure out that, you know, being gay isn't such a sin after all, I'm scared shitless somebody will find out. My employer especially."

"I suspect you're hardly unique, there."

"Fine one I am, talking about integrity." Farrell shook his head. "Do you realize, I volunteered to do the legal work on that gay-bashing program of theirs? J. Marshall Smith. I asked to help him! Figured it'd throw them off the trail if they thought I was on their side." He shook his head sadly. "I am ashamed and mortified to admit it, but it's true. And all those years sneaking down to the Village, hoping nobody'd recognize me." He laughed bitterly. "One small advantage of life in the anonymous corporation. But let's not talk about this anymore. I see it makes you uncomfortable."

"No, that's all right," Cartright replied. "I got over that a while back. It seems to be in the open more, out our way."

Farrell leaned back and sighed. "Frisco...Frisco. It was absolutely *amazing,* the first time I went there. People actually proud of who they were, and not ashamed to show it. What an eye opener!"

"But there're two sides to that. It's been tough on the old-timers, seeing the city get that kind of a...reputation. It took me a long time myself. It wasn't until a couple of people I knew, I mean, I thought I knew, spoke out. I guess I never realized those were real people."

"That college friend of mine, the one I used to visit...he died last month. It was a blessing. They said at the end he was in terrible agony. I've seen it come with a rush, too...my doctor says that could happen to me. You know, Will, I still can't believe this is happening to me. Up to this last round I was convinced I'd be granted a special exemption. Maybe it's not too late. Will you help me file my appeal, counselor?"

Farrell shook his head sadly. "Ah...that's stupid, so stupid. What's special about Francis Farrell? Not one goddamn thing, that's what."

"I don't believe it, not for one minute."

"Believe it, Will! Nobody's beats this thing!" Farrell looked directly at Cartright. "All right. I have a question for you, a test, sort of. Some people say AIDS is God's curse on gays, His way of getting even. What I want to know, do you believe that? Well, do you?"

Cartright shook his head. "That would seem rather small-minded of the Almighty."

"I used to think that, too," Farrell's eyes glistened, "but now I wonder whether there isn't something to it. Must be my good Catholic upbringing. The guilt runs deeper than I ever dreamt." He laughed bitterly. "No, I don't believe in curses, but one thing I know for sure, if there *is* a curse, it's being cut off from your friends, from your life. I mean, we're all human, everybody's going to die someday. I don't understand it, why did they have to shun me?"

He sank back into the chair, exhausted. "But I have something planned," he said in a whisper. "A little going-away present, you might say..."

Cartright sat quietly, watching. Farrell was slumped in the chair, his eyes closed, breathing peacefully. In a few minutes Cartright looked at his watch, then reached over and patted Farrell's hand gently.

"Take care, my friend. I'd best be going. Keep your spirits up."

Farrell looked up. His eyelids were heavy and his voice thick. "...must have dozed off...do that quite a lot these days..." Then a faint smile. "Thanks, Will. I really appreciate this..."

"I'll see you next time, Francis."

"If you're lucky. Let's hope so..."

Farrell closed his eyes again. He was asleep.

Cartright brought the cup of cold tea to the kitchen.

"Thank you for visiting us," the old lady said, wiping her hands on her apron. "It's such a shame. Francis used to talk about the company all the time. He'd come home with the funniest stories, don't you know, but where are those people now? He's been a foolish, foolish boy, but he's my only son." Her eyes filled with tears. "And he won't be with us much longer."

Cartright put his arms around the woman and held her tight. "Keep up the fight. He's counting on you."

"Oh, I will," she said, breaking free and wiping her eyes with her hand. "Until I breathe my last, I will."

On his flight back, Cartright was completely drained. The edgy, despairing mood he encountered, the reports of Philip Hartley's increasing remoteness – all this gave him the uneasy feeling that something was getting ready to blow at BellAir. Confirming that BellAir was indeed positioning itself to take a run at Bay was not unexpected, but added to his malaise. Worst of all, his sad leave-taking with Francis Farrell.

Cartright was not looking forward to calling his client.

SOME WEEKS LATER another visitor rang the Farrells' doorbell. He waited, nervously shifting his weight from one foot to the other. He came as soon as he heard. Not a call you want to make, but absolutely essential.

"Yes?" The door opened a crack.

"Marshall Smith, Mrs. Farrell. Ah called earlier."

"Oh yes. Please come in, then."

Smith stepped into the parlor and looked around. Neat, tidy. He spotted a card on the table in the small entrance hall. Callaghan & Son Funeral Home. Damn. They must have beat me here. Several people were walking about the apartment. The old woman had been crying; her eyes were bloodshot and sore-looking. Her house dress was rumpled, and her hair looked as if it had been hastily brushed.

"Let me express my deepest sympathy, Mrs. Farrell, and that of our company. Your son was well liked, very well liked, indeed, by all of us. We consider his passing a terrible loss."

An elderly woman came out of the bedroom, towing a vacuum

cleaner by a hose. "That's Mrs. Nardone, my neighbor. My daughters are flying in tonight from Chicago."

Smith cleared his throat. "Why ah came, Mrs. Farrell, we want to offer our assistance in your time of grief. We'd like to help in any way we can." He gestured toward the sitting room. "Would you mind if we talk privately?"

"No, that'd be fine."

He took off his topcoat and put it over the back of the small sofa and sat down beside her. "Mrs. Farrell, first ah'd like to ask, would you care to pray with me? Ah would like to offer you that opportunity."

She nodded, a puzzled expression on her face. "Oh, I pray all the time, then there's the TV mass when the weather's bad."

Smith smiled. He folded his hands and closed his eyes. "Heavenly Father, we ask Your blessing on Your servant Francis. We pray he may be joined with You in righteousness and glory." Smith's voice rose. "And as we pray for this woman, the mother of Your servant, Francis, we ask You to grant her strength to carry on, through Jesus, our Lord and Saviour. Amen."

"Amen," she replied, looking at Smith curiously. "Thank you, Mr. Smith."

"Not at all, Mrs. Farrell." Smith cleared his throat. "Ah used to be in that line."

She cocked her head. "Mr. Smith, I want to ask you something."

"By all means, please do."

"I never understood why hardly anybody from the company came to see Francis when he was sick. Not many people called, either."

"Oh, ah wasn't aware. Ah am so sorry to hear that!"

"That caused him a great deal of pain, nobody coming to see him like that."

Smith swallowed. "Well, we'd like to make up for that, Mrs. Farrell, in our own small way, that is." He pulled a notebook from his pocket. "Naturally, we'll expedite payment of the insurance benefits, we'll make sure you get that right away."

She shook her head. "I'm afraid there's a lot of medical bills the Blue Cross won't cover..."

"Perhaps we can do something along those lines, too," he responded, handing her a business card. "In fact, why don't you forward them to my attention. Ah'll see what ah can do."

His words relaxed her. "Well, now," she smiled, "that would be very nice indeed."

"We know what a difficult time this must be..." Smith looked into the distance. "What ah mean to say, the company wants to put your mind at ease, help you with some of the many details..."

He paused. "In fact, we'd be happy to contact the papers and arrange for the...death notice. Ah've prepared a lovely statement describing your son's career that ah'm sure you would be proud of." He clicked open his ballpoint pen, poised over the notebook. "So if ah could just take down some of the more personal information, ah can..."

"Oh, I'm sorry," she replied, "Mr. Callaghan is already taking care of the notice."

Smith paused, his lips pursed. "I see. Well, then, ah'll just contact Mr. Callaghan, to make sure he has the information to adequately portray your son's exemplary career. Now, there is just one small request we would make. We would prefer that no mention be made about the nature of his...uh, final illness. Ah'm sure you can understand how sensitive that would be for the company."

A faint smile flickered across the old woman's face. She leaned forward, her hands on her knees. "Mr. Smith," she said earnestly, "I plan to see that *all* Francis's wishes are carried out. After all, I've been looking after him his whole life."

"But surely you can appreciate, a high-ranking officer like Francis..."

She shook her head defiantly. "Mr. Smith, you seem to think I was born yesterday. What I'm beginning to *appreciate* is why you're here, what you're really after." She stood up and smoothed her apron. "In fact, young man, I think perhaps you ought to be going now."

Smith reddened. "Don't say that, Mrs. Farrell! That's not the case at all!"

She drew herself up to her full height. "Yes it is, Mr. Smith! You know *darned well* it is!" She walked to the front door and held it open. "And now, sir, I'll bid you a good day!"

Smith left wordlessly, his ears stinging. As he waited for the elevator, he examined the funeral director's card he had palmed on the way out. His mind raced ahead, trying to figure out the next step.

A FEW DAYS LATER the phone rang in Will Cartright's office. Alice Greer, Francis Farrell's secretary, was on the line.

"Mr. Cartright, Mrs. Farrell asked me to call. I've been helping her with things. She's been rather overwhelmed, you can imagine."

"I'm sure," Cartright replied. "Did she get my message, my regrets I couldn't get back for the service?"

"She did. The Mass was yesterday. I'm happy to say there was a good turnout from our department, and Mr. Mueller was there for the company. Mrs. Farrell asked me to thank you, particularly, for visiting Francis. He thought very highly of you, and I know he enjoyed his association with Mr. Delgado."

"I'm sorry I couldn't be there."

"She understood."

Cartright went on, "If it's not too much trouble would you send me a copy of the obituary?"

"Certainly." She paused. "You do know it's caused some difficulty around here."

"No. What do you mean?"

"Well, perhaps difficulty isn't the right word, but they were upset when it came out in the papers. In fact, I heard they had words with Mr. Peterson."

"I don't follow you."

"I. . . I'd better not say any more. Why don't I just send it to you."

Baffled, Cartright replaced the receiver. A few days later the clipping arrived in the mail covered by a short note from Mrs. Greer. Cartright slipped on his glasses. There was a small headline: *Francis X. Farrell, 56, Airline Official.*

He read on.

> Francis X. Farrell, BellAir's long-time Associate General Counsel, died Thursday at St. Luke's-Roosevelt Hospital, after an extended illness. He was a graduate of Loyola University, Chicago, and Northwestern Law School. Mr. Farrell was the son of the late James P. Farrell of Chicago, and Elizabeth Dolan Farrell of New York City, who survives him. He leaves two sisters, Mrs. Arthur McKenna of Oakbrook, Illinois and...

Quickly Cartright scanned the rest. When he reached the last sentence he sat bolt upright, holding the clipping with both hands.

> The family requests that in lieu of flowers, donations be made in Mr. Farrell's name to the AIDS Outreach Program of the New York Gay Men's Health Crisis.

Will Cartright read these lines over and over. Finally, he sat back in his chair. A broad smile spread across his face.

"Good for you, Francis," he shouted. *"Good for you!"*

6

I N LATE MAY the order came down. Appeal denied. The district court ruled correctly, so said the Second Circuit, as it returned the case for further proceedings.

"No injunction," Peterson told a gloomy Hartley. "They'll set a trial date, probably August, certainly no sooner."

The attorney advised against an appeal to the Supreme Court. Not worth the effort and expense. Now the only way to end the strike before fall would be at the bargaining table. Memorial Day passed with no movement. Even if an agreement were reached, the lead time for rebuilding the airline and winning back its passengers assured two quarterly losses, plus a likely third in this, the peak season of the year. In short, 1983 was down the tubes.

Cracks were beginning to appear in top management's supposedly monolithic ranks, not only fractures along the fault lines patched before the strike but new divisions as well. Fritz Mueller and his operations people were a focal point for the pressure, since it was common knowledge they wanted to get back in the air, even if it meant sacrificing Hartley's financial goals.

One afternoon in late June, Hartley found himself between meetings. He picked up a newspaper from his credenza, the previous day's *New York Times,* and turned to an article reviewing in excruciating detail the course of the strike and the grim outlook for BellAir. With the NTSB field hearing on the Boston accident about to begin, a lengthy companion piece by Tom Morrison blasted away on that as well. An unnamed industry source raked Hartley over the coals, compounding his misery over the irate calls from bankers and shareholders that were now a daily occurrence. It was an all-round ugly scene. For the first time in a decade, BellAir's stock price had dipped below twenty dollars, substantially under book value. Loss of confidence and failure of leadership were the media's constant themes.

Hartley stared pensively out his window. And Roger, he thought...what has got into Roger?

Although no end to the strike was in sight, when that blessed day came, Hartley wanted to bounce back fast, so that morning he had gathered his senior staff for a brainstorming session. He frowned... what a disaster. Even before everyone was assembled, Bankhead was all over Marshall Smith.

"No agreement, Marshall?" Bankhead snapped. "What's today's excuse? Leave it in your car?"

Smith glared at Bankhead but held his tongue. "They expect us to make the next move," he replied. "Must figure they're holding the cards."

"A two-year-old could figure that out."

"Well, ah wouldn't put it quite that way. We still have a few tricks up our sleeve," Smith sniffed. "If you recall, we never figured on being out at all, let alone this long. If Ben hadn't screwed up with the flight attendants..."

"Your memory must be going, too. Ben warned us all along that clause might not hold up. That's a hell of a lot more than you did."

"Don't lecture me, Roger. Ah'm not the lawyer around here."

"Did I miss something? When did you step down?"

Exasperated, Hartley separated his warring aides. Attempting to put the meeting on track, he quizzed Bankhead on his ideas for coming back after the strike. More flying than ever, was Bankhead's answer. Put as many seats in the air as we can, low introductory fares, concentrate on the major business markets.

After some discussion, Hartley brought up an idea he'd been mulling over since the strike began. "It's time for a change of direction," he began. "I'm convinced we should go back to short-haul flying on a selective basis, our highest-volume markets out of JFK, Chicago, San Fran..."

"What!" Fritz Mueller exploded out of his chair. "That's insane! The commuters were your idea! They were saving our ass before the stews went out!"

"Roger makes a persuasive case for increasing utilization," Hartley explained patiently. "I'm taking it a step further. By putting our jets back in, we can keep a hundred percent of revenues in those markets, so why not do it? It's a different situation than before. You have to adapt."

As the meeting broke up, Roger Bankhead stopped Hartley at the door. "I don't know where you're coming from with that commuter business," he said with a frown. "Fritz is right. It makes no absolutely no sense."

Hartley was hot, just recalling that encounter. He demanded that Bankhead provide him with a detailed plan for implementing his idea by eight o'clock the next morning and not one minute later.

Sometimes Fritz disagrees just to be a pain in the ass, Hartley reflected. I expect that. But Roger. . .he's too independent for his own good. Worse than that, he's getting more belligerent by the day. The course he's on, I'd better start Marshall figuring out how we cut him loose. For a moment he found himself longing for the relative calm of his days at Salomon.

Frank Delgado and Bay had come in for comment at the meeting, Bankhead challenging Hartley for going in two different directions – taking a position in Bay's stock, now threatening to undermine the company. His answer, that this way he could keep all options open, was not satisfying, even to himself. Along with all the others, Delgado was getting to him, and he wasn't even a real player. Just an insignificant little pop-off. A bug to be squashed.

Hartley poured a glass of water. He glanced again at the *Times* article. Everybody's getting in the act. The directors, too, calling, visiting, agitating. Highly irregular. And Arthur. . .even Arthur's had it with the strike. The financial community was counting on him for reassurance, he said the other day, and what did he have to offer? A "grand design" that wasn't so grand anymore. The airline's bond rating had been downgraded. Now Standard & Poors was threatening to knock it down another notch if things didn't improve soon.

"At this point we have to be flexible, Philip," Winston admonished. "Our first approach didn't work, so let's come at it a different way. Be creative! Give the board something it can get its teeth into!"

No, things were going poorly, not at all as planned. And compounding the misery was a puzzling recent development. There were rumors following the stock's downward slide, vague and unsubstantiated, to be sure, but persistent, that somebody was quietly amassing a position in BellAir stock. *BellAir stock!* To be on the safe side, Hartley had instructed the proxy solicitors to check it out. Their report was expected any day.

Hartley sighed. He looked down at his credenza. Locked inside was a document, fifty single-spaced pages plus another hundred pages of attachments. Salomon and the Merritt firm had presented him today with this intricate plan they called a "poison pill," which was supposed to discourage unwanted takeover attempts.

Damn lawyers, Hartley thought angrily, where are they when you need them! Now they're trying to sell us this bill of goods! Insane, the whole thing's insane. Nobody'd dare make a run at us...but I'd better give the board a look at it next week, just to be on the safe side. He shook his head in disbelief. Nobody knows whether the miserable scheme would even work, least of all the people who wrote it! They admitted as much. Ridiculous! Don't give me paper. I need a win. A big win!

Around seven, after ploughing through his red URGENT! folder and some backlogged correspondence, Hartley was thinking about wrapping it up for the day when his phone rang. He let it ring several times before remembering that Valerie had left a half-hour earlier. He looked down at the flashing light... his private line.

"Hartley," he answered wearily.

"Mr. Philip Hartley, please." There was a lot of noise on the line. Sounded like a poor connection.

"Speaking."

"Mr. Hartley, this is Officer Martin of the Los Angeles Police Department. I was asked to contact you."

"Yes?" Hartley responded, frowning.

"This afternoon we arrested a Miss Shelley Gregory on a drug charge. Possession of controlled substances for distribution. She asked us to call you, said you were a personal friend. The arraignment's set for tomorrow morning."

No. No. It isn't possible. She'd quit the drugs. She promised! But distribution... selling! Hartley's mind raced ahead, already on overload.

"There's some mistake," he managed to say. It had to be a mistake. This couldn't be happening. Not to him. Not now. Beads of sweat stood out on his forehead.

"That's for the court to decide, but as far as we're concerned there's no mistake at all. Not the quantities we found on her."

"Is she... is Miss Gregory there?"

"She was just booked. By now she's on her way to the lockup."

Hartley looked around the room. *Think. Think. I can't let myself be dragged into this.*

"Does she have a lawyer?"

"That's why I'm calling. She thought you could arrange something."

"Can you get her a message?"

"I'll see what I can do."

"Tell her...tell her I'll find her somebody. An attorney. Will you tell her that for me?"

"Like I said, I'll see what I can do."

"This attorney. How can he reach you?"

Hartley thought he heard a snicker.

"Those type lawyers know where we are, Mr. Hartley, but anyway, the number is 213-555-3266. That's the Parker Center. If I'm not around, ask for the booking officer. That particular number's good a couple of hours more. After that she'll be at the women's jail."

Hartley jumped in quickly, fearful he was about to hang up. "One other thing. Will there be...publicity about this? I mean, will it be in the papers?"

Another knowing laugh. "Now, how do you expect me to answer that? Depends what kind of a day they're having down there. I mean, this isn't the world's biggest drug deal, but as far as we're concerned it's a violation of the law and it's public information."

"But she's not a criminal!"

"None of them are, mister," the policeman replied. "That's what they all tell me. Now, is that everything?"

"Yes...you've been very helpful. Thank you..."

Hartley forced himself to sit quietly for a moment. Numbed. Gone, any hope of repose after another brutal day. *Just when I think things can't get worse, they do.* Sighing deeply, he reached for his Rolodex, flipping forward to Ben Peterson's home number, then he hesitated. *Those pin-stripers Peterson surrounds himself with...what good are they? I need somebody tough, somebody with street smarts. Ben would wonder why I asked, too. No, I need somebody I can count on to be...discreet, keep my name out of this at all costs. But who do I know? Who do I know?*

Back and forth Hartley paced, searching his memory. *Who do I know...wait! A fraternity brother...he became a big criminal lawyer,*

made a name for himself. Southern California...L.A.! A few years
back there was a trial. His picture was in all the papers. Haven't talked
to him in twenty years. But here goes.

"Information."

"For Charles Bradshaw, a lawyer."

He scribbled the number on a pad, then quickly punched in the
number...waiting...waiting...

"Bradshaw and Mainelli."

"Mr. Bradshaw, please."

"Who may I say is calling?"

"Tell him Phil Hartley, an old friend."

"Just a moment, please."

Hartley cradled the phone on his shoulder, his elbows on his desk.
Suddenly a hearty voice roused him.

"Phil Hartley! How the hell *are* you! How long has it *been*?"

"'Say, Chuck. Oh, I've had better days, but overall, pretty well."

"Still have that high-powered job? You people aren't getting much
good press these days, are you?"

"No, but we're about to turn things around. Listen, Chuck, the
reason I called..."

"I figured there was a reason. No, thanks, I gave at the office. Last
year, too."

"I wish it were that simple."

"Ah! One of *those*! So, tell me, what've you got going?"

"Well, I...this friend of mine just got arrested on some kind of
drug charge."

"What's the charge?" Bradshaw asked sharply.

"Possession...for distribution."

"I see. I see."

"What I need to know is whether you can do something for
her...you know, represent her."

"That *is* how I make my living, but you should realize I'm not a
public defender. In cases like this we screen pretty carefully who we
take on..."

"Look, Chuck, she's a good person. I'll make it worth your while."

"No, no, I didn't mean that, but since you mention it, that is something I tend to ask up front. I don't come cheap, you understand."

"That doesn't matter. Whatever it takes to get her off and back into treatment."

"Oh, so there may be something to this...just between us?" A tone of kinship crept into Bradshaw's voice.

"I'm afraid so. She's had some problems, but never anything like this, nothing with the police."

"What's her name?"

"Shelley Gregory. It just happened. She's being held by the L.A. Police."

"You mind telling me where? There's a couple of places she could be."

"An Officer Martin, the phone number..." he fumbled on his desk for the slip of paper, "the Parker Center, the number's..."

"The Glass House. That's what we call it out here. Don't worry, I've got the number." Bradshaw chuckled. "I take it, Phil, this is a...*special* friend?"

"Yes. Very."

"Naturally you'll want your involvement kept out of this."

Hartley practically leapt into the phone. "My involvement! What do you mean, my involvement!"

Bradshaw went on smoothly, "I don't mean you're tied into whatever scam she's got going. I mean, shall we say, your personal involvement. And your financial support of her defense."

"But I *can't* be brought into this!"

"I hear what you're saying."

He paused. "Tell her I'll be in touch as soon as I can, and, Chuck..." he paused, "do whatever's necessary."

"Maybe we can get her out on her own recognizance. Depends. You'll go bail for her, if we have to go that route?"

"Yes. Certainly. This is all some terrible mistake. I'm sure that's what you'll find."

"There is always that chance, but don't get your hopes up. Though of course, the court'll never find out what we really think, will it?"

7

B RADSHAW MOVED quickly. By noon the next day Shelley was out on bail and he was talking plea bargain with the DA. Evidence against her suppliers for a reduced sentence was the idea. The local press briefly noted the arrest, but the airline was not mentioned. Hartley phoned Shelley several times, but not until the following weekend was he able to break away to visit. Several false starts with the unions and an upcoming directors' meeting occupied all his waking hours.

To call the directors restive would be a gross understatement. Takeover rumors, now circulating freely, added to the general discord. Several names were tossed about, but it was all guesswork. Was it another airline? A takeover artist? Or, as Hartley personally believed, nothing at all? The market was crediting the rumors, however, and BEL had already jumped two points on speculation. Finally, at the end of the all-day board session, the poison pill was adopted after five hours of presentations from the Merritt firm and Salomon, and a debate that, at several points, threatened to fly apart in confusion.

Shelley's predicament weighed heavily on Hartley. Seeing her so soon after the arrest was risky, but he desperately needed to assure himself that everything was under control. The day of reckoning was closing in. Soon he would have to make hard decisions about her, about them. It was unwise to be seen together, so he checked into a hotel for the weekend. Now, sitting in her bright, modern kitchen, he realized how weary he was, groggy from tossing and turning all night, then oversleeping, rising at ten. Several wire-handled cardboard containers stood empty on the counter, the remains of Chinese take-out, a late lunch.

Over Shelley's vehement objection, Hartley insisted that she return to the detox center. As it turned out, the court had the same idea, ordering her to a secure facility with a rehabilitation program. And there she would stay until Chuck completed his deal – hopefully, a suspended sentence, though he still wasn't sure he could pull that off.

Damn! Hartley thought, how did things ever get to this point? When he learned what the police had found, he was devastated. A quarter-kilo of pure Colombian cocaine, dozens of street-size bags of marijuana and other paraphernalia. She swore up and down she wasn't selling the stuff, that it was planted in her car, but finally she broke down and admitted everything to him. Jesus! What if she'd been caught at the airport? What if she'd been in uniform! Everything would have come out. Everything! What a disaster!

Furloughed during the strike, Shelley was now on indefinite leave until the charges were resolved. This time Hartley stayed completely out of it and let Personnel handle the situation as they would with any employee in trouble. Actually, she said, they were quite nice, considering. The personnel rep told her they appreciated her showing up for work the day everybody walked out, that she was one of the few who did. That had been noted with approval in her file.

"Phil?" She called out to him from the bedroom.

Hartley looked up from the *Los Angeles Times* Sunday sports section.

"Will you come here? I want to show you something."

He put the paper down and walked into the bedroom. The bed was covered with clothes and open suitcases. She was holding up a dress...the green dress she wore the night they met.

"Look familiar?" she asked. "I hope."

"That seems like a long time ago." He sat down on the edge of the bed.

"I haven't worn it since," she sighed, putting it back in the closet. "It's not as if we go anyplace I could wear it."

The remark stung him. She knew the ground rules, what they could and couldn't do. They had come so far. Now, thanks to her, again they were nowhere.

She knelt on the bed and put her hand on his shoulder. "We've never been able to act like normal people. Now, my screwing up like this..."

Hartley took her hand. "What's done is done." He looked at the clothes on the bed. "Finish packing. Janie'll be here soon."

"I don't want to go. I've heard about places like that."

"Unfortunately, the state of California has a piece of you, now."

She tossed a sweater into the suitcase and closed the lid. "Chuck says if I rat on those people there could be trouble. Not that I couldn't figure that out."

"But you'll do it. Right?"

She nodded. "There's a couple of my so-called friends I would like them to put away and lose the key. Oh, I'll do it all right."

She sat down next to him again, putting her hand on his knee.

"I'm sorry I'm doing this to you. I really am. You should've ditched me when you had the chance. But since that's out of the question now..." She smiled. "You'd almost think I planned it this way."

Hartley looked into her eyes. Behind the bravado, she was terrified. He was torn apart, knowing how little time remained for them. She also knew. Of that he was sure.

"Just get better." He kissed her on the forehead. "That's all that matters."

As Hartley held her, a thought rose up in him. So incredible... impossible. Yet each time he pushed it aside, it stormed back, not to be denied.

This is my fault. It's me. I did it to her.

Gently, he pushed Shelley away, holding her at arm's length, his hands on her shoulders. She looked at him, puzzled, as his eyes burned into hers. It was as if he were seeing her for the first time.

What is this woman to me? A fantasy, an object to be dismissed after I take my pleasures, then left to her own destructive devices? I know what she is not. She is no part of my real world. She knows that. She knows there never will be a commitment, a normal life, whatever that might mean. But I started this, I forced my way back into her life. Was it I who shoved her back into this mire that is smothering her?

An unaccustomed feeling of shame swept over Hartley. He shuddered. Is there another name, an ugly name, for what I took to be simple, innocent pleasure?

A FEW HOURS LATER Hartley was reclining in a first class seat on TWA's red-eye to New York. A full flight. Oversold, in fact. A lot of our customers here, Hartley thought gloomily. They wouldn't be so full if it weren't for us. We *must* get things settled soon. During the flight he read a few pages in a paperback from the airport gift shop, then after the snack service was over and the cabin lights were turned down, he settled back with a pillow and blanket. His seatmate was already asleep, snoring softly.

Hartley tossed and turned, his mind racing. . .so much going on, so much to keep track of. Shelley. The strike. Winston's antagonism. Elaine. Roger, acting so strange. Where was it all going? If only he could see ahead six months, a year. Hartley felt his eyes growing heavy. . . dropping off.

Suddenly he shuddered violently in his sleep. Roger Bankhead was in the seat beside him, arguing about something. Damn! What is wrong with Roger? Not the same person I hired. He'd better straighten himself out soon, or else...

Some time later Hartley awoke with a start. He stretched and looked at his watch. One-thirty. Four-thirty New York time. Be there in less than two hours. Go home, shower, then back in. No letup, never any letup. He was vaguely unsettled. . .trying to remember something. What was it? Oh yes, Jeff Mandel, my hotshot young colleague from Salomon, my old shop. God, that was a long time ago, and now he's our financial advisor. Unbelievable. It tied in to something Marshall Smith said, something about upping the ante. Pilot profit sharing? That's it. It was after that briefing on the poison pill.

Mandel was saying if somebody were going to take a run at the company, or even if they weren't, why shouldn't a group of insiders think about putting together a deal to buy the company themselves? A team led by Hartley and his top people, of course.

Now he was sitting up, wide awake. Mandel's thinking – the stock's so depressed we could pay BellAir's unhappy stockholders a premium over market and come away with a very nice package for ourselves. Despite the strike, the airline was sitting on a healthy cash cushion, some of which could be used to finance the deal. Management puts up some funds, the employees kick in from their pension plans, the corporation could borrow the rest. There are ways. What makes the idea doubly interesting, it might break the logjam, might persuade the pilots and flight attendants to close ranks and get back to work.

Hartley looked out. A splash of lights filled the window, a black crescent framing a large city. Chicago, it looks like. Lake Michigan. It's intriguing. Have to ask Jeff and the lawyers to scope it out. If we give the rank and file a stake, not too much, just enough. And what a sweet deal for me and my people! It'd kill a whole lot of birds...

Hartley closed his eyes...try to get some shuteye. For the next hour he dozed fitfully.

TRAPPED IN THE DEPLANING crowd, Hartley pressed toward the jetway, kicking himself that he hadn't arranged to be met by his driver, but this was meant to be a very low-profile trip. As he emerged into the gate area a maroon-jacketed agent stopped him.

"Mr. Hartley?"

"Yes," he replied, startled. Only his secretary and the emergency coordinator in Dispatch knew he'd be on this flight.

"Message for you, sir." The agent handed him an envelope.

Hartley stepped into a nearby boarding area, draping his garment bag across an empty row of seats as he ripped open the envelope.

"Call Mr. Peterson at the office. Urgent!" A scribbled time...5:30 a.m. He glanced at his watch...6:25! He picked up his bag and crossed quickly to a bank of phones, punching in the lawyer's number.

"Peterson here."

"Ben. Got your message. What's going on?"

"Just got here myself. Listen, I had this call about an hour ago at home. Sandor Meyerson... you know the name, of course."

"Meyerson? Sure. Newspapers..."

"Newspapers, TV stations, publishing houses, you name it, he owns it. His lawyer was calling, a friendly call, he says. They want to make sure you're around today, as he put it, to give 'full and prompt attention' to a proposition. He said Meyerson owns twelve percent of our stock. Apparently Friday they bought a big block that took them over the limit, so they're filing with the SEC today. Said they didn't want us to see it in the papers first."

"Damned decent of him," Hartley said curtly. "So that's who it was. He finally surfaced."

"Yeah. This lawyer, Kleinman, he's a big takeover type. They're delivering a letter to us at nine a.m. As a large shareholder, they are making certain demands..."

"Such as?"

"He didn't go into detail. They don't like the way we're running the company. Obviously."

"Horseshit!"

"Exactly. But if he's not bluffing, they've got leverage."

"Let's cut this short. I'll be in as soon as I can."

"I called Mandel etcetera. They'll be here at nine. We'd better be prepared to move fast."

Hartley paused. "Ben, by the way, I've been thinking about that leveraged buyout idea..."

"Way ahead of you, boss. I already asked Jeff to brief us. It may be an idea whose time has come."

Hartley hung up the phone and reached for his bag, his heart beating fast, adrenaline coursing through his system. He strode rapidly down the underground passageway to the street, his step resounding on the marble floor. The sound took him back in time, to days of cleats clattering in the tunnel under a grandstand leading from the locker room... suddenly he emerges into the brilliant sunlight, a stunning spectacle of green and blue and gold. The roar of the crowd washes over him.

Once again Philip Hartley takes the field, only moments until the kickoff...thrilled to the roots of his being.

AT THE STROKE of nine the letter arrived, carried by a leotard-clad messenger, his wispy beard creeping out under a bike helmet. Valerie Wood slit the envelope and brought it to Hartley, who was waiting impatiently in the directors' conference room with his advisors. He quickly scanned the short letter then handed it back to her.

"Eight copies. Make them on my private copier."

Hartley looked around. Every eye was on him. "No surprises, gentlemen. Mr. Meyerson wants to have us for lunch, that's all."

A moment later the secretary returned. Hartley fanned the copies around the table.

"Ben, you're responsible for security on this thing. Collect everything when we're finished. Then shred it."

Walter Wallace, the Merritt firm's corporate law expert, Mandel, Salomon's mergers and acquisitions specialist, and Hartley's inner circle. They began to read. Under S.M. International's stylized logo, an eye, presumably all-seeing, set in a series of interlocking squares, the letter began.

> May 5, 1983
>
> Dear Mr. Hartley:
>
> I am pleased to inform you that S.M. International is the owner of 12.3 percent of the common stock of Bell Industries, Inc. As chairman of SMI, I have followed with great interest your company's activities, since we first began investing in it. I must say I share the prevailing criticism of your recent performance. In fact, it is to protect our initial stake, at that time made solely for investment purposes, that I felt obliged to acquire the additional shares we purchased last week.

Hartley looked up... furrowed brows all around.

> As the largest shareholder in BellAir Industries, Inc., I hereby make demand for immediate appointment of two representatives to your board of directors, pursuant to your articles and bylaws. I will expect your consent no later than five o'clock, Friday, May 20, 1983. Absent your agreement, be advised that I will move ahead with a tender offer for the balance of the Bell Industries shares that we do not, as yet, own.
>
> I trust this will meet with your board's approval, and look forward to establishing a mutually advantageous relationship with you and your management group. Following your favorable reply, an early meeting between us would be indicated.
>
> Yours truly,
>
> Sandor R. Meyerson, Chairman

Calmly, Hartley set the letter on the table. Fritz Mueller was the first to speak. He flipped his copy to Peterson. "Shred mine now, Ben. Piece of shit, that's all it is."

The outside counsel, Wallace, glared at Mueller disdainfully. "Mr. Mueller, I'm afraid you miss the point. This fellow Meyerson is now the largest shareholder of the company that employs you. In a very real sense, you are now working for him. He's your new boss!"

"The hell he is! Not if I have anything to say about it!"

Everyone began speaking at once, conversations crossing, the comments flying thick and fast. Finally, Hartley slammed his hand down on the table.

"*All right!* Let's have some *order* here! Walter, Ben, surely we don't have to cave in to garbage like this!"

The two lawyers eyed one another – the wealthy, patrician dean of New York's corporate bar, BellAir's embattled in-house counsel. Wallace jumped in first.

"That's right, Philip. Ultimately, Meyerson is entitled to representation, but only by presenting a slate for election at the next annual meeting. Meantime, it's your discretion and the board's whether to comply with his wishes, or not to comply, or to go some part of the way. Of course, if he goes directly to the shareholders with a tender offer or attempts a proxy fight, that would be an altogether different matter."

"But there's no requirement I even meet with him."

"No *legal* requirement, though it might be the prudent thing to do. He is a serious and, I might add, successful investor."

"Investor!" Mandel retorted. "The man's a raider! He buys under-valued companies, busts them up, and sells off the parts. Not to mention his greenmail plays."

"We don't know for a fact that's what he has in mind here," said Smith.

"Come on, that is how the man operates. He's a very sharp, slippery customer. And his advisors are top-of-the-line – First Boston and the Spofford law firm. You know Gene Kleinman, Walter."

Wallace nodded. "Bear in mind, Philip, if Meyerson offers to buy the rest of our shares for anything like a reasonable price, you'd be obliged to present his offer to the board. They, then, would have to give it full and fair consideration."

"I talked to Arthur a few minutes ago," Hartley interjected. "He did a deal with Meyerson a few years back. He says you have to watch yourself every step of the way with that guy." He turned to Wallace. "I'll meet with him, all right, but it'll be on my terms and not until I'm ready. Damnit, Walter, even if he *does* tender, we've got our poison pill! That would trigger it, right?"

Peterson shook his head. "Not if it's an all-cash offer. That's how you defeat the pill."

"Yes," Wallace added, "assuming it's a fair price and all cash, no junk bonds or funny money, then as a matter of law, let alone good corporate policy, you may have little basis to resist."

Mueller was sputtering. By now his face was a deep scarlet.

"Save your heart attack for later, Fritz. Okay?" Hartley sat forward in his chair. "Look. I'm not going to be taken over by *anybody*, least of all some bust-up artist!" He turned to Mandel. "Jeff, that management buyout idea. If it makes sense otherwise, could we use it to block a takeover?"

"I'll defer to counsel, but the short answer is, yes, it makes sense and, yes, it can serve as a blocking maneuver. Don't get me wrong, it's not airtight. A better offer could blow it away, but it has a lot going for it." Mandel looked at his watch.

"Okay. Three minutes of LBO 101. Stop me if I run over. First and most important, never, never, *never* call a leveraged buyout a 'management' buyout. It's an *employee LBO*. It goes down much better that way. Walter, jump in if I go off base."

Mandel waved his hand at the group. "It's really very simple. A group led by current management makes its own offer for all the shares of BellAir Industries. You bring as many employee groups into it as you want. In fact, Marshall and I were talking about this. If you spread the ownership around, possibly you could wrap this thing up in one package and settle the strike at the same time."

"But that's impossible!" Mueller exclaimed. "How many shares do we have outstanding? Sixteen million?"

"Correct," replied Mandel, "and you closed Friday at 21⅞, still under book value, I might add. So let's say a ballpark figure would be...what? Thirty-two?" He punched some numbers into a calculator. "You're looking at half a billion, give or take, not counting expenses."

"That's what I said," Mueller shook his head forcefully. "Nobody's got that kind of money!"

"I'm coming to that," replied Mandel. "First of all, we're talking *everybody* kicks into the kitty. You shift some pilot pension money to an employee stock ownership plan that pays into the pot. Same with the flight attendants and the mechanics, though they have less to play with. The nonunion people are in on the same basis."

"Don't count on the IAM," warned Mueller.

"Whatever. Of course, the flip side is, plan on giving the unions one, maybe two seats on the board." Mandel observed the sour expressions around the table. "I know that's not how you people look at the world, but these aren't normal times, and, like I said, it could be a way to get you over the hump with the strike." Mandel shook his head. "C'mon, guys, you don't have to do *that* much, just enough to make it look good. Okay, okay, say one seat."

There was a crooked smile on Bankhead's face. "Those employee contributions are only a fraction of what you'd need. Let's have the rest of the story."

Mandel continued. "The biggest slug of money would come from notes we'd sell. Some private placements, some from a public sale, then we'd need other sources too, big players, if you get my drift, maybe Japanese. And part of the loans would be secured by your fleet. You still have plenty of equity there."

Bankhead sat back, satisfied. "That's what it comes down to. The debt load."

Mandel glanced at Bankhead but plowed ahead, ignoring the remark.

"Now, here's the best part, what's in it for you. Gentlemen, if you pull off this deal, senior management will walk away with thirty, forty percent of this company. In other words, BellAir would be owned by the people who work for it, top management having the largest stake. Of course, you'll have to come up with a certain amount of your own funds, though with your stock and options that isn't as hard as it sounds." He winked at Cliff Meltzer. "I have a feeling the company could be persuaded to arrange some low-interest loans."

"Sounds downright socialistic, don't it," Smith added with a grin. "Ah've made a study of these LBOs, and what happens in some cases, you let the thing run a couple of years till you're in the black again 'cause everybody's bustin' their butt, you pump up the stock real good, then you sell the sucker off in a public offering. Some major, *major* money's been made that way!"

"But Roger's right," Meltzer cautioned. "Mind you, I'm not saying it isn't worth doing, but this kind of a deal basically puts the company in hock up to its eyeballs. Our debt-equity ratio would go off the charts, and it'd kill our borrowing capacity for some time to come. We'd be hard-pressed to finance the planes we have on option."

"But it's not impossible," said Hartley curtly.

"No, not impossible."

"Then there's the little matter of leverage if business turns down," Bankhead added. "Traffic's picking up nicely, for everybody but us, that is, but who's to say how long that'll last. Skip a dividend once in a while, no big deal, but it's a different story when the banker's on your doorstep. Those folks don't like to be kept waiting."

"That's why we pay you and Cliff so well," Hartley snapped. "Anybody can win the easy ones."

"Speaking of bankers," Mandel continued, "there's no question in my mind we can arrange a consortium for the financing, but there are two big 'ifs,' and we may as well face them up front. The strike is a complication, a big one. I don't know that one of these has ever been done under the gun like this, but I'm making the assumption we can pull it off, if a settlement is part and parcel of the deal. Although the debt'll cost us more because of the risk."

"What's your other 'if'?" Bankhead asked.

"It's not so much an 'if' as a given. We have to get significant concessions from all the employees, and I do mean significant. Everybody's got to put their shoulder to the wheel to make this thing work."

"Meaning?" Mueller looked belligerently at Mandel.

"Meaning, your salary costs are still way too high. I won't even get in the front door with my lenders unless I have a commitment to bring them down. At least another ten percent."

"You have got to be kidding!" Mueller shouted. "Where have you been the last six months, Mandel? Don't you know what's been going on around here?" He pushed his chair away from the table. "That tubes it, as far as I'm concerned."

Mandel held up his hand, "No! No! You miss the point! I'm

talking ownership, a seat on the board! The employees'll be running the company! At least that's how you'll sell it. They'll love it!"

"It'll never sell," said Bankhead, speaking very rapidly. "We're already into management for ten percent, and the pilots turned the pay cut down flat. Jeff, there's something you don't understand about these people. They don't want to run this airline themselves. They just want us to do it better."

"Roger is exactly right," Mueller grunted. "The pilots, sure, they talk about what great managers they are, but when it comes down to it, they just want to fly airplanes and be paid a pile of money doing it. No, your idea has no chance, none at all."

"All I'm telling you is what I need. Everybody has to be on board or it won't work!"

Hartley glared at Mueller and Bankhead. "Jeff, this is terrific! How fast can you and Walter put this together?"

"I can flesh it out in a couple of days. Give me the weekend, too. How about Monday afternoon, say two o'clock." Mandel glanced at Wallace, who nodded. "I'll have to make some calls to our sources. In confidence, of course."

Hartley folded his hands. "Fritz, from here on out, your job, your *only* job, is to get the pilot leadership on board with the concept. Marshall, you take the flight attendants. For the time being we'll hold off on the IAM. Peg all the cuts at ten percent."

"Oh sure," Mueller fumed. "Ten percent, just like that! And what about Meyerson? What do I say about that joker?"

Wallace shook his head. "Nothing yet," he answered. "Wait until his SEC filing. Then we'll issue a statement."

Hartley stood up. "Okay, we all have our assignments. I'll stall Mr. Meyerson until we get the program set. Monday it is."

THE REST OF THE WEEK Philip Hartley was constantly on the phone, briefing the directors about Meyerson's unwelcome intrusion and floating the LBO concept past them. Ed Horn was surprisingly sanguine, saying he had no trouble with employee participation in principle, in fact, he had pulled off a similar deal in one of his own companies. But he echoed Fritz Mueller's doubts that the IAM, particularly, would play.

Winston was more skeptical. "It's all in the numbers, Philip. Until I see the projections I can't tell you what I think. And we'll need a special committee of outside directors to look at this." As for Meyerson, Winston added, "it's no surprise someone wants to take a run at us. Naturally we'll resist, at least until we see the color of his money. As I mentioned, Meyerson has a reputation as a hard charger. Nevertheless, we need to keep an open mind..."

"An open mind! Open to what!"

Winston went on coolly. "We can't rule out the possibility that, as things develop, our best course may be best to cooperate with Meyerson."

Hartley paused, stunned. "It sounds like you're resigned to our being taken over. That's not how our game plan reads, not at all."

"The only game plan that matters, Philip, is to do the best by our shareholders. *They* are who we work for. It is *their* interests that are paramount. It's all well and good to think of everybody having a stake, pulling together and so on, but my hunch is, your scheme may turn out to be nothing more than a nice idea, a platitude."

"Platitude or not, I'm moving ahead on it," Hartley shot back.

"As well you should, at least at this stage. But it is imperative that you meet with Meyerson. Sound the man out, tell him you'll call a special board meeting to consider any reasonable proposal. That'll buy you time to bring your LBO plan along. Soon enough we'll know whether your idea is BellAir's salvation or, shall we say, something considerably less."

8

S ANDOR MEYERSON'S play created a sensation. After heavy NYSE action on Monday following the disclosure, the stock's opening was delayed the next morning due to an imbalance of orders, many more would-be buyers than sellers. When BEL finally opened around ten-thirty, it shot up to 25 ½, four dollars higher than it started the week.

To Hartley this was an ominous development. Happy stockholders meant nothing compared to the threat to his LBO. Much more of a runup could be fatal, pricing the stock out of reach. Late morning, Arthur Winston called for an update.

"The timing couldn't have been better," Hartley reported. "It turns out, a couple of weeks ago the pilots asked Drexel to put together an LBO of their own. This is the first time they've been willing to talk about a pay cut."

"What about the others?"

"The flight attendants will go for anything that gets them back to work. They're really hurting. They don't have the kind of reserves ALPA does." Hartley shifted the phone to his other shoulder. "The mechanics are the tough one. They already knew about the pilots' plan. Their reaction was we were ganging up on them."

"Coming from them, that's no surprise. What's your next move?"

"Drexel and the pilots' lawyers are here going over the books. If nothing else, this'll show them why we've been pushing so hard on salary costs."

"The way the stock's moving, the price of admission for your LBO just became a lot higher."

"That could be a problem," Hartley admitted. "Salomon's reworking the numbers right now."

"But of course, they'll still be 'highly confident.' " Winston paused to let his needle strike home. "Have you spoken with Meyerson yet?"

"Not until we have a better fix on the LBO. These things take time. The most I'll say is that we're calling a special board meeting to consider his proposition. He won't know we'll really be looking at final approval of the LBO. By the way, I'm setting up a telephone meeting a week from Friday to get preliminary approval from the board."

There was a lengthy silence. "Philip, I advise you in the strongest terms to speak with Meyerson before this day is out. Certainly the man is overreaching, but on the whole his position isn't that unreasonable. And he does have a reputation for, let us say, firm action when he thinks he's being crossed."

"We'll just have to take that risk, Arthur. This LBO is such a radical idea, the board needs time to consider it. Sure as hell, there's no way I'll put Meyerson's deal in front of them first."

"I see," Winston replied crisply. "Well, continue to keep me informed."

LATER THAT AFTERNOON, the lawyers and bankers assembled again. The offering price was tentatively pegged at thirty-five dollars, a ten-dollar premium over market. When Mandel revealed his estimate of the buyout cost, the room fell silent. Nearly $600 million. Fritz Mueller laughed out loud. Roger Bankhead threw down his pen.

As Mandel explained it, the banking consortium would provide short- and long-term loans, much of the debt to be secured by BellAir's fleet. Then came a line of credit, with certain investment houses also "penciled in" for equity contributions that would translate into a ten percent ownership stake. The sale of debentures made up another component.

"I'm afraid these babies'll have to carry a pretty healthy yield to sell," Mandel said apologetically. "On the order of fourteen to fifteen percent."

"You're talking junk bonds," Cliff Meltzer said, cupping his chin in his hands.

"Not quite, but I won't split hairs. Whatever you call them, they're damned expensive. That's the only way anybody'd touch this deal, with no revenue coming in these days. And it'll be conditioned on the strike being settled before closing. So, that's it for the outside financing." Mandel tapped the wall-board with his magic marker. "Now let's look at the inside sources."

He went for a half hour, detailing the structure of employee pension fund contributions and answering questions.

"What about the IAM?" asked Mueller. "You said you need them, but there's no way they'll play."

Mandel perched on the edge of the table. "Let me put it this way. It would be far better if they were in, but the way things're shaping up we probably can make the deal without them. But that means we'll need an opinion of outside counsel that the no-strike clause in the IAM's contract is enforceable. It won't set well if they could walk out the day after we make the deal. See my point?"

Wallace frowned. "Amory and our labor people will have to get back to you on that. I can give you no assurances."

Mandel nodded, walking back to the board. "Okay. Next, the nonunion employees, middle management, clerks, secretaries, and so on. Their contributions are in the same category as the pilots and flight attendants but somewhat less."

"You can count on them," Hartley said. "We'll push that through, all right."

Mueller shook his head. "First we stick these people with a ten percent cut, then we furlough most of them because of a strike they had nothing to do with, now this. Terrific."

Hartley rose out of his chair. "I don't want to hear that! You damn well better convince them this is good for them! The better job they do, the more they'll make, for Chrissakes! What are they complaining about? It can't be any worse than what they have now!"

Bankhead laughed under his breath. Hartley glared at him. That's it, I've taken enough of his shit. He is out of here. He made a mental note to have Smith set the wheels in motion.

Mandel was going on, "The last piece of this puzzle is the officer group. Talking with Philip here, it's his desire that we dial in all the elected and appointed VPs, that's a total of..." Mandel consulted his notes, "fifty-three people, not counting what we might want to do for the directors. We haven't worked out all the details, but we'll need on the order of $75 million from the officers, some combination of pension money and equity contributions."

Meltzer whistled.

"Bear in mind, most of the officers'll realize big bucks from selling back the stock they already own at thirty-five a share. That'll defray a good part of the expense of buying in. Upside is, top management comes out with nearly forty percent of the common stock!"

"I see it, Mandel, but I still don't believe it." Mueller shook his head. "You sure there's a pea under those goddamn shells of yours?"

The meeting continued another forty-five minutes. As it was breaking up, Mandel caught Hartley. "We need to talk."

Hartley motioned to the side door of the conference room that led to Charlie Bell's private retreat. The men walked in and Mandel closed the door.

"I didn't want the group to hear this, but I ran into Freddie Russell yesterday. He's Meyerson's man at First Boston. First words out of his mouth, how are we coming on our LBO! In fact, he quoted some of the numbers we were playing with yesterday!"

"What!" Hartley cried. "How could he know that?"

"Exactly! If Meyerson thinks we're trying to stiff him, he'll blow this thing sky high! Thirty-five's as high as I can go, and I mean it. That's the limit."

"*Shit!*" Hartley slammed his fist on his desk. "Another case of flapjaw!"

"I doubt that." Mandel raised his eyebrows. "More like we've got a Judas in here somewhere."

Hartley's frowned, his mind traveling back...

Mandel was still talking, "...it's absolutely vital we keep a lid on this until everything's tied down."

Hartley quickly refocused. "I'll get security on it right away. But what if Meyerson goes the tender-offer route?"

"That's my point! With the right number he takes all the marbles, period." Mandel shrugged. He picked up his briefcase and started for the door. "Money talks, everything else walks. But what the hell, Phil. With your stock and options you'll be a rich man. Not as good as the LBO...what'd we figure, seventeen percent of the airline for you? But still, not bad."

As soon as Mandel left, Hartley called George O'Brien in and told him in no uncertain terms to find the leak, hire an outside investigator if he had to, and make it fast. Hartley returned to his soft chair near the window and soon was deep in thought. Judas...that was Charlie's word. Nonsense, of course, utter nonsense. Hartley stared out his window. But can it be, this time we have a *real* traitor on our hands?

OVER THE NEXT TWO WEEKS, progress was made on all fronts except, predictably, with the mechanics. Backed by the national IAM, they continued to hold out, threatening and bellicose. To Hartley's great relief, understandings were reached with the pilots and flight attendants on the LBO and for ending the strike. The outline of a comprehensive settlement was agreed and initialed. By Thursday, the day before the special board telephone meeting, Mandel was able to report commitments from the big Japanese banks. So the final piece of outside financing was in place.

With the widening circle of people in the know, Hartley and Mandel feared news of the LBO would leak out. Milt Collins was called in and told to draft a release. It was dated 4 p.m., Friday the twentieth, the day Hartley expected to receive his preliminary approval from the board. The day of Meyerson's deadline. The directors' schedules didn't permit a face-to-face meeting for nearly two weeks, so this unusual telephonic conference was Hartley's way of gaining their support. A summary had been couriered to each director, and all week Hartley worked the phones hard. He knew he was running a risk. With less opportunity for preparation and discussion than in a personal meeting, the directors might be hesitant, even negative, and a bad first reaction might affect their ultimate decision.

The board's special committee – Ed Horn, Harold Nystrom, and Bill Clevenger – had hired its own team of bankers and attorneys to advise the directors on their responsibilities in this unusual situation, and to evaluate the LBO offer's fairness to the outside shareholders. Its report was awaited.

In the conference call, Ed Horn, speaking from Atlanta, vigorously took the devil's-advocate position. Hartley's ears reddened as Horn went on, but the debate he sparked served to air the issues for members not familiar with LBOs. Fundamentally, the directors were overjoyed that the strike seemed near an end, and Hartley was commended for devising this plan that would also produce the salary concessions they had long sought. There were reservations about shifting to an unfamiliar mode and operating as a private company, along with undercurrents of regret that some of them would likely not be reappointed under the new regime.

Even Dee Bell seemed favorably inclined. Hartley had a hunch that employee ownership might fit her vision of the company, and in his opening statement he invoked Charlie's memory several times. In turn, Dee used the term "family" in her remarks. Times change, she observed, people have to change along with them.

Mueller's criticism was pointed, but his manner subdued. He made sure Mandel explained the enormity of the debt burden the company would inherit, then another director asked Winston for his appraisal of the financial risk.

"It's all in your assumptions," Winston replied. "In good times leverage is your best friend. It can make an average return on equity look absolutely phenomenal. However, when things turn down, as they inevitably do, we could find ourselves unable to pay our bills. In any event, we would have to be very circumspect about capital spending. We'll have very little flexibility until we pay down that debt."

Hartley frowned as he listened to Winston. His comments were reminiscent of Roger Bankhead's earlier carping.

Speaking from Brussels, Stanley Harper asked Hartley to explain why top management was dealt in for such a large ownership stake. "In principle I don't have a problem," Harper said, "but what you're taking out seems way out of proportion to what you're putting in. If I understand this right, the officers end up with thirty-eight percent of the stock, and I see you will own seventeen percent yourself. Sure, you people are putting up a lot of money, but it's only a fraction of the total deal."

Harper's comments made Hartley uneasy. He'd had the same concern himself, grilling Mandel privately when he first sketched the size of the officers' share and his in particular. This was standard for deals of this sort, Jeff replied. There was plenty of precedent. It wasn't a matter of overreaching but of persuading everybody that the officers' value justified it.

In his response Hartley showed no indecision. "Stan, I am absolutely convinced we need a sizable stake for proper motivation." He added that with this inducement he'd been able to convince all the officers to continue for another year at their already reduced pay levels. "Our incentives and the corporation's line up perfectly."

"That may be true," Harper retorted, "but most of the purchase price will be borrowed, and it's the company's debt, not yours."

Hartley kept his composure. "I grant you, if we win, we win big, but the fact is, *everyone* wins, right up and down the line!"

In the end, Hartley was authorized to proceed, subject to the special committee's report and final review by the full board a week from the following Thursday. At the last minute, Mandel was able to talk his banking group into an additional commitment, and he recommended they bump up the price another dollar for safety's sake. To the directors, thirty-six dollars was a very sizable bird in the hand, in view of the stock's recent miserable performance. It was anticipated the market would surge to near or even above the thirty-six level when the news broke.

Meyerson also came in for discussion. The directors were split on whether to accede to his demand for representation, and tabled the issue, subject to further discussion. They briefly debated what to do if Meyerson launched a competing bid, but decided they'd face that situation if and when it arose.

"Philip, if we go ahead with the LBO, what happens if Meyerson won't tender his shares to us?" asked Louise Boyd. "He's under no obligation to do so."

"None but common sense. How often do you have a chance to double your money in less than a month?"

"But that depends on what he's really after," she argued. "If he decides not to tender, he could cause a lot of trouble as a minority stockholder."

"That's true, but there are only so many bases we can cover," the weary Hartley replied.

Arthur Winston asked whether Hartley had been in touch with Meyerson. He was visibly distressed when Hartley said he'd sent him a hold-off letter only, that he was awaiting the outcome of this meeting to speak with him personally. He would try to reach Meyerson today, Hartley pledged. Certainly by Monday.

That afternoon, after the directors had gone and Milt Collins' press release was dispatched, Hartley's intercom buzzed.

"Mr. Meyerson, on your line."

A momentary shock went through Hartley. "Put him through."

He reached for the phone. "Hartley here."

Meyerson jumped him immediately. "I just saw your release. You people are making a big, big mistake."

Hartley settled back in his chair. "I disagree, Mr. Meyerson. This program is in the best interests of our company. I might add that my board feels the same way."

"I don't appreciate being jerked around. I put a reasonable proposition in front of you people, and you don't seem to have the slightest idea what to do with it. I gave you a deadline and you blew it!"

Hartley paused, trying to gauge his adversary. From photographs, he knew what Meyerson looked like, but hearing the voice for the first time, he found it surprisingly soft, chalky.

"As I said in response to your letter, we've scheduled a special meeting of our board the week after next. Your demands will be given due consideration at that time."

"I'll bet you cut yourself a nice fat deal, didn't you?"

"Pardon me?"

"With your LBO. C'mon, that's what those things are all about! Don't bullshit me, I've done them myself!"

"It's no more and no less a stake than our officers are entitled to, for a proper incentive."

Meyerson laughed out loud. "We've never met, but my sources tell me you're an intelligent man. Is it possible they could be wrong?"

"You'd better ask them." Hartley was trying to keep his temper. "We're doing what is best for our company."

"But not for its largest stockholder! You call *that* intelligent? I sure as hell don't!"

"I have other commitments this afternoon. I'm sure you do, too..."

"No, no," Meyerson interrupted. "Believe me, there is nothing in the world more important to me than talking to you right now."

"I'm sorry to hear you have so little going."

"*Touché!* I like that. I like that very much. I will have to remember it." Meyerson paused for a moment. "I want to meet with your board. Before your big meeting."

"I'm afraid that won't be possible," Hartley replied crisply. "I'll be back to you after they make their decision. Until then I don't believe we have much to say to each other."

"That's where you're wrong, my friend." Meyerson paused. When he spoke again, his voice had turned ice-cold.

"I have one more thing to say, and you had better pay attention. When I go after something I do not quit until I get it. Check it out, Hartley. I have a very good batting average. You are going to regret this. More than you can possibly imagine, you are going to regret this."

"Then I'll just have to take my chances, won't I?" Hartley answered.

"That is your choice."

There was a click. Meyerson had hung up.

WEDNESDAY, JUNE 1, the evening before the crucial meeting, Philip Hartley hosted the directors at dinner in BellAir's executive dining room. Normally these functions were lavish affairs, spouses included, held in the finest restaurants. Since this meeting had been put together on such short notice, Hartley considered skipping the dinner, but on consideration he decided an evening of sociability would set the right tone for the next day's momentous gathering.

Most of the directors were present, though Louise Boyd was flying in later that night and Stan Harper, still out of the country, would miss tomorrow's session. With the cocktail hour over, Hartley was pleased with the evening so far, convinced he had made the right move in bringing the group together. Several directors had approached him one-on-one, expressing their concern about the size of the officers' holdings in the LBO, worried they might be accused of endorsing a sweetheart deal. Hartley was considerate and reassuring. The tone of fellowship and cordiality was just right. Yes, he thought, much better the discussions begin here, rather than in the formality of the conference room.

Ever alert to showcase products in which the directors had a personal interest, Hartley was toying with his wine, an excellent white Bordeaux, vintage 1975 from California's Hartzell Cellars, of which Harold Nystrom was part owner. As the appetizer course was being served, he began formulating his toast. To the company, it would go, to the board, to new horizons...something along these lines.

He stood at his place. Someone tapped a glass for quiet. As he cleared his throat, Hartley felt a hand on his arm. Wendell Mendoza, the captain of Charlie Bell's Filipino serving crew and his maître d' for the evening, was beside him.

"Mr. Hartley," he whispered, "there is a telephone call. Would you care to take it in your office?"

"I can't take it now. Who is it?"

"A Mr. Morrison, from the *Times*. He said you'd know him."

"I know him, all right," Hartley grumbled. "Tell him to call Milt Wilcox at home. You know where to find the number."

"I'm sorry, sir, Mr. Morrison said it was very important that he speak to you himself. Nobody else will do."

"I will not leave my guests," Hartley replied between clenched teeth. "Tell him I'll call him back."

Thrown off stride, Hartley tried to collect himself. Again he raised his glass.

"Ladies and gentlemen, I propose a toast. It is fitting that we begin the evening, on the eve of this most important board meeting, with a few words."

"Hear, hear!" Someone at the other end of the table remarked.

"To our company, to BellAir, to its leadership..." He caught Dee Bell's eye, "to our legendary past..." Seated next to her, Arthur Winston, staring at him, "...and to our most profitable and success-ful future."

Everyone raised their glasses. Arthur Winston rose, as was customary, in response to the chairman's toast. As Winston began to speak, the waiter again tapped Hartley on the elbow and handed him a piece of paper.

"The number, Mr. Hartley."

Hartley folded the paper once, twice, then slipped it in his vest pocket. Once again he turned full attention to his guests.

9

HARTLEY ROSE EARLY. Elaine was still asleep as he showered and dressed. Dark blue suit, white shirt, blue tie with the red flecks, his lucky tie. The day would set a fast pace. Mandel and the lawyers were arriving at seven for a final review of the documents they had been working on all night.

Hartley looked at his watch. Plenty of time for a vigorous walk. A beautiful day was in the forecast. He clipped his Cross pen and pencil to his inside jacket pocket and collected his wallet and keys. That slip of paper on the dresser. He opened it...Morrison's message.

"I must speak to you tonight before ten. Urgent!"

By the time Hartley had broken free it was too late to call. He'd do it today, when he had a minute. All in good time.

At six-fifteen it was still dark on the street, but over Queens the clouds were already edged with pink. Hartley strode along briskly, basking in the cool air of the early hour. Few people were in the street, but those he saw had a purpose, he noted approvingly. Little eateries and groceries were the first to stir, proprietors hosing down their sidewalks, greeting the day's deliveries.

Hartley felt exceptionally fine, eager for what lay ahead. He'd been circumspect at dinner, only one glass of wine and an after-dinner liqueur he barely touched. No place for a groggy head today. Celebrations could wait. In fact, he thought, I'll have Valerie make a reservation at one of our favorite spots. We should end this momentous day with a classy evening, Elaine and I.

In a few minutes he was crossing the plaza to the Tower's front entrance. He nodded pleasantly to the security guard, then, after a swift ride to Fifty-five, paused to pluck a *Times* and a *Journal* from the stack on the receptionist's desk, folding and tucking them under his arm. He walked rapidly to his office, unlocked the door and flipped on the light. After setting his briefcase on the credenza, he spread the newspapers across his desk. *Oh, my God!*

The *Times* headline stared up at him: *S.M.I. Bid for BellAir – LBO Threatened.*

His eyes raced down the page.

"*Times* exclusive...Sandor Meyerson...$42 a share...launching tender offer today. Seeking support of BellAir's board...demands representation."

"That son of a bitch!" he snarled. He ripped the paper open looking for the rest of the story, but as he did, his eyes froze. Another headline: *Airline Executive Tied to Drug Suspect.*

There was a large photo just under the headline. Oh, my God! It's Shelley and me! The paper shook in his hands. The two of us, right in front of her apartment. In the foreground was the white Corvette he'd rented a few months ago. Frantically, Hartley's eyes moved down the short article.

> Evidence has come to light linking Philip Hartley, Chairman and Chief Executive Officer of BellAir, with a company flight attendant recently charged with narcotics violations. Shelley Gregory, 31, of Marina del Rey, California, was arrested on May 23 at a popular downtown Los Angeles nightclub for possession of cocaine and marijuana for distribution. Court records indicate that drug paraphernalia was also found in her automobile at the time of her arrest.

Hartley dropped into his chair. My God. This can't be happening. I was so careful.

> Reliable sources identified Mr. Hartley, BellAir's top executive, as a frequent overnight visitor to the woman's apartment in an exclusive section of this oceanside city. BellAir, a unit of BellAir Industries, Inc., and the nation's third largest air carrier, has been in the forefront of the industry's war on drugs. Its tough "one chance only" program has drawn the praise of law enforcement agencies but heavy criticism from the airline's unions and civil liberties groups.

God. Stop. Think.

He threw open the desk drawer and fumbled for his address book. His hand trembled so, he could barely read the number. Bradshaw. Hartley began punching buttons.

"Fuck!" he shouted, banging the receiver down. He rushed to the door and slammed it shut. Again, he stabbed at the number.

Five rings, six, seven. Finally someone picked it up. It was Bradshaw.

"Chuck," Hartley said, breathing heavily, "this is Phil!"

There was a long pause. "Wassamatter...it's the middle of the night here, for Chrissakes."

"Somebody found out! It's all over the papers! Shelley and me! *They found out!*"

"Oh, shit." Another pause on the line. "What does it say?"

"They've got everything! The drugs, the fact I'm a...friend of hers. There's even a *picture!*"

"Jesus," Bradshaw moaned. "What paper?"

"The *Times.*" Hartley winced. Tom Morrison's byline, big as life. He'd missed that.

Bradshaw coughed. "Why would they make a big deal about it? It doesn't make sense..."

Hartley interrupted. "There's a reporter here who's got it in for me. And the drug angle, the push on drugs we've had."

"That's cute, all right, but still..."

"I wonder." Hartley whispered.

"What's that? I didn't hear you."

Hartley put his fingertips to his eyes. "Sandor Meyerson. The name mean anything to you?"

"That asshole! He owns one of the studios out here. Always has his mug in the society pages. Not one of my favorite people."

Hartley laughed grimly. "We are at war with Mr. Meyerson. He just announced a tender offer for the company. That's what's on the *front* page!"

"Un-huh, uh-huh. Okay, now it adds up. This gentleman is definitely a hardball type and something of a sleaze. When was the picture taken? Can you tell?"

"Late April. About a month before she was arrested."

"And how long has he been after the airline?"

"I don't know for sure. There's been some accumulation over the last couple of months. You don't think..."

"I don't think, I know. You've been suckered. Royally suckered." Hartley closed his eyes.

"I'll lay you odds that bastard's had a team of investigators on you ever since he got interested in the company. Industrial espionage. It's a growth industry these days. I use it myself, within limits, of course. All you need is a long lens, some listening equipment, a couple of loose lips. There'd be no way of stopping them." Bradshaw snorted. "I'll give you odds Mr. Meyerson knows more about you than you do yourself."

"Shit!" Hartley slammed his fist on the desk. "What am I going to do? You've got to help me!"

"Right off the bat I don't have an answer. What rotten timing! I had a deal worked out, but if this thing gets a lot of media play, they may have to put her away to save face."

"What about me?"

"Hell, you haven't done anything illegal, far as I know, anyway. Just don't go shooting your mouth off until I come up with something. In fact, I am warning you, no comment about this. Not a single word! This won't help her condition any either, I'll tell you that right now."

Hartley laughed bitterly. "Not to mention mine. I've got a board meeting this morning."

"I don't envy you, but then again, I never did. The stakes you people play for, you got to be so clean, it'd make Caesar's wife out a whore. And sometimes even that's not good enough. Fax the article to my office. I'll get back to you soon as I sort this out."

Hartley hung up the phone. Again he looked at the paper... he hadn't even finished the article. Some unnamed source said he'd been helping Shelley out financially. Jesus, they even implied *he* was involved in her drug situation, though they didn't come right out and say that. Then his eyes came to rest on the final sentence of the article.

Despite repeated attempts to reach him, Mr. Hartley was unavailable for comment.

Hartley held his head in his hands...numb, completely immobilized. The intercom buzzed.

"Mr. Mandel and Mr. Wallace are here, Mr. Hartley," Valerie said. "And your wife's holding on your private line."

"Tell them to wait." He took a deep breath, then punched the flashing button.

"Elaine?"

"Philip! What is this about the *Times*? My father just called me." Her voice was husky. It sounded like she had just awoken.

"Yeah, well, it's there all right. I...we need to talk." He paused. "It's not the kind of thing we can discuss over the phone."

"But there isn't any truth to it. There *can't* be!"

What could he say? Trapped. No way out.

"It's not as simple as that," he mumbled. "She's somebody I met. You know. It...looks like she got herself into trouble."

"Got herself into trouble! What about you? *What about us?*"

"Right," he answered. He could hear her breathing.

"Philip...I mean, we're both adults. I wasn't born yesterday and I don't suppose you were either, but this is a disaster! *An absolute, utter disaster!*"

He groped for words but none came. There were none.

"If you can't tell me right now this is a mistake, I...I mean, I don't know what to say! There's never been anything like this, never any scandal in my family!"

"No," he replied, "I don't suppose that's part of the script."

"Don't joke, Philip. This isn't funny!" There was a pause on the line. "Tell me straight. Have you been involved with this woman?"

Hartley swallowed. "Yes," he answered.

"Do you love her?" she asked in a low voice.

"I don't know." A bitter smile came to his face. "I haven't known what that means, not for thirteen years."

She began to sob. "I...I think I'll have to go home, Philip."

"Yeah. That's probably the best thing."

There was a click and the line went dead. Dazed, Hartley continued holding the phone to his ear. Finally he put it down, then he shook his head violently. Chuck was right. Why hadn't he cut Shelley loose long ago when there was still time? Did he want to be found out? Did he want circumstances to make the decision for him? No, no...that would be insane. But still, why didn't he act, act decisively. His hall-mark all these years. He didn't know. He just didn't know.

There was a knock at the door. Valerie looked in, hesitatingly.

"Mr. Hartley, they're all waiting."

"All right," he said, steeling himself. He brushed back his hair, nervously straightening his tie. "Show them in."

Hartley watched them filter in. All the usuals, except for Roger. Everyone was subdued, somber. Nobody met his eyes. Mandel spoke first.

"Well," he said, pointing to the *Times* headline, "this certainly puts a different cast on things."

"Has there been any direct communication from Meyerson?" Wallace asked.

"I talked to him Friday, but he said nothing about this."

"I'll want to hear about that later," Wallace responded brusquely. "More to the point, the tender offer terms are on page 36 of the *Journal*." He glanced around the room, "I assume you've all seen them." Everyone nodded except for Hartley. Mechanically, he opened the paper. There it was, big as life: *A Message To BellAir Industries, Inc., Shareholders*.

Hartley closed his eyes. In his distress he hadn't thought to look for the announcement.

"We don't have much time," said Mandel. "Let me summarize it. I'll compare it against the LBO, that's what the shareholders will be doing. The board, too, for that matter." Mandel began pacing the room. For the next few minutes he analyzed the competing offers. Meyerson's $42 topped the LBO by six dollars, but it was hedged with many conditions. As Mandel droned on, Hartley saw the print on the paper, heard the sounds Mandel's mouth was making, but everything glanced off. Nothing registered.

Finally Mandel wrapped up. "Clearly, gentlemen, clearly, you end up with a much stronger company under the LBO."

Hartley looked at him. "So you're saying our program's still all right?"

"All right? It's a much better deal, all the way around."

"That may be," Wallace interjected, "but the board is obliged to reconsider its position. This throws a whole new light on the matter."

"But what about our poison pill?" asked Mueller. "Won't that block Meyerson? He's not offering to buy all the shares."

"Let me put it this way," answered Wallace. "The pill may indeed be triggered, unless the board decides to go with Meyerson. In *that* case it's automatically negated. By definition we'd no longer be dealing with a hostile offer. That's the way the pill works, if you'll remember."

"But why would they *want* to go with Meyerson?" asked a panic-stricken Marshall Smith.

"I'm not saying they will, I'm not saying they won't. But he has made a respectable offer, and, as I say, in some particulars it's more appealing than the LBO."

"Ah don't see that at all, not at all." responded Smith.

"And since the company is in play, the question of a white knight arises."

Mueller frowned. "A what?"

"A third party," Mandel said. "Somebody with a better offer."

Hartley's intercom buzzed. He reached for the phone.

"Mr. Winston on one." He motioned for the others to go ahead.

"Hello, Arthur," Hartley said quietly, cupping his mouth with his hand. He gazed blankly at the roomful of people.

"Well, this is an ugly little development, isn't it?" Winston's voice slashed over the line.

"We're picking Meyerson's offer apart now, Arthur. We still have plenty of ammunition."

There was a pause. "I wasn't talking about Meyerson. I'm talking about that picture. You've seen it, I dare say."

"Ah. Yes. The...timing wasn't very good, was it."

"Not very good!" The line was silent a moment, then Winston resumed in a normal tone. "Philip. I warned you about Meyerson. He plays for keeps. Now, you listen to me. You must issue a denial. Have Collins do it, and do it right now, before the television goes too far with this."

Hartley rubbed his eyes with his fingers...Bradshaw's warning. Which way to jump? No way out.

"Philip, did you hear me!"

Hartley moved the phone to his other ear. "Arthur," he said evenly. "I'll deny any drug involvement. Otherwise I have to decline comment."

"Decline comment? Decline comment! That's not good enough and you know it! *You must issue a denial!*"

"You saw the picture, Arthur. It's real. It's no fake."

"I don't believe this, Philip."

"She's someone I know. Right now she's in a rehab center. I...I've been helping her...try to get over a drug problem."

"I see."

Hartley waited. Winston obviously was choosing his words carefully.

"I must say, Philip," he finally said, "I must say how deeply touched I am that our chief executive officer takes such a personal interest in his troubled employees."

"Goddamnit!" Hartley shouted. "That's uncalled for!" He started to hang up.

"Philip!"

He held the phone a couple of inches from his ear.

"There is one more thing. I've heard from several of the directors. There will be no decision on your LBO today. We have no choice but to look at the two proposals together. I don't know whether Meyerson will renew his demand to appear before the board, but if he doesn't we may invite him in ourselves."

Winston hung up. Hartley turned back to the group, which was in an animated discussion. Mandel looked up from a yellow pad covered with numbers.

"Philip, I've just outlined a point-by-point comparison of the two offers. Can your girl type it up and run off twenty copies?"

"Sure," Hartley said, pushing the intercom. "Let's see if I can at least handle this right."

FRANK DELGADO picked up his phone. "Delgado."

"Frank, there's some very interesting news about BellAir..."

"I saw the *Chronicle*, Will. What do you make of it?"

"They're in play, that's for sure. You saw the bit on Hartley and the woman."

"Yeah. I didn't know he had it in him. What do you think it means for us?"

"No question, your contract's still valid, even if somebody takes over the company. What kind of games they'd try to play, there's no way to tell at this point. We'll have to follow it closely." Cartright paused. "I venture to say, Mr. Hartley may not be long for this world."

Delgado was quiet for a moment.

"Frank, you still there?"

He shifted the phone to his other shoulder. "I'm here. I'm just not sure what to make of it. I mean, I'm happy the bastard's on the ropes, but...I don't know, I just have to give it some time."

IN HIS SPARSELY furnished office at the Bank of Manhattan Building, Arthur Winston remained deep in thought. Finally he rose and began laying papers in his briefcase for the nine o'clock board meeting. His visitor, who appeared extremely ill at ease listening to Winston's end of his call to Hartley, also rose and buttoned his jacket.

"These next few days are going to be very difficult," Winston said solemnly. "But whatever happens, you should know your service to this company will not go unrecognized."

Winston dropped his copy of the *Times* in his case with a flourish.

"Rest assured, Roger, Sandor is well aware of your contributions."

THE BOARD MEETING was inconclusive. Hartley opened with a graceful if uninformative statement that attempted to defuse his personal situation, but the directors' embarrassment and shock were not so easily mollified. A remote, chilly atmosphere hung over the meeting until the group turned, with relief, it seemed, to the offers to buy the company.

Shortly before ten o'clock a letter arrived, which Hartley read aloud. In it, Sandor Meyerson demanded an immediate meeting with the board, access to all of BellAir's financial records, and a list of shareholder names and addresses. According to the lawyers, the company wasn't required to open its confidential books, but after a brief discussion, Hartley dispatched Marianne Keller to make a start on the shareholders' list.

Deferring action on the LBO, the directors adjourned the meeting until the seventeenth, two Fridays hence. The delay was needed to give its special committee time to evaluate Meyerson's offer and have its attorneys and bankers meet with the raider's advisors. Also, in a step Hartley knew had to be taken, but incensed him nonetheless, the special committee was instructed to look for a white knight who might top both his offer and Meyerson's.

Whatever its effect on Sandor Meyerson, Milt Collins' press release had no impact on the feverish trading in BellAir's stock. Many shareholders were taking profits, but others wanted in, based simply on Meyerson's bid. BEL was moving up rapidly in heavy trading. By the end of the day it had jumped to 38 3/8, more than two dollars above the LBO target, though still well short of the tender offer price. According to Mandel, the arbs were now in the game – arbitrageurs, professional speculators betting the price would rise to the level of Meyerson's bid, possibly even higher.

Hartley left the Tower at five-thirty, the earliest in months. He couldn't concentrate, just had to get out. He was alone in the apartment, having just hung up with Elaine, who was at her father's estate on Long Island. After some difficulty he'd persuaded her to meet him in town. They'd set a date later. She was surprisingly calm, he thought, considering what she was going through, no doubt including severe pressure from her father.

The Judge, he thought bitterly. That old hypocrite. I'll bet his closet holds more than its share of skeletons. He thought back over his day, the longest, most miserable day of his life, made even worse, if that were possible, because he expected it would be one of the best. From the heights to the depths in one easy step.

The board meeting had ended about one, much earlier than planned, since most of the day had been blocked for deliberations on the LBO. After adjournment, Hartley went through with a television interview Milt Collins pressed on him. He agreed to do it, on condition that the reporter stay away from questions about Shelley. After that ordeal, he closeted himself with Valerie to dictate replies to his backlogged correspondence, then began calling in his key people one by one to discuss the plight they found themselves in.

Mueller. Hartley shook his head. What a hard one he was to figure. He expected some smirking comment, but there was none of that. Instead Fritz launched into a supportive, let's-get-with-the-program speech. Even more amazingly, he seemed to mean it. Perhaps, Hartley thought, perhaps it's because he's been there himself. Though he never had one explode on him like this. He always had Charlie covering for him.

Marshall Smith was agitated, gloomy. At first, the guiding genius of BellAir's drug program had little to say. "It's gonna be tough," he finally managed, "but we have to turn this to our advantage. Ah don't know...maybe somehow we could use her as a positive example, you know, of rehabilitation, when she gets out of the treatment. If only it wasn't for that criminal part," he added. What he really meant, Hartley knew, was "if only it weren't for *your* part."

But Smith's real depression was over the LBO. He'd been counting heavily on gaining personally from the scheme. Now it seemed he had given it up for a lost cause. Hartley had to pump him up with a fight talk of his own. It was still the better program by far, it was vital to keep working the employee groups, essential that they be persuaded to hang in there.

Bankhead remained the real enigma. He was professional and correct but volunteered nothing, in fact, said nothing about Hartley's personal situation. Very strange. Cannot figure him out. Not that it matters. He won't be around here much longer, anyway.

Hartley poured himself another scotch, a double. It might have been a triple, he wasn't counting. Then he turned on the six o'clock news.

Damn! There's our logo, big as life. Hartley winced as mention was made of him and Shelley, but that part was mercifully brief. Then they ran the tape of his interview. It went well enough, he thought, seeing it on the screen. He got in several good licks about the LBO and managed to project confidence that the airline would soon be back in the air. Hartley watched intently as the scene shifted to an interview with Sandor Meyerson, a full face closeup. Fleshy jowls, a bow tie practically invisible in his double chin, florid, looking much older than his fifty-eight years. The face of success, Hartley thought bitterly, sipping his drink.

The interviewer asked Meyerson whether he was disappointed at the reaction of BellAir's board. "No, not in the least," he replied. "They're giving my proposal serious consideration, which is exactly what they should be doing. It's miles ahead of that management scheme. I have no doubt they'll come around to my way of thinking."

"But what about the agreement the LBO plan has for ending the strike?"

"You have to recognize," Meyerson replied, "it was Hartley and his crowd that brought on this strike in the first place, with their poor management. That's number one. Second, my people have already met with the unions. I'm confident we'll be able to work out an agreement to end the strike promptly, and on a productive basis for all concerned."

Hartley sank deeper into his chair.

"It's an absolute outrage!" Meyerson said fiercely. "Do you realize how much Hartley alone stands to gain from that LBO of his? He'll walk away with nearly twenty percent of the company! And for what? For selling back the stock and options the company gave him in the first place! Then in a year, he turns around and takes it public at, what would you say? Fifty a share? Is that about right? Maybe even more. Well, sir, that's thirty-eight million bucks profit for the man. Minimum. *Thirty-eight million!* And he has the nerve to ask everybody else to take a pay cut? Criminal, that's what it is! There is no other way to describe it!"

Hartley snapped off the television. That two-faced bastard! What the hell is he in this for, charity? Have to get Milt to work on that angle. The lying son of a bitch, twisting everything! As if *his* hands were clean!

Suddenly the phone rang. Hartley grabbed it from the table next to his chair.

"Hartley!" he snapped.

"Oh...Philip. This is Shelley."

He closed his eyes and took a deep breath. "Shel. I was going to call you tonight."

"I want you to know how awful I feel about everything. Chuck just told me about it. He was over here this afternoon. He just left."

"It's not a pretty scene." He massaged his eyes with his fingers. "Are you holding up okay?"

"I don't know. I was feeling pretty good about things until I heard this. I just feel terrible...what I've done to you."

"You didn't do anything to me. Whatever happened, I did it to myself. Look. I'll be out to see you as soon as I can."

"Chuck says I may have to go to jail for a while. Maybe ninety days, he said."

"I'll call him, push him some more. I'm sure it won't be as bad as that."

"I hope you're right. That would be really hard." There was a pause on the line. "Philip," she finally said.

"Yes."

"You know, that was a nice picture. We look good together."

Hartley was stunned. He shook his head, not knowing what to say. Finally, he began to laugh, the first time he had laughed all day.

"You're really something, Shel," he said softly. "You are really something."

10

THE MANEUVERING was fierce, incessant. Hartley pleaded with the unions to stand by their commitments, while Meyerson's men twisted arms hard the other way. Thursday afternoon, the pilots were still planted squarely on the fence, waiting for the wind to start blowing one way or the other. After much factional wrangling, they reached a "meeting of the minds" with Meyerson. If he emerged the winner, they would cooperate. For Meyerson's part, in contrast to the LBO's pay cut, he pledged to accept a year's wage freeze, to "stabilize" the company.

AFA's leadership was now speaking out for Meyerson, though their official position still favored the LBO. For the flight attendants, Meyerson's package was little better than the company's, which led to speculation that their backsliding had more to do with the revelations about Hartley than the economics. Naturally, this was denied. Not surprisingly, the IAM came out for Meyerson. Distrustful of Hartley and his management team, they quickly cut a side deal with Meyerson.

The Tower was in an uproar. There was some support for the LBO among middle management and nonunion employees, but resentment was rife in this large, amorphous group over the disparity between what top management stood to gain and their own supposed benefits. For them, the LBO was a symbol, a summation of the resentment felt by these loyal foot soldiers from whom everything was expected but little returned by way of respect. The motivational meetings orchestrated by Hartley for this group turned into shouting matches, self-abasing sessions of breast-beating, gloom, and despair. As one programmer on Forty-three put it, "Here we go again, sucking hind tit."

Meyerson's remarks about excess and greed fanned the flames, as did a detailed critique of management's LBO "windfall" in Wednesday's *Times* under Tom Morrison's byline. Morrison's piece was prominently featured on bulletin boards all over the system until Hartley ordered it taken down.

"He sells out, pockets thirty-eight mil, and I'm supposed to take another cut? No way!"

"What else is new? Them that has, gits!"

Disappointed by the board's delay, Hartley consoled himself with the thought that dispersal of the out-of-town directors might hamper Meyerson's lobbying efforts. But he hadn't counted on his opponent's cleverness and tenacity. The eight outside directors were personally visited by Meyerson's top aides, who spent hours with each, preaching S.M. International's good faith and serious intent. In a brilliant flanking maneuver, Meyerson dispatched S.M.I.'s luxurious long-range 727 to retrieve Stanley Harper from London for the showdown meeting. Aboard was a Meyerson "executive assistant" who just happened to be a former Miss Los Angeles.

The furor over Hartley galvanized opposition in all quarters. His share of the deal had come in for ferocious criticism, well beyond what he had expected, but it was too late to turn back. He could ill afford to divide his supporters at the eleventh hour. Even more, he was infuriated to see the board wilt under pressure and question what they had already agreed was a reasonable arrangement. Several directors complained that it was bad form to come away with such a large share, the same criticism Roger Bankhead had made early on, which Hartley had dismissed as just more of his backsliding, another nail in his coffin.

So, advice to the contrary, Hartley was not about to compromise. He had dug in his heels. It was a matter of principle. If the deal was fair then, it was fair now. No better offer had yet been found. His personal gain and his personal troubles were completely beside the point.

Late on Thursday, for what seemed like the thousandth time, Hartley counted votes, trying to distill the results of his lobbying efforts. As matters now stood, three of the outside directors would back him: Martin Byrnes, Louise Boyd, and Bill Clevenger. Harold Nystrom was a probable no. Nystrom had become touchy and withdrawn since the sorry state of his hotel empire had been brought to light. Ed Horn was not opposed to the LBO idea, but as usual, he was holding his cards close to the vest. Stanley Harper was a question mark all the way. It was never possible to predict how he'd come out on a close issue.

Hartley was increasingly worried about Dee Bell. In Tuesday's shortened session she said little, and when Hartley phoned later she waffled, saying she needed more time to make up her mind. Hartley knew she was troubled, for she invoked Charlie's name several times, mentioning how people rallied behind her husband in difficult times, how important that kind of spirit was to the company. Her parting words – whatever was best for BellAir, that is what she would do.

As far as Arthur was concerned, in several heated exchanges he seemed more intent then ever on asking questions and debating fine points. To Hartley's dismay, Winston was also expressing "serious concern for leadership and morale in the organization." Why now, of all times, this sudden interest in industrial psychology? Or was it just a cover? He couldn't read Winston. In fact, he doubted he'd ever read him right. He remembered Elaine's words early in the game. Don't trust the man. Use him, but don't ever let him maneuver to where he can hurt you.

Elaine...how painful that was. Despite all their years together, the ink was barely dry on Morrison's terrible article, and she'd already cut and run. He stared at the mess on his desk. Unanswered calls, untouched correspondence. In a few minutes he would walk up Park Avenue and over to the Plaza to meet Elaine, their first encounter since the break. A drink only – she had dinner plans, she said – then back to the office for one final strategy meeting.

He was a few minutes late arriving. Elaine was already seated, a drink in front of her. To his surprise, she greeted him warmly and returned his peck on her cheek.

"You're looking good," he ventured.

"And you seem to be bearing up. How go the takeover wars?"

"You don't want to know," he answered wearily. "Tomorrow will seal it. This time there's no middle ground."

"Was there ever?" she asked, putting her drink down. "That day I was so angry I couldn't stand it. It was the worst day of my life."

He looked at her...those were his words, too. Yet there she sat, crisp and pretty, even after what she'd been through. She never shows what's inside.

"But I'm over it," she was saying. "More hurt than anything, I guess, and sorry for myself. Sorry for you, too."

The waiter appeared with Hartley's drink. He lifted his glass halfheartedly. She didn't respond. For a moment they sat silently, both of them staring at the table.

"Philip," she said finally, "I've been thinking about our situation. The fact is, it's been downhill for us a long time now. I think it's time to call it quits. That's what you want, obviously. I know it's what I want."

"You mean what your father wants," Hartley shot back.

A flash of anger swept through her, and she turned a deep red. "Well, what of it! Can you blame him? The publicity! The humiliation! Never mind my father, how do you think this makes *me* feel?"

"I never meant to hurt you. You realize that, don't you?"

"I'm sure you didn't," she laughed bitterly. "That's obvious. You were playing with fire and you got burned. Trouble is, you burned a lot of other people, too."

"It's not fair to say that..."

"Fair!" She gave an anguished little laugh. "You have the nerve to talk about fair! My God, Philip! This isn't just some little screwup! Everything we've worked for all these years, down the drain. We're in the papers, all over the TV! The people at my firm, my clients, I know what they're thinking. Look at her, she lost her husband and not just to anybody, but a drug dealer, no less!"

Hartley stared at her. Too exhausted to be angry, he could say nothing. After a moment, she composed herself.

"We're just going to have to recognize where our life is, aren't we?" she said calmly. "Or should I say, where it isn't." She looked around the booth for her purse. "You'll be hearing from my lawyer. In fact, I just came from there. I hope we can make the break with minimum disruption. We both have our careers to tend to."

"What's left of mine..."

"That's *your* concern, isn't it. From now on, it is none of mine." She fumbled with her purse, trying to pull the strap over her shoulder.

"Now," she said, looking up at him, "I'd better leave..." He saw her eyes filling with tears, "...before I change my mind."

"I'll walk out with you," he said, rising from his chair.

"Don't bother." She blinked hard. "I'll go out the way I came in."

She strode purposefully away. He sat back heavily, overcome with grief. Part of him had just died. Could he retrieve it? Did he even want to? He wasn't sure. At this point he wasn't sure about much of anything.

THE NEXT MORNING BellAir's board assembled at nine. Only one item on the agenda: "Consideration of Proposals to Purchase BellAir Industries, Inc." After brief opening remarks, Hartley turned to Jeff Mandel for an analysis of the two plans. Mandel threw a viewgraph slide on the screen. Immediately Harold Nystrom rose and pointed at Mandel.

"This is out of order! You haven't heard from the special committee!"

Hartley glanced at Horn. "Don't worry, Harold, we'll get to that in due course."

Mandel removed an expandable pointer from his coat pocket. "To begin, in view of Salomon's recommendation that our $36 a share is a full and fair offer, Meyerson's $42 would also appear to be fair, everything else being equal." He tapped on the screen with his pointer. "But, ladies and gentlemen, everything is *not* equal. It's not even close, and here's why. The LBO is all-cash to BellAir's shareholders, while S.M. International's offer is highly conditional. They won't buy *any* shares unless enough are tendered to make *sixty-seven percent!* And even if they get there, what happens to the people holding the rest? He's under no obligation to buy their shares."

"They could go up in value," commented Nystrom.

"Or down," Ben Peterson snapped.

Mandel continued. "Next point. There's been a lot of talk about deals he's made with the company's unions, but nothing's concrete. All I can say, and Philip can speak to this, is that our people are hanging in with us."

"But are they also willing to deal with Meyerson and end the strike?" asked Stanley Harper. "That's a critical point."

Hartley cleared his throat. "They say they'd be willing to work with him, but we know of nothing definite."

Fritz Mueller shouted, "If you people ever make a decision, we'll be back to work within the week! *Whichever* way it goes!"

Hartley glared at him. I could kill that man.

"I'm concerned for the soundness of the company," Bill Clevenger added, "particularly our debt load. How would the different ownership structures affect operations?"

Ed Horn stood up.

"I'd like to say something about that." He looked around the room. "I'm the only one here who's lived through an employee buy-out. It was in '76 with our paper mill in Louisiana, and I'll tell you, it *can work*, if it's done right and you keep control of the process. In fact, inside a year we'd decertified every damn union on the property. In two years we'd turned a losing operation completely around. Not that we'd expect to bust the unions here, of course," he added with a wink, "but from a philosophy point of view, it's nothing to be afraid of, not at all.

"But I have a bone to pick here, and it's a big one." Horn looked directly at Hartley. "I believe management has cut themselves too fat a deal. Don't get me wrong, I'm all for taking as much as you can get away with, but this one is *way the hell* out of proportion. I have to believe there'd be real trouble if management's share isn't toned down some and everybody else brought up."

Hartley rose at his place, tense, his stomach tight. Was this a preview of the special committee's report?

"Ed, I can't believe you're bringing this up now. We've been over this ground till we're blue in the face. With the deadline we're under, there's no way to go back and redo the deal." Hartley looked around the room. "But the real point is, why should we go back on it? May I remind you, this is the very same plan you already said was fair! Down to the last detail!"

He glared at Horn. "You're so concerned about morale. How about the people who make this organization run? That's what we're talking about here!"

Nystrom raised his hand again. "May I remind you, Philip, that was only a preliminary approval we gave, subject to the special committee's review. But since we're on this subject, how can you justify what happens if you decide to take the company public again? You'll all be millionaires!"

"Coming from you, Harold, I find that comment hard to understand. I seem to remember you did rather well in a recent deal." Hartley shook his head. "Just look around this room. Are any of you people ashamed of your success? Of course not! Then why is it such a crime for the officers to benefit if we increase the company's value? If we fall short, we'll suffer the most."

"I agree with Phil on that," answered Clevenger, "but like I said, I want some assurances on the debt question. If I read the numbers right, our debt-equity ratio would go to one of the highest in the industry. What about that, considering our capital requirements the next few years?"

Hartley answered. "Bill, we see the economy picking up, and the crazies are dropping out. Think of it this way. Every competitor that goes belly-up is one less to hurt us. Give us a little time, and we'll get the debt back down to a reasonable level. Sure, it's a gamble, but the odds are in our favor, no question."

"You make a persuasive case, Philip," said Clevenger, nodding. "I think it's worth taking the risk."

Suddenly everyone started talking at once. As the conversations gained momentum, Hartley saw that the meeting had temporarily adjourned itself. He looked at his watch.

"Let's take ten minutes."

During the break Ed Horn came up to Hartley. "Phil, put me on next. I'd better give our report before we go any further."

Hartley looked at Horn apprehensively. "Am I going to like what you have to say?"

Horn smiled. "You'll know in a minute."

When the meeting reconvened, Mandel quickly summarized his presentation, then took his seat. Hartley looked down the table and nodded. Horn rose.

"First of all, I should tell you that we had no luck finding a white knight. We did a lot of scratching around and there was some interest, but we came up dry. I think the situation was just too confusing, with the strike and all, too risky for anybody to want to play. If any of you are interested, there's a summary in here of the contacts our bankers and all made." He held up a spiral-bound report, identical to the one in front of each director.

"Now, putting aside the LBO for a minute and turning to Meyerson. He's given us a good offer, and with some improvements he's made that I'll tell you about, our advisors have no question it's fair and reasonable to the shareholders."

Hartley frowned. Improvements? What was he talking about?

"You know," Horn was going on, "very early, I learned the importance of loyalty, of sticking by your word and doing right by people. The trouble is, in practice it isn't always that simple. Sometimes that sentiment conflicts with a person's other obligations. It's painful when you face such a choice. In this situation here, I'm sure I speak for all of you when I say this will be a very tough decision for this board. For choosing between these two proposals, means choosing between our current management group," he gestured at Hartley, "and another one with which you have no experience. Solid, effective people, Meyerson and his team, but still, unknown quantities to most of you.

"As you're aware, Bill, Harold, and I were appointed a special committee. Our advisors met with Meyerson. We did it that way rather than invite him here, thinking that might not be the best thing. We took with us your questions and concerns, and we have some answers for you."

Horn glanced around the room. All eyes were on him. "You all know Meyerson is a very busy man. But despite rumors to the contrary, if he carries the day here, he has promised to devote a substantial part of his time to BellAir. Just as important, he plans to surround himself with the most capable airline talent in the industry. That's what he told us. This could include carrying over some of our current top people, though, of course, it's too early for any assurances on that score.

"Next, I'm pleased to report that Meyerson has made a major concession. If the board acts today to endorse his proposal, he is prepared to amend his tender offer and increase his purchase commitment to eighty percent. He will also drop the condition that he be tendered any minimum amount before he buys any shares. In other words, whatever is tendered to him up to that eighty percent, he will buy."

Hartley and Mandel exchanged glances. This was an ominous development.

Horn raised his finger for emphasis. "And finally, he will purchase all the remaining shares within the next year, at no less than market price on a date of his choosing."

"That's all well and good," Martin Byrnes retorted, "but what about his business plan? Does he have the faintest idea what he'd do if he owned the airline?"

"I'm sure he does," Horn replied. "We didn't go into that in any great detail. I do know he's made a success of everything he's ever touched."

Byrnes jumped to his feet. "But he's going ahead with the tender offer, no matter what we do, isn't that so?"

"Yes. There's no backing away. He made that perfectly clear."

Byrnes pointed angrily at Horn. "I don't like having a gun held to my head. It's an insult!"

For the next two hours the group debated the two proposals, angrily and eloquently. A little after twelve, there was a lull in the conversation. Hartley looked down the table at Horn.

"Ed, you still haven't favored us with your committee's recommendation."

Horn cleared his throat, then he stood.

"Philip, and I say this with all due respect, it is your committee's recommendation that the board endorse the S.M. International offer, and that we tell our shareholders that today." He smiled. "By the way, Bill dissents from our position, in case you hadn't guessed."

"Damn right I do!" Clevenger shouted.

Horn sat back down. The room was quiet. Finally, slowly, Hartley rose, hands in his pockets, his shoulders slightly hunched.

"I can't say I'm surprised, given everything that's happened. However, speaking for your officer group, I have to tell you we are very, very disappointed not to have the committee's support."

Hartley shook his head slowly from side to side. "I truly believe our offer is more beneficial to our shareholders. Let me say this to you. Even if you are not persuaded the LBO is the right way to go, at the very least give our shareholders the chance to decide for themselves by not supporting either proposal. Don't stack the deck against us."

"Can we do that?" Louise Boyd asked.

"Yes," replied Wallace. "It's not ordinarily done, but the board has that option."

Hartley continued. "What I just suggested would be a responsible position for the board. Nevertheless, in the strongest terms, I repeat my request, and that of your management team, that you support the LBO in the decision you're about to take."

He looked searchingly at each director, one by one. "Is there anything to add?"

Several of the directors shook their heads. None spoke.

"Then a motion would be in order."

Nystrom raised his hand. "I move that the board approve the S.M. International proposal and endorse their tender offer."

"Second," quickly added Stanley Harper.

"Moved and seconded," Marianne Keller intoned.

Hartley frowned. Stan. . .is he just putting the ball in play? Or is that really his position? He stared at Harper, trying to discern some clue, but could see none. He cleared his throat. "Is there a need for discussion?"

Pursed lips all around, impassive faces.

"Seeing none, Marianne, call the roll."

Hartley sat down, resting his chin on his hand, staring at the wall.

The secretary to the board placed a form in front of her, preprinted with the directors' names in order of seniority. She had already lined out the inside directors who would have no vote on this issue. She began.

"Mr. Winston?"

Hartley looked intently at his mentor. . .his champion.

Winston stared straight ahead. "Yes."

The bastard. The two-timing bastard.

"Mr. Nystrom?"

"Aye."

"Mr. Clevenger?"

"No!"

"Ms. Boyd?"

"No."

"Mr. Byrnes?"

"No!"

Three to two, so far, my favor. But coming up. . .

"Mr. Harper?"

"Abstain. Make a note, Marianne. As Mr. Hartley recommended, my position is we should take no position."

Hartley winced. *No! Not with it this close!*

The corporate secretary looked up from her pad. "Mr. Horn?"

"Yes."

Hartley gritted his teeth. With Harper's abstention it was three to three. Dead even. Of the eight outside directors, only one remained. Hartley looked at the small, gray-haired woman at the far end of the table. On her face there was a faint smile and her eyes were ablaze. They were trained directly on Hartley. His heart sank.

"Mrs. Bell?"

"Yes!" she said, lifting her face to Hartley. *"Yes!"*

Keller looked at her notes, rechecking the tally. "By a vote of four to three with one abstention," she announced, "the inside directors not participating, the ayes have it. The motion is carried."

Harper raised his hand. "Change my vote to an aye. Might as well be on the winning side for a change." He looked around... nobody was laughing, not a smile anywhere. Hartley stared at him in utter disbelief. A tie vote would have defeated the motion.

"Duly noted. The motion carries by *five* to three."

There was complete silence. Those who weren't staring at their hands sneaked glances at Hartley. Crestfallen, he tried to compose himself. The memory he had been restraining all morning burst upon him. The memory of another ambush, not so long ago in this same room. He stood slowly and took a deep breath, rocking forward onto his hands, the tips of his fingers against the edge of the table. All eyes were on him.

"This...this comes as a great shock, a great disappointment. Your officer group has labored so hard, with what we believed was your support." Hartley swallowed. "But you have acted, the board has acted, and I have no alternative but to carry out your wishes."

He looked at Mandel, slouching gloomily in his chair, at Wallace, toying with a pencil. "We will proceed to notify our stockholders of your decision. I ask the special committee to return at three o'clock to review the notice."

Suddenly the pressure was off. Everyone began talking at once. Over the hubbub Hartley strove to be heard.

"If...if there is no further business," He looked around the room. He had lost them. For today. Forever.

Hartley reached for the gavel, Charlie Bell's mahogany gavel. He raised it high above his head, then brought it down with all his might, smashing it against the table. The head snapped off and flew across the room. Hartley held the shattered handle aloft as he cried, "*We are adjourned!*"

OVER THE NEXT THREE WEEKS the insurance companies, the pension funds and investment houses, BellAir employees current and retired, small investors holding one, two, five hundred shares, and, in the final days, the speculators and arbitrageurs after a quick profit –

nearly all the shareholders of BellAir Industries, Inc., tendered their shares. By the time S.M.I.'s offer expired, so many shares had been submitted that, together with Meyerson's earlier stake, he easily exceeded eighty percent. Hartley's efforts to motivate the shareholders with newspaper ads and mailings were unavailing.

The faction of BellAir's pilots that had conceived its own buyout and embraced Hartley's was outraged. However, as Fritz Mueller foresaw, most were relieved at not having to yield ten percent of their salary in the speculative experiment. After being out of work five months, Meyerson's salary freeze seemed almost generous. After all, they reasoned, that was their position in the first place.

To a man, BellAir's pilots were jubilant at defeating Hartley's two-tiered wage scale. For now, at least, they would sit back and watch, along with the rest of the industry, as a similar system just adopted by American Airlines played itself out.

Everyone was grateful to go back to work. By week's end the first flights were in the air. It was expected the airline would be back to full strength by late August, though still hanging fire were the imminent but as yet unspecified changes to be made at the top of the company. Machines were the easy part. Aircraft, ground equipment, baggage systems, and the like had been carefully tended and exercised during the mothball period, and with a few days' preparation would be ready to go. Much harder, the people. Crews were badly scrambled by the layoff, and under FAA rules the large number of pilots who had missed their recurrent classes and simulator checks during the strike would have to be retrained.

Adding to the complexity were the additional three hundred names swelling the pilot rolls, the replacements, "scabs" to most, who had kept the airline running until the flight attendants closed it down. Where they fit in remained to be seen. Under a secret side deal between Meyerson and the union, no new-hires were flying even after the first few weeks of operations. The matter remained in dispute. There was talk of a lawsuit.

A few weeks after the decisive board meeting, Arthur Winston summoned Roger Bankhead to a small conference room in BellAir's Skymaster Club at Kennedy Airport. On his way to Geneva for a banking conference, Winston had asked for a briefing on developments at the airline. After receiving Bankhead's lengthy report,

Winston sat back in his chair and closed his eyes, putting his fingertips to his temples.

"I'm not getting any younger, Roger. These last few months have been difficult." Winston took a deep breath. "Change always is, and this situation, well, I don't need to belabor the obvious. As you surmised, all the directors have submitted their resignations, signed and undated. I believe we'll see a clean sweep. That's how Sandor likes to operate."

"With one exception. You'll stay on, of course."

"Yes, I've been asked to remain as vice-chairman. Truthfully, I had hoped to begin easing out of the picture, but I've agreed to help until he gets his feet on the ground." Winston patted the thick folder Bankhead had brought for him. "I trust I won't be too much of a burden to you."

"Good advice is always in order."

"By the way, I've provided Sandor with Bank of Manhattan's proposal for restructuring the company's debt. I'll make sure you get a copy. We're recommending the hotels be put up for sale right away to retire some of the short-term obligations. So start giving that some thought."

"I hear you, but it's a shame. The hotels were just beginning to turn the corner when the strike hit."

"Yes. Well, you do what you have to do," Winston replied. "After we deal with this immediate business, looking ahead I can see '84 as a very profitable year. Of course, it was disappointing not to achieve our salary reductions."

"Tell me, Arthur, which way is Fritz leaning? I haven't been able to read him."

"Oh, he'll stay on," answered Winston, "no doubt about that. That will make you our two group vice presidents. Fritz with the operational side, and everything else in your hands. One more year is all we need from him. After that we'll be set."

"Has Meyerson decided on a new president yet?"

"My guess is he'll bring somebody over from one of his other companies, someone he's comfortable with. Of course, that will put a greater burden on you and Fritz to supply the know-how."

"Well, I'm ready. And I appreciate your vote of confidence."

"I'll say it again, Roger, you've earned the opportunity. I know this was terribly hard for you. You and Philip were quite close."

"For a while." Bankhead looked away. "He gave me my chance here. I just don't understand what happened. Nobody could fathom him, the last few months. I tried to tell him he was going down the wrong road, but he wouldn't listen, not to me, not to anybody except that Smith. Once he got an idea, he just ran with it. No other views, no discussion. That LBO business capped it all, as far as I was concerned." He looked squarely at Winston. "At least I can say I leveled with him. It's not as if he didn't know where I was coming from."

"Well, be that as it may. Smith's gone, of course."

"No loss there," Bankhead replied.

"No. Incidentally, I meant to offer congratulations on your engagement. Is it that same young lady I've met?"

Bankhead nodded. "It seemed like the right time to make the move."

"This the first for you?"

"No, the other one didn't work out."

Winston smiled. "I like to see my officers settled down, with a family and so on. Allows them to concentrate on the business without other, shall we say, distractions. By the way," Winston leaned forward for a handful of peanuts, "I do agree with you. Philip's LBO would have been a disaster. Even if he'd been more restrained, it was still a terrible idea. But one thing puzzled me, Roger. When you first showed me the plan, I couldn't understand why you were in for such a small share. You were offered more, I take it."

"Sure. We were all offered the same. To be honest, I couldn't stomach that debt load we would have taken on. As you pointed out, it would have sunk the company."

Winston apprised Bankhead warily. "Well, whatever the reason, I must say your judgment was admirable. And coming to me so early in the game, that was crucial. It gave us time to, let us say, prepare for the situation. Fortunate, indeed, S.M. International surfacing at just the right time."

As Winston reached for the peanut dish again, he patted Bankhead's hand and winked. "Actually, if Sandor Meyerson hadn't come along, I think I would have had to invent him."

Bankhead looked down, toying with his glass. "The only bad part is how things worked out for Philip."

"Don't give that a second thought. Philip has done quite well financially. That other situation he'll have to deal with himself."

Winston sat back. "You know, Roger, in this life there are no guar-antees. I've always felt that the most anyone can expect is the chance to show what you're made of. If it works out, wonderful. If not, well, at least you've had your day." Winston nodded reflectively. "Philip had a good run at it. He didn't do badly, everything considered."

Bankhead stared into his glass. "Friday was his last day."

"I daresay there were no going-away parties."

"None I was invited to, at any rate."

"It really is too bad," said Winston. "For all his talent, he wasn't very good at building bridges."

Bankhead looked out the window at the nose of a 747 not more than thirty feet away. "That last board meeting," he said. "The vote was so close. It could have gone either way."

"Not really. It wasn't nearly as close as it seemed. In fact, if I hadn't been certain of the outcome, there would never have been a vote."

"But if Mrs. Bell hadn't voted the way she did...Philip was con-vinced she'd be with him. That's what she led him to believe."

Winston laughed. "Not a chance. I've known Dee Bell thirty years. She was against his scheme all along, whatever he might have thought. Actually, it went a lot deeper than that..." Winston's voice trailed off. "You know, you really have to give that woman credit. When Charlie died, the way he died, she could have gone to pieces. But she didn't. She stayed right in there. I wasn't sure how it would come into play, but I knew at some point, having Dee Bell on the board would be very useful. Of course, I never suspected it would happen this soon. Or this way."

Winston glanced at his watch. "Well, I'd best be on my way."

Bankhead looked at the low table between their two chairs. The latest *Time* lay on a pile of magazines. Hartley's picture was on the cover, a black banner across his chest.

Scandal, Greed – Or Both? asked the headline.

"I don't suppose she was thrilled by the publicity," Bankhead pointed at the magazine.

"You mean the flight attendant, that drug business?"

"Yes."

"Well, of course that's right. Anything casting a shadow over Charlie's name, or the company, but my feeling is, that didn't really make the difference. Though it may have sealed it a bit tighter."

"What will happen to her now?" Bankhead asked.

"I suppose she'll live out the rest of her years quietly. Sandor will accept her resignation, not that she would want to stay on, anyway. She has her sons, her grandchildren. You see, Roger, Dee Bell chose her role, and she played it very, very well. She did exactly what she set out to do."

Winston leaned back, his elbows on the arms of the chair, steepling his fingers in front of his face, a smile on his thin lips.

"I trust, when my time comes, they'll say no less of me."

PART SIX

Thursday's Children

1

THE DAY PEAKED at 86 degrees, close to a record for September. As Will Cartright's Metroliner descended in its approach, the small craft was tossed about by air currents billowing up from the coastal hills, baked all summer by the searing sun. Before long the rains would return, restoring the hills and side valleys to their lush, cool-weather raiment.

A half hour after landing, Cartright found himself in the middle seat of a blue and green Bay Airlines van, trundling through the Monterey waterfront.

"How's old Ernie doing these days?" Cartright asked the driver.

"Okay, I guess."

New blood, Cartright thought. Can't be more than eighteen. "He usually gives me a ride in."

"Actually, I don't know him that well. The older guys, they sort of keep to themselves, if you know what I mean." The van slipped through the tunnel at the city marina, then it slowed, mired in traffic along Cannery Row.

"Never fails, there's always something new around here," Cartright remarked as they crawled past a shopping arcade, brightly lit in the early evening dusk.

"Yeah," the driver grumbled. "But it's all tourist this, tourist that. They could care less about the people who live here." The van inched along and finally ground to a halt. An oversized tour bus was blocking the road. The driver leaned on his horn, but ceased when he saw the bus was discharging passengers and not about to move.

"Damnit!" he exclaimed, looking at his watch.

"Tell you what, I'll walk from here."

The boy set the hand brake, hopped out, and slid the door open, handing Cartright his suitcase and briefcase. He stood by, shifting his weight from one foot to the other. Engulfed in the warm, foul bus exhaust, Cartright dug into his wallet for a bill. This is new, he thought, annoyed.

"Much obliged, mister. You have a good night, now."

Cartright lifted his bags and started down the sidewalk. Up ahead he saw the familiar neon bird, its blue light still winking erratically, but as Cartright neared, he stopped, puzzled. Something's wrong. Then he saw it. On the wall beneath the bird, a freshly painted sign: La Fiesta – Fine Mexican Cuisine.

"Well, what do you know."

He stepped forward, a bag in each hand, prepared to arm-wrestle the front door, but as his foot hit the carpeted threshold, the door automatically swung open. "Now *that's* what I call progress!"

On entering the restaurant, other changes were evident. Gone were the faded pink walls, now white plaster and dark wood. A small fountain stood in a cactus garden, colored lights playing on the burbling water. Cartright peered into the brightly lit dining area. Potted plants, sombreros, colorful blankets, and busy! Looks like a full house. Paddle-bladed fans spun under dark *vegas* that traversed the ceiling.

As Cartright was making his observations, a pretty, young hostess appeared, attired in a colored peasant skirt and a white linen blouse, a black ribbon at her throat.

"Good evening, sir," she said cheerfully. "Do you have a reservation?"

"No...that is, if I do, it's in the name of Delgado."

"Oh, of course." She put aside her reservations book. "Mr. Delgado isn't here yet, but I can seat you if you wish. And may I check your bags?"

Cartright handed her his suitcase. "I'll keep the little one."

After trading Cartright a claim check, she lifted two large laminated menus from a stack next to the register and briskly led him to the farthest corner of the room.

"Mr. Delgado's booth," she said, setting the menus down.

Cartright slid in and put his soft-sided briefcase beside him. "I'll have a Dos Equis while I wait," he said.

"Certainly, sir. Your waitress will be right over."

In a few minutes Frank Delgado appeared. He paused at the entrance to greet a party of businessmen, then waved to a nearby family. Cartright noted his client's conservative gray suit, his white shirt, and striped tie.

"Hiya, counselor," Delgado said, pumping Cartright's hand.

"Damned if we don't look like twins," Cartright replied.

"No way," Delgado laughed. "Anybody can see I'm the good-looking one. Chamber meeting," he said, easing out of his jacket and loosening his tie. He patted the menu. "So, what'll you have? Don't mean to rush you, but I'm kind of in a crunch tonight."

"There certainly are a lot of new items in here..."

"Try the chimichanga. That's been very popular."

"...but the main thing is," Cartright observed, "everything seems to be three dollars more than it used to be."

Delgado shrugged. "Somebody has to pay for all these improvements. The place is real upscale now, isn't it?" Delgado beamed. "Miguel sold it to another cousin of mine. He just does the cooking now."

"What if I liked the way it was?"

"Sure, everybody did, but you couldn't make any money that way. What'd they have, fifteen tables? Hell, it got so he was turning away fifty, a hundred people every night." He nodded at the other side of the room. "The bar had to go, though. That was too bad. You see, what's happened, Mexican food is big time now, all over, especially in this area."

"That accounts for the name change, I suppose."

"Exactly! Now anybody can tell what we serve here, even if they're just walking by. The old name was just too confusing. And we're starting to pick up some tour bus trade, too. That is very nice, very stable."

"I noticed," Cartright said dourly. "Well, at least you managed to keep the bird."

"Of course! The locals would never let us touch it, and, you know, it is a good conversation opener. So!" Delgado lifted his water glass. "Here's to progress!"

They ordered and in a few minutes the waitress brought their dinners. Delgado shook his head. "Man, that looks *good!* You just can't beat Miguel!"

After they ate for a while, Delgado put his fork down. "Fritz Mueller called me the other day."

"How's he holding up?"

"Pretty good, considering. He decided to stay on, help the new owners get their act together." Delgado leaned forward. "Confidentially, he told me how close we came to a big, big problem with those people."

"What do you mean?"

"I mean, if Hartley had pulled off that LBO deal, he was seriously thinking about running their jets back into Monterey. In all our best markets! Not to mention taking everything away from us in San Fran!"

"We'd have had them before a judge so fast their heads would spin," Cartright replied sternly.

"That's my man!" Delgado beamed. "But thankfully, Fritz says the new owners don't seem that interested in short-haul flying. They're going to keep doing what they were doing before. More long-haul, even less of the small stuff. For us that's perfect!"

"Looks like you dodged a bullet. Did he say anything about that Bay stock they own?"

"He said don't lose any sleep over it." Delgado shrugged. "I guess we'll just have to play that one by ear. Anyway, why I wanted you to come down, he clued me in on something they're thinking, something really big. They're putting a bunch of used 737s on the market. He wants to know if we're interested."

Cartright whistled. "You'd have to be out of your mind..."

"Except for one thing," Delgado interrupted. "They want us to fly for them, but on a contract basis. We'd be protected on that kind of deal, at least I think so. That's what I need you to tell me. They're talking San Fran, Reno, Bakersfield, some of the Oregon cities. The same thing we were doing during their strike except with jet equipment!"

"But that'd be a new airline!"

"Well, you're right, and that's the problem. Hiring, retraining, a whole different set of rules. That's even before you figure in the extra costs."

Cartright pushed his plate back. "Why would you even consider it?"

"That's why I wanted you here tomorrow. Bert'll be here, too. I need you guys to keep me honest on this one." He waggled his finger at Cartright. "The way I see it, if we don't pick up on this, they'll get somebody else and then where am I? It's a helluva commitment, but I can't afford to let somebody else get in tight, not with our contract up for renewal."

"With all the confusion, they still haven't moved on that extension we worked out."

"Well, anyway, tomorrow we'll go over everything." Delgado signaled the waitress who was clearing the next table. "Two coffees, please."

Cartright had fallen quiet.

"What's on your mind?" Delgado asked.

"What you were saying reminded me of something. Remember when I visited Francis Farrell, that last time I was back there? Just before he died."

"Yeah," Delgado shook his head. "What a shame about Francis. What a damn shame."

"We had a long talk, the two of us. He told me he admired how you were able to stay close to things, even with all the wheeling and dealing that has to go on."

Delgado laughed. "I hope you let him know it's all an act."

"Of course. But then we got talking about you and Hartley."

"Oh?" Now Cartright had his client's full attention.

"We were comparing styles. Francis said he thought you'd do a better job even if you switched places."

"I don't know about *that*!" Delgado retorted. "I'm beginning to think the bigger you are, the harder it is. That's what scares me about this 737 business." He paused. "It's the damnedest thing. The better people tell me I'm doing, the worse I feel. Here I have this fancy organization but everybody else is doing the things *I* want to do! And you got me all this stock, but can I sell it? Of course not! I could lose control of the damn company! All I ever think about these days is money, money, money! I tell you, it's no fun."

He swallowed a mouthful of coffee. "But when I get feeling sorry for myself, all I have to do is think about Fritz. There's a guy carrying one heavy load."

"With the takeover?"

"No. Well, maybe that, too, but I mean that accident they had, the one at Boston. You see, I know for a fact he has hung that one around his own neck. Personally. That's the kind of guy he is. He feels responsible for what happened."

"Well, was he?" Cartright asked.

Delgado leaned forward in the booth. "You're damned right he was. No offense, Will, you're the best lawyer there is, but you people, you attorneys and such, there's some things you just don't understand. What I'm saying, this goes way beyond what's legal and what isn't. It's even bigger than making a buck. It's called doing the right thing. Even when there's nobody beating on you to do it. Fact is, they're usually beating on you not to do it."

"But what's that got to do with the accident?"

He shook his head. "See, you just don't get it! The man thought he had all the bases covered, but his own operation fucked him up. He was pushing it too hard and he knew it. Naturally, he comes off okay in the papers, defending the company at that hearing and all, but he has to play that game. What I'm saying, Fritz Mueller is going to carry that one to his grave, no two ways about it."

"Frank, you disappoint me. That was precisely what Francis and I were talking about." Cartright lowered his voice. "Let me tell you about this theory of mine. You really don't understand a person until you know what he worries about the most. And on that score, you come off pretty well." He pushed his chair away from the table. "Remember what you just said. It bugs the hell out of you that you can't be out there all the time, on the line with your people, with the operation. You'd rather be there than anything else in the world. Even more than meeting with me! Am I right?"

Delgado nodded.

"All right. So you compromise. This isn't some kind of dream world. Your financials are important. But the difference is, there's something inside pulling you in the right direction. Fritz has it. Charlie Bell, too, everything I ever heard about him. That's what I mean. That's what Francis meant."

"Hartley. Where does he fit in?"

Cartright paused for a moment. "Francis thought his head was in the wrong place. From what I saw, I would agree."

Delgado was silent for a moment, turning over an idea. Finally he shook his head. "You have to give the man *some* credit. Like I said, I'm having trouble keeping track of my little outfit. What must it have been like for him? How many people did he have, fifty thousand?"

"Give or take a few."

"How do you handle a monster like that?"

"I suspect there are ways," Cartright replied.

"What do you mean?" Delgado asked, puzzled.

"It's the signals, goddamnit!"

"Signals?"

Cartright hit the table with his hand. "The signals from the top! That's what counts! That's what makes Fritz what he is. It makes you what you are. You tell your people what you want, okay?" He looked intently at Delgado. "And what you want, they have respect for!"

"But fifty thousand people?"

Cartright smiled. "I guess you just take them one at a time."

Delgado let out a deep breath. "Now that you mention it, you're right. It's elementary."

"Though in my experience more honored in the breach than the observance."

Delgado stood. "Well, on that cheery note, we'd better wrap this one up. C'mon. I'll give you a ride to the hotel."

He put his arm around Cartright's shoulder, and the two men walked out together. As Cartright claimed his suitcase, Delgado fished around a glass bowl beside the cash register. He handed Cartright a small green foil packet.

"Mint?"

"Thanks."

They stepped outside. The street was crowded with cars. People were strolling along the sidewalk, enjoying the pleasant evening, a steady stream in front of La Fiesta – Fine Mexican Cuisine, formerly the Blue Heron, its entrance dark one moment, bathed the next in the glow of a spindly blue bird, a symbol of the stored-up hopes and dreams of the local people. Outmoded, yes, but observing the passing scene with a defiant eye, warning that through it all, it will survive.

2

PHILIP HARTLEY gripped the steering wheel with one hand. His other arm was draped across the seat back. The midday sun beat down, but his new prescription sunglasses cut the glare perfectly. Somewhat longer than the executive trim he had affected for so many years, his hair blew back in the rush of wind through the open convertible. From time to time Hartley glanced over the cliffs to the turquoise and white breakers, but his mind was not on scenery. At San Luis Obispo he'd pick up old Highway 101, then a straight shot through to L.A.

It had been a brutal summer. Several weeks after the fatal board meeting, he cleared out of the Tower one Sunday morning, personally packing and carting his belongings. Bad enough, what happened, how it happened; he wanted no more encounters. The *Time* cover and that miserable article. So unfair, the final straw. Charlie Bell… Winston…Roger. Loyalty. Deceit. Where does one end and the other begin? This would take a long time to sort out. If ever.

Then there was Elaine and that lawyer of hers. Just thinking about them made his blood boil. The demands. Outrageous! For the time being, he'd taken another place, a two-bedroom apartment a few blocks from the condo. Most of his belongings were in storage. Elaine had moved back in with her dog. Never liked that little rodent, he thought, doesn't even deserve to be called a dog.

The past weekend he'd spent in San Francisco visiting friends, a college classmate and his family. The first normal time in so long he couldn't remember. Golden Bears football Saturday afternoon, a sail on the Bay, then the Forty-Niners at Candlestick. The plan was to relax Monday, then meander down the coast the next day, arriving in L.A. by dinnertime. But when he checked in with Valerie as he did periodically, one of the calls she passed along was a shocker – Frank Delgado.

Talking with Valerie, Hartley had tensed. Delgado...what the hell does *he* want? If it's to gloat, this will be a very short conversation, if I call him back at all. He sat on the edge of the bed, phone in hand, looking out the window at a large spruce tree. The house was empty, his surgeon host already at the hospital, the kids at school, the wife at the club.

Delgado was brief. Since learning that Hartley was in the area, he'd like to meet him, have a short talk. Hartley thought a moment...well, why not. It can't be any worse than what I've been through lately. Maybe tie down another loose end. They settled on the coffee shop in the Hyatt off Highway 1 outside Monterey, Tuesday at eleven.

Not at all sure this was a good idea, Hartley arrived at the restaurant a few minutes late. He spotted Delgado sitting by the window. Hartley sat down in the booth. Delgado put his menu down and nodded at him. The two men stared at each other. Finally Hartley broke the ice.

"What are we doing here, Delgado?"

Delgado looked at him a moment longer. "I had some things to say to you."

Hartley shook his head wearily. "If you want to beat up on me, save it. I've had a bellyful of that lately. In case you hadn't noticed."

"Oh, I noticed, all right. But that isn't why I called you."

The waitress came over, pad in hand. She looked at Delgado. "Coffee for me," he said. "Black."

"Make that two."

"Nothing else?"

Delgado handed her the menu. "That'll do it."

The men continued to look at each other. Finally Delgado leaned forward and put his elbows on the table.

"You and me, we had our differences. The fact is, I couldn't wait to see you go down."

"I hope you enjoyed the spectacle," Hartley replied sourly.

"I thought I would, but I didn't." Delgado shook his head. "That's why I wanted to talk to you. I guess you know what I thought of you and your management...philosophy, if that's the word. But how it happened, I think it was bullshit what they did to you. You got a raw deal."

Hartley looked stunned.

"Let me put it this way. That asshole Meyerson, I know people who've run up against him. He is bad news. But I guess you found that out."

Hartley nodded. "In spades."

"And the way they used that woman, that really bothered me. The whole thing stunk, if you ask me."

"I couldn't agree with you more." A pained expression came to Hartley's face. "Those people, the media, they didn't even try to understand what we were doing. Then dragging us through the mud like that." He frowned. "But I'm starting to think it was for the best. Might as well...I don't have much choice, the way things turned out."

The waitress brought their coffees. Hartley took a sip, then put the cup down. "Looking back, I see some things I would do differently."

"What do you mean?"

"My...friend. Shelley. I thought we were being careful, but not enough, as it turned out."

"What about BellAir?" Delgado's eyes narrowed. "Any second thoughts there?"

Hartley sat back. "I've thought a lot about that. To be honest, I can't think of much there I would change. I was always looking out for the airline's best interest."

Delgado snorted.

"You haven't the faintest idea what pressure we were under. Trying to hold that company together, trying to make a buck doing it."

"You seem to think you're the only one with problems." Delgado's face reddened. "Look what you tried to do to me! My friend George Steiner, goddamn, you put him out of business!"

"It's a tough world out there. You do what you have to do."

"That Meyerson guy would probably say the same thing."

Delgado stared across the table. Hartley began to nod. He seemed to be searching for words. "Hell, I don't know...maybe you're right." He met Delgado's eyes. "Could you have done any better?"

"I've been thinking a lot about that lately."

The two men fell silent, picking up their cups, drinking, putting them back down. Delgado nodded, as if now he were having a conversation with himself. "What are you going to do now?" he finally asked.

"I don't know. I've had my fill of airlines, I can tell you. Something will turn up. Anyway, I'm pretty well set."

Delgado looked down at the table. "There is something I'd like to say to you."

"You haven't pulled any punches yet."

He looked directly at Hartley. "The thing that really bothered me, right off the bat, you didn't have any feeling for this place." Delgado gestured with his hand. "This is my home. You're from here, too. I could not understand that. I resented it, if you want to know the truth."

"Too many ghosts." A sad expression came over Hartley. "Too many ghosts here for me."

Delgado looked puzzled, then his face softened. "Well, maybe we don't need to talk about that."

Hartley nodded. "If it makes you feel any better, I'll be spending more time out here now. Maybe it'll be different this time." He sat back in the booth. "What about you? What's next for Bay Airlines?"

Delgado thought quickly...I can't get into that. "Let me just say, the bigger we get, the more I appreciate how good it is to be small. I just hope I can keep up with everything and still be able to sleep at night. Sometimes I feel trapped by my success."

Hartley shook his head. "That sounds familiar, I'll tell you."

The waitress came over with the coffee pot.

"You know, I could use something to eat," Delgado said. "How about you?"

"Sure. It'll be a while until dinner."

Delgado called the waitress over and they both ordered cheeseburgers.

"So," Hartley said, "you have what, two kids?"

"Three. My oldest's starting senior year at Stanford. He's done well, considering he's not much of a scholar. Every year after football season he has a lot of catching up to do."

"Stanford." Hartley shook his head solemnly. "Can't say I like the sound of that very much."

"They don't play him much, but he's happy. I guess that's what counts. My other son's at Cal."

"That's more like it. Is he an athlete, too?"

"No, he's into music. It's his major, in fact. Plays the clarinet. Classical, jazz, Dixieland, you name it. But mostly classical."

"And your third..."

"A little girl, Teresa. Actually not so little any more."

"You're a lucky man."

Delgado nodded. "I know. I really am."

The waitress brought their sandwiches and the two men ate in silence.

"You're married, I remember hearing," Delgado ventured.

"Not much longer." Hartley shook his head. "The last few years we were just sharing space. No, that's too good a word, it was more like we'd divided things up, my life over here, hers over there. Well," he sighed, "it's really divided now. I moved out, the lawyers moved in. End of story."

"What about the woman?"

"That was the worst thing, what they did to her. . . what I let them do to her." He looked out the window. "When you stop to think about it, the whole thing's so ridiculous. There you are, up to your neck in big, complicated deals, no time for anything else, hardly able to breathe all those years." He shrugged. "Then in a day it's over. Nothing left, not a trace."

Delgado nodded. Tell me about it, he thought.

"But Shelley, she has problems. Big problems."

"She went to jail, they said."

"She did, and she got out, too. But some things she'll never put behind her. She has to win her life back, a day at a time." Hartley's eyes met Delgado's. "I'm going to try and help her through it."

"You mean the drugs."

"Yes," he replied.

Delgado shook his head. "I hear what you're saying, but that's one hell of a commitment. I've seen some situations right here in town, people getting involved and trying to help. It can be very hard on them, too. I hope you know what you're getting into."

"Yeah, well, I don't have many illusions left." Hartley paused. "You know, what you were saying about your son, if you really meant it, you've done right by that kid. If he's just happy to be on the team, happy to get in the game when his number's called. Unfortunately, that is not how Phil Hartley was put together. Not me. I always had to win. I had to win big. Always something to prove. That's how I operate. . . operated."

He looked at Delgado solemnly. "You see, around me, people get hurt. Even when things were going good, people get hurt. Then, when things start falling apart..."

Delgado caught his breath...he'd been waiting for this moment for years, this chance to put his foe away once and for all. But he hesitated, frowning. "That is so strange," he found himself saying, "what you just said about yourself. For a minute I thought you were talking about your friend and her drugs."

Startled, Hartley sat erect in the booth. A look of alarm came to his face. He put his napkin down. "I'd better be going."

Hartley reached for the check, but Delgado took it out of his hand. "Uh-uh. This one's on me."

"Hey. I'm not that hard up. Far from it!"

"I'm sure you're not. But you can't deduct it and I can."

Hartley nodded. "Who knows? Maybe I will again."

The two men stood.

"I'm glad we got together," Hartley said. "Cleared the air, some."

"Good luck," Delgado said. He shook Hartley's hand.

"And you. You take care."

3

PHILIP HARTLEY sped south. Images rushed past, a blur. All those years of gamesmanship, of maneuvering...Frank Delgado's remark kept forcing itself upon him. They were my addiction. *That was my cocaine!*

It seems so obvious now. Then what is the difference between us, between Shelley and me? Is there a difference? Addiction, obsession...are they not cut from the same cloth?

AT SEVEN TWENTY-FIVE Philip Hartley pulled into the parking lot of the squat red-brick building – Church of the Covenant, by the sign in front. Approaching on foot, he slowed, unsure of himself. Several men were hanging around the front door, smoking, examining Hartley as he neared.

"You're here for the meeting," one of them said with a knowing wink.

"Why...yes," Hartley responded. "I suppose I am."

"You're late. They already started."

Down the stone steps at the side of the building to a set of double doors. Cautiously, Hartley opened the door and stepped into the rear of a crowded, low-ceilinged auditorium. Glancing around, he eased into a folding chair in the last row. Immediately, his eyes began to smart from the thick cigarette smoke. Through the haze he saw a young man speaking from a lectern. In one corner of the room stood an American flag, and in the other, the Bear Flag of the State of California. On the back wall a hand-lettered banner hung: *NARCOTICS ANONYMOUS – SANTA MONICA CHAPTER.*

Hartley lifted himself in his chair for a better view. Yes, he sighed with relief, there she is, up front...and Janie French beside her.

The speaker took his seat to enthusiastic applause, then a bull-necked man in a short-sleeved shirt approached the lectern.

"Our thanks to Keith for his report," he began. "I don't need to remind you, but I will anyway, like all chapters of N.A., we're self-supporting, so everything you put in the basket tonight goes toward expenses – these meetings, our literature, the help line, and so on. We have this unusual approach to money. We raise what we need but no more than we need. The reason being, we never want to compromise the atmosphere of recovery, which is why we're here in the first place. Not very businesslike, I suppose, but for us, it works."

Hartley frowned and looked around. People were nodding their heads approvingly. Pretty normal-looking people, he thought. For the most part, that is, noticing the gold ring in the ear of the bearded young man beside him.

"After a couple more speakers we'll take a short break." The moderator pointed to a table covered with a green cloth, a large urn, and several pitchers. "So help yourselves to the coffee and juice.

"Now, for any newcomers, this is the most important part of our meeting, because here's where we ask people celebrating an anniversary to come up and tell us what it feels like to be clean and sober. And what they went through to get there. A year, six months, a month, it doesn't matter, we want to hear from you.

"We all know it's tough." He tapped his forehead, "we know it up here, but it's important to hear other people say so. Once you admit you're not the only person in the world this ever happened to, you've taken the first step toward recovery. So, at this time," he glanced at a piece of paper, "I'd like to ask a new member of our chapter to come up here. Please say hello to Shelley!"

Shelley Gregory made her way to the front of the room. Good, Hartley thought, she's picked up some color. Looks a lot better. Two weeks they will spend together. Then – his stomach tightened at the prospect – it's back to New York for the final hearing on the divorce.

"My name is Shelley," she began in a strong, clear voice. "I'm an addict and an alcoholic."

"Hi, Shelley!" they roared.

From the back of the room Hartley could see her biting her lip, fighting back a smile. "And you don't know how happy I am to tell you I've been clean and sober for three months!"

Another cheer rang out and somebody whistled. Hartley shook his head...how pretty she looks.

She broke into a broad smile, wiping her eyes with the back of her hand. "Tonight I get my ninety-day key ring. I have to say, there were times I didn't give myself nine days, let alone ninety. In fact, the only reason I'm here at all, is two good friends I want to thank tonight.

"These people stood by me, and it's been pretty miserable for them. I wouldn't have blamed them for quitting. It's not easy to love an addict, the kind of things you put your friends through, and particularly them. So I want to say, thanks, Janie..." Her friend in the second row stood up. "And..." She searched the audience, "I hope he was able to make it tonight, thanks, Phil."

Tentatively, Hartley stood and waved to Shelley. She spotted him and waved back, beaming. Everyone turned to look. Embarrassed, Hartley began to sit back down, but suddenly he jumped. The young man next to him was grabbing his arm! Hartley allowed him to take his hand, and he began pumping it up and down.

"I don't know who you are, man, but you're all right! God damn, *you are all right!*"

Hartley reddened, forcing a smile. By this time a middle-aged woman was moving to the lectern.

"My name is Doris," she announced, "and I'm an addict and an alcoholic."

"Hi, Doris!" yelled the crowd. When she finished, a young man in a business suit rose and began to relate his tale. Then another. They spoke of the common horror, the abyss. Of the pulling back, often not knowing how or why or by what power. The unceasing effort to avoid the brink. And their fellowship in N.A.

At the break, Hartley approached Shelley and greeted her with a hug and a decorous kiss. He shook Janie's hand.

"That's all I get?" she pouted.

Hartley replied by wrapping his arms around her.

"I hope you won't mind if I ride back with Phil," Shelley said.

"Heck, no. Given the chance, I'd do it myself."

"How about joining us? We're going out for a bite."

"I'll take a rain check. Tomorrow's an early day. Anyway you probably want to be alone."

The meeting resumed, and the person next to Shelley slid over, offering Hartley his chair. The next speaker commenced. Then another took his place. Hartley took Shelley's hand. They laughed and applauded as the meeting went on. Frequently they whispered to each other, Shelley resting her head on his shoulder. At the end, the three of them walked out, arms linked.

The two women embraced. "Thanks so much for coming," Shelley said, "and for everything."

"Anytime. But you're in good hands now."

They pulled out of the parking lot, heading for her neighborhood. Hartley glanced at Shelley's face...alive again, full of hope. But how long will the euphoria last? Delgado was right. This is going to be tough, gritty work. He patted her hand and she grasped his. It's been a long time since somebody needed me. Maybe, he thought, maybe this time I won't foul it up.

Hartley stared at the road, still pondering Delgado's words. Shelley and I, we share more than she knows, more than she will ever know.

"Did you drive straight through?" she asked, noticing how quiet he was.

"No, I stopped on the way to see...a friend. Remind me. I'll tell you about him some time."

A NOTE ON THE TYPE

This book was set in Sabon. The Sabon typeface family was developed in 1964–67 by Jan Tschichold. Sabon was designed based on classical typefaces.